THE TENDER BARBARIAN by Dixie Browning

"You're limping," Bey accused. "Take off your shoe and let me see your foot."

"Look, Bey, if you want coffee, drink it and go," Emily said evenly. "I'm not hurt, and I'm not taking off anything."

He grinned. "Sooner or later, you will, you know. But I can wait. I want it to be the proper time and place."

GOLDEN MAN by Ann Major

"What are you doing here, Blade?" she asked, her voice strange and tight.

"I figured you'd heard I was back."

"I had, but that doesn't answer my question."

"Well, this is where I used to live," he said in that soft male voice that could make her shiver. "And it's where I'm going to live now. I've come home, Jenny. To stay."

THE GENTLING by Ginna Gray

"How long are you going to ignore it?" Irace asked softly.

She shook her head. "Ignore what?"

"This thing there is between us."

"I—I don't know what you're talking about."

"Oh, no, Katy," he said quietly. "I've tried to be patient with you, and it's gotten me absolutely nowhere. Well, no more. I'm not going to let you slip through my fingers again."

About the Authors

Dixie Browning
is a charter member of Romance Writers of America, an award-winning author and has toured extensively for Silhouette Books. She also writes historical romances with her sister under the name Bronwyn Williams.

Ann Major
is not only a successful author, she also manages a business and runs a busy household with three children. She lists traveling and playing the piano among her many interests. Her favorite composer, quite naturally, is the romantic Chopin.

Ginna Gray
A native Houstonian, Ginna Gray admits that since childhood, she has been a compulsive reader as well as a head-in-the-clouds dreamer. Long accustomed to expressing her creativity in tangible ways—Ginna also enjoys painting and needlework—she finally decided to try putting her fantasies and wild imaginings down on paper. The result? The mother of two now spends eight hours a day as a full-time writer.

BAD BOYS

Dixie Browning
Ann Major
Ginna Gray

Silhouette® Books

Published by Silhouette Books New York
America's Publisher of Contemporary Romance

SILHOUETTE BOOKS
300 East 42nd St., New York, N.Y. 10017

by Request—Bad Boys

Copyright © 1993 by Harlequin Enterprises B.V.

THE TENDER BARBARIAN
Copyright © 1985 by Dixie Browning
GOLDEN MAN
Copyright © 1985 by Ann Major
THE GENTLING
Copyright © 1984 by Virginia Gray

ISBN: 0-373-20094-3

CONTENTS

A Note from Dixie Browning

I've always been intrigued by contrasts, in people and backgrounds, people with other people—people and circumstances. With Beyard Jones, I went for all three, pitting a hard-bitten man who's been forced to learn survival skills early in life against an elegant, very proper spinster. I gave him the least likely profession for a man of his sort, and for good measure, instigated a turf war between Bey and Emily.

It wasn't that Bey was precisely bad—or even so very wild—yet sometimes it seemed that he'd spent his whole life one step ahead of trouble. It was no wonder he kept a low profile. It was no wonder, when he roared into her life on his street bike, that Emily was both frightened and attracted.

The twisted road that led Bey Jones to Emily McCloud started when a sniper's bullet landed him in a veterans' hospital flat on his back for three months. He read every Louis L'Amour and Zane Gray he could lay his hands on, but when the volunteer group mixed up their book delivery and he reluctantly read his first paperback romance, the die was cast.

A few years later he had it made, but old habits die hard. Bey's survival theory? Flash it around and you risk getting it ripped off. Blend in and you stand a chance of surviving. By the time the story begins, he's fought his way up until he owns a twenty-five-foot oyster boat, a BMW R75, a portable typewriter and a few secluded acres of wilderness. Which was enough for any reasonable man.

And then he met Emily McCloud.

So there you have it. Tough, tender or truly bad, the man still fascinates me.

Dixie Browning

THE TENDER BARBARIAN

Dixie Browning

One

"To bed her, or not to bed her," Beyard Jones muttered thoughtfully. "*That* is the question."

After due consideration, he abstained. Three short paragraphs later he typed "THE END" and ripped the page from the battered portable, only five days past his contractual deadline. A single well-documented consummation and a few near-misses would have to do it this time. When he'd first started out, writing steamy love scenes had been a real turn-on, but by the time his fourth book had gone into its fifth printing, he'd found it more boring than stimulating. Possibly because he'd been so damned busy writing about it he'd had too little time to engage in any firsthand experiences.

Some forty-five minutes later, as he settled a visored helmet over his thatch of sun-streaked hair, it occurred to him that he was going to be busier than ever for the next few months. Just as well he'd fulfilled his current contract. He'd allow himself a week's break, another week to come up with a decent proposal, and then he'd drag out contract negotiations for a couple more weeks before putting himself into another deadline situation.

Touching the bulky padded envelope in his motorcycle's saddlebag, he turned on the quiet BMW R75 and headed for the post office to mail the manuscript. That done, he'd be on his way out of town. With any luck, he'd beat the evening traffic across the Bay Bridge.

Taking the Ritchie highway south from Baltimore, Bey flexed his shoulder muscles. Speed-induced wind whipped faded jeans against his thick leather boots, reddened a twice-broken nose and a chin that still sported a few ancient battle scars. Tough, compactly constructed, Bey Jones had come up the hard way. It showed.

By the time he turned off on 50-301, some of the strain of the past few weeks had already begun to ease. As he neared the bridge, breathing in the pungent bay air, a few of the lines that added premature age to his weathered face began to smooth out.

Those last two chapters had been killers. As usual, he'd found himself smoking nonstop, existing on beer, black coffee and Vienna sausage while he worked the clock around to gather up all the threads he'd cast onto the loom of the story and weave them into a tight, satisfying ending.

It didn't get any better. He'd thought that after all these years the process of writing would grow easier. It hadn't worked out that way. The more he wrote, the more he learned of his craft, the higher his standards grew. According to the reviews, each of his five published romances had surpassed the one before, and every one of them had made it to a respectable rung on

the bestseller lists—which added a subtle pressure all its
own.

It had been his accountant who'd insisted that he in-
corporate himself. The fact that he even needed an accountant still took some getting used to. From the
tender age of eleven, he'd worked his tail off for every
dime he'd ever had. Now, at thirty-two, he was a corporation, a property owner, and weather permitting,
soon to become a home owner.

The quiet purr of the well-bred street bike throbbed
between his powerful thighs as he leaned into the wind.
Fletcher's Landing—*his*. He'd first seen the wooded
peninsula from the bay, from the cockpit of the rugged
work boat he'd bought, repaired and renamed the
Bonnie Bonus. She'd been running rough ever since
he'd left Baltimore, and he'd finally headed her for the
nearest lea shore to change the plugs. It had been exactly one year ago. The trees had been incandescent
with color against the somber darkness of the river.
Tucked away from the raw winds of the open bay, he'd
anchored near the ruins of an ancient wharf.

It had caught at his imagination. He'd gone ashore
and explored, looking for some sign of habitation,
finding none. The following weekend he'd left the *Bonus* at home and taken the bike. He'd had a hell of a
time locating the place from the highway, but he'd finally found it. Aside from a small frame house practically straddling the narrow neck of the peninsula, it was
uninhabited.

He'd spent that weekend and many more camping in
a secluded cove as far from the house as possible. If the
place was posted, he'd missed the signs—but then, he
hadn't wasted much time looking for them.

Through the double blind of a Baltimore realtor and his corporation, Bon-Bey, Inc., he'd made an offer for the place, hardly daring to hope he'd be successful. He'd wanted the whole thing—a place where he could relax and be himself without worrying about having his privacy invaded. Never gregarious, he'd grown positively reclusive since his first romance novel had hit the top. He could count on the fingers of one hand the people who knew of his identity as Bonnie Jericho, and that was five people too many.

According to the realtor, the owner wouldn't part with the cottage, but he'd managed to secure all but the few acres immediately surrounding it. It was the first time in his life he'd owned anything more valuable than the bike, the boat and a portable typewriter. Even now, it scared the hell out of him.

A hollow belly reminded him that he'd been in too big a hurry to get out of Baltimore to eat, much less to pack provisions. He pulled into a convenience store in Easton and stocked up on crackers, chocolate bars, Vienna sausages, sardines, beer and marshmallows. It should get him through the weekend. If not, he could always run into St. Michaels for a meal or two.

Emily McCloud gripped the steering wheel and made a deliberate effort to unwind. In spite of all the years she'd spent getting her teaching degree and securing a post at Eastwood Academy, it would take about one more week like this last one had been to make her chuck the whole bundle. What on earth had induced her to think she'd find fulfillment in introducing to a group of boy-crazy teenagers the joys of English literature?

She ground the starter again and swore with a fluency that would have sent generations of distaff Mc-

Clouds into a spin. Her car hated damp weather. It started on the fourth try, and Emily left the faculty parking area and waited for an opening in the late-afternoon traffic. It was beginning to drizzle, and she had a round of errands to do—and unless she could get her mind back on track again, she'd probably forget half of them.

Her high, pale forehead furrowed gently above a pair of dark, silky eyebrows. It wasn't enough that all the faculty and staff had to take a cut in pay. It wasn't enough that the radiator in her room was manic-depressive. Since the first day of the term she'd been fighting the pernicious influence of those paperback romances that were handed around the class until they were falling apart, and today had been no better. If she were to give a pop quiz on Devereaux and Dailey and Jericho, her class would ace it, but Steinbeck? According to Mollie Crandall, he was a baseball player!

The rumors of impending bankruptcy had been officially denied again today. She'd dropped by the staff lounge to see if she could glean anything from the gossip mill, and discovered Abbie Linga, the headmistress, lying down with her feet up, her shoes off, and a box of chocolates on her flat stomach. She'd been steaming her glasses over the latest torrid paperback. Emily had turned and walked out again.

"Hang in there, McCloud," she grumbled, edging into a tight parking slot. "A weekend of peace and quiet will cure what ails you." She corrected herself; make that one hour of peace and quiet and thirty-five hours of grading test papers, reading things she had no interest in reading, and then grinding out her weekly book review. For the weekly pittance.

The first stop was the *Talbot Light*, to drop off her copy and collect the books for next week's reviews. After that, she'd pick up her coat from the cleaner—then go by the hardware store and the grocer's—if she could find her list.

She was simply going to have to ask Wendell for another column; two pittances would be better than one. The trouble was, she wasn't an expert in anything, except possibly teenage girls and modern literature—and she was beginning to doubt her expertise even there.

It would have to be something special to entice Wendell to give her more space. In all the years she'd known him, including the two years she'd been engaged to him, she'd never known him to let his personal interests interfere with business. Not that she was of interest to him personally now, except as an old friend.

Bracing herself a few minutes later, she lifted her chin and opened the door marked Managing Editor. "Wendell, if you have a minute, I'd like to talk to you," she announced briskly.

In the moment before he acknowledged her presence, Emily studied Wendell Twiford objectively. The hair that had once been stove-polish black was now well shot with silver, and not even the tinted horn-rimmed glasses could hide the pouches beneath his pale blue eyes. It had been . . . Lord, it had been seventeen years since he'd given her the small solitaire.

Removing his glasses, Wendell glanced up at the tall dark-haired woman before him. "Hello, Em. How's school these days?"

"Don't ask. I only hope I get something better to read this weekend than I did last time. Stream-of-consciousness babbling from a paranoid prisoner isn't exactly my idea of weekend entertainment. If he ever reads my review, he'll know for sure the system's out to get him."

"Call 'em as you see 'em, Miss Emily. You wanted to talk to me?"

"Wendell, I have an idea for a new column. You remember that syndicated thing on gourmet dining we ran several years back? It was pretty popular, wasn't it? I could do a weekly column on gracious dining—menu, recipes, wines—maybe even flowers and suitable dinner music." Her voice grew vibrant as eagerness brushed the subtle hollows of her cheeks with color. "I'm talking about a dining-room piece, Wendell—not just another kitchen column."

"Candlelight and wine?" Wendell's voice was dry as he lifted a brow in amusement. "Don't tell me you've finally discovered romance, Em."

"I'm talking about civilized dining as opposed to burgers and fries," Emily snapped. "And don't mention romance to me, please. At the moment my tolerance is paper-thin!"

"So what else is new?" Wendell jeered softly.

"Wendell, I'm not in the mood for your sarcasm. My head aches, I've got a stack of test papers to grade and a list of errands to run before I can go home."

"I'm sorry, hon—just teasing. Want to go to the club dance tomorrow night?"

"With three books to review, a stack of papers to grade and the storm windows to put up? Hardly."

Emily knew exactly how to interpret the invitation. The family membership had never been renewed after her parents' death, but now and then Wendell offered to escort her, along with his own date, out of consideration for the fact that they'd known each other all their lives.

He needn't have bothered. Emily's social life had withered and died except for an occasional movie or a concert with someone from the school. There simply wasn't time for more, but she hadn't really missed it.

At the moment she almost resented Wendell's kindness. The trouble was, they knew each other too well. The families had always been friends, and they'd drifted into an engagement that had weathered her first year at the university and Wendell's struggle to get a moribund publishing firm on its feet again. But after the tragedy, when she'd had to take over the raising of her two younger sisters, it had been strained beyond the limit. Wendell had insisted she make other arrangements for the girls, and she'd refused. The engagement had ended with all the excitement of a wet firecracker.

"What about it, Wendell? I thought Friday would be a good day." Need battled with pride as Emily tried her best to sound unconcerned.

"Emily, the appeal is too limited. Stick to your book reviews and your schoolteaching, hmm? At the moment I'm doing my damnedest to make room for a travel feature beginning the first of the year."

Emily's level gray eyes flared to brightness and then faded again. She'd have loved tackling something like that, but unless it would support her—and small columns for a small daily wouldn't—she couldn't give up her teaching. Unless it gave her up first. "Who's doing it?"

"Nancy. She's on a cruise right now—which is why I asked about the dance. If you want to go, I'll take you."

Nancy Roscoe was blond and petite and divorced, and she'd had her eye on Wendell since junior-high-school days. Emily stood and brushed a hand down her wool paisley skirt. "No thanks, Wendell. I'm booked solid all weekend." With characteristic self-honesty, she admitted that she resented Nancy Roscoe's getting the travel column more than she did her finally getting Wendell.

"I heard you sold the Landing, Em. Why don't you take the money and treat yourself to a cruise? Nancy could put you onto some decent ones—you might even get a reservation on the Love Boat." His grin was only slightly mocking, but it was enough to send a hot rush of color to Emily's cheeks.

"Wendell, did anyone ever tell you—"

"You did, Em—frequently."

"Well, double it—in spades!"

"Don't forget to pick up the books on your way out," he reminded her calmly, reaching for a stack of papers in an obvious gesture of dismissal.

By the time she got outside, Emily had cooled off. Why did she let Wendell's remarks get under her skin? He hadn't wanted her enough to share the burden of her family at a time when she'd really needed him, and Lord knows, she'd long since got over any damage to her heart.

At the hardware store Emily bought another gallon of paint for the shutters. The price had risen since the gallon she'd bought only last spring. She walked briskly to her next stop on the same block, only to discover that the dry cleaner couldn't locate her coat. Shifting his cigar, he asked her to describe it.

"It's a beige vicuna polo coat," Emily said irritably, failing to add that it was seventeen years old and had been relined three times. It was still a good coat.

"Reg'lar girl's off this week. Check back later."

Two doors down was a convenience store. She could pick up a few items there and skip the grocer's. Emily stood on the sidewalk considering which to save—time or money. There was a motorcycle squeezed in the space in front of her car. Desperately needing a scapegoat, she told herself that unless the owner moved it within thirty seconds he was going to be sorry. The bike was in better condition than her old sedan—a little scraped paint wouldn't bother her at all. In fact, she'd welcome the chance to grind something other than her teeth!

She ground the starter. The thing groaned impotently, and Emily swore under her breath. She felt an absurd desire to bury her face in her hands and cry—which would solve precisely nothing.

"Need some help?"

The deeply voiced offer came clearly through the one-inch crack of her window, and Emily turned to see a leather-covered arm bracing itself on her door. Her startled glance shot upward to a tough-looking face, the eyes glinting only inches away from hers. Her peripheral vision took in a chin—an extremely stubborn-looking chin, hazed by a golden stubble that failed to disguise two small scars. Above it was a mouth that responded to her unconscious examination by twisting into a crooked grin. Whether friendly or mocking, she couldn't have said. The confrontation took place in mere moments—moments in which she had time to notice a nose that looked as though it might have pushed its way into more than one unpleasant situation.

It was the eyes that did it. Deep-set, hazel, surrounded by a thicket of bronze-colored lashes, they were the wickedest eyes she'd ever seen—and amazingly enough, the warmest.

Disconcerted, she blurted something that couldn't possibly have been heard through the glass. She twisted the key once more, and this time the engine coughed into life. Her eyes still entangled in a compelling thicket of bronze and green and amber, Emily watched the man back away and turn toward the motorcycle. Her hand on the gear lever, she waited until he'd mounted the sheepskin-covered seat. One booted foot on the curb, he tossed a quick grin over his shoulder and then wheeled off into the street, his muscular body leaning with the angle of his mount like some modern-day centaur.

Emily remembered to shop for the week's groceries, then drove halfway home without them and had to go back. By the time she pulled up beside the cottage it was dark, and a cold, despondent drizzle had set in.

After a hastily prepared dinner, eaten on a mahogany table that was far too large for the small room, on china that had been in her family for generations, Emily braced herself to begin her required reading. She never read at the table. She couldn't allow herself to backslide into careless habits, living alone as she did. There were standards to be maintained, and once she began letting down her guard, she'd be lost.

Carefully she washed and dried and put away the Wedgwood and rock crystal. She spread the linen towel on the rack, lotioned her hands, and went into the cluttered living room. Then, with only the smallest sigh, she reached for the first book. She hadn't even checked to see what she was in for this weekend.

A new release, it was fairly good, but even though her headache was under control, her concentration was shot. She kept seeing a vision of hazel eyes and an impudent grin in a face that was, for all its battered irregularities, compellingly attractive.

At ten she gave up and reached for the stack of test papers. While rain drummed sullenly on the metal roof, she skimmed the answers and made her marks. Finally, yawning widely, she stood up and stretched. Cocoa and bed—she'd finish the tests tomorrow. It was going to be too wet to paint shutters and put up storm windows, anyway.

After making herself a cup of cocoa, she prowled restlessly through the house. It was hopelessly over-crowded. Sometimes she wished she had the nerve to cart it all off to a junk dealer and start fresh, but she knew she'd regret it. This was all she had now that both girls were married and living so far away. Neither Vangie nor Libby had wanted any of the McCloud furniture. She'd sold the really good pieces, splitting the money three ways. She'd kept only the white elephants. The Victorian pump organ with the asthmatic bellows, the miserable old satin-striped Biedermeier sofa, the breakfront with the missing pediment—they were family things, imbued with memories of her earliest childhood, when her grandparents were still alive. Even her bedroom was taken up by an enormous sleigh bed that was valueless because it had once been damaged and clumsily repaired.

More than once she'd made up her mind to chuck it all and leave Maryland, to try to enjoy what was left of her youth before it was too late, but at the last minute she always backed out. She'd already used up her youth, and as for moving—dammit, she'd retrenched as far as she intended to.

Four generations of McClouds had lived in Talbot County, the earliest of them, Fletcher McCloud, making a modest fortune in shipping. They'd built up an estate that included a three-story colonial home near Easton that was now listed with the Maryland Historical Trust, and much later, the small cottage at Fletcher's Landing, a wooden peninsula near St. Michaels.

Holmes McCloud, Emily's father, had been an impractical dreamer and an alcoholic. What was left of a once proud shipping company, originally built around a splendid fleet of rams and schooners, had never quite made it into the age of computerized, containerized shipping. Under Holmes's incompetent directorship, it had finally sunk without a trace.

The Easton house had gone next, during Emily's last year of high school. She'd been in her first year at the university when her father's fatal heart attack had occurred. She'd dropped out, knowing that her mother would have her hands full with the two after-thoughts, as Holmes and Ansie McCloud had called their two youngest daughters, born nine and ten years after Emily.

Two days after Holmes's funeral, Ansie took the week's dose of sleeping pills she'd been given to get her through the shock of losing her husband so suddenly. It had been totally unexpected, if only because Holmes's and Ansie's marriage had been one continuous polite battle, fought with saccharine words and poisonous looks.

Emily had moved herself and her two young sisters out of the expensive apartment her parents had leased and into the Fletcher's Landing cottage, over the vociferous protests of both girls. She'd taken them out of Eastwood Academy, where three generations of McCloud women had studied, and had enrolled them in the public school.

Eventually, Vangie had married a California fruit grower, and Libby, the younger by some thirteen months, had met and married the son of a French diplomat and was presently living in Paris.

In and between and around the bringing up of her two sisters, Emily had managed to complete her own education, switching her major from art to a more practical field.

She'd hung onto Fletcher's Landing as long as she could, loving the deep, shadowy woods with their earthy, resinous smell, and the soothing sound of lapping waters around the ruins of an ancient wharf. It had been her refuge, her haven, the balm that had healed the surface wounds of day-to-day living. It had helped assuage the deeper ones that had come with the gradual realization that from a high point that had not been all that high, her life had begun a slow, gentle decline, and there was no reason to believe it would ever climb again.

The unexpected offer had been too good to turn down. With the three school loans to pay off, and two weddings to finish paying for, she'd been severely strapped. But she'd refused to sell the cottage. She'd kept the few acres immediately surrounding her house, and given instead a right-of-way onto the peninsula through her land. She'd split the money three ways, using her share to pay off her debts.

On Monday morning she was awakened by the sound of a vehicle passing her house. After striding to the front porch in her gown and slippers and seeing no one, she sighed and went inside again. It was hard to get over a feeling of possessiveness toward the land her family had owned for so long, but Fletcher's Landing was no longer her responsibility. If trespassers invaded it, leaving their litter behind, it was up to the new owners to put a stop to it. Hunters and fishermen had ignored the "No Trespassing" signs for years, and someone had been sneaking in to camp for the past year.

A feeling of unfocused resentment persisted, and Emily entered Wendell's office the following afternoon with an aggressive burst of energy that brought her skirts swirling about her long, shapely legs.

"Read 'em and weep," she pronounced defiantly as she placed her copy on Wendell's desk. "Since when did we dignify trash with a review?" Her fists on her hips, she dug her knuckles defiantly into the soft wool knit of her mulberry-colored pullover as she waited for an answer.

"Trash?" Wendell responded absently, running his finger down a long column in a word estimate that would be accurate to within six words.

"The Bonnie Jericho thing. Tell me, Wendell, do women actually swallow that tripe?"

"Oh, the romance." His voice was dry, his eyes amused. "Jericho's a bestseller—supposed to be regional. And why ask me what women read?" he dismissed, returning his gaze to the page before him.

Emily snorted in disgust, and Wendell looked up again, his finger anchoring a word to the newsprint. "I suppose I should have known better than to ask you to read the romance," he said wearily. "You know, you continue to amaze me, Em—you could be a beautiful woman if you bothered to make the effort, but your nose is getting slightly out of shape from being pressed to that self-imposed grindstone of yours."

The arrow found its target, but a slatelike opacity disguised the hurt in Emily's dark gray eyes. "In case you've forgotten, the grindstone was hardly self-imposed. Besides, you had your own particular grindstone, remember?" The demands of an ailing newspaper had been Wendell's argument against taking on the burden of a ready-made family.

"I haven't forgotten. At least I knew better than to allow a grindstone to become a millstone around my neck."

"Well, bully for you."

Wendell shook his head mockingly. "You could never get beyond this stage of a discussion without falling back on a cliché, could you, Em? For an English teacher your vocabulary is remarkably limited."

Emily took a deep, calming breath. She'd long since learned to deal with Wendell's taunts. "Not as limited as you might think," she purred, eyes still stony. "Maybe you'd better have your lawyer go over the book reviews before Tuesday. If Miss Jericho should happen to see a copy of our modest little rag, you're probably going to hear from her." With that she swung around and strode to the door, back rigid, head held high under a burden of rich chestnut-brown hair.

Wendell's reminder to pick up the next batch of books on her way out somewhat dampened the effect of her exit line, and she whispered an oath as she veered off to collect two spy thrillers and the biography of a comedian who was notorious for his love affairs.

At least there were no more so-called romances to strain her credulity. At some age, women of even moderate intelligence were supposed to get over believing in Prince Charming and knights in shining armor. Lord knows, after growing up in a household where the kindest words spoken between her parents were apt to be "please pass the salt," she hadn't expected to be whirled away on a cloud of moon madness, but even so, she'd been disappointed. Her engagement had been a farce, and the two later relationships she'd almost ventured into had reaffirmed her belief that men were takers, not givers—not even sharers.

* * *

Bey tried the door again, and then walked around to the back of the small frame house that all but blocked access to his property. The realtor had said she wouldn't budge, but it wouldn't hurt to give it one more try. According to what he'd been able to learn, the woman was the last of an old, once prominent Eastern Shore family, a spinster who'd dug herself in after selling off everything but her home.

Lord knows, Bey could sympathize with her for wanting to hang in there. If he'd ever had a genuine home, he might not be so all-fired bent on what he was doing.

"Lady, you've got what I want, and I'm just mean enough to go after it," he muttered, eyeing the peeling paint on the back of the house. The poor old creature couldn't even look after what she had. She'd be much better off in a retirement home or one of those cubbyholes designed for elderly singles.

He'd pay her twice what it was worth—hell, he'd already paid her enough for the rest of her land to goldplate this place. Maybe she was one of those cranks who hoarded it all away in a shoebox. Maybe she'd endowed a home for cats. Bingo games? The horses? Could be. At any rate, he rationalized half-guiltily, he'd be doing her a favor to get her out of here and into town where someone responsible could look after her.

"Hey, anybody home?" he called out, pounding on the dark green front door one last time. At least she'd taken the trouble to spruce up the front of the house—shutters in good shape, windows sparkling. And gutters full of leaves and pinestraw, he noted as he backed down the single step and out onto the autumn-littered brick walk that led out to the narrow rutted road.

Straddling the BMW again, Bey headed for town. It was too wet to camp out. Dammit, he hated having to spend a single minute of his precious free time shut up in the impersonal walls of a motel. Once he'd made up his mind, he'd been so eager to get on with the building that he'd overcome the contractor's objection by agreeing to hire two crews to get the place under way before winter set in. He'd located the corners today, and left the men putting up batter boards.

The thought of owning his own home had grown like a fever in him. Dim memories of the only home he could remember had long since overlaid with the series of institutions he'd known since his mother had dumped him in the lap of the state authorities. If she'd actually been his real mother; he'd never been sure. Fortunately, he'd learned survival skills fast.

Dining alone in the motel restaurant on fried oysters, Bey considered the unlikely route that had brought him to the brink of taxpaying respectability. It had been the books that had been his salvation. The sporadic education he'd picked up had introduced him to the Western classics. On his own, he'd read everything Zane Grey and Louis L'Amour had ever written, and by the time he was old enough to enlist in the army he'd written three bad Westerns.

It had taken him a long time to figure out just why they were so bad, but he'd done it. The trouble was, he'd never met a horse face-to-face in his life, and the closest he'd come to a bunkhouse was an army barracks in Fort Bragg. Hell, he was a waterman. Son of a merchant seaman—at least that was what he'd been told—he'd lived around the bay area all his life, usually one step ahead of one set of authorities or another, depending on his age.

The army had been a blessing to him. Once his initial training had ended, he'd taken every course he could fit into his schedule. By the time he'd got out, he might have earned himself a degree, but he'd audited most courses, wanting the knowledge far more than a piece of paper.

He would have stayed in longer but for a sniper's bullet that had landed him flat on his back for three months. It was while he was in the V.A. hospital that the local ladies' auxiliary had mixed up their book delivery. Having read everything the skimpy library provided, Bey had grumblingly read his first paperback romance.

By the time he'd finished the lot, he was itching to write again. Dammit, he might not know much about range wars and cattle stampedes, but he knew about women—bad ones, not-so-bad ones, the beautiful and the unbeautiful.

It was almost like a new frontier, with the heroine fighting against overwhelming odds to hang on to her newly won territory. He understood genre books, having spent so much time between the covers of Westerns. Romances weren't all that different—variations on a theme, with far more scope than the standard horse-and-gun epic. In the good ones, the writing was superb—witty as well as tender.

Oddly enough, it was the tenderness that appealed to him most of all. It was an exotic new taste on his tongue, an intoxicating new world waiting to be explored. If fantasy was what women wanted, he had a few of his own he'd like to share.

He'd gone back to Baltimore after being discharged, simply because it was familiar. He'd leased a row house that was little more than a tenement and bought himself a portable typewriter from a pawnshop. The advance on his first book barely covered the rent and a few supplies, but he'd gotten a nibble on a second book, and with that under his belt, he'd signed on with an agent.

His next advance was considerably more than he'd expected, even minus the agent's cut. With it he'd bought himself enough decent clothes to get him through a weekend in New York at contract time, and then he'd bought his first yacht. Much in need of repairs, the twenty-seven-foot oyster boat was unremarkable on the outside, which suited him just fine. His defensive instincts were too well-developed for ostentation, even now that he could afford it. Flash it around, and you get it ripped off. Blend in, and you stand a chance of surviving. Those were among the earliest lessons he'd learned.

He'd blended in. Over the next few years, as his bank balance had soared to numbing heights, he'd learned his way around a different jungle. He could hold his own on any turf, from New York's Upper East Side to Baltimore's slums. The purchase of Fletcher's Landing had leveled his funds considerably, but with the delivery fee for his last manuscript he'd have more than enough to build the sort of house he had in mind.

Back in his motel room again after the indigestible meal, Bey prowled, pausing now and then to stare out into the courtyard with the covered swimming pool. He waited until there was no one in sight and then he turned up his collar and dashed out into the rain. Minutes later he wheeled the dripping BMW into his carpeted room. He didn't own much, but what he did own, he damned well knew how to protect.

Two

"The hell you say," Bey growled, lifting his naked back from the pillows. He'd showered and, still damp, had settled onto the bed with a cigar and a copy of the morning paper.

The review had taken him by surprise. If publishers wanted to send out advance copies, that was their privilege. Bey's agent passed on the royalty statement and the checks, and that was all the news he needed to know. After reading one or two articles on romances and the women who wrote them, he'd deliberately turned his back on newsletters, reviews and anything not directly related to his own work.

It was strictly hype—this business of writing in purple satin nightgowns, in lilac-scented bubble baths, and drinking only Dom Pérignon chilled in sterling-silver ice buckets. Bey's sense of privacy was too deeply ingrained to expose himself to that sort of rubbish. It was awkward enough being a man in what was predominantly a woman's realm. Damned if he wanted it bruited about that he wrote his books wearing silk pajama pants and kept a harem for inspiration and research.

Scowling, he allowed his eyes to be drawn once more to the scurrilous attack. "'Victimized females'? Lady, you're nuts!" he grunted. "'Addictive, pernicious pap ladled out ad nauseam by a woman whose tastes obviously became fixed somewhere between late puberty and early adolescence. Miss Jericho is a traitor to her gender.'"

Crushing the paper as he leaned forward, Bey lunged for the notebook and pen that were never far from his side. "If I'm a traitor to your gender, lady, what the devil does that make you?"

Tossing aside the front section of the paper, he smoothed out the offending article and checked the byline. "McCloud? Do I know you from somewhere?" The name had a familiar ring to it. He repeated it aloud and then, shaking his head to clear away the distraction, he began scribbling.

"Miss McCloud...who is obviously totally unfamiliar with romance in any form..." he mumbled as he wrote, "would do well to curb her vituperative tongue...lest she earn the pity of her readers. There is nothing more pathetic...than a woman incapable of appreciating her...*womanhood!* If my heroine appears...victimized to you, Miss McCloud, and my hero overbearing...it could be because you have obviously...never been made aware of the basic physical differences between the sexes. Not genders, Miss McCloud," Bey scribbled angrily. *"Sexes!"*

Appending the ambiguous initials B.J., Bey searched through the plastic-veneer drawers until he located an envelope bearing the motel's logo. Checking the newspaper's masthead, he addressed it and enclosed the lined page from his notebook. Oblivious of his state of nudity, he crossed the room and laid the letter on the seat of his bike.

Then, stretching out on the bed once more, he crossed his arms under his head, stared up at the rough plaster ceiling and began visualizing the house that would soon be taking shape on the shore of his own stretch of the bay—or more accurately, the mouth of the Miles River.

Reluctantly Emily unrolled the morning paper with one hand while she stirred her coffee. Wendell had phoned the night before to alert her.

"Answer it in Friday's edition, Em," he'd ordered. "This sort of thing is great for circulation. I wouldn't be surprised if we don't generate a few more letters before it runs its course."

"Wendell, I don't write letters to the editor unless I feel it's my civic duty, and this hardly falls into that category. If some woman wants to indulge in a public brawl over a sleazy romance, that's her business. I don't have to be a part of it."

"You *are* a part of it. You landed the first punch with your review, and it was a doozy. I didn't think even you would go that far."

"I warned you when I handed it in—if you didn't like it, you could have killed it. And what do you mean, even me?" She clamped her teeth into a slice of dry toast while she rustled through the paper to find the editorial page.

"Figure of speech, Em—forget it."

"And stop calling me Em! It makes me feel like someone's grandmother!"

Wendell's chuckle came through quite clearly, and Emily visualized those pale blue eyes lit with amusement. Wendell had always known how to get a rise out of her.

"That's right, you have another birthday coming up in a few days, don't you, Em? What is it—thirty-nine? Forty?"

"It's thirty-seven and you damned well know it," she snapped, having located the correct page. "I'll see you after school." She hung up the phone to concentrate on the response to her scathing review.

"My dear Miss Jericho," Emily typed rapidly five minutes after she'd arrived home from school. Then, sighing in exasperation, she ripped the page from the typewriter and rolled in a fresh sheet. Miss Jericho was neither dear nor hers. Besides, it might not be Bonnie Jericho who'd written the insulting letter. Regional or not, there was no reason to think a bestselling author would bother to read a small-town daily, and there'd hardly been time for it to reach her through a clipping service.

A cool glint brightened Emily's normally grave eyes. "Dear B.J. Is that Betty Jane? Barbara Jo? Anonymous letters are both cowardly and abhorrent. I dignify yours with an answer only at the behest of my editor."

Which was not precisely true. All day long she'd been seething, to the point where she'd actually overlooked her students' inattentiveness and the stack of dog-eared romances that had exchanged hands during break. On the way out of the stifling room, she'd heard Kim

Bleeker whispering, "Sandi, you've *got* to read this one and give it back tomorrow. Talk about every which way! Seven times, and once on *horseback!*"

She hadn't even bothered to light the fire before starting her reply to B.J. Could it be Jericho, after all? In spite of everything, Emily knew a momentary rush of excitement at the thought that she might actually be corresponding with the author of five bestsellers. And no matter how much she might despise the genre, she grudgingly admitted that for trash, they were well-written.

B.J. could be anyone. She could think of half-dozen people offhand whose initials fit, although she seriously doubted that Bob Jernigan at the service station would bother to write such a letter, and Barby Jarvis was only four years old. It was probably some frustrated, defensive romance reader. It might even be one of her own students, although the wording was a bit sophisticated for the average fifteen-year-old.

"Dear Betty Jane: I'm sorry you took exception to my review of *Reap the Wild Wind*. While I stand by my opinion, I will confess that my attitude is partially colored by the fact that Miss Jericho is obviously a skilled writer. It is unfortunate that she restricts herself to such unworthy subjects. Fairy tales of the type propounded by the so-called romance genre are an insult to the intellect of any thinking woman. They do our gender a disservice by raising expectations that can only lead to disillusionment, and are therefore to be despised."

She felt somewhat better after that. Lighting the fire she'd laid that morning, Emily sighed and slipped off her gray sling-back pumps. At times like this, with another birthday staring her in the face, she was apt to suffer from a mild sort of depression. Thirty-seven come Saturday, and what did she have to show for it? One engagement that had ended anticlimactically after two unexciting years, one career that grew less rewarding with every passing day, a part-time job that took too much of her time for the paltry rewards it brought, and a drafty house chock-full of furniture that was neither old enough to be valuable nor attractive enough to be desirable.

She had Libby and Vangie, the sisters she'd raised from ages ten and eleven respectively. She'd done her best with them, and all in all, they'd turned out to be people she liked as well as loved, but they were caught up in their own affairs now. Neither of them had wanted to come back to the Eastern Shore, where too many unhappy memories lingered. She couldn't blame them for that.

Thirty-seven. For the hundredth time she considered selling out, moving away and starting over. She was still young enough to do it. If lately she'd felt far older than her years, it was her own fault. She'd been so caught up in the treadmill of classroom and homework, of rushing through books just so she could grind out her reviews, of trying to fit in all the chores that went along with owning an elderly house, that she never took time for herself.

When was the last time she'd seen a movie? Or even walked in the woods? How long had it been since she'd found time to relax, to take an apple, a bit of cheese and a glass of wine to the shore, where she'd watch birds, or poke about the water's edge, examining pebbles and the occasional potsherd she found there? So the peninsula had changed hands—there were no fences to keep her out, no signs proclaiming the new ownership. Nothing had really changed.

As soon as the rain stopped, Emily promised herself resolutely, she'd put together a picnic and find a sunny spot near the water where she could lie back and watch the sails buffeting back and forth out on the bay. What was the point in owning a waterfront cottage if one didn't take time to appreciate it?

By Saturday the sky was a joyous shade of blue, with only an occasional wisp of lavender cloud to mark the passing cold front. There were a dozen chores to be done, and Emily delighted for once in ignoring them all.

Humming an unrecognizable version of the overture to *Der Rosenkavalier*, she ducked her head under the spray and lathered the abundance of glossy brown hair. Today was her birthday and she was determined to enjoy it. One day soon she'd treat herself to a new coat, since the cleaners had been unable to locate her old one. She didn't have to go overboard—a modest chinchilla should do it.

"Or a black mink?" she suggested to her image as she blotted the moisture from her hair. The steamy mirror was flattering, especially as her cheeks were still flushed from her bath. "As the woman in the TV ad says," she told herself, assuming a sultry pose, "I'm worth it."

Actually, she was holding up pretty well, all things considered. She'd inherited the McClouds' spare frame—long, nicely shaped legs, narrow hands and feet. Her cheekbones were the sort that aged well, and her eyes were nice enough. Perhaps she'd start wearing more makeup—a little more eye shadow, a touch of blusher. Lately she'd got out of the habit.

The scent of the woodsmoke tantalized her nostrils before she'd even left the yard. She'd always loved campfires and burning leaves, but if someone had dropped a cigarette in the woods and set fire to a patch of brush, that was another matter. If Bon-Bey's woods burned, then so did hers, and Bon-Bey, Inc. wasn't here to police their property.

Following the trail of the acrid smoke, Emily angled toward the far shore of the point, an area she seldom visited, as there were many more accessible places that were every bit as lovely. It was encouragingly damp once she entered the deepest woods, but along the shore there'd be patches of marsh grass and low shrubbery that would dry quickly in the sunlight.

She almost tripped over it. In the mellow gloom of an autumn forest, the last thing Emily expected to see was a motorcycle. A few feet away stood a small tent. Before she could react to those two items, she saw the man. Broad, red-clad shoulders tapered downward to narrow hips, revealing a band of tanned flesh between shirt and jeans. His back was to her as he hunched over a small fire.

Emily's heart leapt into double-time and she froze mid-stride. Her eyes took in the leather jacket flung across the motorcycle and the short-handled ax wedged in a fallen oak. There was no one around for a dozen miles—unless he was only one of a gang who was using the isolated place for... for whatever motorcycle gangs used isolated places like this for. She could scream her head off and no one would hear her.

Before she could break the momentary paralysis and edge away from the small clearing, the intruder stood and turned in a smooth motion that reminded her of a fox she'd once seen in these woods. There was something about his face—wary, but unafraid. She recognized him instantly. It was the same man who'd offered help outside the dry cleaners several days before. Had he followed her home? Was he planning to...? But that was ridiculous! Not in broad daylight—not here in her own backyard!

They stood poised, neither of them speaking as the tiny fire crackled and sparked behind a circle of rocks. Emily, her brain working quite coolly now, evaluated her chances of escaping should he prove aggressive. They were of a height, but her legs might be longer. On the other hand, he had wheels. She didn't fancy being chased through the woods by an angry motorcyclist. He was obviously tough and fit and totally unafraid. He was also a trespasser, someone who had no business even being in these woods, much less camping here.

"Would you care for a chocolate-and-marshmallow graham cracker?" the trespasser inquired as politely as if he were in his own drawing room offering milk for her tea.

She'd been unconsciously holding her breath since that first involuntary gasp. Now the air rushed from her lungs. What sort of motorcyclist would offer her something like that? A member of Heck's Angels?

Emily subdued an unlikely urge to giggle. "Smores?" she inquired, her husky contralto quivering in relief and amusement.

He blinked. Even from this distance she was aware of the intensity of his gaze. Tilting his head inquisitively, he smiled, and Emily felt something inside her shift, leaving an oddly hollow feeling in its place.

"The...the graham crackers with chocolate and marshmallow melted on them. When I was young, we called them smores. You know—some more?" She hadn't moved; they were still a dozen yards apart. She wondered if he'd heard the peculiar breathlessness in her voice. Swallowing nervously, she recalled something about wild creatures being able to smell fear in a human being.

God knows she'd been scared out of her wits for a minute there. And she wasn't out of the woods, yet—either figuratively or literally.

"I've got a pot of water all ready for coffee. Even with the sun out, it's cold back here in the woods." Bey waited for her to advance or retreat. He'd heard her approach even before she'd caught her breath—a split second before. There'd been times in his life when a split second's warning had been all that had saved his skin.

Silk and handmade lace and hundred-dollar-an-ounce perfume, he'd summed her up instantly. Even in gray wool slacks covered in beggar's-lice and a suede jacket that was shiny at the cuffs and collar, she was a class act. She was the sort of woman who seldom came his way. He'd thought about her once or twice since he'd seen her grinding away at that old clunker she drove. A woman like that should be driving a Mercedes, at least. Better yet, she should be chauffeured.

The half-grin thawed into a genuine smile. "Come hunker down at the fire. I've got a spare cup here somewhere."

Stiffly Emily began to move, feeling strangely as if she were a puppet and someone else was pulling the strings. She wasn't accustomed to "hunkering down" to anything—especially not with a barbarian who rode a motorcycle and wore muddy jeans with what looked suspiciously like the top of a set of long johns. She halted several yards away. "These woods are posted, you know," she said evenly.

"I'm not hurting anything." Bey watched her eyes, his subliminal senses taking in the easy way she moved.

He liked tall women. This one carried herself as proudly as a clipper ship.

Emily found herself engaged in an unexpectedly intimate examination of the man, of his muscular, compact build, his irregular features, and deceptively relaxed way he held himself, like a coiled spring ready to fire off at a touch. He was a sort she'd seldom encountered personally. "There are signs up all along the boundary warning trespassers away," she pointed out.

Hazel eyes captured gray ones easily, holding them prisoner for long, uncomfortable moments. "I have permission to be here," Bey said quietly, perversely refusing to release her gaze. She had strength and pride. He admired that in a woman.

"From whom?" Emily demanded breathlessly, breaking away finally from his disconcerting spell. If this man even knew who owned the property, it would surprise her. He had to be bluffing.

"Let's just say the new owner knows I'm here. More to the point, who are you, and what's your business here?"

Feeling suddenly weak, Emily dropped down onto the dead oak, digging her fingers into the punky wood. She could pretend that she still owned the whole tract—it would lend her more authority. But there was always the off-chance that he was telling the truth. "Did you say coffee?" she blurted more from confusion than from thirst. If it wasn't outright surrender, it was close to it. At least the man had the courtesy not to gloat.

"Hope you don't take anything in yours." He turned away, busying himself at the fireside for a moment before returning to hand her a steaming, battered mug. She took both sugar and cream, actually, but she was on thin ice here—best to be diplomatic until she could politely take her leave.

He joined her on the log, cupping his strong, surprisingly well-kept hands around an even more battered mug. "In a minute I'll make us some... What did you call 'em? Smores? I thought they were my own invention."

Emily sipped cautiously at the scalding brew, amazed at finding herself here in the middle of the woods calmly sharing black coffee with a man who could be a member of an infamous motorcycle gang, for all she knew. "Hmm, instant," she remarked, immediately regretting her tactlessness.

"You don't drink instant coffee?"

"It's fine, it's just perfect," she lied hastily.

"At least you've got no grounds for complaint."

Emily shot him a quick glance. At the sight of wickedly gleaming eyes in a suspiciously solemn face, she felt the edge of her reserve begin to crumble. "That's abominable," she accused with a straight face.

"I know. Don't you like abominable jokes either?"

"About as much as I like instant coffee. What did you measure it with, a shovel?"

"A knife blade, as a matter of fact. Three bladefuls per cup."

"Try one," Emily suggested dryly, sipping the bitter beverage cautiously.

Without speaking, he took her mug, poured out a third of the coffee and refilled the cup with water from the smoke-blackened pot. He watched as she tried it again. "Better?" he asked solicitously.

Emily considered a courteous lie and decided against it. She had an idea this man would see through any such polite fabrication. Besides, what did it matter? "It's still terrible, but if you like it this way, that's your privilege."

"You live around here?" the man asked genially. He had a surpisingly nice voice—deep, soft, with an accent that was impossible to pin down.

She nodded, caution preventing her from revealing the details. "I used to walk here a lot. It's one of the few places I know where you can't hear the traffic noises."

"I noticed. Many people find their way out here?" The question was casually put, but Emily had the feeling that her answer was of more than casual interest.

"All the time," she prevaricated. "Hunters, fishermen, bird watchers, scout troops. There's a botany class scheduled to be here any minute now—oh, and I forgot the joggers."

He shot her a skeptical look. "What about the house at the edge of the woods? The one with the green door and shutters?"

Emily leaned over and picked up a purplish sweetgum leaf, twirling it between her fingers as she considered a reply. "What about it?"

"Would that be your house?" It was a shot in the dark, but he knew with a growing certainty that this woman was the elderly party he'd been trying to contact off and on for several weeks.

Emily nodded. It would do little good to deny it—anyone in town could tell him as much if he were really interested. At least he didn't know she lived alone. And even if he did, there was something about him that, oddly enough, she instinctively trusted. For all his toughness, there was a directness about him that appealed to her.

"My name's Bey Jones. That's Bey with an *e*, not an *a*. What's yours?"

Well, that was direct enough. "Emily McCloud," she replied, digging up a half-buried pine cone with the toe of her suede moccasin.

For a minute she thought he hadn't heard her. And then he turned and extended a hand. "Miss McCloud," he acknowledged softly, his smile just as wide, but somehow different. "I'm your new neighbor."

She'd left him soon after that. Thrown off balance by a subtle change that followed the introduction, Emily had made the excuse of something in the oven and hurried away. Later she wished she'd taken the time to ask a few pertinent questions. Such as what he planned to do with the property. And exactly who he was, and where he was from, and what he did, and if there was a Mrs. Bey Jones.

Bey with an *e*. Then it hadn't been a typo. She'd been upset at having to sell the property and a misspelled word had been the least of her worries. She was so accustomed to seeing the word "bay" on so many businesses around the Eastern Shore that she hadn't even thought about it.

Bon-Bey was his corporation, then. What sort of corporation? Surely the place hadn't been rezoned; she'd have been notified if that had been the case. A residence? A development?

Oh Lord, not a housing development! Bon-Bey was a real-estate outfit, then—she'd bet her bottom dollar on it. The way her luck had been running just recently, it had to be that.

If she'd needed a shove to boost her out of a rut, this was it. What a birthday present! A card from Libby, a scarf from Vangie, and a tract of cracker-box houses going up right under her nose.

On Sunday morning, she drove into Baltimore. She'd always found aquariums soothing, and the National Aquarium was precisely what she needed at the moment. And after she'd sorted herself out, she'd treat herself to an expensive lunch and a new winter coat. That done, she'd consider the facts calmly and decide whether or not to put her house on the market and hand in her notice at school. If the school didn't hand its notice to her first.

Staring unseeingly at the glass wall as a white shark passed within three inches of her nose, Emily sighed again. At this rate, she'd soon be hyperventilated. She'd been sighing all weekend.

The perfectly idiotic thing was, she couldn't get Bey Jones out of her mind. The academy was facing bankruptcy, her salary had been drastically cut, there was no chance of making up the difference with another column. She was now officially thirty-seven years old and facing a housing development right on her doorstep, and all she could think about was a tough-looking man who rode a motorcycle and camped in the woods and made atrocious coffee.

A man, her relentless thoughts added, who had a crooked smile and a way of laughing with his eyes that made a battered face seem amazingly desirable.

The trucks came before she even left the house on Monday morning. Three pickup trucks followed by a behemoth with a gaping steel jaw. Emily stood on her front porch, briefcase and purse hanging limply from one hand, and watched the ominous parade.

It had started then—the ruthless bulldozing, the crushing of everything precious and lovely in her woods—the woods where she'd picnicked with her grandfather as a child, a consolation for having all her parents' attention claimed by the two babies.

As though sensing that something was seriously wrong, her girls were unusually subdued all day. When Denise Boger actually claimed Conrad Aiken's obscure *Samadha* as her favorite poem of the term, Emily could have wept.

"It's sort of like the way it is now, Miss McCloud. We've got these trees out behind the swimming pool, and every fall they sort of like... well, the pool gets all full of leaves, and the trees shine down in it, and...well, you know."

Perhaps she was doing them a disservice to foster sensitivity and an appreciation for beauty, Emily thought despairingly. By the time they were her age, all the beauty might have been bulldozed off the face of the earth. Sensitivity could be a handicap.

By the time she dropped off her copy and collected another stack of books, Emily had herself in hand again. She collected the mail, dropped it along with her purse and briefcase on the Biedermeier sofa—it made a wonderful table—and lighted the fire. By the time she'd changed into gray slacks and a violet cashmere pullover Libby had left behind, she was completely composed.

Next year she'd indulge herself in another maudlin bout of self-searching. One a year was all she could afford. Time brought changes; it was inevitable. It didn't pay to look back at what might have been, or worry too much about what was to come. Sufficient unto the day...

The peremptory rap on the door came while she was setting a single Wedgwood plate on the table with one hand and stirring the Stroganoff with the other. Muttering an impatient "I'm coming" under her breath, she hurried through the living room, dodging nimbly around the bulky pump organ and swinging her hips to avoid the projecting arm of a rather ugly Morris chair.

"Bey?" she said in some confusion at the sight of her visitor.

"Miss McCloud," he repeated. He was wearing the same shirt and the same jeans, as far as she could tell. With one muscular arm braced against the doorjamb, he looked perfectly relaxed.

Her confusion increased at his formal greeting. "Mr. Jones?" she said uncertainly. She'd somehow thought that first names were in order after the few minutes of camaraderie they'd shared.

"I saw your light," he murmured, his eyes never leaving hers.

Disconcerted at his nearness—they'd been several feet apart on the oak log in the woods—she stepped back and issued a hesitant invitation. "Won't you...come in?"

She could feel the animal warmth of him as he brushed past her. His scent, a mixture of woodsmoke and some excitingly masculine essence, assailed her nostrils and threatened to rob her of her newly regained composure. She stood there staring helplessly at his back while he turned slowly to examine her room.

He was little taller than she was, and yet his presence seemed to push out the walls and lift the ceiling. There was a force about the man that was somehow larger than life. It frightened her, and she wanted him out— out of her house, out of her life.

"Did you...were you...?" she stammered, hardly knowing what to say without sounding rude.

"I stayed over another couple of days since the weather's clear. Had to go into town and stock up on provisions."

"Oh," she said lamely. And then, lifting her head at the smell from the kitchen, she blurted, "Excuse me, will you? Something's burning."

Not quite, but almost. The sour cream, wine and mushroom sauce was dried around the edges of the pan.

"Were you in time?" Bey asked. He watched her stirring the mixture, agitating the narrow strips of beef, her lips pursed in annoyance.

He'd intended to stay away—he'd managed to put her out of his mind for two whole days, but as he'd passed her house a few minutes ago, his curiosity had risen up stronger than ever. How could a woman as beautiful and as obviously intelligent as Emily McCloud write such a narrow-minded, vindictive review of what was a damned fine book, if he did say so himself? He was no longer furious with her—he was merely curious.

In the moment before she turned to answer him, his gaze lingered appreciatively on the subtle curve of her lean hips. There was a special allure in subtlety. He'd appreciated plenty of voluptuous women in his rambling years, but there was something about this particular woman that set her apart.

"It wasn't quite scorched," Emily admitted, switching off the burner and lifting the lid to stir the pot of rice. It was ready—the table was set. "I suppose you've had dinner," she murmured, avoiding those compelling hazel eyes. "I'm running late tonight."

"Guess I am, too," Bey replied equably, taking in the single plate, the sparkling wineglass, the crisp linen napkin and the heavy, ornate silver. "It won't take me long to get a fire going, though. Once it burns down, I'll have the can all opened and ready to heat."

Emily closed her eyes momentarily and wondered if he was doing it deliberately. "You're welcome to share my dinner," she heard herself offer.

Bey levered himself away from the doorway where he'd been leaning, arms crossed over his chest. "I wasn't hinting, Miss McCloud."

Irritably Emily reached for another plate. "I wasn't implying that you were, Mr. Jones."

"Oh, well, in that case, I thank you." He was beside her without seeming to have moved, taking the silverware from her hand and placing it on the table beside the second plate. Dense bronze lashes shielding his eyes, he arranged the utensils with perfect precision and accepted the linen napkin with a nod of thanks.

Emily could have kicked herself. He was acting like a wistful little boy, and she knew damned well there wasn't a boyish bone in his body. Bey Jones was tough as nails. She must have been insane to invite him into her home.

"I hope you like Stroganoff," she grumbled, not caring if she sound ungracious.

Three

"Sure do," Bey replied, a crooked grin simmering across his irregular features. "Shall I pour the wine for you?"

"It's in the refrigerator." Emily reached for another of her Grandmother Barrington's hand-etched lead-crystal wineglasses. "Or perhaps you'd prefer coffee?" she added, glancing over her shoulder with a suspiciously grave expression.

At Bey's look of swift comprehension, her gravity dissolved into a smile that lingered as she took down another bowl and began dividing the salad.

"Hey, if that's for me, don't bother." Bey uncorked the wine and steadied the glass as he poured, his sinewy hands incongruous on the fragile stem.

"You don't care for any salad?" Emily's eyes shifted from his face to his hands and back again, her senses suddenly jolted by the sight of so much concentrated masculinity against the familiar background of her breakfast nook.

"I can live without it."

"I'm afraid I don't have another vegetable."

"You have rice," Bey replied agreeably.

"Rice is not a vegetable."

"Sure it is, I've seen it growing." Bey pulled out her chair, his arms spreading in a half-embrace as he seated her at the table.

"It's a grain," Emily pointed out as she served his plate with a generous mound of brown rice and ladled on a lion's share of the richly sauced beef.

"A technicality," Bey rejoined calmly. He spread the napkin across his thighs and grimaced apologetically. "I'm not exactly dressed for dining out."

She shrugged. "Neither am I."

"You're in. I'm the one who's out." Fork poised, he studied the woman across from him. He hadn't paid much attention to what she had on—she was the sort of woman who made clothes seem irrelevant. Whatever she was wearing was the right thing to wear. An errant thought brought a speculative gleam to his eyes and he quickly lowered them to his plate.

"This is good," he said a few moments later, offering her one of those hazardous smiles of his that threatened to undermine every shred of her hard-earned equilibrium. "Living outdoors is a real appetizer."

That said, he devoted himself to cleaning off his plate, the task of a few moments. Emily wondered guiltily if she should have given him all the Stroganoff and settled for the spinach-and-mushroom salad as her share. He had a sort of coiled-spring vitality that indicated a voracious appetite.

The plain truth was, he rattled her. It had been bad enough in the open woods, but here in the intimacy of her own small home, it was far worse. There was no place in her settled life-style for a man like Bey Jones.

She'd be polite, but cool, she decided firmly. She'd get rid of the man as soon as she possibly could without being actually discourteous.

"Do you live in this area, Mr. Jones?"

"I'm working on it, and make it Bey, will you...Emily? That's a nice name. Are there many Emily McClouds around these parts? I seem to recall the realtor's saying you come from an old Eastern Shore family."

"I have a sister in California and another in Paris, both married. As far as I know, I'm the only McCloud left. I didn't make dessert, Bey. Would you care for coffee?" Above a carefully controlled mouth, Emily's eyes sparkled unexpectedly. "I'm afraid I can't offer you anything but the drip variety."

"I'd like that—in front of your fireplace?" Bey asked hopefully. "I'm going to have a fireplace before this winter's done. Here, let me help you with those dishes."

Rising hastily, Emily reached a protective hand toward the fragile crystal. She regretted it even before she saw the quick flare of his nostrils. She didn't have to insult the man by implication. "I...I'll just leave them for later," she murmured apologetically. "Would you see if the fire needs tending while I start the coffee?"

He shrugged, the collarless red knit shirt following the smooth play of muscles that produced the expressive gesture. Wordlessly he sauntered into the living room, leaving Emily both angry and bewildered.

What *was* there about this man that affected her so strongly? He certainly wasn't the sort of man she usually invited into her home, but since she had, it was rude, not to mention unfair, to imply that he was a barbarian who couldn't be trusted in polite society.

She knew absolutely nothing about him—for all she knew, he could be lying about everything. In the short time since she'd first laid eyes on him, he'd managed to invade her consciousness in a way that no man had done in years. Irritably she dismissed the thought that perhaps it was herself she didn't trust.

The coffee poured, she handed Bey a cup and nodded to the cushioned Morris chair. Then, gracefully balancing her own cup and saucer in one long, slender hand, she lowered herself onto the inhospitable sofa. "I saw the trucks and that monstrous-looking digging thing go by this morning."

"The backhoe?" Bracing his shoulders against the chintz cushion, Bey stretched out his legs and crossed his booted ankles.

Emily wished rather desperately that he'd either get himself a looser pair of jeans or sit in a more circumspect manner—so much potent masculinity at close range was disconcerting. It had been too long since she'd entertained anyone more exciting than the local minister; she simply wasn't prepared for a man who flaunted his sexuality without even being aware of it.

"A backhoe," she repeated, forcing her mind into a safer channel. "That's sort of like a bulldozer, isn't it? Bey, I do hope you plan to leave a few trees standing." Small hope; a cycle-riding ruffian who wore undershirts, tight jeans and resoled boots would probably timber the place and then resell it for farmland.

Bey, cradling the delicate violet-sprigged cup in his square, tanned hands, glanced slowly about the room, making no effort to reassure her. Unless he were a junk dealer, Emily thought rancorously, no man could be all that interested in her accumulation of mismatched furniture.

For a long moment his gaze rested on an untidy stack of papers on the breakfront. He shifted his weight, and in silent desperation she watched the play of muscles under the faded denim. Then, tearing her eyes away from his powerful thighs, she studied his face in an effort to probe his mind. The man was not quite so simple as she'd first imagined. Oh, she'd soon recognized the little-boy-lost game he was playing—it had probably got him into more than a few kitchens. More than a few beds, as well.

But there was another game being played here. She sensed it without understanding it, and it made her uneasy. "What exactly are you planning to build, Bey?"

His gaze wandered back to move over her face with the same degree of detachment he'd shown the pump organ, the striped sofa, the imperfect breakfront and the assortment of mismatched chairs. Slightly less, she noted in dismay, than he'd shown her overflowing bookshelves.

"Just a home," he said. "You know—fireplace, kitchen, lots of windows. You're invited to trespass anytime you feel like it." The detachment shifted and his expression warmed—a trick done with mirrors, Emily decided.

"Thanks," she said dryly, "but I'm afraid the woods have lost a great deal of their appeal."

His smile grew infectious, creasing his weathered cheeks into what might have been considered dimples in a lesser man. "I promise you, I'm not taking down a single tree unnecessarily—just enough to squeeze in one small house. You'll never even know it's there."

She'd know, all right. She was going to have to be on her guard every minute until she'd figured out exactly why Bey Jones affected her the way he did. It wasn't reasonable. It wasn't even rational! "For you and your family?" she hazarded.

"For me. I'm not married."

"Oh, well, I didn't...I mean, it's of no concern to me..." She broke off. Listen to her! He was doing it to her again! Looking at her that way, as if she were some intriguing botanical specimen he'd come across unexpectedly. The next thing she knew, he'd be pulling her petals off.

She tugged at the neck of her sweater. She'd asked him to tend the fire, and he'd thrown on more logs. At this rate she'd have to order another cord of wood before Thanksgiving.

"Did I overdo it?" Bey asked apologetically. "Sorry—I've got a thing about fireplaces. Love 'em. Never had one."

She edged as far away from the blaze as she could, but in a room the size of her small living room, there was nowhere to go. "Maybe I should open the front door," she muttered in desperation.

"Better yet, why don't we take a walk, watch the moon come up over the bay. By the time we get back, the fire will have burned down some."

She had to do something—she was sweltering. Perspiration bloomed on her back, making the sweater itch abominably. With no makeup to disguise it, her face was probably beet red. "Well...maybe just a short walk," she conceded. "I have some work to get done before tomorrow."

"I don't think you mentioned what you did, Emily."

"Neither did you," Emily retorted.

"I asked you first." He was standing so close she could see the shadow of golden stubble against his tanned skin. Suddenly she felt an overwhelming compulsion to touch him. "I teach English at a girls' school," she blurted.

He nodded thoughtfully. "Better wear a coat, you're soaking wet."

Emily got out her suede jacket and he took it from her hands, holding it while she ran her arms into the sleeves. The touch of his hands on her neck as he settled it into place brought still more heat to her face.

I'm having a mid-life crisis, she thought wildly. That sort of thing is supposed to be mental rather than physical, but heaven help me, this is both!

There was just enough light from the stars to make out the yellow clay road. "This way," she murmured, curling her hands into her pocket and hurrying across the rutted road to an overgrown path that led down to the water. Halfway down, she halted, and Bey cannoned into her back.

"Ouch! I think I'm caught." Cautiously she felt for the briar that had snagged her slacks.

His hands covered hers in the darkness. "Don't move—let me help you." His voice was as soft as the silver seedheads that swayed heavily on the nearby reeds—soft, with a kernel of hardness at the center.

She couldn't move; clawlike thorns were digging into her thighs. As uncomfortable as she was, Bey's fingers moving carefully over her leg through a layer of thin wool gabardine made matters still worse. Her hair, which she usually wore anchored in a tidy knot, was coming down, and she shoved at it ineffectually.

"I don't feel it anymore," she murmured finally, easing away from the grip of a warm hand just above her knee.

"Think I got 'em all." He was closer than she'd expected, and when he stood, his words brushed warmly past her ear.

"Look, this wasn't such a good idea," Emily protested weakly. "I can't see a darned thing and the moon probably won't be up for hours."

"O ye of little faith. See that glow over there? What do you think that is?"

"That's the stadium at Easton," she said dryly. "They're having a night game."

Draping an arm across her shoulders, Bey swept her down the sloping path to the narrow strip of beach. "I always was a sucker for the romantic glow of stadium lights." Halting at the edge of the water, he whispered, "Look, there's a sloop coming in from the bay under sail—see her?"

Pointing with one hand, he leaned his face close to hers, and Emily felt her breath catch and hang somewhere in her throat.

"I don't see a thing," she managed, her voice barely audible. Furtively she wriggled away from the warm presence at her side.

"Don't look directly at what you're trying to see— look just above it and wait," Bey instructed softly.

"How can I tell where just above it is if I can't see it?" Her chattering words emerged on tiny clouds of vapor, and she drew in a sharp breath, savoring the musky scent of woodsmoke and soap and something devastatingly masculine. She was acutely aware of the contrast of the cold night air and the radiant warmth of his body; the space between them might just as well not be there for all the good it did her frayed nerves.

"I... I expect the fire's burned down by now," she said huskily.

"How long do you think we've been out here?" Laughter simmered under the dark surface of his voice.

"Half an hour?" The words were a hopeful plea.

Bey laughed aloud. His arm tightened briefly around her shoulders, and then he moved away. "Five minutes at most."

Emily continued to stare out over the dark water where the pale shape of a large sloop was beginning to emerge. Wrapping her arms about her chest, she shivered. "That's long enough. Let's go back." Torn by a strange reluctance to end the brief closeness and an overpowering need to escape, she turned and started up the bank.

Bey didn't offer to help her. From behind and below, he could see her slender, swaying back quite clearly. The feel of her was still on his hands. Eyes narrowing, he inhaled deeply. Was it only his heightened imagination, or could he still catch a hint of her clean floral scent mingling with the smell of mud and water and dried weeds?

His night vision was excellent; he followed her easily, admiring the sheer grace of her stride as she picked her way through the encroaching weeds. As he moved silently up the narrow path, it occurred to him that she was nervous as a cat.

A schoolteacher, hmm? That might explain a certain academic bias, but there was more to it than that. She had style, beauty, wit and intelligence, and she was as nervous around him as a convent-reared virgin on her first date. What had turned her against men, soured her on romance? A bad affair? A failed marriage? Possibly. Whatever it was, it had hit her hard. She'd built up a lot of scar tissue.

He was still watching her when she reached the top of the bank. In a gesture of uncertainty that he filed away in his writer's mind for future use, she half-turned, shook her head and continued across the road without waiting.

Bey picked up his pace. Damned if she was going to barricade herself inside that stuffy little museum of hers—at least not until he had a few more answers. He had her where he wanted her now. She'd been dying of curiosity to know what he was going to do with Fletcher's Landing. It meant something to her, that tract of land—probably been in the family for generations. The McClouds were Old Family, landed gentry.

Gentry, maybe, but the land was now his. He'd paid twice what it was worth just to be sure he got it. He might not have much of a pedigree, but a hundred and twenty-two acres of the Chesapeake Bay was a pretty damned good consolation.

"Emily? Slow up," he called out softly.

At the edge of the uneven brick wall that led to her porch, Emily paused. Courtesy was too ingrained to allow her to dash inside and bar the door without a word. Striving for just the right note of chilly regret, she said, "I expect you have things to do, Bey—provisions to unpack and..." Her composure began to crumble. "...and, well...it's been a lovely evening, Bey."

He roared. His laughter assaulted Emily's newly vulnerable sensibilities, and she swung around and stalked up the shallow steps to her front door.

"Emily, wait—honey, I'm sorry." He took the two steps in a silent leap. Moving swiftly, he caught her at the door.

She tried to ignore him. Her hair was falling in ruins about her shoulders, and her teeth were clenched tightly to keep them from chattering. When a suspicion of a chuckle reached her, it was too much. She lifted her chin and turned, ready to shrivel him with a word, a look.

He was too close. The clean woodsy-musky scent of him, the animal warmth of his body, began leaching the strength from her bones. Their eyes were almost on a level.

"You seem to find me amusing, Mr. Jones. I was merely being courteous, you know. It was *not* a lovely evening." She gathered her courage and rushed on, her voice quivering from sheer nerves. "You barge into my house and devour my dinner—you turn my living room into a blast furnace, and you seem to think it's all some sort of a joke. I'm afraid I can't share your amusement, Mr. Jones."

Light from the door she'd left ajar spilled out to halo Bey's thick blond hair. His face was partly in shadow, but she could easily make out the dancing light in those hazel eyes, the gleam of his strong white teeth. She could even see the tiny shadow where one of the front ones lapped slightly over its neighbor. Her hands clenched impotently at her sides. Damn the man, even his *teeth* were disarming!

Taking a deep, steadying breath, she said firmly, "I . . . I . . . good night!"

And still she stood there, her body stone deaf to the conflicting demands of her brain.

"Aren't you going to invite me in for a nightcap?"

Freshly affronted, she drew in a sharp breath. "Don't be absurd."

The white gleam of his grin widened. "Am I being absurd, Emily? Why are you so upset? You invited me to share your dinner, and as for the fire—I told you, I've never had a fireplace. How was I to know—?"

"Oh, forget it. I can always turn on the air conditioner."

"Don't bother. The temperature will drop several degrees the minute you set foot in the room. There's not a whole lot of warmth in you, is there, Emily McCloud?"

She fumbled for the knob behind her, unreasonably stung by his words. She'd heard them from Wendell more than once, and it hadn't bothered her all that much until now.

Before she could slide through the door, Bey's hands moved to capture her arms. He was incredibly strong, but she was no weakling. "I don't appreciate being mauled, Bey," she said bitingly, twisting stiffly against the relentless grip of his fingers.

"I could never back down from a challenge."

"I am *not* a challenge," she seethed, turning her face away from the compelling intensity of his eyes. "And I refuse to engage in a brawl. If you're going to...to kiss me, then do it and get it over with."

She heard the sharp intake of his breath. For an instant his fingers bit into her arms painfully. Tears of frustration filmed her eyes and she blinked them away. How on earth had she got herself into such a degrading situation, engaging in a wrestling match on her front porch as if she were no more mature than one of her own students.

Slowly he released her, his hands trailing off her arms to hook into his belt. He stepped back, and momentarily paralyzed, Emily was unable to escape his scathing words.

"Lady, I've picked up a few scars in my lifetime," Bey grated softly, his merciless eyes cutting through every layer of protection she'd acquired over the years, "but so far I've managed to avoid being frostbitten. If it's all the same to you, I think I'll pass up your offer."

Emily closed the door and leaned against it, eyes closed, fists pressing against her thighs. Damn, damn, *damn!* She'd never been so humiliated. Not even when she'd had to ask Wendell for a raise. Not even when she'd failed her first driver's exam three times for the same stupid mistake, with half her high-school class looking on.

Neighbors or not, she'd have nothing more to do with him. It shouldn't be all that difficult. People in big cities lived next door to each other for years without meeting. She had no reason to go into the woods, and Bey certainly wouldn't be turning up on her doorstep again. Whatever he'd been looking for, he hadn't found it here; he'd certainly made that plain enough.

Bey sat on a bench, notebook in hand, and glared at the woman he'd been observing so carefully for almost forty-five minutes. She was his third try today; he'd wasted an entire morning. He'd picked up her trail down by the ship the *Constellation* and managed to keep her in sight, meanwhile making notes on the way she moved and the way her hair slithered over her shoulders when she turned her head to speak to the man beside her. He'd tried out his heroine's name on her—Belinda. Not a perfect fit, but...possible.

He already knew Belinda's perfume, her favorite wine, the authors she read and the music she liked most. Somehow, this woman looked more like a cocktail type, but never mind. She probably preferred rock over Rachmaninoff, too, and never read anything heavier than a fashion magazine, but his imagination could span the gap. The buzz words he'd jotted down were "elegant," "well-bred," "modest," "spirited."

And then she'd paused not three feet away from where he loitered, pretending to take notes on various yachts anchored in the harbor. Scowling, she'd lifted a small, shapely foot, bringing with it a trail of stringy pink gum. Focusing wide, limpid eyes—nearsighted, he suspected—on her companion, she'd let fly a string of oaths that would have singed the hair off a drill sergeant's chest.

Bey ripped out the page of notes and crumpled it in one fist. That cut it! Dammit, at this rate he'd never find his heroine! He'd been coming down here to the inner harbor every day this week, looking for the personification of his female character. He'd long since discovered that it made his work immensely easier if he could find a woman who fit the mental image of his current heroine and watch her move about, hear her speak.

The outline had been going so well. He'd had it more or less roughed out in his head before he'd come back to Baltimore, but the minute he'd started fleshing out his protagonists, he'd found himself in trouble. His male character was no problem; it was Belinda who refused to solidify. She'd been waiting quietly in the back of his mind ever since he'd conceived the plot line, but then somehow, as soon as he'd started bringing it together, she'd started falling apart. Blond hair had given way to brown, green eyes to gray, and a beguiling little vest-pocket Venus had grown into a tall, willowy woman who walked as proudly as if there were five miles of red carpet unrolling before her feet.

All right, so be it. He wasn't locking into any particular physical type, but dammit, he had to make her come alive! This morning, in disgust, he'd covered the typewriter and gone hunting; he'd followed three women, none of whom had been quite right. Wasn't there a woman anywhere these days who fit his requirements? Either they dressed like hookers or frumps, or they moved like water buffalo, or they opened their mouths and spewed out sewage.

He raked a hand over his wildly untidy hair as a gust of cold, damp wind bit through his fatigue jacket. Maybe he was looking in the wrong place, but he'd tried hanging around some of the better shops inside. He'd moved out here when he'd begun to attract the interest of the security guards.

It was a simple enough quest: brown hair, gray eyes, fairly tall, good bone structure. So why had every brown-haired, gray-eyed woman in Baltimore suddenly chosen to stay holed up all week?

Ramming the battered spiral notebook in his hip pocket, Bey took the steps, dodging browsers as he cut through the shopping mall. He crossed the street against the light and retrieved the BMW from the parking lot.

Dammit, he might as well have gone to the Landing this weekend for all he'd accomplished. He'd planned to have a chapter roughed out and the opening scene of another one by now.

* * *

After giving her black silk suit a last-minute once-over, Emily touched her hair, pressed her glossy lips together, and switched out the bedroom light. There was absolutely no reason why she shouldn't go out to dinner with an old friend. Lord knows, Wendell was no threat to her heart, nor she to his; it was simply a matter of survival. She'd been letting herself get into a rut. How long had it been since she'd gone out to dinner, much less dancing? Of course, it would have been nice if Wendell had done the asking, but she'd been too desperate to stand on ceremony.

Punctual as always, Wendell drove up just as she was draping her new gray chesterfield around her shoulders. After checking the latch, she hurried out and slid into the front seat.

"What made you change your mind, if you'll pardon my curiosity?" he asked as he backed around and headed toward town.

"It just occurred to me that I was getting stale. I felt like getting out, meeting new people."

"You do know how to flatter a man, don't you?"

"Did you want me to lie to you?"

"Heaven forbid," he said dryly. "You were always a stickler for truth and duty, weren't you?"

"How did duty get into this?" Emily relaxed into the heady comfort of Wendell's luxury sedan. "Is this thing new? I must say, I'm impressed."

"Are you? Tell me, Em, do you ever regret it?"

In the soft light from the instruments, she studied his lean profile, the long aquiline nose, the softening jawline. Did she regret it? After a comfortable silence that extended for several miles, she said, "It wouldn't have worked, Wendell. We're too much alike. I never realized that before, did you?''

''Mmm-hmm. I've always known it. That's precisely why we didn't make it. You were honor-bound to take on the girls and all the responsibility that entailed, and I was honor-bound to take on the *Light* and all its encumbrances and liabilities. I suppose we had no choice. Neither one of us could offer the single-mindedness each of us needed in a mate.''

Wendell lighted a cigarette and switched on the radio to a new station. Emily, unconsciously stroking the raw silk of her skirt, stared at the approaching lights of St. Michaels and considered his words.

So where did that leave her now that her responsibility to the girls was all but finished? With a house that was sadly in need of repairs, a career that was growing shakier by the day, one that had never brought her the satisfaction she'd hoped for. Her friends were all married, most of them living elsewhere, and she was so busy trying to make ends meet she hadn't had time even to keep up with her hobby. Her paints were all dried up, her brushes probably moth-eaten by now.

And just lately, there'd been a new feeling of restlessness, a sense of something vital that was lacking in her life. She didn't even know what it was, much less how to go about finding it.

Four

Another letter to the editor. Emily had hoped the matter would die a quiet death. She was sorry now she'd ever read *Reap the Wild Wind,* much less written that review. Still, seeing the way her girls pored over such books, what choice had she had? These so-called romances that were cropping up everywhere today were insidiously believable. Judging by the popularity, there were hundreds of thousands of poor women being set up for the inevitable fall.

Scowling, she folded the newspaper into quarters and propped it against the coffeepot while she buttered her toast. This thing had gone far enough, regardless of what Wendell said. Her eyes scanned the page quickly and snagged on the initials B.J. The letter above the ambiguous abbreviated signature was short and to the point.

"Your reviewer admits that Miss Jericho's novel was well-written. One can only assume that it's the subject matter she finds so offensive. Would Miss McCloud have us clear our shelves of Jane Austen and the Brownings, of Dumas, Shakespeare and the Brontës? What do you have against love, Miss McCloud?"

Emily groaned, her anger increasing as she read the next few lines. This thing was getting completely out of hand. How could a simple book review have evolved into a public wrangle concerning her personal life? She could well imagine how everyone at the paper was taking this. They all knew she'd once been engaged to Wendell. By now they probably thought she'd been unilaterally dumped by their managing editor and was still nursing a broken heart.

"One more letter and that's *it*," she vowed, mentally composing a stinging reply that would put an end to the whole ridiculous affair.

By Friday afternoon Emily was more than ready for a break. One of her seniors had come in sporting an engaged-to-be-engaged ring, and it had proved of far greater interest than the early-twentieth-century poets. Her head was throbbing, and it was all she could do to give out the weekend assignment.

"Read Rupert Brooke's war poems in chapter three, and on Monday we'll compare them to his prewar work. That's all, girls," she finished, lifting her voice above the noisy exodus.

The last student darted out just as the headmistress came in. "You're getting famous, Emily," Abbie declared, tossing a copy of the *Light* on Emily's desk.

"Oh, no, not again," Emily wailed. She slipped a sheaf of unfinished reports into her briefcase and reached for the morning paper. What did it take to put an end to this stupid duel?

"You mean you haven't seen it yet?"

Rustling the pages, Emily shook her head. "Didn't have time. Car wouldn't start and I had to call Bob to come out and jump the battery."

"I wonder if B.J. really is Bonnie Jericho," the straw-thin redhead murmured, leaning over to reread the latest letter on the editorial page. "'The lady doth protest too much, methinks.'" She ran a nicotine-stained forefinger down the page. "Knows her *Hamlet,* anyway."

"Right now," Emily seethed, "the only *Hamlet* I can think of is 'murder most foul.' Where does she get off, telling everyone that I've obviously allowed my personal deprivations to color my intellectual judgment? That was a perfectly objective review, dammit! If you ask me, our friend B.J. sounds suspiciously defensive. She's obviously showing off the with *Hamlet,* trying to make me think she's not just a romance junkie."

"Don't underestimate us romance readers, Em—we're not exactly cases of arrested development, you know."

"Did I hit a nerve?" Emily inquired dryly. "Just how many a week do you account for?"

"About six, if I'm lucky. Want to borrow some? I just finished a really knockout book about this woman lawyer who's defending—"

"Abbie, don't do this to me," Emily sighed, shouldering her heavy purse and collecting her stuffed briefcase. Another weekend of work. She'd be lucky if she got through this mess by Monday.

"You try too hard, Em. No woman could possibly be as immune to romance as you pretend to be."

"Who's pretending?" Emily denied irritably. "I just can't see wasting so much time reading fairy tales."

"When's the last time you read one?"

"Last month when I read that Jericho thing. Abbie, I've got to run. By the time I do all my errands and get home, it'll be pitch dark."

"They're good for you, honey—if I couldn't look forward to a couple of hours a day with a good juicy romance, I'd have long since knocked off a whole boardful of directors, not to mention a certain administrator."

"Oh, goody. Then you'd have all the time in the world for reading romances, in between making license plates and busting rocks."

"I don't think they do that anymore," Abbie said, grinning as she ducked into her office to collect her coat and purse. "The trouble with you, Em, is that you give up too easily. So you were saddled with the girls and it broke up your engagement. Get out there and try again! Every woman worth her salt has a few broken romances behind her—it's part of the learning process."

As two sets of footsteps echoed hollowly along the empty corridor, Emily's eyes warmed in a tired smile. "I've already got an advanced degree, thanks. After Wendell, I fell for a man who decided to go back to his wife—and I didn't even know he had one—then there was Jonathan, my handsome weekend sailor. Actually, I was a part of a nervous breakdown he was having at the time, only I was too dumb to know it."

"So?"

"So I should throw my hat in the ring again and wait for another Prince Charming to pick it up?"

"You don't wait for him to pick it up, silly. If he looks good to you, you go put it in his hand. You might lose a few hats that way, but it beats the hell out of sitting home night after night grumbling about what other women are reading.''

"Abbie, I honestly don't give a damn what you read—I think I'm just jealous. I've got two murder mysteries to review this weekend, and I *hate* murder mysteries! I always get a headache trying to remember all those tricky little clues, and I can never guess who dunit. I'd almost settle for another romance—at least whatever gets done, you know who did it.''

"I wish you would—read one, that is. You know what they say about the physical benefits of owning a pet? Reading romances is even better—good for high blood pressure, ulcers, and whatever else ails you.''

Holding the heavy front door open, Emily giggled. "I could never afford to read one now, not after this flap with B.J.''

"Painted yourself into a corner, hmm? Believe me, it'd take more than all my four degrees put together to keep me from enjoying 'em.''

"So that's it—I've only got two measly degrees. No wonder I don't appreciate good literature.'' Emily paused beside her car as the wind whipped her skirt against her slender legs. Her tan suit was ancient, but its pedigree was flawless.

"Did it ever occur to you, Em, that maybe you're in the wrong profession?''

"It's a little late to be discovering something like that, isn't it?'' With a shrug and a smile, she slipped in under the wheel, hoping the loaner Bob had installed while he recharged her battery wouldn't let her down.

Abbie saw too much, she decided as the car started up obediently. Before she'd been jolted out of her half-formed plans for studying art in Rome, teaching had been pretty far down on her list of favorite occupations. But then she'd found herself with the girls to consider, and a teaching degree in English had seemed like a more realistic goal to shoot for. She'd never kidded herself about her moderate artistic talents.

The long drive home offered plenty of time to consider the question of her future. It was beginning to look as if one way or another, she might not have a job much longer. Given the opportunity, what would she like to do with the rest of her life?

A nebulous idea began to take shape in her mind. As long as she was fantasizing, she might as well admit that what she'd really like to do was to study. And not necessarily art. Now that she no longer had the heavy financial responsibility of the two girls, she'd give anything to be able to study all the fascinating subjects that had seemed too frivolous or impractical at the time. She'd almost forgotten what it was like to read a book for the pure pleasure of reading, and not because she had to write a review of it.

"And dammit, I'd like to put on my pajamas and eat chili and nachos from a paper plate in the living room while I watch the news, instead of forcing myself to go through the same old charade every night," she muttered belligerently as she turned into the leaf-covered driveway beside the cottage.

It was only generations of proud McClouds that made her hold out so long. One of these days—on her fortieth birthday perhaps—she'd give in, she promised herself. Until then, she'd probably continue to maintain the standards that had been instilled in her from the cradle.

A shadow emerged from the porch, causing her heart to leap into her throat. "Emily, it's me—Bey. Sorry, I didn't mean to scare you."

"What are you *doing* here?" she demanded angrily, jamming the door key in the lock.

"I wanted to ask you something about a plant. I figure you know these woods better than anyone else."

"Are there any woods left?" she jeered. "My road's practically impassable, thanks to all those heavy vehicles you're using. By now you've probably bulldozed everything in sight."

She thrust open the door and began unbuttoning her coat, ignoring the way her heart was slamming against her ribs. At the continuing silence behind her, she snapped, "Well, what are you waiting for? Either come in or stay out, but please close the door."

He came in. Immediately the atmosphere was altered. The chilly room, with its scent of chrysanthemums and furniture polish, seemed to take on a new warmth that had nothing at all to do with temperature. The pungent scent of flowers was laced suddenly with an exotically masculine essence, and in spite of herself, Emily felt something inside her begin to thaw.

"Are you still camping out at the Landing?" she asked, her disgruntled tone in direct contrast to his cheerful response. She sounded like a shrew, and for the life of her, she couldn't seem to help it.

"Got there this morning. I couldn't wait any longer to see how much house I had. The foundation's finished and they've started on the floor joists. By the end of the week I should have a floor and possibly even a wall or two. Now that the rock work's done, I've got two crews going." He made no effort to disguise his excitement, and Emily found the blend of tough competence and boyish eagerness utterly disarming.

Struggling to conceal her happiness at seeing him again, she lit the fire and then headed for the kitchen. Bey sauntered in after her, as friendly and relaxed as if their last meeting hadn't ended so ignominiously. She'd spent a week putting that miserable episode out of her mind.

"Would you like a cup of coffee?" Emily reached for the pot, not waiting for an answer. She needed one. In fact, she needed something stronger, but coffee would do for now.

They took it into the living room. Bey settled into the Morris chair as though by right. He was wearing jeans again, but this time they were black corduroy, soft and conforming. He wore a black wool pullover and the same boots he'd worn before—heavy, well-worn engineer's boots that made no pretense of being fashionable. He looked dark and dangerous, and every bit as attractive as she'd remembered, and Emily felt herself being drawn away from her safe shore and into deep, uncharted waters. "What was it you wanted to ask me?" she mumbled into her steaming cup.

"Did anyone ever live at Fletcher's Landing? I think there must have been a flower garden there at one time. I've got something blooming, and about the only flower I can identify is a rose—it's not a rose."

Between sips of coffee, Emily gave him a condensed version of the history of the place. "I haven't the slightest idea who lived there. By the time I was curious enough to ask, no one seemed to remember. At any rate, I don't think it was a McCloud, but I couldn't swear to it."

"And you've never seen the flowers?"

"Not from your description."

Carefully Bey placed his cup on a table. Rising, he took the poker and shook down the logs, releasing a shower of sparks. The resulting crackle sounded homey and pleasant to Emily's ears as she tucked her feet up beside her on the sofa.

"There's more than enough wood on there," she warned, remembering the last time. "That stack on the back porch is supposed to last until January."

"There's enough wood around here to last us both a lifetime. I'll have a fresh load stacked on your porch for you, all right?"

"I wasn't hinting, Bey. I just meant—"

"I know—I wasted three whole logs the other night. I'll replace 'em."

Impatiently she rattled her cup in her saucer. "I didn't *mean* that! Frankly, I'd much rather you left my share standing. A tree on the hoof is worth two in the fireplace."

"That's birds and bushes and hands."

Her lips twitched, but she managed to maintain a stern look. "Birds and bushes, too, please—especially those tall reeds with the silvery lavender tops."

"What about hands?"

"What about them?" Shifting her position so that she could follow his movements, she made an effort to draw him out. "This corporation of yours, Bey—what does it do?"

He'd crossed the room to stand before the bookcase that took up almost an entire end of the room. The shelves were overflowing with books from her parents' library as well as the few she'd collected on her own. There was a tiny oil landscape on an easel, the only decent thing she'd ever done, between the encyclopedias and the history books.

Bey took it down, studied it silently for several moments, and then carefully replaced it. Ignoring her question, he continued to examine the shelves. Emily continued to examine him, her eyes traveling slowly over the back of his well-shaped head and the wide black-clad shoulders. She could see the hollow of his spine and the indentation of his waist just above where his jeans were belted low on his narrow hips. He'd moved as silently as a cat burglar in those heavy boots, but somehow, despite her earlier fears, she knew she could trust him. There was a disarming directness about him, a steadiness of eye that was reassuring. Whatever else he was, Bey Jones was no threat to her possessions.

As to her peace of mind, that was another matter. If he were a book, she decided with instinctive certainty, she'd be compelled to read him; the cover was so irresistibly intriguing.

He turned before she could disguise her interest, and for a long moment their eyes clung. If she were an imaginative sort, she might have read all sorts of things in the quick darkening of those amber-and-emerald eyes.

He leaned against the bookcase, crossing his arms over his chest. "These books don't fit you, Emily. Too dry."

"I happen to be a dry sort of person."

"Like hell you are." His skeptical tone served to sharpen the awareness between them until she was all but trembling. "Suppressed, maybe...inhibited, probably...but dry? Never."

She felt as if she'd downed a glass of champagne too quickly. "Interesting conclusion, Bey," she observed coolly, "but you're wrong on all three counts."

"Shall I prove which one of us is wrong?"

She did her best to sound uninterested. "Don't bother. The opinion of strangers has never concerned me overmuch. If you want to believe I'm... all those things you said, then be my guest."

With a swift shift of direction that left her slightly off balance, he asked, "What do you like to read?"

"Lately I haven't had much time to read anything— at least not for pleasure."

She followed his movements as he prowled about the room. He had an efficient way of walking that used a minimum of effort. She watched him scan the shelves once more. His eyes lingered for a moment on the painting, and then he crossed to stand before her, feet apart, lean torso settling into a deceptively relaxed stance.

Her gaze focused on the hands that were resting on his hips. Against the darkness of his clothing, the crisp golden hair on their backs seemed incandescent. Those hard, muscular forearms might well belong to a fighter, but his square, well-kept hands seemed more suited to...

An unaccountable warmth crept up her body, and she moved restlessly, dismissing the irrelevant thought. He'd carefully avoided her direct question about who he was and what he did, she noticed. The more she saw of the man, the more of an enigma he became.

He stood before her, casually blocking any attempt at escape she might have made. The slow smile that spread across his craggy face had the effect of cutting through every protective layer she possessed, and she found herself totally defenseless.

"I thought we might have lunch tomorrow," he said, his resonant voice registering on the very marrow of her bones. "I owe you. Would twelve, twelve-thirty suit you?"

Emily broke away from the magnetism of his gaze. Huskily she said, "You don't have to—"

"Of course, if you've got other plans..."

"Well, if you're sure—"

"Fine. Pick you up about twelve-fifteen." He reached out and cupped her cheek with the hard palm of his hand, and Emily waited breathlessly for it to burst into flames. The hand dropped, and helplessly she watched him move toward the door. "I'd better go get a fire built if I want to eat tonight. See you tomorrow."

Long after he'd let himself out, she sat staring at the door, feeling as if she'd been buffeted by a small tornado. What on earth was she doing accepting a lunch date with someone like Bey Jones? What would they talk about? How would they get to town—on the back of his motorcycle? She'd never been on one of those things in her life, and she had decidedly mixed feelings about roaring through the countryside with nothing to hang on to but the driver.

By the time she heard the rap on her front door, she'd changed clothes three times, settling finally on navy wool slacks and a green turtleneck sweater. That would do for lunch in any restaurant in any of the nearby towns, as well as for her first ride on a motorcycle. For added confidence, she wore her high-heeled navy suede boots. No man liked to be seen with a woman who was taller then he was, and she needed all the help she could get.

It wasn't enough. Bey greeted her with that incongruously guileless smile of his, and she felt herself sinking once again under his potent spell.

"You're beautiful in green. Brings out the color in your face," he told her, opening her closet as if he had every right and extracting the suede jacket.

The color in her face had nothing to do with her green sweater. Emily allowed herself to be helped on with the coat, wondering why she'd ever thought she could intimidate him with a few additional inches. Bey was probably no more than five-feet-ten, but he radiated more confidence and more power than any basketball star she'd ever seen. He was in complete control of himself, and as a result, Emily felt her own confidence begin to ebb before they'd even left the house.

"Where's the motorcycle?" she asked, glancing around for the black-and-white machine.

Bey took her arm and angled through the yard toward the woods. "Left it home. Maybe I'll build a garage for it one of these days. Could double as a doghouse if I decide to get a dog, speaking of which, I hope you like hotdogs. I considered grilling a couple of steaks, but I've only got one steak knife—the one I used to measure coffee."

"We're picnicking?" Despite her slightly longer legs, their strides matched perfectly. Bey held aside a small branch until she passed.

"You don't want to? We could run into town if you'd rather, but I'll have to douse the fire first." The hint of disappointment in his voice struck a nerve she didn't even know she possessed, and she hurriedly assured him that there was nothing she'd rather have than a campfire meal.

They walked silently, their feet scuffling a path through the carpet of red and golden leaves. A jay announced their coming, his raucous voice echoing in the silence.

"I envy you," Emily said wistfully.

"All this?" He gestured around him, and she nodded. His hand moved to hers as they came to the half-rotted trunk of a pine that had died of old age. They stepped over, and he continued to hold her hand. "It'll always be yours, Emily. A little thing like a deed can't change that."

The glowing ambience of the deep woods and the warmth of his touch combined to bring an unexpected ache deep inside her. She pulled her hand away and increased her pace. "I'm hungry," she announced brightly. "Starved, in fact."

"Great. You're my first houseguest, and I'm going to treat you right. There's a wheelbarrow around here somewhere—the rock masons used it—so feel free to pig out: if you overdo it, I can still get you home."

They were nearing the place where she'd discovered him that first day, and she began to see signs of construction. Critically she glanced around. "I don't see any sign of a road. How have the trucks been getting in and out?"

"The long way. I didn't want to tear up the area between your place and mine, so I routed them around near the water. Come on, we're almost there. I spent the morning cleaning up for you, but I'm afraid it's still a little messy."

They came to the clearing a few moments later, and Emily uttered a soft cry of dismay. Smoke from the campfire drifted lazily upward, but no amount of smoke could disguise the raw wounds in what had once been untouched forest. There were mounds of bare earth and splotches of rough, hardened concrete. There was a small mountain of gravel, a scattering of rock, and stacks of assorted building materials underneath the gaping hole in the canopy of trees overhead. Deep, muddy tire tracks were everywhere, and centering the small clearing was the foundation of a house not much larger than her own.

"I'm sorry," Bey said quietly. He was standing beside her, his arms hanging limply at his sides. Distress was plain in his eyes, and Emily shook her head.

"No—I'm the one who's sorry. Bey, it's your land. I can't expect you to turn it into a wildlife sanctuary."

"There's a lot of land here, Emily. The wounds will heal over, and the house will blend in. God knows the last thing I want is to stick out like a sore thumb. One of the reasons I wanted this place was for the privacy it offered."

The initial shock was wearing off, and Emily picked her way through the sticky mud and approached the rock foundation. "How about a guided tour?"

Bey leapt up and turned to give her a hand. "It'll be easier to visualize after the floor's done. Watch your step in those heels."

Holding on to her hand, he pointed out various undefined areas as kitchen, bedroom, study and bath. "The chimney's this big slab here—fireplaces in every room but the bath. I couldn't figure out a way to get a fireplace in there."

"Cozy," she murmured, distracted by the feel of the hard hand enclosing her own. She'd never dreamed that the feel of flesh against flesh could be so catalytic. "What about the living room?" she asked shakenly.

"Oh, well—I thought this area over here could serve as den, study, library, living room, office—you name it. No point in spreading out over half an acre."

They discussed the house plans, arguing amicably for several minutes, and then Bey leapt down and lifted his arms. "You said you were starved. For the time being, my dining room's that small clearing over there."

She was no more than three feet off the ground, but the invitation was irresistible. Leaning forward, she placed her hands on his shoulders and jumped. The ground was uneven. Her heels sank into the soft earth, and she stumbled, laughing breathlessly. When his arms closed around her, she had time to give only a small whimper of protest.

Five

Bey turned, still holding her in his arms, and seated them on a sheet of plywood that covered a section of floor joists. Using his strength with incredible finesse, he eased her down onto the fragrant raw wood, and then leaned over her, bracing himself with one arm to gaze down at her face. Her hair flowed around her like dark threads of gold-shot silk, and those cheekbones, those eyes—ah, she was so beautiful, so distant and yet so familiar, like some half-remembered dream from another life.

Disarming her first with a kindling smile, he began gently grazing the corners of her mouth with small kisses, straying now and then to brush the tip of her nose with his lips. Emily held her breath. A cool wine-colored leaf drifted down onto her forehead, and still smiling, Bey pressed his lips against it, holding it to her heated skin for a moment.

"There, now you're wearing my brand," he murmured deeply.

"Bey..." A little frantically she searched for a handhold on reality, but reason had deserted her, her wits scattering out of reach like the flurries of wind-blown leaves. Before she could help herself, she was entangled again in the splendor of his eyes, lost in a thicket of russet leaves that reflected in his irises like brambles in a hidden woodland pool.

Intellectually she would never on this earth have put herself willingly into the hands of a man like Bey. It was an admission of vulnerability, and vulnerability led to disillusionment and pain. After the example set for her by her parents, after the fiasco of her own engagement, she'd taken care to build up an impervious defense against the sort of power an attractive man could wield over a lonely woman. And now, at the first test...

Intellectually she was immune, but emotionally she was as defenseless as ever.

Emily surrendered herself to the spell of Bey's hungry lips. He was kissing her with a barely controlled fierceness that should have been frightening, but somehow wasn't. In danger of being torn apart by the conflicting demands of mind and body, she simply ceased thinking. It was treacherously easy just to give herself up to the depravations of that sweet, firm mouth, the comfort of those hard, sheltering arms.

She trembled under the slow, gentle movements of his hand as it smoothed its way inside her jacket, under her sweater, to stroke the soft skin just above her waist. The heat of their combined bodies released the intoxicating scent of leather, of warm flesh, of her cologne, and something that was richly masculine. Breathing deeply, she drew it into her consciousness to weave it into the shimmering tapestry of this moment out of time.

And it was only a moment, she reminded herself distractedly. It could sparkle and beguile, but then it would end, and once more she'd be... Emily. Lonely, unsparkling, unbeguiling Emily.

Bey's mouth fitted itself to hers, and his tongue began probing the curved line between her lips, as if searching out weaknesses. One hand wandered up over her shoulder, tantalizing the side of her breast in passing, and the warning disintegrated like fog under sunlight. His fingers curled into the neckline of her sweater, seeking the perfumed warmth of her throat. They strayed up to the satin skin of her chin, sensitively delineating the delicate bones of her jaw, the defenseless softness beneath. With thumb and forefinger he pried her jaws apart, quickly moving to consolidate his gain by deepening the kiss before she could protest.

As if she had the strength of will to protest something she'd craved without even realizing it. Emily prided herself that self-delusion was not among her failings.

His tongue explored the smooth edges of her teeth, the inside of her lips. It engaged its counterpart in a slow, erotic dance that had her fingers clutching mindlessly at the taut muscles of his back. She could feel his body growing hard and tense over hers, and the knowledge of his arousal was electrifying. His breath grew increasingly ragged as her fevered response had her twisting and arching beneath him. And then, when every nerve in her body was screaming for release, he drew back, disengaging her clutching hands, her reaching arms.

Cool air rushed between them, and she stared up at him, bewildered. With an unsteady hand Bey raked back his thick sun-streaked hair. His next words struck her with an almost ludicrous sense of incongruity. "I expect that fire's burned down enough by now," he said huskily. "Shall we go see about some food?"

Emily plummeted to earth and landed without actually breaking anything. Sitting up, she brushed a wood shaving from her sweater and, forcing a commendable degree of composure into her voice, said, "Oh, yes—please. I'm starving."

The look he shot her spoke volumes, and she felt the heat rush up to redden her translucent complexion. Abruptly turning away, she slipped off her jacket and draped it over a stack of two-by-fours. *It was a kiss, you silly fool—a casual kiss, that's all! People do it all the time.*

But there'd been nothing faintly casual about it. How far it would have gone, she'd never know, but she certainly hadn't been putting up much of a fight. The thought was acutely embarrassing. Arranging her hair into some semblance of order, she glanced across to where Bey was bending over the fire. Was he paler than usual, or was she imagining things?

The hotdogs were superb, burned to a crisp on the outside, succulent and bursting with flavor on the inside. Bey loaded her bun with slaw and chili from plastic containers. He sliced a red onion and layered it generously and then splashed on a mustard that was all but combustible.

By the time he served the first round, Emily had regained her perspective. So she was out of practice; that was no reason to get carried away by a simple kiss.

"I planned on three apiece," Bey informed her. "Then we'll see about dessert."

Sending him a skeptical look, she opened wide and bit off a chunk, closing her eyes in appreciation. Moments later, she was blinking away tears. "Is there a fire extinguisher handy? Bey, if I manage even one of these monsters my insurance rates will double."

"Fire or medical?" He sat cross-legged on a slab of wood, having given Emily the seat of honor, a rough carpenter's stool.

"Both, but it'll be worth it. They're scrumptious."

They continued to eat in silence, and Emily gazed around at the tall hardwoods. The leaves were going fast now; a few more weeks and they'd be gone. Her eyes strayed to the yellow one-man tent pitched some hundred feet away. Surely he wouldn't camp out here in the dead of winter? Trees or not, the wind that whipped in off the bay could be ferocious.

The question died on her lips as she turned and caught the unguarded expression on his face. He was staring at the rock foundation with a look of raw longing mixed with disbelief, and once again Emily was shaken by the complexity of Bey Jones.

"Bey, who are you, anyway?" she asked softly, feeling oddly like an intruder as her words broke through his preoccupation.

"What do you mean, who am I?" There was an unexpected edge to his voice.

"I only meant—what do you do? Where do you come from?"

"I told you about Bon-Bey. As to where I come from—"

"No, you didn't. Do you realize that I know more about the UPS delivery man than I do about you? *What* and *where* is Bon-Bey?'' She waited impatiently as he loaded another bun and held it out to her. The man was a master of evasion. Maybe he was an escaped convict. Maybe he was an illegal alien, or a spy. What better place to hide out?

She wrenched her mind back from its fanciful suppositions and reached for the wiener. ''You'd better have that wheelbarrow handy,'' she taunted.

''I can always throw you over my saddle and carry you home that way. Or you could stay and be my first—''

''Houseguest? Thanks, but I'll manage to waddle home somehow. You were saying?''

''Yeah. Well, I guess you'd say Bon-Bey is concerned primarily with publishing. And as for where I come from, Baltimore's as good an answer as any. I've bedded down in a lot of places in my thirty-two years, but I always seem to find my way back there.''

''You're only thirty-two?'' Somehow he'd seemed much older. And yet, in spite of the occasional flashes of boyishness, Bey possessed a sort of tough maturity she'd seen in few other men. Disconcerted, she lifted her eyes to find him studying her with a maddening smile.

''Any objections?'' He lifted one russet brow, and she tore her eyes away and poked at an escaping onion with a mustardy finger.

''Of course not. Your age is nothing to do with me.''

''How old are you?'' He reached for the carton and divided what was left of the milk into the two enameled mugs.

''If you go around asking questions like that, I'm surprised you've survived this long.'' She grinned, took a large bite, and then fanned her face. By the time she could swallow, tears were streaming down her cheeks.

"It's good, though," she assured him, gratefully accepting his milk after she'd downed her own. "I'm thirty-seven," she admitted candidly.

Nodding thoughtfully, Bey wolfed down the last of his second hotdog and began spreading another bun with condiments. "Sounds about right to me," he murmured, cutting into a fresh onion with his sheath knife. It occurred to Emily that it was probably the one he used to measure coffee.

"About right for what?"

"Us. That's a mean difference of two and a half years. Physiologically speaking, it would be better if I were a few years younger or you were maybe forty, but I don't anticipate any trouble."

Bemused, Emily laid down her unfinished hotdog and stood up. Forcing a note of exasperation to cover the rush that had come over her at his calm declaration, she said, "I don't anticipate any trouble either, as a matter of fact, not that our respective ages have any significance. Even when I lived in town, I was never particularly neighborly, so chances are we won't be seeing all that much of each other."

After carefully balancing a long strip of kosher dill pickle on top of his bulging bun, Bey turned his attention to the part of her that was nearest—her boots. His gaze rambled thoughtfully up the length of her legs, encased in navy wool flannel that was now slightly less than pristine. As she'd dispensed with her jacket earlier, there was nothing at all to protect her from the thorough survey as his eyes lingered on the swell of her breasts before finally moving on to her increasingly angry face.

"You were saying...?" He took a large bite of his third hotdog and chewed thoughtfully as he awaited her answer.

"Dammit, Bey, don't play cat and mouse with me!"

His eyes widened ingenuously. "Is that what you think I'm doing?"

"I don't play games," she said adamantly. "Look, I think we'd better level with each other. This has been lovely, but we're even now. I gave you dinner; you gave me lunch. We've traded courtesies, so let's quit while we're ahead. Quite frankly, I don't think we have anything at all in common except for the fact that we're neighbors."

"I must say, I like your idea of courtesy. I'll trade with you any day."

By the time she could come up with an annihilating retort, he seemed to have forgotten her presence. There was an odd expression in his eyes, one that might even have been called dreamy if it weren't for the twice-broken nose, the pugnacious chin, the formidable jawline and that "damn-your-hide" arrogance he wore so carelessly.

"That's *it!*" he murmured under his breath. Rolling to his feet with a swift agility that took her by surprise, he stuck out his hand. "Sure you won't stay for dessert?"

Not even to herself could Emily admit her dismay at what amounted to a brush-off. "No thanks," she said coolly, ignoring the extended hand. "It's been delightful—thank you for inviting me... but I'd better be getting home—a million and one things to do, you know." If her small laugh sounded more brittle than carefree, it was the best she could manage at the moment.

"Yeah, well...thanks for coming, Emily. I'll see you. *Soon.*"

Don't count on it, Emily thought strickenly as she hurried away from the campsite. Blind, for once, to the beauty of the woods she'd loved all her life, she couldn't wait to escape them, to shut herself up in her bedroom and cry herself sick.

Which was precisely what she did, for no good reason other than that she couldn't help herself. Every woman, she thought brokenly, deserves a good cry once in a blue moon. Even the non-criers. She was a non-crier herself—had been, that is, until she'd run head-long into a young barbarian who'd made confetti of her defenses without even trying.

Some half-hour later she stood before the bookshelf and tried to see it through the eyes of a stranger. She lifted the small landscape from its easel and studied it, wondering if Bey had noticed the tiny "E. McC." in the lower-left corner. It was a study she'd done years ago of the ruined wharf at the Landing. There was hardly anything left of the ancient pilings and rotted timbers by now.

Dry? Her eyes scanned the shelves, wondering how they reflected on the owner. There was a preponderance of reference books. Ansie had given away most of the modern fiction when they'd moved from the house to the much smaller apartment in Easton. Emily had relied on the public library until she'd grown too busy to read for pleasure.

He'd called her inhibited and suppressed, as if he were an expert on women. The egotism of some men was astounding.

Aimlessly she opened the enormous dictionary. Her gaze fell to the middle of the randomly chosen page.

Barbarian; foreign, primitive, savage. He was definitely foreign to her limited experience, as different from Wendell and the other men she'd known as a kitten was from a cougar. Primitive? In a sense. There was a basic earthiness about the man that was both appealing and frightening. Savage? Probably—given reason.

Sighing, she closed the dictionary. Whatever he was—*who*ever he was—there was no room in her orderly existence for a man like Bey Jones. He was too young, for one thing. Or she was too old. And anyway, they had absolutely nothing in common.

Emily spent the rest of the afternoon struggling through the first of the two murder mysteries she was expected to review. Clue after clue slipped through her fingers as her attention strayed back to the woods, to the building site. He might be gone by now for all she knew. Or maybe he had someone else there with him. He'd certainly tired of her own company quickly enough—couldn't wait to get rid of her. But then, the young had a short attention span, she rationalized desperately.

She slammed the book shut and stood up. Dammit, it wasn't fair for him to barge into her life and disrupt everything just because he wanted to show off his new house! She had better things to do with her time.

Reaching for the phone, she dialed Abbie Linga's number. After the tenth ring, she hung up. She needed to get out. A movie would be just the thing to get her out of this maudlin mood, but she didn't relish going by herself. That was the trouble with living alone; all your friends were married and had families, or had moved away. When you suddenly had a craving to go to a movie, there was no one around.

Not allowing herself time to think, she dialed Wendell's home number. Nancy Roscoe answered.

"Oh, hi, Nancy. How was Italy?"

"It was Greece, and I adored it. Em? Thought I recognized your voice. If you wanted to speak to Wendell, he's in the shower. Can I take a message?"

Emily held the phone away from her ear and grimaced. Now, why would he be taking a shower at five-thirty in the afternoon? "Oh, it was nothing—just something about the book reviews. It can wait."

She hung up the phone and stood there wrapping her arms about herself and staring down at a torn and muddy leaf she'd tracked in. The scent of dead ashes filled the room as a gust of wind stirred the hearth. Suddenly she felt utterly alone in the world, and it was frightening. Alone was such a desolate place to be.

"Dammit, I refuse to be depressed over a silly, meaningless incident!" she muttered ferociously. Stalking into her bedroom, she changed into her oldest clothes. It would be dark before she could do much more than drag the ladder out and put it into place, but there were shutters to be painted, storm windows to be put up, and all the gutters were overflowing with leaves. And for once she was positively brimming with energy. She *had* to do something physical, or she'd never manage to sleep tonight, and besides, she could use a feeling of accomplishment about now.

Squatting on the cold ground, Bey scribbled furiously for three-quarters of an hour, his scowl gradually giving way to a grin of satisfaction. It had been there all along, buried under the superficial layers of his mind, but he'd been blind to it. He'd been struggling for two weeks with his damned Belinda and she'd persistently refused to behave.

And no damned wonder. He'd been trying to force her into a form that was all wrong. The petite green-eyed blonde with the sultry voice and a knowing way with men had been patterned on a woman he'd been briefly involved with. Della was a feature writer for a Baltimore paper, and Bey had severed the relationship when she'd started asking too many questions about how he made his money and what he did with his time when they weren't together. It had occurred to him later that she probably thought he was a dealer in something highly illicit.

Della had been a likely enough candidate for heroinehood. Volatile, intelligent, attractive, she'd have made a good one, only somehow, in the process of getting her down on paper, she'd undergone a slow meta-morphosis. He'd fought it because he hadn't understood what was happening, but now that his Belinda had finally evolved into a tall, gray-eyed, brown-haired woman with breeding and integrity in every bone of her body, he felt an enormous sense of relief. The plot all fell into place now that his heroine had come to life.

Something else was beginning to emerge in his consciousness as well, and he made a deliberate effort to put a lid on it. He'd almost gotten in over his head today, and he couldn't afford the luxury. Not yet. With a woman like Emily, it paid to take it slow and easy—if one took it at all.

Forcing his attention back to the written word, Bey nodded thoughtfully. ''Skim off the dross and we get down to the gold. Play the gold against the steel and we've got the story.'' With a crooked grin of triumph, he capped the pen and rammed it into his shirt pocket and then riffled through the pages of his small notebook. A frown quickly replaced the look of satisfaction. Three pages left. Three small pages!

Softly and with deadly efficiency he swore. He'd sooner have been caught out here in the dead of winter in nothing but his skivvies than without enough writing materials. Ideas popped into his head at the damnedest times, and he went crazy if he couldn't get them down.

It meant another trip into town. It was practically dark, and he had a hell of a lot of thinking to do. He'd planned to crawl into his mummy bag and mull over a few things during that creative period between the time when his mind went into overdrive and the time he fell asleep.

Leaning over, he grabbed the bucket of water he always kept handy and emptied it onto the ashes of his fire. And then, for the first time since Emily had left him, he stood up.

Damn—he was stiff as a board! Thirty-two might sound young to some people, but he'd got a hell of a lot of mileage out of every one of those years.

He headed for the tent, where he'd left his keys, and it was then that he saw Emily's brown suede jacket. Veering toward the lumber pile, he hooked it with one hand and brought it up to his face. As he inhaled her fragrance, a slow smile gentled his rugged features. God, what a woman. Talk about your dross and your gold...!

Whistling loudly in an effort that was more bravado than bravura, Emily hung on to the broom handle with one hand and the gutter with the other as she balanced on next to the top rung. She could hardly see as far as the corner of the roof, but she was determined to finish what she'd started. She needed the satisfaction of finishing at least one thing today. The reports could wait another week; the school might fold before anyone got around to reading them anyway. But at least her gutters would be clean. She'd learned a long time ago to take pleasure in small triumphs when the larger ones eluded her.

She didn't see him round the corner just as the last streak of pale pink light faded from the western sky. The first she knew that she wasn't alone was the rasping oath that assaulted her ears.

"Judas priest, woman, would you tell me just what the hell you think you're doing up there?"

Startled, she twisted around. The rusty metal gutter protested noisily as it sagged under her gripping fingers. "Bey?" she squeaked.

"Are you crazy? Wait—don't move!"

It was too late. She felt the ladder begin to lean, and she clutched at the roof, only there was nothing to hold on to. "Get away, get away," she screamed, as the world lurched past her. In the split second before she landed, she made an effort to relax, recalling fragments of something she'd read about the proper way to fall.

The falling was fine; there was nothing at all proper about the landing, however. She felt herself literally plucked out of the air by two incredibly strong arms, and then she was sprawling all over a mass of warm granite.

It was several long moments before she could think, much less move. By the time she came to her senses, she was horribly aware of the still form beneath her. "Bey?

Oh, God, Bey, I've broken you," she wailed, easing herself to her knees.

She placed a hand on his chest. It was too dark to see clearly, but it was definitely a chest under her palm. And it was definitely not working properly. Broken phrases of concern were interspersed with unconvincing ones of reassurance as she placed her ear just over his mouth.

He wasn't breathing.

"Oh, my God..." Heartbeat—clear the air passages—expand the lungs. Fragments of the CPR routine filtered into her shocked mind as she maneuvered herself into position and cupped his chin with one hand. Her mouth covered his slack lips, and then she remembered to shut off the nasal air passage. Lifting her head slightly, she was struggling to support his neck and pinch his nose when he began to stir.

A reedy gasp struck her ear and he muttered, "Forget the nose, love—it's the mouth that's important."

"Bey! Oh, Bey, you're alive!" Crumpling, she rested her forehead on his chest as her knees dug deeper into the frost-softened earth. She was dimly aware of the dampness permeating her jeans, and acutely aware of the rock-hardness of the chest under her face. She felt a hand come up to stroke the back of her hair, and Bey's voice, for once distinctly lacking in strength, murmured, "You okay, Emily? Nothing broken, I hope."

Lifting her head, she laughed shakily. "I thought you were. Didn't you hear my warning?"

Still holding her face against his chest, Bey sat up. The positions were awkward, but neither of them seemed to notice. "Didn't you hear mine?" he shot back weakly.

"By then it was too late. Next time I'll yell 'Timber.'" Her hands moved restlessly over his shoulders and arms for reassurance. "That darned ladder—I knew the ground was too soft on this side of the house. I finished all the others, though, and I only wanted to...Bey, what are you doing here?" She was still on her knees, off balance as his arms held her tightly to him. In no condition to fight gravity, she lowered her hips to the ground, her legs trailing across his thighs.

"Came to return your jacket," he murmured warmly into her hair. "I think I threw it over by that green thing with the red berries."

"Yew," she whispered, fitting herself more closely to the hollow of his shoulder.

"Yes?" His voice was a resonance that vibrated all the way to the base of her spine.

"What?"

"What were you going to say?"

"When?"

"You said *you*," he reminded her, examining her vertebrae with gentle expertise.

"That's what it is—my jacket. The bush."

"Did you land on your head?" His lips brushed over her cheek and burned against the side of her cold nose. Helplessly she raised her head, and with a soft groan he took her mouth.

Her lips parted at the first touch of his thrusting tongue, and he lowered his back to the ground, bringing her down on top of him. One of her hands pressed into the soft, cold ground for balance; the other found its way under his black sweater. His flesh was warm and resilient, and she kneaded it feverishly as his hungry mouth unleashed a wild response deep inside her.

She had on too many clothes. Her breasts craved the touch of his hands, of his bare flesh, but they were separated by too many layers of wool and cotton and nylon. His hand moved to her hips, cupping and stroking before shifting her so that she was lying full length on top of him.

A soft startled groan emerged from the depths of her throat. Oh, God, it was starting all over again. *This was insane.* She hardly even knew him—he was years younger than she was, and she was on fire for him.

Bey's hand moved under her sweater, under the flannel shirt she wore beneath it, and slipped between the hardness of his own chest and the softness of her throbbing breast. There had to be a better way—

He rolled over, still holding her tightly against him. His mouth trailed hot, moist kisses from her lips to the hollow under her cheekbone, to her temple. "I want you so much I'm half-crazy, Emily." The slow, agonized emphasis on each word raked trails of liquid fire through her body. "I didn't mean this to happen so soon, darling, but I... It's too late now."

The hot rush of his breath against her ear, the intoxicating taste of him, the feel of his powerfully aroused body against hers—these sensations unwillingly gave way to other, less pleasant ones. Emily's clothing had twisted under her, and a stretch of bare skin was slowly freezing in the night air. Cold dampness was seeping through the thin layer of her jeans, and assorted aches and stiffnesses were beginning to clamor for attention.

Under the circumstances, it was relatively easy for her to back away from the volatile situation. She was just lucky it hadn't happened on a warm summer night when she was wearing next to nothing. She began to disengage herself, slightly chagrined when he let her go without an argument.

"Bey, I don't know about you, but I'm freezing to death—and I think I might have sprained my foot. Is that possible? A foot?"

He sat up again, expelling his breath in a deep, shuddering sigh. "Yeah, I guess it's possible to sprain almost anything."

She got to her feet, gingerly testing the left one before applying any weight on it. Quickly shifting to her right one, she began flexing her arms and fingers. "What about you? Any injuries? Good Lord, I landed on top of you, and I'm no butterfly."

"I must have sprained my judgement," he said wryly. "Believe it or not, I don't normally pounce on women the minute the sun goes down."

Laughing breathlessly, Emily touched her throat. "At least there are no puncture wounds." Turning toward the back door, she added, "And in this particular instance, I did the pouncing. Come on inside where it's warm, Bey."

"Yeah, well . . . just long enough to be sure you're okay, then I'll be on my way." He followed her around the corner of the house, and in the darkness she couldn't tell if he was limping or not. She was. She'd whacked her foot good, and sneakers weren't much protection.

"I could do with a cup of coffee," she chattered through clenched teeth. It was something other than the falling temperature that had locked her muscles into painful rigidity.

Snapping on the overhead light, she turned away, struggling for composure. She heard the scrape of a chair, and a sound that was half-sigh, half-groan.

Averting her eyes, she busied herself with filling the coffeemaker with water and then paused, gripping the edge of the counter.

Lord, how could she ever face him after wallowing around on the ground that way? As if she hadn't made a fool of herself once today, already. His hands had roamed all over her, and both times she'd permitted it. Permittèd it—she'd *loved* it! Even after that peremptory brush-off he'd handed her today.

Dumping coffee recklessly into the filter, she wondered how she'd managed to delude herself all these years as to her own sensual nature. With Wendell she'd rationalized her disappointment as inexperience. With Bo, it had been a certain lack of openness that had prevented her from drifting into a physical relationship. Later, of course, she'd been glad it had never progressed that far.

And Jonathan—handsome, charming, romantic Jonathan. He'd been every woman's ideal lover, up to a point. And then at that point he'd been a failure, and he'd blamed his failure on her. And by the time she'd come to realize that his problems were deep-seated and of long standing, she'd felt so sorry for him that she'd accepted the blame. The day he'd sailed out of her life on his sleek forty-five-foot yawl had been the day she'd put all nonsense about men and romance out of her life.

"You're limping," Bey accused, breaking into her thoughts.

The coffee gurgled peacefully, and Emily took down two delicate cups, wishing for once she had a pair of heavy utilitarian mugs to wrap her cold hands around.

Adjusting a determined smile on her face, she turned to deny the charge. "No I'm not. I'm fine, just fine. I think maybe my foot was just frozen."

"Take off your shoe and let me see."

"Look, Bey, if you want coffee, just sit quietly until it's finished making, drink it and then go," she said evenly. "I'm not hurt, and I'm not taking off anything."

He settled back into the chair, his arms spreading along the armrests and his legs stretching out across her polished pine floor. The crooked grin that creased his cheeks and sparkled in his eyes did nothing at all to reassure her.

"Sooner or later, you will, you know. But I can wait. I want it to be the proper time and place."

Six

Wearily raking a hand through his unruly hair, Bey shoved his chair away from the desk. Pulling out of his story after a long work session was like coming out of an afternoon movie; one was always surprised to discover that the rest of the world was still out there.

For four eighteen-hour days, he'd been subsisting on his usual fare of black coffee, beer and Vienna sausages. His jeans hung on his bones like the hide on a starving hound, but he'd written three chapters, rough-editing with pencil at the end of each session. At this rate he'd be ready to negotiate by the middle of November.

He could use the advance; buying the property had knocked the starch out of his bank account, and the house was eating into his funds faster than he'd expected. He had a few good investments that paid monthly dividends, but otherwise, it was feast or famine. Royalty checks twice a year, and an advance when he mailed in a book.

It was a hell of a way to making a living, but he was hooked—he'd wanted to be a writer ever since he'd read his first Western. Of course, if he'd stuck to Westerns, he wouldn't be where he was today. On the other hand, he wouldn't have to be so damned secretive about what he did for a living.

He glanced around him, wondering if he had anything in the house to eat. God, what a cheerless room. He'd deliberately downplayed any sign of affluence, not wanting to arouse the hunting instincts of some of his more unsavory aquaintances, but maybe he'd overdone it.

If word got out that he could have bought the whole damned building as a tax write-off, he'd have been ripe for plucking by every small-time hood in the neighborhood. And if he got ripped off and registered a complaint about it, he'd have to answer a few questions. He didn't care to have to explain the source of his income to some hard-nosed cop.

He stood up and stretched, flexing the muscles of his back and shoulders. He could do with some fresh air and a bowl of chili, maybe some doughnuts or a few of the Kahlúa brownies he'd developed a taste for. He'd been cooped up for four days, and the first day hadn't been all that productive. He'd had a hell of a time focusing his mind on his work.

Emily McCloud. It was the right name for her, he mused. Bey had an instinct for names. Sometimes it took him more time to find the right name for his heroine than it did to decide on her career. Emily was . . . Emily. And unfortunately, he was more inter-

ested in furthering the relationship between Emily and
Bey than he was the one between Belinda and Cain.

He was almost out the door when the phone rang.
For two bits he'd have ignored it. Chances were pretty
good, though, that it was either his agent or his editor.
Not many people knew his number, and he wasn't in the
book.

He growled into the instrument.

"Hello, love, want to take me to a party?" a familiar voice crooned.

Bey's lips tightened. He'd all but told the woman to
get lost six months ago. What did it take to make it
stick? "Am I the best you could do, Della?"

"You're the best any woman could do, darling ... only I haven't done you lately."

"Crudeness doesn't become a woman, Della. What
did you want?"

A musical laugh shimmered against his ear. "That's
what I adore about you, Beyard, you're such a lovely
bundle of contradictions—that old-fashioned chauvin-
ism that pops up when I least expect it. I wonder what
that macho facade of yours is *really* covering up?"

"At the moment it's covering up an empty belly. I
was on my way out the door to get a bowl of chili, so
why don't we cut this little visit short, huh?"

"Oh, goody! Our old place? I'll meet you there. I've
got some interesting gossip to—"

"Della, gossip gives me indigestion."

"I haven't seen you since I covered this convention in
D.C. a few months back—romance writers. Hundreds
of 'em, and agents and editors swarming all over the
place. I'm beginning to think I'm in the wrong end of
the writing business. And, Bey—some of the rumors I
heard will amuse you."

"I seriously doubt it," Bey said dryly. His eyes narrowed and the planes of his face flattened imperceptibly as he waited for her to get to the point. Della never wasted time on idle gossip unless she was ferreting.

"Are you still there? Darling, it was fascinating. The women who write these things—would you believe that some of them are lawyers, librarians, pilots—even journalists? I met an English prof from some university or other who writes one a year—the torrid kind."

"Is that it? Della, I hate to cut you off, but—"

As though he hadn't interrupted her, the lilting voice went on to say, "But you know what I found the most fascinating, darling? Some of the writers—not many, but a few—are men using women's names. I actually met two of them, and they're…mmmmm, well let's just say I'd *adore* helping them with their research."

"Good luck," Bey replied calmly.

"But about this party, Bey, it's—"

"Della, look, I've got to run. I'm leaving town this afternoon, and I don't know exactly when I'll be back. Thanks for the invitation, but you know how I feel about parties."

"I haven't forgotten, my charming misfit. You hate people, you despise socializing, and you can't stand frivolity—except when it comes to women's lingerie." She ignored his snort of disgust to continue breezily, "Well, darling, if you'd rather have a private party, you know where I live."

"Della, I just told you I was on my way out of town."

"More government business?" she purred. He'd mentioned once, when her inquisitive mind had backed him into a corner, that he'd done some work for the government a few years back and that he still had to be ready to leave town at a moment's notice.

Which was literally the truth. Four years in the army qualified as government work by anyone's standards. And when a beautiful green-eyed blonde started digging into matters that didn't concern her, he'd found it expedient to get out of town. One of the reasons he'd bought the *Bonus* was to give him a place to spend weekends, out of the reach of the phone or any unexpected visitors.

He'd first met Della Brame outside a café on a snowy day when her car wouldn't start. He'd taken her home on his bike, and they'd begun seeing each other. It had been pretty good for a while—they'd had little in common outside the bedroom, but that had been enough at first. At her insistence, Bey had started squiring her around town to various bars and nightclubs. He'd been bored stiff by the superficiality of the crowd she hung out with, but he'd made good use of the time by filling notebooks with quick character sketches. His waning interest had plunged still further when she'd started asking some pretty pointed questions about what he did for a living.

He'd finally managed to break it off without being too brutal. It didn't pay to antagonize someone in Della's profession. As a socialite turned feature writer for one of the area's largest dailies, she'd built a reputation on detecting all but invisible flaws in the most respectable facades. Bey had worked too hard to perfect his cover to risk blowing it.

He managed to evade Della's repeated invitation by promising to call when he had more time. And when that day came, he added silently as he replaced the phone in its cradle, he'd be on the other side of the Chesapeake Bay, leaving not so much as a trail of bread crumbs behind him.

Meanwhile, the chili could wait. He had a powerful urge to head for the Eastern Shore again. He'd never had the slightest desire to confide in Della, but Emily was different. He'd have to level with her. In spite of a few notable lapses, he planned to go easy until he could think of some way to let her know about his writing. Still, it wouldn't hurt to drop by and inquire after her injured foot.

Maybe he'd take her something; a woman like Emily deserved to be courted. By all rights, he should be an expert on courtship, but when it came to actual practice, he wasn't so sure he could pull it off. He'd been accused of a lot of things in his lifetime, but never of being courtly. It would have to be something that wouldn't scare her off—no expensive jewelry. And something that would fit in his saddlebag, which meant no flowers.

An irreverent thought occurred to him, and the last of the hardness engendered by Della's phone call disappeared from his face. He wished he had the nerve to present her with a copy of one of his books—say, the latest one, *Reap the Wild Wind*. Not yet, though—not until he felt a hell of a lot more secure with her.

Emily angled the chair so that she could prop her slippered feet on the fire screen. For once, she'd drawn a book she was thoroughly enjoying. The biography of an English archaeologist who'd devoted his life to a study of Mexican prehistory, it covered a fascinating correspondence with a holy man in India that posed some intriguing questions. She'd love to take a course in archaeology someday.

Her storm windows went unhung and her shutters unpainted, but her conscience was clear. It was too cold and damp out there to risk pneumonia, especially when she had a good fire, a good book and a pot of hambone soup on the stove. She'd earned herself a break.

At the rap on the front door, she looked up in exasperation. There'd been a meeting of the board on Thursday night, and Abbie had mentioned dropping by sometime this weekend. But not now, Emily thought plaintively. Dammit, she was in no mood for discouraging news. Eastwood Academy's days were strictly numbered unless the board had found a fairy godmother—they all knew it, but couldn't the official notification wait until Monday? She'd had the devil of a time regaining her peace of mind, and it wasn't fair to have it shattered again so soon.

Resignedly she threw open the door. "Come on in Ab...Bey?" Still holding the book with a finger to mark her place, she gazed at the black-clad figure who stood grinning at her. It had started to drizzle, and there was a film of moisture on his leather coat and the helmet he held under one arm.

"Brought you something," he said almost shyly.

"You...why...hello, Bey," she stammered inanely. Hurriedly she held the door wider. "Come inside. It's turned colder, hasn't it?"

His eyes mocking her confusion, he stepped inside, pulling the door shut after him. From beneath his helmet he produced a small gold-mesh bag filled with foil-wrapped chocolates. "Hope you like candy. I'd have brought flowers, but I didn't think they'd stand the trip."

"Bey, you didn't have to..." Breaking off, Emily led him across to the chair before the fire. "Take off your coat, it's wet. Your pants are... Oh. They're leather too." She found herself staring at the close-fitting black pants in fascination. "Don't they get hot?"

Oh, Lord, she'd had to ask. Whatever social graces she'd once possessed had long since deserted her.

Peeling off his coat, Bey turned and said with perfect urbanity, "As a matter of fact, they do."

For several moments they simply stared at one another, Emily feeling as if her veins had been pumped full of sweet sparkling wine. She hadn't expected to see him so soon, not after the way they'd parted the weekend before. She'd been so afraid he'd take advantage of her momentary weakness that she'd practically rushed him through the door, coffee and all. And then she'd spent almost the entire week thinking about him.

"How've you been?" he asked. As his smile widened, his eyes seemed to grow more amber than green.

"Just fine, and you?" Oh, lovely, she jeered silently. He'll really be entranced by my scintillating conversation!

"I never got around to showing you that flower, did I?"

Puzzled, she held out her hand for the coat he'd removed. "I'll hang it over a chair until it's dry. You mean the flower you found growing at the Landing? No, you never did. My visit ended sort of abruptly, remember?"

"Ouch. In case you hadn't noticed, there are a few rough edges on my party manners. I'm trying, though—bear with me, will you?"

He did it so easily, deflecting her criticism so that she wanted to cradle him in her arms and soothe away any pain her barbed words had caused. Men like Bey Jones should be made to wear a warning label: CAUTION; could cause serious weakness in women.

"What did it look like?" she asked, gesturing to the Morris chair and taking a seat on the other side of the room.

He held up a fist and lifted one knuckle above the others. "Sort of like this. It was red—sort of purplish red—and it grew on a vine with beans and lacy leaves."

Emily laughed. "It's a wild sweet pea. I didn't know there were any blooming this late in the season. I used to collect great bunches of them when I was little—I remember I was disappointed that they didn't taste at all sweet."

Bey relaxed against the chintz-covered cushions. The heat from the fireplace had brought a flush to his face after the long, cold ride. "This is nice," he murmured, glancing around the room. "Did I tell you I'm going to have a fireplace?"

"I believe you did happen to mention it once or twice," Emily murmured gently. There—he'd done it again, damn him. It took no more than that oddly disarming candor of his to turn her into pudding. Another man might boast about his yacht or his horse or an expensive sports car, and she'd be completely turned off. Bey mentioned a fireplace and her silly heart went into a tailspin.

"How's the building?" she asked, her voice a shade huskier than usual.

"All framed in, I hope—haven't checked it out yet. I'm on my way now."

"Bey, you're not camping out in this weather?"

"Got a better idea?" The grin widened, its very guilelessness raising her defenses.

"I certainly have. There are plenty of rooms in St. Michaels. You could get a good night's sleep in a motel and come back in the morning. You can't see anything in this rain, anyway."

"It's supposed to clear up before long—clearing and colder, according to the noon report."

She nodded resignedly. If he was going to be huddled up in that flimsy little tent on a rainy night while the temperature dropped down into the twenties, she wouldn't be able to sleep a wink. Dammit, why did he have to do this to her? Here she'd finally managed to put the whole silly affair into perspective; she'd caught up on her paperwork and drawn a really good book for once, and now she wouldn't be able to enjoy it for worrying about him.

"I'll be just fine. My sleeping bag's good down to fifteen degrees, and I've got on wool long johns."

"It's wet out there, Bey. You won't be able to heat water, much less get warm," she said resentfully. Why did he have to come along and ruin her whole weekend?

"I'll drink beer."

"For breakfast? That's disgusting."

His grin never wavered as he picked up the gold-mesh bag from the coffee table and opened it. He peeled one of the chocolates and popped it into his mouth. "No it's not. Goes great with sardines and crackers. Of course, the crackers aren't much good in this kind of weather, but then, you can't have everything."

"*Every*thing! You don't have *any*thing!" she argued indignantly.

"Give me time," he murmured, reaching for another chocolate. "I've got plans to have it all." There was something decidedly disturbing about that voice, nor could she find anything at all reassuring in the way his eyelids drooped lazily over those wickedly gleaming eyes.

"I... Do you... That is, I've got a pot of soup on the stove. It's late for lunch and early for dinner, but maybe you'd better have something to fortify you before you take off."

The whispering sound of soft leather accompanied his rising. He stood before her, looking disconcertingly masculine as he bit into another chocolate. "Sounds great. I was always a sucker for homemade soup."

She led the way into the kitchen. "It may not be the world's greatest soup, but it certainly beats beer and sardines on a day like this," she said defensively. "Do you mind eating in the kitchen again? My furnace is on the blink and the dining room's on the north side of the house."

"I know you'll find this hard to believe, but I rarely stand on ceremony," he teased, enjoying the way the color came and went under her translucent complexion.

He watched her move around the room, reaching to take down bowls, opening the silverware drawer and then shoving it closed with an unconsciously graceful swing of the hips. That was a nice move. And the way her sweater hugged her breasts when she lifted her arms to the top shelf made his pupils dilate with pleasure. Everything about her was lovely. Why couldn't he have settled for some ordinary woman instead of shooting for the stars? She had everything—looks, intelligence, background, a career and a home of her own.

She was gold, he was dross. What the hell did he have to offer her? Looks? He'd seen better-looking faces at the zoo—behind bars. Intelligence? Okay, he'd grant himself a few points there. He was a little short on formal education, but he'd get by. Background? That was a laugh. His background consisted of a series of foster homes and institutions, plus a rumor that his old man had been a merchant seaman. As for his mother, she was ninety percent imagination and ten percent bad memories. When it came to background, he didn't have a whole lot to offer any woman, much less a woman like Emily McCloud.

He was hungry. Breakfast had been black coffee. After Della's call he'd been too damned anxious to split town to hang around for lunch. "This is purely ambrosial," he murmured, scraping up the last spoonful of the richly flavored soup.

"Purely ambrosial," Emily repeated in awed amusement, reaching for his bowl. "Does that mean you want seconds?"

"Can you spare it?"

She couldn't resist. "You realize you're now back in my debt. One plate of Stroganoff and two bowls of soup to one and a half of your hotdogs."

Their eyes met in shared laughter that had seemed to spring up from nowhere. Emily marveled at how quickly he could affect her mood. One minute she was wishing she'd never laid eyes on the man, and the next she was wondering how the kitchen could feel so sunny on a cold and rainy afternoon in November.

Bey asked about the book she'd been reading, and eagerly she launched on a summary. "It makes me wish I could take off for Mexico—especially on a day like this."

"You like nonfiction best, then?" he asked idly, rising to pour the coffee she'd made.

"Oh, I like everything if it's well-written."

"That's a pretty broad statement." He sipped the steaming coffee and gazed at her quizzically.

She shrugged. "When I was growing up I read everything, and I *do* mean everything—much to my father's horror."

A slow grin deepened the creases in Bey's weathered cheeks. "And here I thought you'd been so sheltered," he scoffed gently. "What do you mean by everything—girlie magazines? *Popular Mechanics?* Cookbooks? Romances?"

In the living room, the mantel clock chimed the hour and a log settled noisily in the fireplace. Someone rang the doorbell.

"Abbie," Emily muttered, excusing herself and rising reluctantly to answer the door. She was aware of a surge of irritation that had nothing at all to do with the possible bad tidings her friend might be bearing.

"Lord, it's miserable out there," the wiry redhead declared, shaking the raindrops from her scarf and sniffing appreciatively. "What's cooking? Am I too late or too early?"

"Right on the button. Come on out to the kitchen and have a bowl of soup," Emily invited, bowing to the inevitable. She made the introductions, not missing Abbie's swift look of interest. "Abbie, this is Bey Jones. Bey, Abbie Linga. Abbie's headmistress at the school where I teach."

Abbie fluffed the orange hair that had been flattened by her scarf and treated herself to a thorough survey of the compactly built man in the black leather pants and brown knit shirt.

"Well, well, well," she drawled, "I'm beginning to see why no one can drag Em away from this rural retreat of hers. And all along I thought she was too busy doing her schoolwork to come out and play.'' She accepted the bowl of soup Emily served her and proceeded to ignore it. ''Do you live around here, Bey? And is your first name Chesapeake, by any chance?'

Emily's head swung from one of them to the other as they settled the matter of Bey's unusual name and his reason for being here. She felt rather like a spectator at a tennis match.

''So—you're going to be neighbors,'' Abbie murmured, a speculative gleam in her eyes. Emily could have killed her. Evidently all those romances she'd read had softened her brain.

This had gone far enough. ''I suppose the news is bad,'' she broke in, deliberately steering the subject away from the man in her kitchen. ''You weren't in your office when I popped in yesterday.''

Abbie turned a blank look on her. ''Oh...that. Well, I must say, you've at least got some compensation. Now I won't have to worry about leaving you here all alone and in despair.''

''How long do we have?'' Emily asked stoically.

''The rest of this term. We might have lasted out the year except for the asbestos ceilings that have got to come out. It was decided,'' she announced sarcastically, ''to postpone any decision on when to comply until the next term, at which time, of course, Eastwood will have ceased to exist.'' She planted an elbow on the table and plopped her chin in her palm. ''Drat!''

''Seventy-seven years,'' Emily said morosely. ''Do you realize that my grandmother and my mother both graduated from that school?''

''And you.''

"And me," Emily echoed, staring absently at a ring of moisture on the polished surface of the table. "I think I'd like a drink."

Bey rose quietly to his feet. "If you'll tell me where and what . . . ?"

"I've only got sherry," she apologized dully. His eyes crinkled into a shadow of a smile, and it irritated her unreasonably. "You think it's funny, my losing a job? I may end up shucking oysters for a living."

His hand rested on her shoulder for a long moment, and Emily found herself wanting nothing so much as to close her mind to her troubles and bury herself in those strong, sheltering arms.

"Matter of fact, one of the reasons I came out here was to sound you out about something," Abbie said briskly.

Bey's smile turned inward as he busied himself with the decanter. He'd known she'd drink sherry. It would be dry, and good, but not too expensive. He served the wine and then swung his chair around to straddle it.

"So sound me out," Emily sighed.

"Ever been to Durham, North Carolina?" Abbie inquired, downing her wine as if it were whiskey.

Emily shook her head, trying to force an interest in what Abbie was saying. Subliminally she was aware of an almost catlike stillness in Bey. He was resting his arms on the back of the chair, his eyes half-closed as he sipped from his wineglass. There was something almost alien about his presence at her table; alien, but somehow . . . right.

"I've been offered a position as headmistress in a small coed school in Durham County. I happen to know that there's an opening in the English department, but the salary won't be too great—at least not for the first year or so. If you're interested, I'm driving down next Friday for an interview."

Bey's eyes opened, and he placed his empty glass on the table. "Let's go in by the fire. Abbie, you can't expect Emily to make a decision like that off the top of her head. Tell me," he said, escorting the small, attractive redhead into the living room and leaving Emily to bring up the rear, "exactly what does a headmistress do? The term conjures up all sorts of interesting possibilities."

Emily's gray eyes grew stony as Abbie bloomed under the attention. Dammit, Abbie had two ex-husbands, a live-in companion, and a decent new job to go to. Did she have to have Bey drooling all over her too?

Somehow she found herself sharing the hard sofa with Bey while Abbie settled into the Morris chair. Crossing her arms, she leaned back, only to feel Bey's fingers twisting gently in her hair. He was sitting almost three feet away, with one arm stretched out along the back of the sofa, listening to Abbie's job description with every evidence of fascination. Emily tried to pull away from his hand and winced when the fingers tightened in her hair.

"I like your line of thought, Bey. Unfortunately, for the next few weeks I'm going to be busy trying to placate a hundred or so disgruntled parents and help them squeeze their offspring into some other over-crowded, underfinanced institute of learning. Come to think of it, shucking oysters doesn't sound all that bad, Em. Got any good contacts?"

"Next weekend, you say? What time are you planning to leave?" Emily asked, frowning thoughtfully.

Bey yanked at her hair again. "Honey, you can't just go dashing off that way. You've got a home here, and a—"

Honey? Emily shot him a repressive look, jerking her hair free of his playful fingers. "And what? How long do you think I can keep this place with no job?"

Abbie reached for the small bag of chocolates Bey had left, helping herself to one of the few that remained. "What about the column?" She turned to Bey. "Emily does this book review every week. She's had this thing going with some reader who took exception to a certain review, and everybody in town's talking about it."

"Oh, Abbie," Emily grumbled.

"Well, they are. Wendell ought to raise your pay for the increase in sales. He could double his circulation if you'd do just one controversial review a month."

Embarrassed, Emily slanted a glance at Bey. "Abbie's exaggerating. It wasn't controversial. I just didn't like the book."

Bey's eyes probed hers as a smile teased the corners of his mouth. "Didn't like it? Or didn't understand it?"

"It was just a romance, for goodness' sake," she said disparagingly.

Abbie chimed in. "And Emily doesn't care for romances. They're conspiring to undermine the womanhood of America." She peeled another chocolate and slipped it into her mouth, rolling her eyes heavenward. "Look, folks, I hate to eat and run, but duty calls. Why don't you bring a bag on Friday and we'll leave from school. The interview's on Saturday morning at ten, and we can do the town Saturday night and come home Sunday."

Bey stood up. In the cozy cluttered warmth of the small room, he seemed strangely... The word "menacing" popped into Emily's head and she shook herself. Black leather pants, a battered face, and the build of a professional athlete did not necessarily add up to menace. She was being fanciful.

"Abbie, I'll let you know by Wednesday," she said hurriedly.

Bey wrapped an arm about her and she shot him a tight-lipped look. "Yeah, she'll let you know, Abbie. Been nice meeting you. Come by again."

The moment the door closed, Emily turned angrily to confront him. "Don't you think it's time you were running along too, Bey? Duck season's started, and you might have to try a couple of places before you find a room." She did her best to ignore her accelerating pulses and the dryness that had her swallowing convulsively. Dammit, why was he crowding her against the door this way?

"I told you I'm not staying in any motel, Emily." He didn't touch her, but the very animal warmth of his body seemed to reach out and surround her, numbing her will to defy him. "I don't mind a little rain," he said, the gravelly texture of his voice more evident than usual under its softness. "I've slept out in worse weather than this without benefit of sleeping bag or tent. I don't melt."

He melted, all right. He melted *her.* Hardening herself against his beguiling spell, she said witheringly, "Well, just so you understand that my hospitality begins and ends in the kitchen."

"You're inviting me to spread my bag on your warm kitchen floor?"

The boyish eagerness was not entirely convincing, not when the virile strength of him, the very scent of him, was undermining her reason. She crossed her arms and did her best to seal herself against his magnetism. "I'm inviting you to leave, Bey. It might strike you as amusing that I've just lost my job, but believe me, I don't find it at all humorous. I've got a lot of serious thinking to do, and I don't need—''

"Humorous?" he broke in. "What the hell gave you the idea I thought it was humorous?"

"Oh, don't try that innocent look on me. I saw you grinning like a Cheshire cat back there in the kitchen. Things may be rosy for you publishers, but let me tell you something, the teaching business has seen better days! I don't find it all amusing to have to start out at the bottom of the ladder again after all these years."

Without taking a single step, he was suddenly much closer. "Emily, Emily," he whispered, unfolding her arms as easily as if they were made of paper, "you'll be all right. I promise you, you'll be just fine."

Seven

Helplessly she watched as it began to melt away—the anger, the determination, the firm boundaries she'd set out to define the limits of their relationship. As the spell of him eddied around her, she watched it begin to crumble, undermined as swiftly as sand castles in the tide. Her stricken gaze followed him until the very last moment, seeing the quick softening of his lips, the fierce intensity of heavy-lidded eyes embedded in the hardened planes of his face.

"Bey, please don't?" she pleaded, her voice wavering off into a plaintive question.

It was hopeless. How could she fight against something she wanted beyond all reason? At the first touch of his hard hands on her face, curving along the lines of her jaw, defining the hollow of her cheeks, she surrendered. Her lips parted in the instant before he claimed them. One kiss, she promised herself in desperate resignation. One kiss and then she'd shove him out the door. And heaven help her if she broke that promise.

The darting thrust of his tongue triggered an instant response, and her arms crept around his waist, her hands moving restlessly over the powerful muscles of his back. Her breasts were crushed against him, and she swayed unconsciously, wanting the tactile stimulation of flesh against flesh.

As if sensing her needs, Bey slowly lowered his hands from her face to the hollows of her throat. Then, lifting his mouth to brush kisses over her eyelids, he fitted his palm around the small fullness of her breast, and she sagged against him.

"Oh, God, sweetheart, you don't know how much I've wanted this, wanted you—you just can't know," he whispered hoarsely.

"Bey, this is a mistake," she murmured even as her hands curved over the taut leather-clad muscles of his buttocks. "You've got to go, got to leave me alone." For all the control she had, she might as well be drunk! Somewhere in the back of her mind, a wisp of reason struggled for recognition, but her heedless body was racing at breakneck speed along the path of its own desires.

His hand slipped up under the layers of wool and nylon, his hard palms creating an erotic friction on her sensitive skin. Under her sweater and camisole, she wore nothing. By the time he cupped the lower slopes of her breasts and allowed his thumbs to reach upward, her nipples had already gathered themselves into tight, expectant buds. She felt his quick, surging response as he recognized her state of readiness.

The pale patterned wool of the ancient rug was soft, warmed by the glow from the fireplace. Bey lowered her to the floor and followed her down. Slipping an arm under her shoulder and another over her hips, he caught her tightly to him.

"Emily, Emily—do you have even the faintest idea what you do to me?" His warm breath stirred her tumbled hair as his tongue found the pink shell of her ear. She shuddered violently. "So perfect, so lovely—I don't deserve you, but God, I want you, sweet Emily—every curve, every smell, every warm, secret place—I want all of you."

Each shimmering word he whispered shot through her body, setting up a rush of tremors as his hands began unbuttoning her sweater. She could only lie there rigid with excitement. Her feet were arched, toes extended downward in the fur-rimmed pink suede slippers. When he slipped the sweater from her arms and tugged it from beneath her, she clung helplessly to the narrow gleam of his eyes, drowning in a cascade of pure sensation.

He knelt beside her, the supple black leather straining across his thighs as he raised his arms and pulled his knit shirt over his head. Her gaze tangled in the dense thicket of surprisingly dark hair on his chest, and her fingers curved unconsciously into her palms. His nipples were flat copper disks, their tiny centers standing proudly alert. Her lips parted in a small groan.

He came down over her slowly, his mouth finding hers in a hungry joining, even as his hands worked at the fastening of her slacks. She could feel the heat spreading through her body, radiating out from an incandescent center that throbbed almost painfully. As his hands slid under her hips to remove her slacks, her legs stiffened again.

He came back to her mouth as though impatient at the momentary delay, alternately suckling and thrusting as his hands began to explore the warm satin of her stomach between filmy white briefs and the lacy camisole. One of his legs moved to cover one of hers, and she marveled with strange detachment at the cool feel of leather against the heated flesh of her thigh.

Bey's lips moved to nuzzle her tumbled hair away from her ear. "I need to see you," he whispered, drawing out the sibilant sound until she arched her back and shuddered in helpless excitement. Quickly he reached under her to slip the flimsy garment over her shoulders.

Somewhere along the way, she'd lost her slippers, and Bey, she noted in vague surprise, had shed his boots. She wanted him to shed everything. She was starving for the sight of him, perishing from a need so elemental that it drove out all else from her mind.

Once more he knelt beside her, his smoldering gaze igniting flames as it ranged over her with lingering deliberation. Bemused, Emily watched the slow journey of his hard, tanned hands as they moved along her milk-white torso. The flat surface of her stomach trembled in anticipation of his touch, and when one of his fingers dipped into her navel, she whimpered, her breath escaping in shuddery little gasps.

In the incredibly erogenous bend of her thigh, he planted a series of moist kisses. And then his tongue began to trace the imperceptible crease. In a rush of exquisite agony, she curled herself around his head.

"Bey, please—I can't stand it," she whimpered.

Lifting his head, he met her beseeching gaze. The planes of his face seemed oddly altered; harsher, yet strangely vulnerable. "Bey..." she cried softly, catching at his shoulders to pull him up over her.

"Wait," he grated.

"Ah, please..." She read the promise in his eyes, but she needed more than promises. Her body's own sensuality had lain dormant for too long, and now, in awakening, it was threatening to overwhelm her.

Reaching up to the sofa, Bey pulled down a small pillow and slipped it under her hips. "Soon, my sweet ladylove," he whispered, his voice harsh with the strain of control. His hand feathered down to her breast to cup, to fondle, to arouse, and the realization that he was trembling too pierced her.

The sweetness that had coiled so tightly in her loins began to unwind, to flow out along her limbs, simmering, shimmering, gathering strength until it encompassed every cell of her body. Half-closed eyes savored the sensuous sight of dark, hair-roughened flesh against creamy smoothness, flaring nostrils drank in the scent of musky masculinity against the familiar fragrance of her body lotion. By the time she felt his tongue circle a throbbing nipple, her eyes were tightly closed and she was breathing in shallow little gulps.

In an involuntary reaction, she drew up her knees. The languorous sweetness penetrated the core of her being, and her thighs stirred in an instinctive urge to part.

Abruptly Bey stood, his hooded gaze never leaving her. She lay vulnerable beneath him as he unzipped the close-fitting leather breeches and stepped out of them. Whatever he wore beneath them came off as well, and Emily found her gaze riveted to his powerful, beautifully masculine body. And in the brief moment before he came down to her, she knew that in spite of reason, it was far more than the virile young body she wanted. She wanted all of him—for all time.

The words he'd whispered to her flickered in her mind, in echo to her own needs. There'd been no word of love, no hint of commitment. If all the caring was on her side and there was only wanting on his, then this would have to be enough.

Bey was actually trembling with the strength of his desire, and yet even though he must know that her own need was every bit as fierce as his, he held back. With a tenderness she found incredibly moving, he knelt to kiss her thighs apart, murmuring broken words of reassurance. She'd been left in no doubt as to the extent of his expertise, but now he seemed almost hesitant—unsure—not at all like a tough, magnetically attractive man who must have known scores of women.

She ran her hungry hands down his body, encouraging, beseeching, discovering. His flesh was warm and resilient, its texture silken under her sensitive fingertips. As she encountered the rougher terrain where the crisp-soft hair patterned downward, she followed it.

"Emily...!" He swore softly as her hands claimed the velvet-sheathed steel of him. She felt a soaring need to give him all the pleasure, to lift him to spinning heights. Instinct as old as womankind guided her until she sensed that he was all but beyond control.

With a rasping oath, Bey lifted her aside. God! And to think he'd once accused her of being incapable of appreciating her own womanhood.

He came into her then, his control completely shattered by an explosive force that went far beyond the limits of anything he'd ever experienced before. In the wild, swift climb that carried them heedlessly to the sun and then hurled them beyond it, he became a part of her very consciousness, welded physically, mentally, spiritually into a union that had at its center the white heat of a nova star.

Together they drifted downward, clinging, bathed in heated moisture, gasping for breath. All the lights in the universe glowed softly around them, and from a great distance came the sound of ceaselessly drumming rain. They slept.

Sometime during the night, Bey awoke and threw another log on the fire. He prowled the house until he located the blanket, and with a feeling of tenderness that scared the hell out of him, he allowed it to drift down over the woman in an unconscious grace that was beauty incarnate.

Fighting down the panic that threatened him, he knelt and slid beneath the blanket, gathering her into his arms again.

A streak of watery sunlight greeted her as Emily opened her eyes. An assortment of unfamiliar impressions rushed in on her. Her bedroom faced northwest; morning sun never found its window. Her bed was hard, but not this hard, and the shoulder her head was resting on was much firmer and warmer than her goose-down pillow.

Her eyes closed against sudden realization. She was in the living room. She was on the floor. They'd made love, and he was still here, and heaven help her, she was in love with him.

It came again, the sound that had dragged her from the depths of sleep. Sitting up, she grabbed the naked shoulder beside her and shook it fiercely.

"Bey! Wake up, dammit—there's someone at the front door!" she whispered furiously.

He was instantly alert, his wits in readiness, his body lagging only slightly behind. It took him less than a second to assimilate the situation. "Tell 'em to wait one minute. I'll scoop up our gear and head for the bathroom while you put on a robe."

Lunging for a slipper, Emily jammed her foot in it, grumbling under her breath. "Any idiot who'd come calling at the crack of dawn on Sunday morning...!"

Bey was on his feet, totally unself-conscious in his nakedness. "Honey, dawn cracked quite a few hours ago. Did you invite anyone to Sunday dinner?"

He handed her another slipper and she hopped on one foot while she put it on, casting him a reproachful glance over her shoulder. "Why did you let me sleep so late? Dammit, why did you...?" And then, lifting her head, "Just a minute!" she called out irritably.

When she headed for the bathroom where her robe hung behind the door, Bey was one step behind her, trailing an armload of clothing and bedding, incongruously topped off by a pair of rugged leather boots. "Are you always this delightful in the morning?" he whispered.

"I'm a dragon in the morning! Would you please get dressed and get out of here? And use the back door."

"Don't I even get breakfast?" he asked plaintively.

Whirling around, Emily jerked her white quilted robe together and knotted the sash. "This is *not* a bed-and-breakfast establishment, Bey. Just get out and stay away from me, is that clear?"

They stood in the bathroom doorway, and she turned to confront him, anger hiding the anguish on her pale features. Her eyes dropped, only to encounter a pair of high-arched bare feet, the toes curled against her cold floor. Her gaze traveled up a pair of hairy, muscular legs, to the ludicrous bundle he held against him, and from there it swept out to each of his broad, coppery shoulders. Centering once more on his strong tanned throat, it lifted reluctantly to that battered, impossibly dear face.

He was grinning at her. Hazel eyes glowing like amber, white teeth gleaming in imperfect splendor, he met her stony glare with all the aplomb of fully clothed king of his realm.

The buzzer sounded again, and with an impatient oath Emily shoved past him. "Just be sure you're out of here before I come back," she snarled.

Her scowl gave way to astonishment as she opened the door to see Wendell Twiford. "Good Lord! I mean, good morning, Wendell. What on earth brings you out here at this time of day?" At *any* time of day. In spite of their occasional dates, it had been years since Wendell had set foot on her porch.

"I heard the news, of course." He removed his Irish tweed hat and smoothed the surface of his graying hair. "Em, I'm really sorry. I've been meaning to call, but you know how it is—one crisis after another. Say, may I come in? No point in letting all your heat go out the door."

Grudgingly she backed away, allowing him to enter the living room. A swift, apprehensive glance assured her that there was no evidence of her overnight guest in sight. Then, as the sound of the shower registered on her consciousness, she clenched her teeth in impotent fury.

"Well, now, maybe we can put out heads together and come up with something to tide you over until you can get situated again. I knew there was trouble, but I didn't realize how bad things were." His pale eyes reflected a sympathy that she found thoroughly distasteful. "I guess this is why you came to me asking about another column. You should have leveled with me, Em. I'd have found you something—art coverage, maybe. You could cover the Waterfowl Festival exhibit for me. Nancy doesn't have to do it every year."

Another fifteen bucks, she thought rancorously. That would help a lot! The shower was still going. She only hoped that if Wendell noticed the sound he'd put it down to something else. "Look, Wendell, thanks for your concern, but I'm fine." She'd be damned before she'd take his charity. "There'll be severance pay and all that, I suppose—I'm not hurting, honestly."

Wendell sat, after carefully pinching the creases in his dark gray pinstripe. "Tom Brady did a feature for today's edition, file stuff, mostly—brief history, alumnae who've gone on to fame and fortune, old families that have contributed so much—that sort of thing. Your own grandfather posthumously donated a wing, remember?"

The sound of the shower was glaringly absent, and Emily felt a sudden inappropriate surge of recklessness. "Actually, it was a drumstick—the concert shell in the auditorium."

Wendell's lips tightened disapprovingly. "You never change, do you, Em? In a pinch, one can always count on you to say something frivolous."

"It's my pinch, Wendell, and if I want to be frivolous, that's my business."

"I was *trying* to do you a favor," he reminded her witheringly.

"And I appreciate it, Wendell—I do," she assured him, vaguely ashamed of herself for not appreciating it more. On the verge of offering coffee, she thought better of it. "Don't worry about me, Wendell, I'll be just fine. I've already got something lined up."

The look of relief on his narrow patrician face was unmistakable. Oddly enough, Emily appreciated the sense of duty that had prompted his offer far more than the offer itself. It was ironic that the single-minded sense of duty they both possessed had been the very quality that had come between them.

But then, remembering what had happened in that very room only a few hours before, Emily knew that what she'd felt for Wendell had been little more than friendship. Theirs had been that pathetic cliché, a suitable match.

The ominous silence in the back of the house nibbled at her nerves. She stood up, arranging a bright smile on her face. "Wendell, I haven't even had time to dress yet—my brain's still asleep. Why don't I call you in a day or so and we'll work out something about the book reviews. I may be moving out of town after the first of the year."

"Moving! Where? More to the point, why?"

"Why do you think? This place isn't exactly a hotbed of industry."

"Em, you can't leave this place. McClouds are a part of the very backbone of the Eastern Shore." His look of indignation would have been touching if she hadn't been so distracted.

"Look, Wendell . . ." She broke off as Wendell's shocked eyes slid past her. *Oh, no—he wouldn't!* Burying her chin in the high collar of her robe, she closed her eyes and waited.

"Ready, honey?" Bey's voice, ingenuous, cheerful, sounded from the doorway. "What, not even dressed yet? Oops—sorry. Didn't mean to intrude."

If it weren't so embarrassing, it would be funny. Or did she mean that the other way around? Lord, at this point she didn't know what she meant. She was giddy! Lifting her head slightly, she saw Wendell's thin lips open, close, and then open again. He reminded her of something she'd seen at the aquarium.

Bey strode into the room, clad in the leather breeches and boots, with a peach-colored towel draped around his neck. His chin bore a streak of suds, and he was holding her lavender razor in the hand he was extending to Wendell.

"Oops—sorry again," he said cheerfully, shifting it to the other hand.

Somehow, Emily managed to get through the next few minutes without committing mayhem. Her anger soared to such monumental heights that it was utterly impossible to maintain. It became funny. And the more she tried to keep a straight face, the funnier it became. By the time she saw Wendell on his way, no wiser as to just what Bey Jones was doing in her bathroom, shaving with her razor, she was ready to collapse.

"You... Damn you, I told you to get out," she sputtered, falling back onto the sofa and covering her face with her hands. She felt the springs yield beside her, smelled the scent of her shampoo. "You used my shampoo," she accused, as if that were the prime offense.

"I had to use something—I've got a tough beard."

The very reasonableness of his explanation set her off again, and she could no longer contain herself. She

howled, toppling away from him to lean against the inhospitable arm of the sofa.

She felt the tentative touch of a hand on her thigh.
"Emily? Sweetheart, are you all right?"

"Oh, Lord, why didn't you just leave?" she gasped.

"I needed a shower—you needed time to cool off. I
had no intention of walking out of here before we'd
talked." His voice seemed to gain strength as he spoke.
"Look, I don't know who this Twiford guy is to come
barging in here the way he did, but he's not good
enough for you."

He was still shaken by the depth of the jealousy that
had cut through him at the sight of that smooth SOB.
He'd never experienced anything faintly like it before.
"I know his type," he jeered. "The veneer goes all the
way through—no blood, no guts."

Sobering, Emily wiped her eyes. "And you'd be the
expert on blood and guts, of course." She turned in
time to see the swift darkening of his eyes, but then it
was gone, so quickly she thought she must have imagined it.

There was a stillness about him that disturbed her.
His voice, when it came, was unusually quiet. "Yeah, I
suppose I am. But don't make the mistake of thinking
that's all I'm an expert on, Emily."

And then, with a mercurial shift of mood that easily
matched her own, he said, "Run put on something
warm—a pair of rubber boots if you've got 'em—and
let's go see my house. Who knows, I might even have
the hearth of my fireplace by now."

"I haven't even had coffee yet," she wailed, amazed
at how much his suggestion appealed to her.

"You get dressed while I make it, okay? If you're a
good girl, I'll even fix breakfast."

"I must have a death wish," she muttered, shaking her head. "Five minutes, and it had better be good."

"Where is it?" she asked some ten minutes later. Five minutes to shower, five to pull on her old flannels, the violet cashmere, and step into a pair of wool socks. She was starving!

"Found your thermos." He tapped the stainless-steel container. "The rest is in the bag." He indicated a brown paper bag on the table. "Now go finish getting dressed. Jump into your boots and get a coat on. You need a hat, too—your hair's wet."

"Can this be the same Emily McCloud I've known for thirty-seven years, calmly allowing some strange man to order her around in her own home?" She retrieved her vinyl Wellingtons from the utility room and tugged them on.

"Quit harping on your age," Bey growled playfully, "and do as I say, or some strange man might help you get *un*dressed."

I'm a classic fool, she told herself, fitting a lopsided orange crocheted hat over her thick, damp hair. I don't know a single thing about him except that he's five years my junior, a rough, tough biker who *claims* to have something to do with a respectable business—and heaven help me, I think I love the man.

Steam rose from the carpet of wet leaves as the sun's rays beat down on the sodden ground. Naked tree trunks glistened blackly, and here and there a stubborn oak clung proudly to its autumn coat of color.

"Your boots are going to be ruined, you know," Emily remarked smugly as her own waterproof ones began to collect a rim of dun-colored mud.

"Hate to disappoint you, honey, but they've got enough neat's-foot oil on 'em to walk on water."

She glanced pointedly at the muddy engineer's boots. "I always knew you had feet of clay."

He swatted her on the backside with the paper bag. "Does that mean you think I'm an idol?"

"Hardly. Speaking of idol—not the clay-footed variety—what do you do with yourself when you're not here? What sort of things do you publish?"

"My darlingest Emily, I make it a policy never to discuss work before breakfast."

The door was closed so softly that she could only accept the polite rebuff. Besides, under the magical spell of the freshly washed forest, she felt incredibly invigorated, completely alive. She swung along beside him, her long-legged stride challenging his to keep up with her.

He did so easily. Carrying the brown bag and the thermos of coffee, he moved with a strong gracefulness that alone set him apart from any man she'd ever met. The word "Indian" came to mind, but if there was a vestige of Indian blood in him, it was well disguised. His name was Welsh, he had the tenacity of the Scots, the silver tongue of the Irish, and Lord knows *what* else from *where* else.

"Where'd you come from, Bey? I mean your family?" She had a bit of the Scots tenacity herself.

"Say, here's that vine I was telling you about," he exclaimed, pointing with the thermos to a withering tangle of pale green. "Nothing but beans on it now."

She gave up. If he wanted to tell her, he would. If he didn't, nothing short of thumbscrews would pry it out of him. An irreverent grin crinkled her eyes. Come to think of it, in a case of thumbscrews versus Bey Jones, she'd bet on Bey.

He held aside a long bramble cane for her to pass, and then they paused to admire the delicate frosting of pale blue that preceded its seasonal demise. "I'm going to know the name of everything that grows in this land, every bird, every insect, every—"

"Rock?" she ventured, melting all over again at his undisguised enthusiasm. Among the more sophisticated men she'd known all her life, enthusiasm was considered gauche unless it was for sports, yachts, or certain prestige automobiles.

"I read a book on rocks once—igneous and sedimentary rocks, schists and gneisses and some I can't even pronounce."

"I know granite and quartz. That's about the extent of my geological knowledge," Emily admitted. "What I'd really like to delve into is archaeology. Geology would probably be a help there."

"Do you know about birds?" he asked eagerly as they neared the construction site.

"By sight, most of them. By song, not that many," she admitted.

"I've got a book. I've got a lot of books. The minute this place is closed in, I'm going to start moving in. You can help me set up my library, all right?"

At the sight of the insulated siding and the newly sheathed roof, they both forgot the books. Emily moved forward and then stopped to wait for Bey, who was standing as though frozen, his expression strangely vulnerable. It struck her that she'd seen a similar look on his face just before he'd made love to her.

Shaken, she moved on to the edge of the clearing and waited until he joined her. A feeling not unlike jeal-

ousy twisted inside her as she watched the reverent way
he approached the structure. She might as well not have
been there for all the attention he paid her, and it hurt.
It hurt like the very devil. It also puzzled her.

It was only a house, and not even a very large house,
at that. She hadn't the faintest conception of square
footage, but it couldn't be too much larger than her own
place. Through the large opening that would be a front
door, she could see the corner of a raised hearth. Bey
leapt agilely up through one of the openings and stood,
his back to her as he gazed downward.

After a long while, he turned. Emily, leaning against
a stack of fragrant wet lumber, hadn't moved at all.
"Shall we have our breakfast in my kitchen?" he asked.

A smile, that reminded her of sunshine after rain,
broke across his face and she felt her eyes filming over
in an absurd rush of emotion.

Dammit, if this was what being in love was going to
do to her, she wouldn't last out the month!

Eight

Swearing impatiently, Bey ripped the page from the typewriter, wadded it into a ball and tossed it to the floor with the others. The area surrounding his desk was beginning to resemble a snowball factory. He shoved back his chair and stood up, eyeing the array of half-empty coffee cups and cracker crumbs. He'd stayed awake by drinking gallons of black coffee. When he'd run out of food, he'd gone to the nearest vending machine and bought a dozen packs of cheese and crackers.

He *had* to get this thing into the hands of his agent, and this time, dammit, he was going to accept the multibook contract his publisher had been trying to make him sign since his second book.

Up until now he'd been content to take it one step at a time, venturing only what he could afford to lose. One book at a time—he could handle that. Until now, the money hadn't been all that important—it had never seemed quite real, anyhow, since it had gone directly from his agent to his accountant. He'd subsisted on the small amount of investment income that hadn't been plowed back into his portfolio.

The real satisfaction had come from knowing that he was a damned good writer who got better with each book. But satisfaction was no longer enough. The cards were stacked too heavily against him; he'd need every advantage he could get if he was going to win her.

On Wednesday he called his agent, Frank Satchell. Half an hour later he was on his way to the airport. A shuttle would put him into Kennedy before noon. After that it depended on how fast Frank could push things through for him. Whatever happened, he intended to be back on the Eastern Shore come the weekend.

It had been a while since he'd suffered a suit and tie, but if it would move things along at a faster pace, then it was worth it. He'd long since learned the advantage of protective coloration, and that went for Madison Avenue as well as the bay country. Where he was going, the brothers Brooks would open more doors than Levi Strauss.

As a protective measure against the cattle-car ambience of the shuttle, he turned his thoughts inward to that last frustrating few minutes with Emily.

They'd sat on the floor eating peanut-butter sandwiches and tollhouse cookies, washing it down with the coffee from the thermos. She'd chided him about his atrocious taste in foods, and he'd rambled on about the house. To his delight, she hadn't seemed bored. If he hadn't had the house to talk about, he'd have made an even bigger fool of himself. It had been all he could do to keep his hands off her, but he'd known damned well that if he touched her, it would start up all over again. He wanted her, God knows, but he wanted *all* of her— for keeps. And he had a hell of a lot of groundwork to lay before he could ask her to marry him.

They'd talked about heating systems. They'd talked about floor finishes and other prosaic things that hadn't interested him one damned bit at the moment. They'd talked about fireplaces and the best woods to burn. With that little frown of hers that made her look so endearingly studious, she'd told him he should start cutting and drying his firewood now for the following year.

"If you want to keep your chimney clean, Bey, you should really dry your wood for at least a year." Her eyes had looked everywhere except at him, and he'd wondered if she was remembering the night before, in front of her fireplace.

"I'll raid your woodpile and then you can share my hearth," he'd suggested, only half-teasing.

And then she'd told him he could have all her wood since she probably wouldn't be here, and he'd panicked.

"What do you mean, you won't be here? Of course you'll be here." He'd stood up, glowering down at her as he tried to hide his dismay, and when she'd refused even to look at him, he'd dropped to his knees, grabbing her and pulling her against him.

"Don't tell me that, Emily—you're not going anywhere, and you know it."

She was stiff as a poker in his arms, and he cursed his own ineptitude. He *knew* better. Dammit, she was the sort of heroine he'd written about over and over. He knew better than to try to force his will on her.

"Emily, Emily, listen to me," he'd whispered hoarsely, and then he'd kissed her. All the pent-up love in him had come welling up then, from a source that went deep into his past, a source that had never been tapped before.

The fine, fragile strength of her had lain still against him while he'd ravaged her mouth like some wild brute. She hadn't resisted, but she hadn't responded, either. After a while he'd made himself release her, and she'd brushed herself off as if she'd rubbed up against something unclean. It had almost killed him.

"Emily, I'm sorry," he'd groaned. "Dammit, you know I wouldn't hurt you for the world." He'd wanted so desperately to tell her how much he loved her, but the words that arose to his throat had lodged there to choke him.

"Do I?" she'd asked distantly, reaching for her coat. "You'll understand if I eat and run—I have a lot to get done if I'm going away next weekend."

"Emily!"

She'd refused to look at him as she went about gathering the rest of her belongings—her thermos, the crocheted hat she'd pulled off to allow the sun to dry her hair. As if they'd been discussing the autumn colors, she'd said, "I understand Durham's lovely. I'll probably miss the bay, though."

He'd been scared as hell and it had come across as anger. "What do you mean, you'll miss the bay? You can't leave here!"

She'd turned to face him then, spine straight, eyebrows arching slightly over her clear gray eyes. She'd given him a look that would have withered steel. "I beg your pardon?"

Helplessly he'd heard himself say, "You can't go now, Emily. What about us?"

"Us? As in you and me?" She'd never looked more desirable, and he'd never felt more miserable.

"What about your house? You can't just walk out and leave a house like that shut up over the winter."

She'd shrugged carelessly. "I'll sell it."

"Just like that, huh? Unload the whole damned works on some damned fool whim! Who the hell's going to oblige you by taking it off your hands, busted furnace, peeling paint, termites and all?"

"Did anyone ever tell you you have a foul vocabulary? You are, and I do *not* have termites."

"The hell with my vocabulary! Lady, if I'm your only hope, you're in bad shape."

That had been three days ago. She'd walked away, and he'd stood there and watched her, angry, hurting and scared as hell. He'd aged ten years since then. He'd written and rewritten the scenario, but the ending was always the same. On paper, it was so easy—but then, his heroes were all tall, handsome, successful dudes who managed to combine savvy with savoir faire.

Oh, he could write 'em, all right, but when it came right down to it, he couldn't speak the lines to save himself.

New York still smelled the same. Time to pull himself together and get his mind on business. He handed over a twenty and a five and was gone before the cab pulled away from the curb. Swearing softly under his breath, he tried once more to put the matter of Emily McCloud out of his mind—or at least to the back of it. Right now he had a contract to consider, but after that, he was going to go back there and make her listen to him while he laid his cards on the table—such as they were.

He'd never kidded himself about his looks; not even his mother could have loved him. He was quite literally a bastard. He had no fancy degrees, no illustrious ancestors—that he knew of—and he made his living producing something she professed to despise.

Emily, on the other hand, was everything he was not. She had more class in her little finger than any woman he'd ever met, but in spite of all her breeding, her old-family, old-money background, she *needed* him. She'd come alive before his very eyes. In fact, it was just now sinking in that she'd been more surprised than he had at the depth of her passion.

Emily handed back the essays that had been done for a project that would never get off the ground. At least not in this school. "I'd suggest you save these," she'd told her class. "They're excellent, on the whole, and someday you may want to polish them and submit them to..." To whom? They'd be split up, transferring to half a dozen other schools in all probability. "To the historical society, or the *Talbot Light*. Maybe someone will want to go on with our project."

Knowing their days together were now numbered, the girls had seemed to mature overnight. Emily knew she'd miss them. It no longer seemed important that they spent more time reading romances than they did early-twentieth-century poets. At least they read.

The Waterfowl Festival she'd agreed to cover would mean she couldn't go with Abbie to Durham. Instead, she'd arranged to get off two days the following week and drive down alone. Ironically, she needed the time to think. Until now she'd deliberately crammed every waking hour with activities just so she couldn't think, but it wouldn't go away. She'd put away her ladder and thought of him—she'd used her lavender-handled razor and thought of him again. He was *haunting* her!

Like a fool, she'd waited that day for some sign that what had happened between them had meant something to him—that *she* meant something to him. She'd promised herself she'd stay cool and let him make the next move. Instead, he'd sat there going on and on about his blasted house as if it were Buckingham Palace. When he'd shown no sign of discussing anything more personal than the view from his bathroom windows, she'd started asking a few pointed questions about his personal life.

She'd made a mess of everything, but dammit, how could she trust a man who wouldn't even answer the simplest questions about himself? It was as if he didn't trust her. And if he didn't trust her, then he couldn't love her. And if he didn't love her, then there was no future in seeing him again. She'd practically run away to keep him from the satisfaction of seeing her cry.

After school she dropped by the morgue and read the past coverage of the annual Waterfowl Festival. Tomorrow she'd take her lunch hour and go by the Mayor and Council Building to look over the permanent exhibit again. She'd seen the exhibit before, of course. No one living near Easton could avoid it, when practically every store window in the county was decorated around the same theme.

There was a florist's box on her porch. With a rush of emotions that veered radically from hope to anger and back again, she carried it inside and switched on the overhead light. Deliberately she placed the long gray box on the table while she removed her coat and hung it in the closet. Then she took time to light the fire. The box teased her silently while she changed into her slippers, but she refused to give in to the flurry of hope that had sprung up inside her.

With the fire crackling noisily as it blazed up, she settled onto the Morris chair, picking up the box and fingering the small envelope bearing her name. Could it be from Bey? He hardly seemed the type to send flowers, but then, he had brought her candy. And then proceeded to devour it. Between him and Abbie, she hadn't even had a taste.

On the other hand, he'd hardly be sending her flowers after the cool way they'd parted. She'd half-expected him to come by again, or at least to call. Dammit, she didn't even know where to reach him—on the off-chance that she ever needed to get in touch with him.

Impatiently she ripped the gold cord from the box and threw the lid aside. If it was another dutiful sympathy offering from Wendell, she'd burn it.

Roses. Neither pink, nor white, nor yellow, but a subtle blend of all three colors, they were dewy and exquisite. The perfume drifted up to her nostrils from the bed of green waxed paper as she opened the small envelope.

"They make no pretense, these beautiful flowers, of being beautiful for my sake, of bearing honey for me; in short, there does not seem to be any kind of relationship understood between us, and yet..."

It was signed B.J., with a little help from Richard Jefferies.

Breathing in the spicy essence of the roses, she read the words over and over, always coming back to the ambiguous ending, "...and yet..."

"B.J.," she murmured, frowning. She'd been stumbling over those initials ever since she'd reviewed that Bonnie Jericho book.

At least she seemed to have heard the last of one of her B.J.'s. There had been no more letters to the editor from the disgruntled romance reader—or writer, if that were the case.

Which left Bey. And since she didn't imagine that the flowers had come from either Miss Jericho or her anonymous defender, they must have come from Bey. As what? An apology? Somehow, it didn't seem quite his style, quoting obscure writers. But then, sending an expensive bouquet hardly seemed his style, either—or did it?

Burying her face in the cool, sweet spiciness, she admitted that, yes, she could easily imagine Bey sending flowers. In spite of his tough appearance, there was something incongruously tender about him, something that had reached out to her in a way that no other man had done in all her life.

She shoved the roses aside impatiently. Dammit, why did he have to drag it out with flowers? How could she start getting over him if he persisted in making these foolish romantic gestures?

Emily had followed the flying-goose signs painted on the sidewalks until her feet began to protest, and then she'd taken the free shuttle. She'd saved the Gold Room, where the most expensive things were shown, until last, knowing that the work there would blind her to some of the lesser works in other building. She was a sucker for a fine painting; last year she'd almost succumbed to a Bob Dance shorescape. Luckily someone else had beat her to it—she'd have had to sell her soul to buy it.

Foot-weary, but with a glow of pleasure lighting her face, she wandered back and forth, studying the various works on display. Her notebook was already scribbled full, the winners in the various categories duly noted.

"How long do you suppose it took to do that one? Every feather's perfect."

Emily turned to see a strikingly attractive woman examining a finely detailed study of a pair of pintails. "Longer than it took the ducks to grow them, I suspect. Did you see the Joe Seme over there?"

"The one by the door? I'm coveting like crazy, can't you tell? Della Brame, Baltimore Sentinel. You know, I'd expected to be pretty bored by all this stuff, but it's really impressive. Have you covered it before?"

"Only unofficially. You can't live around here and escape it." Emily introduced herself and explained, "I'm not really a reporter, I'm only subbing for the woman who usually covers the art news. All I do is a weekly column of book reviews."

The small green-eyed blonde glanced at the notebook, identical to her own, and shrugged. "We all start somewhere. I got my start covering a crab cook-off when the food editor came down with ptomaine. My last piece was a cover story in the Sunday supplement—estuarine pollution."

"You're that Brame, then." Emily tucked her notebook into her purse and turned to study the other reporter. "I read the estuary thing. You must have stepped on a few toes in that one."

"I sincerely hope so. I'm planning a doozy of a follow-up if things fall out the way I expect them to. Say, are you hungry? I'm starved, but I hate like sin to eat alone. Is there someplace where we could actually sit down?''

Charmed by the easy friendliness from a bona fide reporter, Emily smiled ruefully. ''You do understand that the population around here more than triples for this thing, don't you? We can try, though. What do you like, clam chowder? Crab sandwich? Oysters on the half shell?''

She turned toward the door and froze in her crepe-soled tracks. Before she could react to the sight of Bey's leather-coated figure blocking traffic just inside the door, Della darted forward.

''Beyard! What you are you doing here? Why didn't you let me know you were coming? We could have come together.''

Standing stock-still, Emily met Bey's gaze, both of them ignoring the effervescent woman who was rapidly closing in on him. At the last possible moment, Bey dragged his eyes away from Emily's and turned toward Della.

Of all the lousy breaks. Here he'd taken time only to change his clothes after getting in from New York, just so he could start patching things up again, and now *this* had to happen. It was a thousand-to-one shot, finding her elbow to elbow with Della. He'd had the devil's own time finding her at all. As a last resort he'd tried the paper, and Twiford had told him she was covering this thing. He'd spent the morning accosting every tall, slender brown-haired woman in sight.

''Don't I get a kissy-kissy?'' Della clasped her hands behind his neck, and Bey reddened painfully. ''I heard you bought some property in this neighborhood, Bey,'' she purred, ruffling the hair at the back of his head, "but I didn't expect to run into you here."

"No... I... that is, yes. Della, do you mind? This is a public place." Bey unfolded her arms from around his neck, his color deepening, to her obvious amusement.

"Oh, my, aren't we being proper, though—as if you cared one whit for public opinion."

Shooting a swift, agonized glance at where Emily stood rooted, Bey swore under his breath. He resisted the impulse to burst into a spate of explanations, and finally his momentary paralysis was broken by the ruthless elbow of a white-haired woman whose way he was blocking.

"Emily," he said tentatively, ignoring Della to push his way through the crowded room. Halfway there, he watched with a sinking feeling as her chin lifted and the shutters dropped over her eyes. Had he imagined it, or had she looked as stricken as he felt?

"Hello, Bey," Emily said huskily, meeting his eyes now unflinchingly. "Are you enjoying the exhibit? It's a good one this year. Have you seen the—"

"You two know each other?" Della had followed him across the room, and now she looked from one to the other of them, her eyes narrowing on a glint of speculation.

"We're neighbors—sort of," Emily murmured, wondering how to disengage herself from the embarrassing situation. She was finally beginning to understand why Bey was so reticent about his life when he wasn't with her.

"Della, it was good to see you," Bey growled dismissingly. "Now, if you'll excuse us?"

The petite reporter insinuated herself between the pair of them, tucking her arm through Bey's. "Not on your life, sweetie pie. I told you I heard you'd bought some land around here, but that's not *all* I heard. Remember that conference I covered in Washington last June? Well, just last week I ran into one of the agents I'd met there, and guess what she told me? There's a rumor going around about this certain romance writer—you know the one—top of the bestseller list five out of five times? It seems she's something of a mystery, shuns all publicity. Nobody's seen her, nobody knows if she's really a conglomerate of editors or a soap opera star, or what. One of the men in the sports department swears Bonnie Jericho's a pen name for Howard Cosell."

Della's green eyes glittered with secret amusement, and Bey felt the cold sweat breaking out on his back. "So?" he said with admirable coolness.

"Soooo, her frustrated fans are getting pretty steamed about all this secrecy—no autographs, no lurid, detailed biographies. So I intend to do something about it. This agent I was telling you about lunches with Jericho's agent's wife, and over drinks one day... well, I'll save the best part until later." She smiled up into his face with the look of a slightly tarnished angel. "Wanna buy me lunch, sweetie pie?"

The last vestige of color faded from Bey's face. His cheekbones could not have been more sharply defined if they'd been carved from granite as the noise of the enthusiastic crowd came and went in his ears like the roar of a distant plane. "Della... dammit, let's get out of here," he growled. Grabbing her slender arm, he wheeled her away, leaving Emily standing there like a pillar of salt.

So much for that tantalizing half-promise: "...and yet..." Hours later, Emily stared at the wilting roses through burning, reddened eyes. She should have put them in a cooler room, she supposed. Here in the living room, with the dry heat from the fireplace, they wouldn't last three days.

Which was only fitting, she told herself bitterly. Her brief love affair had hardly lasted as long.

On an impulse born of desperation, she dialed the number of the St. Thomas Aquinas Latin Day School in Durham. With any luck, she could change her appointment to an early-Monday-morning one and be back home the same day. If only she'd turned down the Waterfowl assignment and gone with Abbie in the first place, none of this would have happened. She could have gone on living in fool's paradise for a little while longer.

A few minutes later she hung up the phone with a smile of grim triumph. She had an appointment for nine-forty-five on Monday morning. And there was no reason whatsoever that she had to wait around here until the following day. An overnight bag to pack, a call to Wendell in case anyone needed to get in touch with her—the girls would know to call him if they couldn't reach her here, not that they ever called anymore.

Somewhere, she had a résumé—a dozen years out of date, but then, nothing of note had happened to her in all those years. Not until recently, that is, and that would hardly be of any interest to a prospective employer.

By three o'clock she was on her way, having stopped by Bob's place to fill up and have him check under the hood.

"Off for the weekend, Miz McCloud?" he'd asked, wiping a dipstick on a filthy cloth before ramming it home. "Gettin' a late start, ain't ye?"

"Better late than never," Emily acknowledged, shoving aside the bag of review books she'd thrown in at the last minute to unearth her purse.

Wendell would have jeered at her for that one. He'd always pounced on every cliché she uttered, and under pressure, she always managed to utter plenty of them.

Traffic was unusually bad, and she was glad to clear town and head south on Route 50. She'd go down the east side of the bay and come back along the west. Lord knows, she needed a vacation, and she had a day to spare. She switched on the radio to a top-twenty program, taking perverse pleasure in listening to music she abhorred. At least it was far less painful than her thoughts would have been.

Bey pounded on the front door one more time before leaping off the side of the porch and stalking around to the back again. Her car wasn't here. He was dead certain she wasn't either, but he rattled the back door, anyway. Dammit, she couldn't just go off this way. Sooner or later she had to come home, and when she did, he was going to be waiting for her. He'd got rid of Della by promising her an exclusive interview; the next thing he had to do was to explain to Emily.

He should have known it couldn't last forever. The spotlight on the romance industry was no longer as bright as it had been during the big boom, but the very fact that he'd kept a low profile—or rather no profile at all—had been enough to awaken the hunting instincts of a woman like Della. He should have hired himself a stand-in.

Dammit, why now? With every single thing he cared about on the line, he had to stop and placate that ambitious little ferret! A chance meeting, a slip of the tongue over drinks, and that steel-trap mind of hers had done the rest.

In reluctant admiration, he swore softly. He'd seen her go after a highly placed clergyman on nothing more than a standing order of roses—the man's wife was allergic to them, but his mistress, who happened to be the wife of a prominent politician, suffered no such affliction.

The initials hadn't been much to go on, but with that computer brain of hers, Della was too damned good at adding up just such insignificant details. He'd once made the mistake of siding with a panel of romance writers pitted against their detractors on a late-night TV show they'd been watching. His first mistake had been taking her home with him. He'd put away his portable, but he'd forgotten the bookcase. How many men owned a complete set of Jericho novels?

He pounded on the door again. Shading his eyes, he peered through the window into the shadowy kitchen, conscious of a small feeling of reprieve. It wasn't going to be easy. She'd either blister him with scorn, or she'd laugh, and at this point, he didn't know which he feared more.

Nine

It had to be deliberate. It had to be Wendell's idea of a joke. Three romances—never mind that one of them was historical, one a romantic suspense, and one a two-inch-thick contemporary with a quarter-million-dollar ad campaign already in progress.

"I'll kill him for this," she muttered, glaring down at the three paperback books. No wonder he'd put them in a bag before handing them over. She'd been in too big a hurry at the time to do more than grab and run, but now that she thought of it, there might have been a glint of amusement behind those dark-rimmed glasses. The minute her back was turned, he'd probably started snickering, anticipating her reaction.

Well, if the managing editor thought he was going to trick her into another circulation-building wrangle like the one with B.J., he was in for a long, dry wait, Emily thought rancorously, stabbing the TV switch beside the bed.

She scowled unseeingly at a parade of screeching cars until one of them flipped over and exploded. Then she switched it off again. Her gaze slid to the three books lying beside her on the bed. Regardless of the category, their glossy covers were remarkably similar: low-cut gowns that failed to disguise what they barely covered, anguished expressions that represented either the throes of passion or acute indigestion, boringly handsome men with windblown forelocks and glowering eyes. And the hands...

Bey's hands were as square and tanned, and certainly stronger than those of any paperback hero. Against the pale skin of her breasts, they'd looked... With a groan, Emily shut her eyes in a vain effort to block out the memory.

Another mental picture drifted into focus: Bey and herself in the classic book-cover pose—Bey, with that crooked grin on his battered face, his wide shoulders covered in black leather, and his denim-clad thighs braced in that aggressively masculine stance that was so characteristic of him. And of course, our heroine, stunning in threadbare lavender cashmere and baggy gray flannel slacks to match her gray-flannel eyes.

How wonderfully romantic. And instead of a castle in the background, there'd be an unfinished house surrounded by dun-colored mud. Instead of a caparisoned stallion prancing restlessly behind the enraptured pair, there'd be a muddy motorcycle, its saddlebags full of camping gear and junk food.

After a long day fraught with too many emotional blows, it was just too much. Emily's lips trembled dangerously, and then she was gasping with laughter. Tears

streamed down her cheeks, and after a while, when the
laughter turned into sobs, she rolled over and smothered her face in the pillow. In the impersonal shelter of
a motel in Chincoteague, Virginia, she cried until her
chest ached, her throat was raw, and her eyes were
swollen half-shut.

And then she got up and marched to the bathroom,
where she splashed handfuls of cold water on her face,
liberally soaking the front of her tailored white pajamas in the process. After blowing her nose, she stalked
back into the bedroom and reached for the romance
with the lusty blond hero on the cover.

Bey camped on the doorstep of the small frame house
until the first stars began to show. Waiting was cold
business with the temperature already plunging toward
a predicted low of twenty-two degrees Fahrenheit. Just
before full dark, he strode out to where he'd parked the
bike. After scanning the empty road that branched off
Route 33 to run out onto the peninsula, he unpacked his
sleeping bag and rummaged through the carrier for
something to eat. The single can of beer and a half a bag
of marshmallows he found wasn't much, but it was
better than nothing. Time for steak and brandy when he
had something to celebrate.

By the time the moon cleared the opposite shore, Bey
had accepted the fact that she was trying to avoid him—
and doing a damned fine job of it, too, he swore feel-
ingly. By the time it was directly overhead, he was
scared stiff. Pacing the small front porch, he told himself that anything could have happened to her. She
could have had an accident. With all the creeks and
ditches around here, she could be trapped in her car,

slowly freezing to death as the cold, brackish water crept up over her still body.

"Christ!" Closing his eyes against the work of his vivid imagination, he smashed a fist into his palm in a desperate repudiation of his worst fears. She could be lying unconscious in a hospital bed for all he knew.

"Oh, Christ," he uttered in a broken voice. Formal religion had never been a part of his life, but there'd been a few times, times when he'd been completely helpless... It was as though his consciousness went into a sort of automatic overdrive. If that was man's spiritual self coming to the surface—if that was what religion was—then so be it.

Expelling a deep, shuddering breath, he considered the situation calmly. She was probably just out with Twiford. He'd called several times after he'd raced back here and found her missing. He'd gone back to town, searching every parking lot, every side street, for a glimpse of her car, and then he'd started calling around. The school, the newspaper—both closed. No answer at Abigail Linga's address in Oxford. Same response at Twiford's home number.

There was something going on between Emily and Twiford. He didn't know quite what it was, but it was a damned sight more than any simple business relationship. He called her Em, which was a desecration of a beautiful name.

Slamming a fist into his palm again, Bey groaned. He could handle almost anything except the agony of not knowing. If she was all right... *God, let her be all right!* If she was all right, then he'd leave her alone. He'd speak his piece and then he'd go—which would mean selling the Landing. If he couldn't have her, then he sure as hell didn't want any reminders.

The thought of chucking the whole damned works, the property he'd coveted for so long, the house that was to be his first bona fide home, left him curiously unmoved. Nothing mattered except that Emily was safe.

God knows, if she never gave him so much as another word, she'd have already given him more than any other woman had. Every love story he wrote from now on would be dedicated to her. The miracle was that he'd managed to write one at all. How could he have imagined that love would be like this—a constant heat simmering through his body, an all-consuming fire in his brain, an aching void in his gut whenever he was apart from her?

If she turned him away, he'd have to sell out. He wouldn't be writing anything for a long, long time. Could a heap of ashes string a hundred thousand words together in any cohesive pattern? It had all been a fluke, anyhow. He'd probably hit the road again.

He was awake before daylight on Sunday morning. One look was all it took to tell him that her car was still absent from its usual place. The house was as cold and dark and empty as it had been when he'd finally crawled into his bag and slept in front of her doorway.

Gambling that she wouldn't turn up before noon, having been gone this long, Bey jogged through the woods to water's edge for a brief revitalization, and then he headed for St. Michaels and a decent meal. Seemed that worrying burned considerable calories. He was famished.

By the time he returned to his vigil after an enormous breakfast, he felt somewhat better able to sort things out. He'd been plain stupid to allow Della to stampede him that way. When she'd started dropping ten-pound hints, he'd panicked. His only thought was to get her out of there before she blew his cover to Emily. He should have handled it better, but he'd been taken off guard.

A lot of things had taken him off guard lately, he admitted wryly. It was downright scary to realize just how vulnerable a guy became when he found a woman who meant more to him than life itself.

By eleven o'clock on Sunday night, he was ready to go to the police. Leaving his sleeping bag on her porch, he rode into St. Michaels and located a public phone. There was a string of emergency numbers; he'd call 'em all, from the local cops to the state police, to the hospital, the county sheriff, and even the coast guard.

But first he'd try Twiford again. Just reading those emergency numbers made him break out in a cold sweat. He wasn't sure his fingers were up to the job of dialing them.

A few minutes later he hung up, torn between frustration and relief. Durham. It was so damned obvious he must have been blind not to have figured it out. She'd been planning the trip anyhow, and she'd wanted to get away from him. When Della had thrown herself at him, he'd still been staring at Emily. He'd seen the look on her face, as if he'd just struck her. She'd covered it almost immediately—credit her breeding for carrying it off in royal tradition, but she'd been hurt and puzzled.

And if she'd been hurt, Bey told himself with a cautious return of confidence, then it must mean that she cared at least a little. Under those circumstances, a woman didn't look at a man in that stricken way unless she was feeling *something*. And it wasn't disgust he'd seen staring back at him from those clear gray eyes.

Straddling the bike, Bey zipped up his jacket and flexed his frozen fingers. All he had to do now was be there when she got home. She was due at school Tuesday morning, which meant she'd try to get back as early tomorrow as possible. Five...six—seven at the latest. Between now and then, he'd work out a plan of attack.

Trouble was, she might not even realize she cared for him, in which case it was up to him to convince her. Words or action—he wasn't sure which would be the most effective. It would depend on his state of mind when she finally showed up. If he was in the same mental state he'd been in for most of the weekend, then words might have to wait.

Emily got as far as Edgewater before her battery went. She'd braked for a dog just south of the bridge, and the engine had stalled. With traffic piling up behind her, she'd ground frantically on the starter, to no avail. Click-click, and that was it. A truck driver had pushed her car off to one side and then given her a lift to the nearest service station.

Some two hours and fifty-three dollars later, she crossed the bay bridge, hungry, angry and curiously unable to focus her mind on any of the myriad problems besetting her. St. Tommy's, as the school was known locally, had made a favorable impression; the two members of the board who had interviewed her, equally favorable. An older school, although not quite as old as Eastwood, it had been closed for a year for expansion and a major overhaul. It would be almost like going into a brand-new school.

They'd liked her—Emily was reasonably certain of that. Abbie had told them something of the special projects she'd launched each year, involving her students in local history, folklore and traditions.

She caught a glimpse of sparkling water just off to the left. Last week's rains had produced some flooding in the low-lying fields adjoining the bay, and in the moonlight they were unbelievably beautiful. Durham was nice, but it wasn't on the Chesapeake.

For the hundredth time, her thoughts skittered over the question of whether or not to make the move—*if* they offered her the job. Before she could come to grips with that question, her flighty mind was off again, this time rehashing the romance she'd finished the night before.

Oddly enough, she'd enjoyed it. Priding herself on being objective, she was forced to admit that it was not nearly so well-written as the Jericho thing had been. All the same, she'd found herself quickly involved with the protagonists, empathizing with the heroine to an astonishing degree. The prose was a little too flowery for her tastes—a marked contrast to Jericho's work, which had a clean, direct style that was both terse and tender.

Recalling one of the more sensual passages, Emily's mind swerved back to Bey. She grimaced. Shoving the accelerator to the floor, she pulled out and passed a slow-moving chicken truck. Instead of fantasizing, she'd do well to apply herself to the problem of what to do between now and the opening term at St. Tommy's next August. Provided they wanted her.

Once through Easton, the countryside was dark. She hated driving at night, but at least the festival crowd had gone. She reminded herself that she still had a piece to write on that. She'd gone by the *Light* when she'd left the Gold Room, to hand over her notes in case Wendell was in a hurry. She hadn't made her plans at that point, but she'd known she had to get away. Wendell had handed her the bag of books and told her to get it in by Thursday for the Sunday edition. She hadn't argued. The extra money would come in handy, especially as she had no idea how she'd be able to support herself between teaching positions.

Turning into her driveway, she switched off the engine and slumped tiredly for a moment. The penetrating cold began to creep around her ankles as the effects of the asthmatic old heater quickly wore off. Somewhere she had to find the energy to go into the house before she fell asleep and caught pneumonia. Her bag could wait until tomorrow—no, it couldn't. She'd need her toothbrush. Oh, hell.

Opening the car door to the still, freezing air, she was reminded that her house would be cold and damp too. She hadn't taken time to lay a fire before she'd left, and she couldn't trust the furnace until she got around to getting it overhauled. The bathroom heater would have to serve, then. A hot soak, a glass of sherry, an electric blanket, in that order. School or no school, she'd postpone any really serious issues until tomorrow.

A shadow emerged from the deeper ones on her porch. Emily gasped and stepped back uncertainly. The shadow left the porch and moved toward her across the moonlit yard.

"It's about time you got home," Bey snarled, planting himself directly in her path. "Do you have any idea what I've been through since Saturday?"

"Bey? What's wrong?" Gone were all the indignation, all the jealousy and the anguish. Once more her mind was skittering around like a drunken butterfly, lighting on first one thing and then another: the substantial width of those leather-clad shoulders, the way they tapered so swiftly to a pair of narrow hips, the arrogant tilt of his head, the scent of woodsmoke that clung to him, enhancing the masculine aura she found so intoxicating.

Emily barely restrained herself from reaching out to him. By the time he touched her, she was shivering uncontrollably in the grip of a tension that had nothing at all to do with the frigid temperatures.

"Emily, Emily," he grated fiercely, pulling her into his arms to bury his face in her hair. "I ought to shake you until you rattle!"

Held prisoner in his powerful arms, she was helpless either to embrace him or to resist him. And for the life of her, she didn't know which she'd have done, given the chance.

"What are you doing here?" she managed finally, when she could get her face free of his throat. "Bey, is something wrong? Has something happened?" A kaleidoscope of possible disasters flickered through her mind and then it was gone, lost in the rush of more immediate considerations—like the feel of the rock-hard body that was all but supporting her, the scent of his flesh, the arms that held her as if they'd never let her go again.

"You're freezing," he muttered. "Hell, so am I. Let's get inside, and then you and I are going to do some talking. I can't go through another weekend like this again—God, woman, you're ruining my health, did you know that?"

A rough parody of a laugh emerged from his throat, and then Emily found herself being half-dragged to the front door. Bey waited impatiently until her fumbling fingers produced a key, and then he took it from her and rammed it home, his face almost obscured by the frosted vapor of his breath.

"My bag—my toothbrush," she protested weakly, and he pushed her inside.

"I'll get 'em."

The house was like a tomb. The scent of dead ashes and dead flowers assailed her nostrils as soon as she stepped inside. Moving stiffly, she began switching on lights. When Bey burst through the door again, dropping her bag to blow on his reddened knuckles, she was staring at the fireplace, trying to find the will to go out onto the back porch and bring in a load of wood. She wasn't even sure she had any kindling chopped.

"Let's get some heat in here," Bey growled, coming to stand behind her. "You turn up the thermostat and I'll get some firewood."

"The furnace needs a new dojigger. It just belches soot and then goes out."

"The fireplace'll do. Tell me where you keep your paper and kindling, and I'll get it going. Meanwhile, why don't you crawl under a blanket somewhere and wait for me. We'll revive the old custom of bundling." His grin went a long way toward thawing her out before she caught herself.

"Newspapers in that copper boiler, firewood on the back porch," she chattered, digging her hands into the pockets of her coat. "You might have to split some kindling. The hatchet's in the tool chest beside the back door."

"Okay, you just sit tight, honey, and leave everything to me."

There was nothing she'd rather do, but certain things took precedence, even over matters of the heart. And the bathroom would be like an icebox until the heater had had time to thaw it out.

At least the water heater worked. A few minutes later, Emily stuck her head out the bathroom door. "Bey? Look, I'm going to take a hot bath. It's either that or dive headfirst under the electric blanket and stay there until spring." The offhand cheerfulness was surprisingly well done; she almost convinced herself. "Stay as long as you like—get warm, make yourself some coffee—and thanks for building me a fire. Just be sure you put the fire screen in place before you go."

By the time the tub was filled with steaming water, the tiny bathroom was almost comfortable. Emily peeled off the top layer of clothing. Amazing how much cold could accumulate in a house that was closed up for a few days. It was a good thing her pipes were well insulated—she hadn't given a thought to that sort of thing before she'd left.

One foot in the tub, she heard Bey's footsteps approaching. She glanced apprehensively over her shoulder. He wouldn't.

He would. "Hey—are you all right in there?"

The porcelain knob rattled suddenly and Emily hurriedly lowered herself into the green herbal-scented bathwater and jerked the shower curtain around the claw-footed tub.

"Of course I'm all right! Look, Bey, I'm really too tired to talk tonight. If you think we need to talk, then come back tomorrow after school—unless you're going back to Baltimore," she called through the white paneled door. If he headed a corporation, he must have to show up at an office sometime.

"Not on your life, lady. I didn't freeze my buns off all weekend just to build your fire. Tell me what clothes you want and I'll get 'em for you. I found your bath-robe and slippers in the bedroom. Anything else? Nightgown? Toothbrush?''

Emily closed her eyes, shaking her head in an effort to clear it. Things were piling up on her. It was all she could do to cope with one matter at a time, and she wasn't anywhere near ready to deal with Bey. Driving for hours alone, she'd given a lot of thought to the best way to extricate herself with the least possible damage to her ego. Never mind her heart—it was a hardier or-gan than the romance novels would have one think. At least she devoutly hoped it was.

"Emily? I'm not a particularly patient man." The knob rattled once more, underlining his pronounce-ment.

Doubling up her long legs, Emily slid under the wa-ter, puckering her mouth and eyes as it closed over her head. *Go away, dammit! Just go away and stop crowd-ing me!*

Her eyes popped open again when she felt herself being lifted up by her hair. As the scented bath beads brought a wash of stinging tears to her eyes, she swore succinctly. "Dammit all to hell, will you just leave me—"

"No, I won't, and if you ever pull a damned fool stunt like that again, I'll turn you over my knee and whale some common sense into your aristocratic little backside!''

"My aristo...! Bey, hand me a towel, will you? My eyes..." she wailed, pawing the air in the vicinity of the towel rack. Her hand collided with a leather-clad shoulder and then she felt her head being held in a vise-like grip. A cool, damp cloth covered her burning eyes, and she groaned. Why was it that she always ended up behaving like a fool whenever he was around?

"There, my scrawny little mermaid, is that better?" The eyes were better—much better—but the amusement in that rasping drawl didn't do much for her composure. Besides which...

"Bey, will you get out of here?" Struggling against his superior strength, she flung aside the damp washcloth and jerked her head away from his hands. The clear plastic shower curtain wasn't much protection, but it was all she had. "Just get out," she ordered, glaring at him through red-rimmed eyes around a handful of plastic. He was kneeling there on her peach-colored bathmat, looking thoroughly intimidating in spite of the grin that crinkled his whole face. "Is this the way you get your kicks, preying on helpless females?"

"If you're helpless, then I'm a wooden Indian." Shrugging his massive shoulders, he slipped out of his coat.

"You're a *dead* one if you're not out of my house in one minute flat," she said malevolently, wrapping her arms around her chest. Her knees were drawn up until they brushed her chin, and her toes were curled defensively under the transparent green water.

Bey shoved up the sleeves of his shirt—an expensive-looking gray knit, she noticed distractedly. In fact, for once he was dressed in something other than jeans and boots. She found herself hotly resenting the fact that he was more attractive than ever. "Time's up," he murmured, amusement lacing his deep voice.

"Bey, please." She was drowning in those hazel eyes. By the time she felt herself going under for the third time, he'd reached into the tub for the washcloth she'd torn away from her eyes. "Why are you doing this to me?"

"What am I doing?" He soaped the cloth and placed a hand at the back of her dripping head.

"Badgering me. Hounding me." Her voice was muffled when the cloth covered the lower part of her face and then slipped down her throat.

"And don't you think you deserve it?" he asked in a tone of menacing reasonableness, caressing her throat with the fragrant suds as his supporting hand slipped down her back.

"I don't think anything," Emily moaned. "I don't know why you're here, I don't know why you're so angry—and you are, aren't you? That's why you're punishing me this way."

His head lowered, his voice drifting up to her ears in a cloud of scented steam. "Is this what you call punishment?" he asked just before his tongue flickered hotly over one tightly furled nipple. "And this?" He treated the other one to equal time, lifting its slight weight in a hard, soapy hand.

"You said you wanted to talk," Emily cried in a desperate attempt to regain control of the rapidly deteriorating situation. "Just let me get out of here and we'll talk!"

"I've changed my mind. I'm in no hurry to talk." One of his hands had dipped deeper into the water, in search of sunken treasure.

"Your sleeve's getting all wet. Bey—ah, please don't do that." She lowered her back against the high, sloping porcelain, helpless against the skill of his hands on her slippery skin.

"Tell me you don't like it and I'll stop," he rasped, raking his teeth over the sensitive tendon at the side of her neck.

"I..." The words lodged in her throat as his palm flattened on her body, spreading her thighs in a caress that rendered her completely boneless. Her head lolled like a heavy bud on a slender stalk. "Oh, please," she managed just before he lifted her from the water.

Ten

"**I**'m getting you all wet," Emily protested distractedly as Bey held her up in his arms and plucked a towel from the rack. She was shivering almost uncontrollably, but not from the cold. The tiny room was steamy warm.

"I won't melt." Bey blotted her awkwardly while his lips drank the droplets from her cheeks, her eyes, her temples. "On second thought..." He lingered at the corner of her mouth for a moment too long, and then it was too late. Lowering her feet to the floor, he held her so tightly that she could feel his ribs pressing into the softness of her body.

"Ah, so sweet...so sweet," he whispered, melding his mouth to her parted lips to drink a sweeter nectar. With the hard palms of his hands, he raked the curve of her back, his fingertips tracing the shallow valley of her spine to hold her tightly to him.

Emily felt the galvanic response gathering deep inside her. Eagerly accepting his thrusting tongue, she gloried in the swift quickening of his taut body. She couldn't get close enough, couldn't touch enough, taste enough. The texture of his clothing, of his flat buckle, impressed itself on her skin, exciting her still further.

One of her feet lifted to rub the calf of her leg in slow, sensuous strokes as he closed his teeth gently over the point of her chin. When he began to nibble on her ear, tonguing the small pink aperture, she uttered a frenzied little whimper.

Her foot came down on the sleeve of his hastily shed coat, and she kicked it aside unheedingly. Her new coat, as well as the rest of her clothes, were down there somewhere—the least of her concern, at this point. Tugging his shirttail from the belt that circled his lean, flat waist, she struggled to remove it.

Freeing one arm at a time, Bey cooperated, never ceasing his ministrations to her ear, her throat, her tingling breasts. When his rumpled shirt joined the rest of the heap on the floor, Emily's hands moved in eager exploration from his back to his sides, to the wedge of dark hair that arrowed down to disappear under his belt.

"Here . . . please," he grunted, directing one hand to a tiny pointed nipple. "Ahhhh, swe-e-eet lightning!" he gasped.

Emily knew a fleeting moment of surprise at the intensity of her own pleasure when Bey shuddered and closed his eyes, the planes of his face oddly flattened by the force of his desire. She should be shocked at herself, at this glorious feeling of abandon that swept her along in its wake, but she wasn't. She wanted to do everything, to fuel the ravening fire in her own body by giving him all the pleasure there was.

"Like this?" she whispered tremulously, trailing her fingernails lightly over one of the small flat crowns that nestled in the crisp chest hair and then lowering her head to caress its mate with the tip of her tongue.

Bey's body jerked abruptly as he drew in a ragged breath. Something clattered to the floor—her body lotion. The room was incredibly cramped.

"Sweetheart, we've got to slow down," he grated hoarsely, catching both her hands in his and putting her away from him.

"But I don't want to slow down." Long past any hope of prudence, Emily twisted her damp wrists from his grip and reached for his buckle. She moved closer, backing him onto the cul-de-sac between the tub and the lavatory.

Eyes dark with desire, Bey made a valiant effort to regain his control, when the last thing on earth he wanted now was control. He'd been a fool even to touch her, but God! He wanted her so much it was crippling him. She wanted him, too—for now. But until things were settled, he couldn't risk it. If he couldn't have her for always, then he'd better start pulling out while he still had the courage.

"What happened to my inhibited, suppressed Miss Emily?" he whispered in a weak attempt to defuse the sexual tension between them. Raising his hands' palms outward, he made a playful effort to fend her off.

Emily leaned forward. The placement was perfect. She could feel the rosy peaks of her breasts tighten into small pebbles as they snuggled into his hands. "I'm much too tired to be inhibited." She lowered her face to his shoulder, smiling at the groan of defeat that rumbled in his throat. "Inhibitions take energy," she murmured. "I've had an incredibly tiring day."

"*You've* had a tiring day," Bey jeered softly. His arms closed around her once more and he brushed his open mouth over her lips—slowly, warmly, his moist, sweet breath mingling with hers. "Remind me to tell you a story someday."

His arms closed around her as he sighed heavily, and Emily realized that somehow the driving force of their desire had been transmuted into something less acute but just as warm. And it was all right. She leaned against him, feeling the weight of the last thirty-six hours settle upon her. Obviously Bey was a little wiser than she was. She'd have hated to fall asleep and miss the main feature.

"I think I'll quietly fall apart now," she informed him. "If you want to stay, you're welcome." Odd, the subtle differences in holding. The arms that had driven her wild only moments before were amazingly comforting now.

"I have no intention of leaving, sweetheart, but I think we could both do with some food." Bey felt his control wavering again, and he reluctantly put her from him. He was probably the world's biggest fool for not taking what she'd offered, but he had to be straight with her. Besides, he could use a shower, himself. The amenities on her front porch weren't all that great.

Reaching behind her, Emily felt for the doorknob. The inhibitions he'd accused her of arose swiftly as the colder air from the hall invaded the steamy warmth of the bathroom, reminding her of her nudity. "Ah...look, Bey, this was...I mean, if you don't mind..." Hopelessly she shook her head. Were there any social rules to cover a situation like this?

Her eyes pleaded with him, and it was all Bey could do not to drag her back inside the bathroom and carry on what he'd begun. Goose bumps on every inch of her flesh, wet hair plastered to her shoulders, she was still the most beautiful sight he'd ever seen.

He came to her rescue. "Look, if it wouldn't be too much trouble, I could really use some coffee and a shower. I've lived in these clothes all weekend."

Grasping the excuse he'd generously handed her, Emily stepped back, shivering as the draft struck her damp backside. "Me too. Look, I'll make coffee and scramble some eggs while you—"

"Great. Don't stint, will you? Confession might be good for the soul, but it's damned hard on the body. I'll need all the strength I can summon up."

"Confession?"

"Later," he promised tersely, reaching for the door and closing it gently in her face.

"Confession," Emily repeated softly to herself, turning slowly toward her bedroom across the hall. *"Confession?"*

The spurious energy her hot bath had restored began to ebb somewhere between the bedroom and the kitchen. Dressed in her best white silk pajamas and her warm quilted bathrobe, she measured coffee and set the automatic maker to working. She probably should have put on slacks and a sweater. Maybe she'd dash in and change before Bey came out. But first she'd get out the bacon.

By the time Bey emerged, she'd cooked a dozen slices of bacon and scrambled six eggs with cheese. She was still wearing her robe and pajamas, and her mind was beginning to run in circles again. After two all but sleepless nights and three hectic days, she was in no condition to deal with *confessions*.

Bey was going to tell her ever so diplomatically that he wasn't looking for any long-term commitment. Either that or he was married. Either that or he was involved with that Baltimore reporter. Or maybe both.

All she knew for certain was that he'd left her standing there in the middle of the Waterfowl Festival while he went off with Della two days earlier, and he'd been waiting here with his confession when she got home tonight. And dammit, if he turned out to be another Bo Edmonds, courting her while he had a wife and two children stashed away at home, she'd never *ever* forgive him! Nor forget him, she admitted miserably.

"Smells ambrosial," Bey murmured, coming up behind her as she dropped two slices of bread in the toaster and rammed down the lever. "Can we eat it in front of the fire?"

"What confession?" She turned and leveled a grim look at him, doing her very best to ignore the way her heart lurched at the sight of that strong, battered face.

"Later." Ignoring her scowl, he reached around her and snitched a slice of bacon from the paper towel on the counter.

"Bey, I'm serious. If you've got something that needs confessing, you'd better do it now, because I'm too tired to play guessing games."

"Honey, I understand—"

"You don't understand *anything*," Emily insisted, deliberately allowing her anger to build into a defense against what was to come.

"'Women are made to be loved, not to be understood.' Wasn't that Oscar Wilde?"

Crossing her arms, Emily glared at him. Her emotions had been on a roller coaster long enough; the ride was over. "Stop *quoting* at me! You're so damned glib until I ask you a straight question, and then all I get is evasions!"

"Patience, darlingest Emily. 'A noble man is led far by woman's gentle words.'"

"Noble, my foot. You want a quote? I'll quote you a quote! I'm not an English teacher for nothing. 'Being a woman is a terribly difficult trade, since it consists largely of dealing with men.'"

"Touché. You're a worthy opponent, Miss Emily. I foresee some dandy matches between us. Do you like *Hamlet?*"

Her mouth fell open. Behind her, the toast popped up and began to cool. *"Hamlet?"*

Willing himself the courage to tell her, Bey took a deep breath. He'd quoted *Hamlet* in one of those letters signed B.J. It was as good an opening as any. His courage wavered. "On second thought, forget *Hamlet.* Maybe I'd better drag out *The Merchant of Venice,* for that thing about the quality of mercy."

Confusion shadowed Emily's pale features. "Bey, I think you'd better stop hiding behind other people's words and level with me."

They were standing so close he could see the fear growing in her eyes. Good God, what did she think he was going to confess, bank robbery? Tax evasion?

Growing more miserably self-conscious by the moment, he began to quote from the final scene of *Reap the Wild Wind.* "'And when she'd pierced his soul through the window of his eyes, there was no place to hide. Neither of them spoke. No words were needed to express the love that had been there from the beginning of time.'" He waited, feeling his heart expand in fear, his mouth go dry. "Those are my words, Emily. Don't you recognize them?"

Firelight flickered softly on the haphazardly stacked dishes. Bey reached for the half-slice of bacon she'd left on her plate, and Emily divided the last of the coffee. "Publishing. That was slightly misleading, you know. I was beginning to wonder why you never seemed to spend any time in the office. Do you know that I thought you were a land developer at first?"

They were lying under a creamy woolen blanket, feet to the fire, shoulders brushing. One of Emily's slippered feet was captured by both of Bey's bare ones and squeezed gently. "That's a hug," he confided. "I didn't really want to mislead you—well, maybe just at first. I was really ticked off when I read your review."

Emily slapped her Wedgwood cup carelessly into its saucer and groaned. "Oh, Lord, don't remind me. And those letters—I'm amazed you didn't tar and feather me under the circumstances. And all that time, you *knew*."

He shrugged, and when his arm encountered hers, he rearranged it so that it cradled her head. "In case you forgot, Emily McDarling, I said a few less-than-flattering things about you, too. Of course, I soon saw the error of my ways."

She turned to face him, her gaze caressing the marvelous irregularities of his profile as he stared up at the ceiling. "It wasn't *how* you wrote, you know—it was *what* you wrote. I thought you were fostering totally unrealistic hopes in susceptible young women, and it struck me as awfully unfair. I thought I was an expert on love, of course." Her soft laughter was colored with the faintest shade of bitterness. "I didn't know the first thing about it. My sophomores knew more than I did."

Silence stretched out between them. Nothing had been said about love—not in so many words. Bey had told her everything, from his early days as an escapee from various foster homes and orphanages, to his army career and the turning point that had come in the veterans' hospital when he'd read his first romance.

She, in turn, had told him about her parents and Libby and Vangie. He'd grunted when she'd got to Wendell, and she'd tactfully left out both Bo and Jonathan. They were, she sincerely hoped, in the same category as the women in his past, women like Della Brame.

After a while Bey said, "I have trouble saying it. That's ironic, isn't it? I can put the words into the mouths of my heroes and my heroines, but I can't speak the lines to save me." He turned to her then, his eyes glowing with an unmistakable message.

"So put it in a book," Emily whispered, reaching up to trace the laugh line in his lean cheek.

"How about a modern version of *Beauty and the Beast?*"

"How about a modern version of *Prince Charming and the Witch?*"

"How about we collaborate on the timeless story of Mr. and Mrs. Jones?"

Emily could hardly speak past the constriction in her throat. A tremulous smile was born on her lips, and it quickly spread into a broad, contagious grin. "I wish I had some champagne—something special."

"I'll order us a case tomorrow. What do you like, French? New York? California?"

She reached across him to replace her cup on the hearth. "Anything. Everything. Bey, why didn't you tell me sooner?"

Scooping more pillows from the sofa, he made a nest of them and resettled them, pulling her over so that she sprawled across his chest. "Do you have any idea of the sort of courage it takes for a man to tell a woman he writes romances? Especially when that woman has gone on record as despising the whole genre?" His square-tipped fingers smoothed the hair from her temple and he brushed a kiss along the curve of her cheekbone. "Especially," he added ruefully, "when the man isn't exactly noted for his romantic appearance."

"Have you any idea how much courage it takes for a woman to admit that she was wrong? I think I was afraid of discovering how much I was missing, Bey." The fire crackled noisily as he slipped her arms from her robe and pulled the blanket over her silk-clad shoulders. "You don't know how much courage it takes for a woman to be alone when she's no longer very young. Not to live alone—but to *be* alone."

He held her close, inhaling the clean fragrance of her hair, her skin. "I know, I know," he crooned, touching her face as if it were the delicate petal of a lotus. "I know about being alone. I know about emptiness, but no more, love." He kissed her eyes shut. "No more."

"It makes no sense at all, you know," she protested feebly when his fingers released the last button on her shirt. "I don't even know how to ride a motorcycle."

"All you have to know how to do is hold me. Would you care to start practicing now?" Sitting up, he stripped off his shirt and tossed it aside. Shining his crooked smile down on her, he muttered, "That's the trouble with this time of year—too many clothes. Do you suppose togas would be too impractical for Maryland winters?"

She helped him with his trousers, and then he made short work of removing her pajamas. "You're much too young for me, you know," she reminded him. "I'll be accused of all sorts of wicked things."

"I certainly hope so." He removed a leaf that had stuck to her hip. "Have you raked your living room lately?"

"You tracked that in. And anyway, I never claimed you could eat off my floors."

"It wasn't exactly eating I had in mind," Bey pointed out. He gave up on trying to keep them covered, and rolling her over onto her back, began the task of warming her with his body.

"Bey, do you think you could manage to support us both while I did some postgraduate work? There's so much I missed out on."

He traced the circulation of her inner arm with a series of inflammatory kisses. "Hmmmm, might join you, darling. I missed one or two things myself."

"Emily," he murmured sometime later, "you understand that I don't have any background—no family, I mean? If I had any ancestral portraits at all, they were probably the type exhibited at post offices."

Emily lifted her hands to his face, touching one of the faint scars on his chin. "It occurs to me that I'd much rather *be* an ancestor than have any number of them," she said thoughtfully.

Bey paid homage to one small ripe breast and then the other. Lifting his head, he gazed down at her slumberous eyes. "I think I might be able to help out with a quest like that, McDarling."

* * * * *

A Note from Blade Taylor

Maybe some people like growing up in hick Texas towns like Zachery Falls, where you're slotted from the cradle to the grave. Maybe they weren't fathered by town drunks who beat them every time they took a mind to. Maybe their mothers didn't run off when they were too small to remember them. Maybe they didn't grow up feeling like they were trash and less than nothing. Maybe they never felt so lonely or got so mad, they did crazy wild things they regretted.

Only two people ever stuck up for me when I was a poor, lost, angry kid—Caleb Zachery, who adopted me when I was orphaned, and Jenny, the preacher's daughter, who was always kind when the other kids at school were cruel.

I loved them both.

Not that I ever expected Jenny to love me back when everybody knew she'd always loved Caleb's real son, Dean. Not that I ever really thought I could have her even after she started looking at me in the same hot way the wild girls always did. Not that I could ever believe she could love me the way I loved her even after the shameful thing I let happen between us one warm spring afternoon shortly before her wedding day.

Something broke inside me, when she acted like I meant nothing to her and she married Dean anyway. I left town and joined the marines. I would have stayed away forever if Dean hadn't died and she hadn't gotten into trouble.

I came back partly to save her, but mostly to have her.

But first I had to live down my bad-boy reputation and prove to her and everyone else what I didn't believe myself—that I deserved her.

Blade Taylor

GOLDEN MAN

Ann Major

This book is dedicated to
a special man in my life,
my brother—David Major

One

_____

"**H**ow does dinner and a night of passion and wild, irresponsible sex sound?" Chuck whispered in Lilly's ear with a lusty chuckle just as Jenny Zachery walked into her secretary's office.

The room was instantly, nervously hushed as Jenny flicked cool green eyes over her two employees.

Looking sheepish, Chuck removed his hand from Lilly's shoulder and stood up. Lilly suppressed a giggle and began riffling through a stack of papers on her desk, trying to look dutiful even though she felt deeply embarrassed.

Lilly admired her boss, even though Jenny Zachery was so poised that she scarcely seemed human at times and so proper that Lilly could not imagine any man daring such an impropriety with her. It was a pity, really. Not only was Jenny beautiful, but beneath the polish Lilly suspected she was a warm and vibrant woman.

"Did you have a nice lunch, Mrs. Zachery?" Lilly managed.

Jenny nodded just as Lilly, in her agitation, knocked several file folders onto the carpet. "Oh, dear. I'm sorry about that, Mrs. Zachery. I didn't mean to be so clumsy."

"I'll get them," Chuck said hastily, stooping to retrieve the spilled contents of the folders.

"I trust you two have been working while I was out," Jenny said. Lilly flushed. "Any calls, Lilly?"

"Only Mr. Kilpatrick."

"I'll return his call from my office. And Lilly—"

"Yes, ma'am?"

"Hold my calls. I'm taking the rest of the day off."

Lilly was stunned. For the first time she forgot her embarrassment over Chuck's remark and saw how pale and unusually vulnerable Jenny looked. "You're not ill, Mrs. Zachery? If there's anything I can do?"

Jenny Zachery scarcely ever took any time away from the resort. When she did it could only mean that something was terribly wrong.

"Thank you, Lilly, but I'm all right. It's just that this is the day, two years ago, that Dean—" Jenny's green eyes grew luminous. She couldn't go on, but she didn't have to.

Lilly's voice was compassionate. "Of course, Mrs. Zachery."

Everyone in the little Texas ranching community of Zachery Falls not only remembered Dean Zachery, they revered his memory. And when they had entombed the man, they had placed his widow upon a pedestal. What none of them knew was that to Jenny the pedestal sometimes seemed so dangerously high and wobbly that she feared she would slip from it. She was afraid of the weaknesses in her character that lay hidden just beneath the surface.

But then, as a preacher's daughter growing up in a small town, Jenny had learned early that wicked impulses had to be locked away, that any indiscretion would be severely punished. She'd had to pretend not to mind that she was a plain, gawky child, when in reality she had longed to be beautiful. She'd been smart, with straight-A report cards, but deep in her heart she'd envied Susan Harper, who hadn't cared about A's, who was popular with the boys, who wasn't afraid to get into trouble. Girls like Susan led exciting lives. Jenny had longed to have fun instead of being so shy and stodgily serious.

Things hadn't changed when she grew older, though her awkward looks gave way to a mature, womanly beauty. She'd remained shy, but people now thought she was poised. There were even those who mistook her for a snob when they first met her. No one suspected that buried beneath her wall of quiet reserve were surging desires that she only half understood.

Jenny was good at locking things deep inside her. Only today it was more difficult than usual. Today, when the bluebonnets were so thick that the fields seemed like waving oceans, she was poignantly reminded of other days long ago. Her memories filled her with such aching nostalgia that she felt she would burst from the pain.

Jenny envied Lilly her young man, who could lightly joke as Dean had never joked with her. Jenny wanted to have fun, to be young again, to do all the things she'd never gotten to do. She didn't want to be a respectable widow with a two-year-old daughter to raise. She fervently wished she could escape the burden of the ranch and the resort. All of it was too much.

She should marry Mike Kilpatrick and let him bail her out of her troubles. That's what everyone expected her to do. Why then couldn't she say yes to Mike, as she'd once said yes to Dean when she'd been troubled and wanted to escape her problems? She wanted so desperately to be able to lean on a man again. But hadn't she told herself she needed to stand alone? There was something wrong with marrying a man because you couldn't handle your own life.

Jenny swept from the room to her own office before her thin veneer of calm cracked. Once inside she closed the door and sank back against it. With one hand she rubbed her aching neck. Every muscle in her body felt tense.

As always, she was dressed stunningly. She was overdressed for the casual ranching community, but then she was running, or rather trying to run a first-class resort that catered to wealthy Texans from Houston, Austin, and San Antonio. Dean had taught her that it was necessary to dress the part, and her luncheon today with a Houston businessman whose firm was seeking a conference center in which to conduct summer seminars had been important. She wore a linen safari shirt, cotton skirt, and a designer "leopard" fur and rhinestone belt. Dean would have approved. Just as he would have approved of her simple gold jewelry and the sophistication of her upswept hairdo. Like her father, he had never liked her rich brown hair to cascade wildly about her shoulders. But there were other things he wouldn't have liked, had he known of them.

"Oh, Dean. Why did you leave me, when I needed you so? What am I going to do?" she murmured aloud as she thought of the overwhelming financial problems of the resort. How had things begun to go so badly? She felt so inadequately prepared to solve all the problems confronting her.

She'd married Dean right out of high school and had been too busy working while he was in college in San Marcos to go to college herself. Besides, at the time she'd wanted to concentrate on her marriage. Dean's sudden death had thrust her into the business world at a very bad time. The Texas economy as a whole had been depressed because of the oil business, and she hadn't realized that she'd need to do so much promotion for the resort. Overwhelmed by her grief, she'd let last summer slip by, and hadn't realized until it was nearly over that her bookings were down twenty-five percent from the summer before. And the summer months were the peak season. Why hadn't she taken more of an interest in the operation of the resort when Dean was alive? Too late she'd realized her mistake in letting him handle everything.

Just thinking of all this was causing her headache to grow worse. Maybe she should return Mike's call. He always made her feel better. Wearily she crossed the room and lifted the telephone receiver on her glossy pecan desk. Dean's desk. Today everything reminded her of Dean, of her loss, of how alone she was.

The secretary forwarded her call.

"Hello, Mike."

"Jenny." His voice was warm and vital. "Is the church social still on?"

"You know it is. I'm looking forward to it. I need to get out and see people. So does Cathy."

"How's she been this week?"

"Terrible."

"She's two."

"Some comfort." Jenny sighed. "She put a grandaddy longlegs in her mouth this morning. I screamed at her and made her cry."

"I don't blame you."

"Mothers are supposed to nurture. I'm afraid I get too impatient."

"Nonsense. You're a perfect mother." His voice lowered. "In fact, I think you're absolutely perfect in every way. You looked gorgeous Saturday night."

Perfect. It was a compliment, but it grated. That's what everyone thought, that she was perfect. Virtuous, hard-working, self-sacrificing were the labels the town pinned on her. "She's such a serious little thing, the Widow Zachery. So quick to help a needy neighbor, and don't forget her church work. Such an admirable young woman. And so old-fashioned. Wish there were more like her." Jenny knew what was said behind her back. How little they knew about the real, the wicked Jenny.

Only one man knew—and he had not been her husband.

Thank heavens he'd left Zachery for good when she'd married Dean, returning only for Caleb's funeral, and then later for Dean's. How could she have borne the insolent knowledge in his eyes? Worse, how could she have borne the secret desire in her own heart?

For an instant, before she stifled the vision, the image of Blade Taylor rose in her mind's eye. The mere thought of his virile maleness evoked a treacherously wicked quiver in the pit of her stomach. She remembered the feel of lean brown arms circling her bare flesh and pulling her against his muscled torso. As if it were only yesterday she could hear the sound of the creek, smell the cedar and wild flowers, feel the texture of the soft grasses against her naked skin as he pulled her beneath him. She felt the intimacy of sensual lips claiming hers. She could taste tobacco and liquor on his breath as he explored her mouth with his tongue. Too, she remembered the scent of him, the smell of leather and horses that clung to him from the long ride they had taken to the remotest part of the ranch. She recalled the vividness of his blue eyes, their boldness because he knew what no one else knew: that Jenny Wakefield was not as demure and perfect and virginal as everyone believed.

Everyone said that Blade was bad. Maybe he was, but he had made her feel wild with a kind of reckless exhilaration that both addicted and petrified her. That wickedness within her had ensnared her, and given him his power over her.

She remembered the way Blade's tousled gold hair had fallen across his brow as he lay on top of her, his bronzed, tough body intimately possessing hers, easing himself ever so gently inside her, stealing her virginity. He had stared deeply into her eyes with an intense male possessiveness before he lowered his head to take her lips, kissing her again, more tenderly than before, perhaps more tenderly than he had ever kissed any woman. But there was anger in him as well. In those days there had always been anger in Blade.

"Remember *this*, preacher's daughter, when you lie with my brother in your marriage bed," he'd taunted softly. She'd tried to resist him then, but he'd moved his body so that wave after wave of spiraling thrills coursed through her. He'd taught her so thoroughly the rapture of what it was to be a woman and know a man that the memory of that hazy golden afternoon still burned within her.

Later, when she'd shyly sought him in all the places on the Zachery Ranch where he could usually be found, he was conspicuously absent, and she'd realized with a pang of terrible remorse that he was deliberately avoiding her.

Did he think her cheap and easy because of the way she'd wanted him? The way she'd reveled in his lovemaking? The way she'd moaned in that last moment of total surrender?

Had she, sweet Jenny Wakefield, the preacher's daughter, really bitten him on the neck and given him that terrible bruise? She'd been mortified, but he'd only laughed and said gently, "It's only a hickey, Jenny. I'll just button my collar way up high the way you do 'til it goes away if it makes you feel so bad."

Then he'd kissed her, and she'd forgotten her shame in the glory and tenderness of his kiss.

Dean had off-handedly supplied information concerning his brother's whereabouts. "Don't know where in the hell that good-for-nothing brother of mine has gone this time, and just when we need him to work the cattle. Probably holed up with a bottle of whiskey and some woman he's got a yen for in some cheap hotel. He's as sorry as his real old man was. But you know Pa. No matter what Blade does, he can't see the bad in him. He's forever throwing Blade up to me, the way he breaks his back working on the ranch, the way he understands animals, the way he stands up to people who try to push him around. It's not like Blade, though, to disappear like this when Pa needs him. He's usually smart when it comes to Pa. Wonder what it was that drove him away."

Jenny had wondered if Blade were running from her. Did he despise her for what she had done? Was that why he'd said he wanted nothing to do with her as long as she was determined to marry his brother?

Blade had made no promises to her, no declarations of love, but he'd asked her not to marry Dean.

Two days later she'd married Dean Zachery, telling herself that it was just a craziness inside her that had driven her into Blade's arms, that it was Dean she really loved; Dean, who'd been her childhood playmate, her high school sweetheart; Dean, who was gentle and kind; Dean, who was the sort of man who made a good husband. The Jenny Wakefields of the world didn't marry fast, loose men like Blade Taylor, men who drank and chased women and lived as if there were no tomorrow. She'd known that she had to suppress the unholy wildness within her at all costs, and the only way she knew how was to marry Dean.

The whole town remembered Jamie Taylor, Blade's father, whose love of drink had blurred his rugged good looks even before middle age. His blue eyes had grown vacant, his virile physique fleshy. He'd turned shiftless, losing his animals one by one to neglect, finally losing the small ranch he'd inherited. His wife had grown tired of his beatings, and she'd run away with a man she'd met in the local bar, leaving Jamie and her small son behind. One night two years later, after a week-long drinking spree, Jamie had come home, and while he lay smoking in bed he'd set the house on fire. Blade had been ten the night his father died. Everyone in town remembered the pitiful, fatherless little boy, and how lost he'd seemed after the death of his only relative. But only one person had cared enough to do something about him.

Caleb Zachery had adopted the boy and tried to raise him decently. After that Blade's clothes were clean, his hair washed and combed. For the first time, everyone noticed his sultry good looks, and whispered that such sex appeal in one so young was dangerous. And for a while some of the bitterness left the boy. Blade worked hard on the ranch for Caleb, as Dean, who preferred to read books and dream grand dreams, would not. For a time there were those who even believed that the boy might amount to something someday. But as he grew older, his father's wildness had become evident in him. By the time he was seventeen he was not amused by such innocent pursuits as school dances and football games. It was said that he drank too much, and that the females he preferred were women, not girls.

"Bad blood will out," the townspeople all agreed. "Blade Taylor will end up just like his father."

Jenny had married Dean more out of terror than because she loved him; she was terrified of her own feelings, of what she'd done. Of what she might do again if Blade Taylor cast those smoldering blue eyes upon her and made her remember the ecstasy of his embrace. Ever since she was a small child, Jenny had tried to be perfect, and with Dean, the task of being the good person she believed she should be seemed almost easy.

She'd spent every day of her marriage trying to make up to Dean for the one transgression of her life, but no matter what she did, it never seemed enough. She'd slept with his adopted brother, the only person that gentle Dean had ever disliked. If he had ever found out, it would have destroyed him.

She and Dean had lived together for eight years, and Dean had never known the wanton Jenny that Blade had touched. Their sex had lacked the dangerous excitement she'd experienced with Blade, if only that once, and when Dean made love to her, Jenny had traitorously longed for Blade. She knew it was wrong, but she'd wanted to feel again that mad, blind passion that turned her emotions inside out and left her spent and aching and limp as jelly. If after their lovemaking she was more thoughtful and attentive to her husband than usual out of guilt, Dean had cockily attributed her behavior to his prowess as a lover.

Oh, the wickedness of her deceit!

"Perfect in every way," Mike had said, describing her. Mike didn't know her any better than Dean had. Thank heaven he didn't. Thank heaven no one did.

"You haven't heard a word I've said," Mike chided gently, interrupting the chaos of her thoughts and returning Jenny abruptly to the present. "All that financial expertise wasted."

She gripped the receiver in sudden awareness.

"Sorry. My mind was a million miles away."

"What I was saying is that we're going to have to hold off on that land sale."

"Why, Mike? You know I need the capital for the resort."

Normally she would have caught the strange edge to his voice. Today she was too upset. "Perhaps it's a mistake to throw good money after bad, Jenny. That ranch land is going up in value every year. It's something I feel you should hang on to. The resort's been losing money steadily."

"Mike, I have to have the money."

"I've managed to get a loan with very generous terms for you. For now, at least, you don't have to sell anything."

"Oh, Mike that's wonderful!"

"Yes, isn't it?" Again there was something in his voice that should have warned her.

"The resort was so important to Dean. I just have to keep it going for him."

"Dean's been dead two years, Jenny. Maybe it's time you stopped living in the past."

"I'm trying, but sometimes . . . you know, today—" She couldn't continue.

"Yes, I know."

"It's funny how a date on the calendar brings back the past."

"Funny, and then not so funny."

"Mike, I don't think I'm handling myself too well today."

"You're doing fine. I know it's not easy. Dean was a part of your life. Losing him was like losing a part of yourself. It's going to take time. You two had the perfect storybook love. I used to be so jealous of Dean because he had you. Only the ending wasn't happily ever after."

"Yes," she said softly, "the perfect storybook love." If only he knew.

The man who knew stood on the side of Ranch Road 12, his Marine Corps duffel bag lying on the dusty gravel beside his varnished boots. At the sight of a lone car in the distance he lifted his thumb and signaled. Not that Blade Taylor expected the car to stop. Hitchhiking took a while these days. The whole country was paranoid from an oversaturation of media violence. People saw the possibility of murder, rape, and assault in the eyes of every stranger, even in the clean-cut looks of a former Marine Corps officer who stood lean and tall in his crisp shirt and stiffly creased Levi's.

There was no bus service to Zachery Falls, and when he'd reached San Marcos there had been no one in Zachery that Blade felt easy about calling. He wasn't exactly the town's favorite hero. Caleb was dead. There was only Jenny, and she despised him. Not that he blamed her, after what he'd done, and that only a day or two before her marriage to his brother. Some brother. He and Dean had never liked each other, not even before Caleb had been generous enough to adopt Blade. Still, Jenny hadn't deserved the way Blade had treated her, as if she were common and easy and his for the taking—but what experience had he had with girls such as Jenny back then? His women had always been wild and willing, women who had such a yen for loving that they'd let any man love them. How could he have understood a woman like Jenny? She'd been a virgin, and before her, for all his experience, he'd never had a virgin.

The red sports car whizzed jauntily past Blade, and he lowered his thumb. He hadn't expected it to stop. Suddenly there was the squeal of brakes, and the car began to back up. Blade leaned down and picked up the duffel bag, slung it over his wide shoulder, and strode toward the car, his steps long and easy. He moved like a man who'd grown sure of himself over the years.

Shoulder-length blond hair ruffled over the edge of the bucket seat, and Blade's sensual mouth curved cynically. A woman. It had been a long time since he'd had a white woman who was free and willing. In the Middle East the only women a Marine could have were bought and sold.

"Blade?" The velvet voice was uncertain.

"Well, I'll be damned! Susan Harper!" Blade caught himself. "Excuse the language, Susan. I've just gotten my discharge papers from the marines. It may take me a while to remember how to act with a lady.''

"You never had any trouble knowing how to act with a woman in the past, Blade Taylor,'' she teased, her tone silkily suggestive. ''Don't tell me you were wounded somewhere...important.'' Her hot eyes roamed over his virile physique.

"Good Lord, no!''

She laughed deliciously and leaned forward to light a cigarette.

She was so beautiful. He couldn't even remember when he'd last been with a woman, but as Blade stared down at the girl in the bucket seat, her platinum head tipped at a coquettish angle, he was not thinking of her. Instead he saw Jenny as he'd seen her the last time at Dean's funeral, in her loose black dress with her long brown hair swept away from her face. Her gentle expression had been filled with pain. Blade had wanted to take her in his arms that day, to kiss her, to soothe away her anguish, to make her forget Dean. Sometimes it seemed that all his life he'd wanted only one thing—for Jenny Zachery to forget Dean. He wanted that badly, but Blade Taylor was a man who'd grown up knowing what it was to do without the things he wanted.

Instead of comforting Jenny that day, Blade had done the only thing he knew to help. He'd walked out of her life before the temptation to stay made it impossible for him to leave her again. In the two years since then, her face had haunted him, tempted him—and he'd never been one to resist temptation for long. So here he was, back in Zachery Falls, wishing that Jenny would just once look at him the way Susan Harper was looking at him now, with her eyes warm and soft and yet suggestive. What would it take to make Jenny look at him like

that? Idly he wondered if Susan knew what glances like
that did to men. Of course she did. The Susan Harpers
of the world always knew what they did to men.

He opened the door and swung his duffel bag into the
space behind the seats. Then he levered his long, lean
body into the car.

"Big man, little car," she murmured, her eyes ap-
praising the length of him.

"It beats walking. Thanks, Susan, for the lift."

"My pleasure." Again there was a suggestive element in her words.

"I'll have to find a way to repay you."

"That'll be easy, Blade. Real, real easy."

She tilted her pack of cigarettes toward him and he
took one, leaning his golden head toward hers, lighting
his cigarette from the tip of hers, his warm brown fingers steadying her wrist as he did so.

"Hmmmm. You smell good, Blade. Clean and all
male."

He merely smiled at her in that easy way of his and
leaned his head back against the seat, inhaling deeply.
It felt surprisingly good to be with someone he knew.

The wind was springtime cool and scented with cedar and all the things he remembered growing up with.
He hadn't known he'd missed all this so much. The sun
was brilliant, but not hot. It was a glorious day to be
coming home, and for the first time in a long while he
felt some of his anxiety slipping away from him.

The wind rumpled his golden hair and blew it back
from his tanned face. His military haircut was growing
out, and his hair now reached his crisp blue collar. He
cast his vivid blue eyes upon Susan and inhaled again.
The cigarette tasted good. Too damned good. He supposed it was from doing without. He was reminded of

other pleasures he'd been doing without. Again he thought of Jenny and the prim-and-proper virtue that had driven him so crazy all those years ago. He smiled. It wasn't only her prim-and-proper virtue that could drive him crazy, but the memory of that time when she'd melted against his body and become a woman.

"I'm trying to quit, you know," he said, his deep voice lazy. "You always were a girl to tempt a man from the path of the straight and narrow." He laughed softly, intimately.

"Was I? I'm glad you didn't forget me, Blade. I certainly never forgot you."

"Really?" A faintly cynical edge had crept into his speech. "Whatever happened to old Bill? You and he were pretty hot, last I heard."

"I divorced 'old' Bill a year ago."

"Kids?"

"Two. He's got them, except for every other weekend."

"Why?" Blade was no longer staring at Susan but at the road whipping past.

"I travel."

"A traveling saleswoman?" Again he laughed. "That's a switch."

"It's not as bad as it sounds."

"I was hoping it was."

This time she laughed.

"What about you, Blade? Married?"

"No."

"That sounds final. But they always said you weren't the marrying kind."

"Yes, that's what they always said—among other things."

"Were they right?"

"Maybe."

It felt damned good to be coming home. It was lucky, Susan recognizing him on the road.

"Anybody ever tell you that you drive too fast, Susan?"

"Lots of people tell me I'm fast, Blade. You used to like that in a woman."

"Oh, I still do." Again he was thinking of Jenny, wondering how she'd look when he saw her again. What would she say? How would she feel? He wished he could tease her the way he teased Susan.

"How come you're coming back to Zachery Falls, Blade? You've got no family here to hold you, and you're not exactly a favorite in town."

Blade shrugged. "I came back because there's something here I want."

Susan tossed her head and stared at him, and her hair flew against his shoulder. "You must want it very badly to brave the town's hatred, when there's a whole world out there just waiting."

"As a matter of fact, I do."

"Gonna tell me about it?"

"No."

"Blade—"

"Susan, let's just leave things as they always were between us—light and easy. Maybe you should look up old Bill. It's bad when a couple splits up and there are kids involved. I should know."

At his rejection, Susan looked hurt. "Okay, Blade."

He heard the funny catch in her voice, and he said, "But that doesn't mean we can't be friends. We always were, you know. Why don't you let me take you to lunch at the Bluebonnet Café? I owe you for the ride.

You can fill me in on what's been going on in Zachery Falls while I've been away."

"Could we talk somewhere more private first?"

"Why don't you pull over onto that back road that winds down to the creek? Do you remember the place where the oaks and cypresses grow real close to the water and the grass grows long?"

"Of course I do."

Susan swerved and the car skidded on two tires as she made the turn. When she stopped in the deep shade beneath the spreading branches of a live oak, they each lit another cigarette. The cool woodsy smell of the creek and the scent of wild flowers made Blade remember Jenny, and the one time he'd made love to her. Susan began talking, and at first he only half listened. He was thinking of brown hair coiled over his hand, brown hair tangled with the sweetness of wild flowers.

"Blade, you seem different now."

"In what way?"

"There's an easiness about you. I don't know... I can't quite put my finger on it. You're more self-confident, I guess, instead of angry. You used to be mad all the time, Blade."

"I did, didn't I? But back then I thought I had a whole lot to be mad about."

"What's everybody going to think of you now, the way you've changed? Imagine, Blade Taylor growing up and losing his wildness and amounting to something after all. You know what some folks will say? That maybe Caleb left you something in his will. Now wouldn't that just give everybody in Zachery Falls something to think about?"

Blade stiffened, his expression darkening at the mention of Caleb. But when he spoke his voice was still easy. "I suppose it would, but why don't you tell me what happened with you and old Bill, Susan?"

Susan began to talk, and she didn't even notice how smoothly he had changed the subject from himself to her. They talked for a long time, and Blade listened with compassion. Susan didn't know that he was wishing that he and Jenny Zachery could talk like this, easily and in friendship. But there had never been anything easy about Jenny Zachery.

He pushed thoughts of Jenny from his mind. For now it was enough to be home, to be with someone who had once been his friend.

He prodded Susan with questions and forced himself to concentrate on her answers even though he had something far more important that he needed to do.

For the moment he allowed himself to forget the reason he had come back to Texas, the reason that would come as a shock to everyone in Zachery Falls, especially Jenny.

There would be time enough to claim what had long been rightfully his.

Two

"Did you hear the news? Blade Taylor's back in town." It was a whisper that spread like the wind, stirring the flimsy cypress leaves, rippling across the river's smooth surface, blowing coolly into half-opened windows, reaching everywhere, everyone.

Gossip spread like lightning in a town the size of Zachery Falls. As soon as Susan's red Porsche swerved around the last curve before the long bridge over the Blanco River, where Clay Hammock was fly-fishing that Wednesday afternoon, people began to talk.

There was no one except Blade with hair that precise shade of deep gold, the rich color of leaves in the Texas hill country's late autumn. No one with hair that was so untidy. What was it about him that made one always imagine that it was a woman's fingers that had rumpled it, as she lay beneath him in passion? Leave it to Blade to find a woman before he even hit the city-limit sign. But then, if the woman was Susan Harper, it figured. Blade and she had always been two of a kind.

When Jenny heard the news she was in the hardware store, where she'd gone to speak to Don Wilkerson about buying some chain link to fence an area behind her house so that Cathy could play outside without someone having to watch her every second.

Two women were behind a shelf that held spice racks and other kitchen knickknacks. Their voices were tantalizingly low as they spoke. Jenny, for all her surface virtue, was only human. She stepped closer to the shelf.

"Blade Taylor's back. Seen him in the Bluebonnet Café with Susan Harper. Looks like the two of them already got something going again."

"Wonder why he came back? He can't be up to anything good. Never was, you know. And he never liked Zachery Falls much, if I remember."

"Never could understand what Caleb Zachery saw in him."

"Some things are hard to figure."

"Handsome devil. So big and tall. It's plain enough to see why women swarm around him even if he *is* no good."

"Won't get them anywhere. A man like him can't help but break a woman's heart."

"Just like his father, if you ask me. And you know what happened to him."

Jenny forgot what she'd been meaning to ask Don about the chain link when he came back from the warehouse. She was shaking with a mixture of turbulent emotions. Blade was back, and he was with Susan Harper in the Bluebonnet Café. She trembled and caught her breath. Odd, how it hurt, to think of Blade with Susan. Then, as Jenny continued listening, her first chaotic feelings changed to angry indignation.

Those two old biddies, Katey Scudder and Margaret Harris, had no right to talk about Blade like that. A big part of the trouble with Blade was that no one in Zachery Falls had ever given him a chance to be anything but bad. Jenny was about to storm around the high shelf and confront the two women, but she managed to stop herself in the nick of time.

What would they think if she rushed down upon them as angrily as a maddened hornet—the virtuous Jenny Zachery attacking two of the town's most respected matrons, defending her bad brother-in-law? Would it be all too evident that she wasn't so different from the Susan Harpers of the world? And why was she defending Blade, if only to herself?

"Because he *needs* someone to defend him," she shouted silently, even as another inner voice mocked her. *You're still as bad as ever, Jenny Zachery. Nothing ever changes. Not in people's hearts and souls. Not in towns like Zachery Falls.*

So she contained her outrage, lest they suspect the reasons that lay behind it, but it felt horrible to be such a hypocrite.

Two days passed, and the buzzing about Blade slowed down, even though no new and more interesting topic of gossip had presented itself. Jenny threw herself into her work harder than ever before. The contractor had finished remodeling ten of the lodge rooms in time for the summer rush. She needed to see about having the pool repainted, and she had to purchase new outdoor furniture. That last would require a trip to San Antonio. There were a few more details that the contractor had to take care of before she could write him a final check. The baseboards weren't painted, he'd failed to install electrical outlets in the bathrooms, and some of the carpeting was improperly laid. Then there was the new chef she needed to hire.

The Zachery Falls pay scale was not the best in the world, but it was difficult to convince the men who came from larger cities to interview for the job that in a small town things didn't cost as much, either. All the men could see was the smaller salary.

Between taking care of Cathy and running the resort, Jenny baked four dozen cookies for the church social. She found time to help decorate the church parlor as well. But even though she kept herself virtuously busy, her mind was a mad tumble, and Blade Taylor was at the center of that tumble.

Why didn't he at least come out and say hello? Hadn't he grown up on the Zachery ranch? Wasn't he sentimental at all? Had he completely forgotten Caleb? But, of course, what she really wondered was, had he forgotten her?

It was all too obvious that he had. She had been no more than a romp in the hay—and his life had been a continual romp. It was doubtful that he even remembered her. There were probably too many beautiful, experienced women in his past.

Oh, to be a man! For an instant she allowed herself to envy Blade for the wild life he had led. To be free. Not to have to be so everlastingly good! It wasn't fair, the way society chained women, but let men run loose to tempt them from their chains. If women let themselves fall to temptation, they were wicked, wicked creatures. Despite all the talk about women's liberation, in Zachery Falls nothing had really changed.

So it was a thoroughly confused Jenny Zachery who looped her arm through Mike Kilpatrick's expensively suited one and let him escort her to the church social. Cathy toddled ahead of them down the long sidewalk to his sleek blue Cadillac that Friday evening.

Mike was so nice, so safe. He was just the sort of man she should marry, just the sort who would be good to her, and to Cathy, as well. Why, then, did she yearn to see Blade again?

It was midnight when they returned to the ranch. Cathy was asleep in Jenny's arms. Mike's hand rested comfortably on Jenny's shoulder as he parked in front of her limestone ranch house. When he bent his head and took her mouth in gentle possession, Cathy squirmed and began to cry.

Jenny pulled away and cradled the child more closely against herself to make her hush. "I'm sorry, Mike." But she wasn't, not really.

"That's okay," he said, his voice filled with the infinite patience that Jenny admired in him. "She's exhausted from being the belle of the ball."

"Wasn't she a little doll?" Jenny murmured proudly, remembering the way Cathy had run to everyone and laughed and gurgled so charmingly. "Sometimes she can be so sweet." Cathy began to kick and scream in earnest. "Like I said, sometimes."

Mike laughed as he got out of the car and went around to open the passenger door.

As Jenny stepped out onto the drive holding the writhing child, she noted for the first time that there was a light on in the apartment above the garage, the apartment Blade had lived in so long ago. The light hadn't been on when they'd left.

That apartment was where she stored retired files. Chuck must have taken a box up there and forgotten to turn the light off, she decided, thinking that she would have to see to it later. That would be just like Chuck.

"Come on in, Mike," Jenny said at the front door, "and I'll make you some coffee after I put Cathy to bed."

"I'll come in, but you can skip the coffee. I got enough at the social. I'll probably be up the rest of the night from all the caffeine."

"You should have had the punch."

"I've never really been much of a punch drinker."

Jenny disappeared into Cathy's room to help the little girl slip into her nightgown and get ready for bed. Cathy was holding her blanket and sucking her thumb with fierce determination. Some of the ladies at the social had been quite severe in their advice when they'd found out that Cathy enjoyed her thumb so much.

"She's only two," Jenny had defended.

"My Lottie had quit well before she was two," Lois had stated smugly. "You should paint her thumb. That will make her stop."

In Zachery Falls people were interested in the most minute details of other people's lives. It really was amazing the way they were so quick to pass judgment. Jenny often found herself thinking defiantly. "I wish I were like Blade and didn't care about other people's opinions. How nice that would be." But she had always cared. And she probably always would.

Mike was waiting as patiently as always when she returned. She walked over to him. "The little monster is asleep."

"At last." He chuckled. "At long last, I have you to myself." He pulled her down onto the sofa, capturing her mouth with his.

She returned his kiss dutifully, wishing that he would stir her in a way that he never had before. But even though his kiss was long and hard, even though he was handsome and not an inexperienced lover, his embrace evoked none of the savage hunger she longed to feel.

"I want you to marry me, and soon," he said, pulling away, breathing hard. "I don't know how much more of this I can stand. I know you too well to expect you to sleep with me before marriage. You're not the kind of woman who goes to bed with a man without making a permanent commitment."

Oh, wasn't she? Rebelliously she wished she weren't locked into such a virtuous mold, but then she knew she didn't wish that at all. Not really. It was kind of nice, people thinking better of you than you really were. It made life easier sometimes. Then she remembered the strange restlessness that came upon her at times, and she knew that it could make life harder, too. You couldn't run away from the secrets locked away in your own soul.

"Hold me, Mike," she said. "Just hold me. I feel so afraid. I don't know myself these days. I don't know what I really want. I don't know what to do."

"Simple. Marry me. I'll take over the resort and the operation of the ranch. You know I already love Cathy, and I've always loved you, Jenny."

But that wasn't what she'd meant. Not at all.

She stared at him in silent anguish, and he offered her the only comfort that he could. He held her in the darkness until, much later, she fell asleep in his arms. Very gently he released her and laid her head back upon the couch. Covering her with an afghan, he bent and kissed her brow, leaving her and walking out the front door, locking it behind him.

She woke when she heard the bolt click, realizing that he had gone and she was alone. She got up and went to her bedroom. Her window shades were raised, and the light from the garage apartment glared brightly, making her wish she'd remembered to ask Mike to see about it before he left. Well, she'd take care of it herself, before she went to bed.

Blade heard Jenny's light footsteps coming up the stairs, and he pulled the sheet and blankets over his bronzed, naked body, which was still damp from his shower.

Oh, Lord. Kilpatrick must have left. Not that Blade was sorry about that. He'd hated the dark house and the car in front hour after hour. He'd hated the thought of Jenny alone with Mike. Still, Blade had hoped that he wouldn't have to face Jenny until the morning. He was exhausted from the long hours he'd spent cleaning up the apartment and making it habitable again. Jenny was certainly a pack rat, the way she'd stuffed this place so full of boxes that he could hardly move around. It had taken him most of the night to carry all that junk down to the garage.

The thought of seeing her again, the thought of explaining what he was going to do made him feel uneasy.

Jenny stepped into the room, realized she wasn't alone, and screamed.

"I should be the one to scream," Blade said lightly, with one of his easy, white smiles. "I always thought that ladies like you knocked before they entered a man's bedroom. You know, I'm not wearing a stitch, and my clothes are hanging on that chair. If I get up to put something on and get decent—"

"D-don't get up!" she cried, shamefully aware of that long, forbidden male body outlined beneath sheet and blanket. Her awareness made her tremble and caused her skin to go hot, and she hoped frantically that he didn't see how he affected her.

"Blade, I...I saw the light, and I only came up to turn it off. I never thought I'd find you here."

He smiled teasingly. "That's obvious. But I'm glad to see you, Jenny. Come on in. You know I never was a man not to be glad about a midnight visit from a beautiful woman, especially my own dear sister-in-law."

She went scarlet, and he wished he hadn't said that. What devil drove him to taunt her when he knew how it always embarrassed her? He had never known how to act around her—probably because she was the only woman who'd ever been special to him.

Lord, she looked pretty, even prettier than he remembered. Her lipstick was smudged, probably from Kilpatrick's kisses, but she was still in the same clothes she'd put on for the church social. It was incredible that Kilpatrick could have been in that dark house for hours without making love to her. Blade was grateful for that, but he was baffled. No doubt Jenny liked that sort of gentlemanly treatment, but how did a man like Kilpatrick keep his sanity?

She was wearing a white lace dress with long puffed sleeves, the cotton fabric so thin that he could see her arms beneath it. The dress was high necked, of course, and every tiny button was fastened clear up to her throat. A tiny golden cross twinkled at her collar.

It was not the kind of dress, nor the sort of jewelry that the more voluptuous Susan would have worn, but he liked them on Jenny. He liked the way the dress outlined her small breasts and her narrow waist; he liked the way the soft folds of material flowed over her hips and down past her knees. He didn't want her to wear dresses that revealed her body to other men. Ever since he'd made love to her that once, he'd known that he wanted her forever. And he didn't want anyone else to have her, even if only in their minds. Not anyone. Not Dean. Not Kilpatrick. As he thought of Kilpatrick, it occurred to Blade that he'd returned just in time.

It had almost killed him when Jenny had gone ahead and married Dean all those years ago. How he had hated Dean for that. He couldn't help himself. Dean had always had everything Blade had wanted so badly for himself. Dean had been Caleb's rightful son, the rightful heir to the ranch that Blade had loved and worked. The blood of Jamie Taylor did not taint the pure, self-righteous Dean Zachery.

From childhood Dean had held the town's respect and love, while they'd looked upon Blade with scorn and considered him trash. He wasn't trash, but if it hadn't been for Caleb's believing in him and adopting him, he might have turned out that way. Not that anyone in Zachery Falls would have cared.

If it hadn't been for Caleb, Blade wouldn't have stuck through college for five years. And he certainly never would have made it through officer candidacy school. In the ten years Blade had spent away from Zachery Falls, he'd learned that he wasn't trash. The people he'd met in faraway places, people who didn't know about Jamie Taylor and his drunkenness, had respected Blade for the man he was and had judged him on the merits of what he did.

Blade remembered the night Dean had married Jenny. He had wanted to die that night. He'd gone to Caleb and told him what he'd never admitted to anyone, not even to himself—that he loved Jenny, that he'd always loved her, since they were kids. He couldn't stay at the ranch, knowing that she belonged to Dean. Caleb had understood, and sent him off to college.

Maybe that wasn't the only reason Caleb had made it so easy for Blade to go away and stay away. Maybe Caleb had seen the way Jenny would look at Blade when Dean wasn't around and she didn't think anyone saw her. That was why Blade had taken her the way he had, because he'd felt the fire in those soft green eyes too often to stay his desire. Maybe she hadn't known what she was doing when she'd looked at him like that, but when he'd made love to her on that long ago afternoon in a bed of sweet-smelling wild flowers, she'd been more responsive than he could ever have dreamed.

Yes, Caleb had understood about a lot of things that other people never understood, especially not his thick-headed son, Dean. Dean had married Jenny, but he had never really known her.

Sometimes Blade thought that if it hadn't been for Caleb Zachery and his love and understanding, the deep, wild anger that had driven him ever since his childhood would have destroyed him. Blade himself believed that there was something bad within him, something he'd been born with, the same bad element that had destroyed his father and made his mother desert him and run off. But there was something else within him as well, an inner determination to rise above the bad. Caleb Zachery had seen the potential in the bitter ten-year-old orphan who had hated the world and everyone that inhabited it. The only other person during those early years who had ever been kind to Blade was Jenny.

Dean and Jenny and Blade were all exactly the same age, and they were in the same grade in school when they were growing up. When Blade was only six years old, the other children had laughed when he had come to school with a black eye because Jamie had thrown a chair at him. His clothes had been torn, and he'd been without a lunch box. But Jenny hadn't laughed. She'd packed an extra sandwich for him and brought it the next day. Blade had been too proud and embarrassed to take it when she'd so shyly offered it to him. He refused her roughly with all the clumsy anger a six-year-old boy can show a little girl, and she'd run off crying. He'd felt so awful about that later, making her cry. He hadn't known what to do. He'd thought and thought about it, mulling over the wonder of her making it for him, the marvel of her thinking about him. It was a kindness he never forgot—but then, he didn't have many kindnesses to remember.

In the fifth grade, right after Jamie had died and before Caleb had officially adopted him, Blade had been in the school cafeteria when he'd overheard Kelly Robinson holding court with the other girls, sniggering about him behind the soda machine.

"That Blade Taylor's so mean and nasty. The way he looks at you, with all that hate. The way he always gets in trouble. He's just trash. Pure, plain old trash, that's what my mama says. I wish he'd drop dead." That had been the pious Kelly speaking, and her opinion was usually law among all the girls in her clique.

Blade had hated the whole world when he heard that. He'd wanted to do something awful just to scare Kelly and make her sorry for what she'd said. But to his amazement, Jenny's timid voice had rushed to defend him.

"I don't think Blade's bad. He's just lonely, not having a family like the rest of us, not knowing what's going to happen to him. It must be awful for him. How would you feel if your mother ran away and your father burned up and you were left all alone?"

"How would you know so much about Blade Taylor, Jenny Wakefield?" the others sneered, their voices nasty and suggestive.

"That's what I think, no matter what you say." There had been tears in the shy voice. "If you would only give him a chance, he might be nicer."

Maybe that was the day that Blade had started loving her, but it had been a secret emotion locked deep within himself. Only once had he nearly given his feelings away.

They'd been in the tenth grade then. Grades were always important to Jenny, and biology was her worst subject. Blade sat right behind her in that class. She must have been desperate because she'd carried a cheat sheet into the final, and since she wasn't really a cheater, she hadn't known how to manage it as suavely as the more blasé, habitual cheaters of Blade's acquaintance. She'd been nervous and scared and in her confusion she'd dropped the incriminating paper onto the floor. It had landed so conspicuously that Mr. Jeffries had marched down the aisle and retrieved it.

"Jenny." The teacher's voice was cold and unforgiving, and Blade had hated the way Jenny looked so pale and cowed. "Young lady, do you know what cheating on a final exam means?"

It meant an F in the course.

Jenny was too terrified to speak. The whole class was staring at her. She'd never been in trouble before.

Blade hadn't even thought. He'd just reacted. He jumped out of his chair with a defiant swagger. "It wasn't her, Mr. Jeffries. It was me," he'd said in that sullen, disrespectful voice that all the teachers hated. "I stole her notes."

"Blade." Jenny had begun a weak attempt to save him.

"Shut up, Jenny. You always were such a sissy. I should have let him pin it on you."

"All right, Taylor. That's just the sort of thing I'd expect out of you."

He'd been expelled for three days; he'd also received an F in biology and a stern lecture from Caleb, but he hadn't minded because Jenny had come all the way out to the ranch herself to thank him.

He'd been repairing a barbed wire fence when she'd found him. She'd gotten off her horse slowly, shyly, and he'd noticed how slim and cute she was in her jeans, how clean and fresh she smelled, how pretty she was with her hair blowing loose about her face.

Impulsively, she'd reached out and touched him, and when she stepped closer, he couldn't stop his arms from going around her.

Her voice was choked and strange. "I want to thank you, Blade, for what you did. I feel so awful about you getting expelled." Suddenly she began to cry and the more she cried the more upset she became.

His arms tightened about her, and he cradled her against his chest. She felt so good, and it made him feel strong and manly to comfort her. It seemed to him that he had wanted this moment for as long as he could remember.

"I'll never, never try to cheat again. To think that I got you into such trouble," she managed between sobs.

"It doesn't matter. I've been in trouble before. What's one more time?"

His hands had stroked the silken brown hair. His shirt was partially unbuttoned, and he felt her hot tears on his bare chest. The warmth of her had filled him with an aching need. He realized that he had only to lower his head to take her lips, only to slide his hands up her slim waist and untuck her blouse so that he could caress her breasts, only to unzip her jeans to explore soft, feminine flesh. He envisioned her naked loveliness.

"Oh, Blade," she said softly. "Everyone's always said you're bad, but you're not. I always knew they were wrong."

Those words had brought him up short and stopped him from trying to take her then and there.

Her beautiful eyes were shining as she lifted her face to kiss him gratefully on the cheek.

But it wasn't his cheek that she'd kissed. He twisted his head, and it was his mouth that met hers. Funny, how she hadn't pulled away when he'd kissed her long and deeply, until the blood was pounding in his veins and her own pulse was beating just as jerkily. It was he who had been stunned by his loss of control, he who was afraid of what he might do if he didn't release her. He'd pushed her roughly away.

"I'm sorry," he'd muttered. "I never meant for that to happen."

She was tracing the edge of her swollen mouth with her fingertips. Her expression was oddly intense, and she was so beautiful it hurt somehow.

"That was my first kiss," she said in awe. And as she swung herself back onto her horse, she'd stunned him. "And you don't have to be sorry about that kiss, Blade Taylor, 'cause I'm not."

It was after that that she started looking at him with those hot green eyes when no one else was around to see. He'd known that she was ashamed of the way she felt about him because she'd look down whenever he looked at her, and he'd left her alone because he respected her. Besides, she had always been Dean's girl, all through high school. And for all her sweetness in defending him when they were children, Blade had known that she was much too nice a girl to ever be interested in him the way he was interested in her. So he'd chased after wild girls, girls who were attracted to a guy with a bad reputation, and his reputation had only grown worse, widening the distance between Jenny and himself even farther.

If Blade was lost in the past, so was Jenny. She was staring at him hard, her eyes soft and luminous, her mind as filled with memories of him as his was of her—only she was embarrassed by her memories, just as she was embarrassed at being here like this with him. It seemed wanton, his lying there naked, with the soft sweetness of the spring darkness outside. They had only to turn out the light, to touch each other. He made her feel primitive, as if all that really mattered was that he was a man and she was a woman.

"What are you doing here, Blade?" she asked, her voice strange and tight.

"I figured you'd heard I was back, knowing the way people in Zachery Falls always talk."

"I heard, but that doesn't answer my question."

He plumped his pillow, and his action made the sheet fall to his waist, exposing his muscled, golden brown chest and flat belly. She couldn't drag her eyes from his body. A damp sheen clung to his golden hair. The smell of his masculine cologne drifted over her.

He was beautiful, sinfully beautiful, and doubtless he knew it. Why in the name of heaven didn't he pull up that sheet? But she couldn't very well ask him to, because it would let him know what looking at him was doing to her. She wanted to touch him. It had been a long time since she'd been with a man, and forever since she'd known the fulfillment of what had been for Blade only a careless embrace on a long-ago spring afternoon.

"Well, this is where I used to live," he said in that soft male voice that could make her shiver and feel so odd. "And it's where I'm going to live now. I've come home, Jenny. To stay."

"You...you can't be serious. What would people think? We can't live together." Then, realizing what she'd said and how it must have sounded to a man like him, her eyes widened in horror.

His hot blue eyes met hers. "Now there's an idea I never would have mentioned, not right off the bat, anyway—you and me living out here together. But I like it, Jenny Zachery. I like it much more than you could ever imagine. And as for what people think...well, you know that's one thing I never really gave much of a damn about."

His male gaze slid down her body as warmly as hands moving over her, reminding her of the way she'd felt in his arms that spring afternoon when he'd taken her virginity. He had no right to make her feel this way. She wanted to hate him for the power he held over her, for that easy power he had over all women.

"Any woman would do for you, Blade." Her voice was low. "I've heard all about Susan. The whole town knows."

"Knows what?"

"That you and she—"

"Yes?" He cocked his head and stared at her, a devilish light dancing in his eyes. She was blushing furiously. She never had been one who could get close to the subject of sex and handle it smoothly, and he'd always been one to taunt her.

"It's... it's certainly none of my business," she said huffily.

"I only wish that the rest of the town was as nobly indifferent to my business as you are."

"Susan said that you and she parked on the river road," Jenny blurted out.

The pain in her voice caught at his heart, and he stared at her hard, wanting to understand the reason for it. He was not so conceited that he didn't remember the way she'd felt about him, but it never occurred to him that she might be jealous. Blade had always thought when he was young that he wasn't good enough for her, and deep in his heart, for all his accomplishments since then, that's what he still thought.

He'd lived roughly, too roughly for a gentle woman like Jenny to ever understand or forgive, and then there were the horrors of Lebanon he still had to get over, the memories of death, of children... He pushed his mind away from the war and back to the woman standing near.

Ten years ago she'd been attracted to his aura of wildness, but then she'd seen her mistake and run headlong into marriage with Dean. Everyone had said that it was a perfect marriage. Blade had hated hearing that, but he'd believed it and felt ashamed for what he'd done to her right before her marriage, knowing that it must have made her hate him as all the other decent girls had. She'd been saving herself for Dean—and Blade had always wondered about their wedding night. He still felt ashamed now, but guilt had a way of making him do things he regretted later. Sometimes he lashed out, instead of being tender.

His voice was cool and indifferent. "When was it wrong for two old friends to talk?"

"Is that all you did?" Again there was that odd pain in her voice that he was at a loss to understand.

"Would that be so difficult to believe?"

"People in Zachery Falls are saying that a man like you wouldn't be content with talk from a woman like Susan Harper."

"Is that what you believe?"

"Blade, you're deliberately confusing me. I don't know what to believe."

"Well, it's no concern of yours or anybody else's what Susan is to me. I told you the truth just a minute ago, but if you prefer the town's version, go right ahead and believe it."

"I—I don't prefer the town's version."

"Maybe you feel safer thinking I want Susan." He stared at her hard. "That's it, isn't it? You're afraid of me, aren't you, Jenny? Afraid of me wanting you?"

That thought made him hurt inside, and he tore his gaze from her stricken face. He felt even worse when she didn't deny it.

"Well, you're wrong there too, girl," he said roughly. "You don't have to worry about me getting any ideas about us just because of what happened that one time." Her sudden flush went through him like a knife, and his voice hardened with the guilt it made him feel. "That was a mistake and I know it, just as you know it. I know everybody around here thinks I'm some sort of sex maniac, but I'm not. I've never taken a woman who wasn't willing, and I'm not about to start now. I didn't move out here to embarrass you, either. This is my home. Just like it's yours. I hope we can be friends." He stopped speaking.

Jenny's mind screamed silently. *Oh, my God, he's really going to live out here.* Was there no way to stop him? Friends? How could she be friends with him? Didn't he know what just looking at him did to her?

She flung herself toward the door and pushed the screen open.

"Jenny." She raced blindly down the steps and he jumped from the bed, having forgotten that he was naked. "Jenny!"

But she was gone, and he thought better of going after her in the state he was in. He felt awful. He knew she didn't want him to stay, but he couldn't think of any way to make it easier for her because he hadn't the slightest intention of changing his mind. It was best to let her think about it and come to terms with it herself. And things weren't going to get any better tomorrow when she learned the reason why he'd come back. He was dreading that—telling her.

He lay down on the bed and thought of her, of how pretty she'd looked in that white dress. He fell asleep smiling, thinking of her.

In his dreams it was Jenny who'd picked him up when he was hitchhiking the other day on that ranch road, Jenny in her prim, white, schoolteacher dress.

They'd driven to that remote, private place where they'd made love all those years ago. He'd helped her from the car and watched her undress. Slowly, shakily, her fingers had loosened every button in that long row of buttons until her firm breasts were revealed. He'd slid the soft edges of her dress aside and kissed each nipple and darkened aureole long and slowly, until they were pouting and full.

When she'd come into his arms she'd made wild, wanton love to him with her tongue, kissing him everywhere, in places that women like Jenny Zachery never kissed a man. Then he'd taken her mouth with the savage need of a man long starved.

She climbed on top of him after a series of long, molten kisses, covering bronzed muscles with her long slim body, moving on him slowly and then more rapidly, undulating rhythmically, her soft moans of excitement arousing him even more than what she was doing because he wanted her to want him, to enjoy him. She'd smiled down at him, her face beautiful and soft. She wore the look of a woman deeply in love, and he'd taken her lips again, this time more gently. Then she knelt above him and took him in her mouth, her brown hair spilling over his stomach, her tongue loving him as his had once loved her, until his whole body felt as though it were on fire from the delicate manipulations of her mouth and tongue.

He awakened hot and shaking, his body throbbing, and he lay awake for a long time after that, perspiring, chastising himself for being an idiot. Nevertheless, despite the damn foolishness of it, he couldn't help thinking of her alone in her bed in that dark house, wishing he could go to her, longing for her to want him as he wanted her.

Thoughts like that were as crazy as his dream. Hadn't she run out as frightened as a rabbit at the mere thought of him living here? What would she do if he touched her, let alone tried to make love to her? He didn't think he could stand it if she shrank from him as though he were no better than dirt. But like everyone else in Zachery Falls, she probably felt he was trash, and that she was too good to be defiled by his lust.

Well, he'd show them. Damn it! He'd show Jenny Zachery, too.

Three

Blade had slept with the windows partially opened so that the familiar sounds and the sweet country scents of the ranch could seep inside. It felt good being back on Zachery Ranch, he thought as he woke up and stretched. He felt as though he belonged. Then he corrected himself. The ranch wasn't called that anymore, and no one in Zachery Falls but himself had ever thought he belonged.

He'd decided to get up early that first morning back on the ranch because there was something he wanted to do before he embarked on the mission that had brought him all the way from the Middle East.

The sun was just rising when he slid out of bed. A dove was cooing, and in the distance, a whippoorwill sang its woeful lament.

Blade shaved and dressed in clean, pressed Levi's and a long-sleeved blue shirt that he left open at the throat.

Shrugging into a suede jacket that emphasized the breadth of his wide shoulders and the slimness of his waist, he stepped into his boots and strode out the door, thinking about the way things had changed.

Woodlands Hideaway was the fancy name Dean had given to the development he'd begun when Caleb was scarcely cold in the ground. Dean had always been one to think big, and he hadn't been satisfied with simple ranching. He'd said that the time for profitable ranching in the Texas hill country was long past. He'd wanted to leave raising animals to the men with flat black land, where the grass grew long and lush. Ranching didn't belong in the exquisitely beautiful hill country with its emerald-clear rivers and bright blue skies. The topsoil was too thin from the overgrazing and farming of the past fifty years.

Dean had always said that the land outside of Zachery Falls was valuable because it was the hill country closest to Houston, only three hours from the giant metropolis. Not only that, but Zachery Falls was located between San Antonio and Austin, less than an hour from either of them, and those two cities were growing faster than any place else in the country.

As a result land prices were sky high around Zachery Falls, and climbing higher because city folks liked a break from the smog and traffic. They wanted to breathe fresh, dry air instead of that dank Houston stuff, and taste the beauty of country life in their spare time. The hill country was filling up with houses and developments. The tourist dollar had brought gold to the hills, and Dean wanted to mine some of that gold.

Dean had conceived his resort with the idea of creating a country paradise for the city-weary tourist. With

Woodlands Hideaway he'd wanted to bring the pleasures of the city to the slower pace of the country.

Blade hadn't agreed completely with Dean, although
he'd seen some truth in his brother's argument. The
ranch did need to be a profitable enterprise. And Blade
was glad about one thing Dean had done—he'd located the development on the southern tip of the ranch
on a high spot along the Blanco River. He'd taken
Blade's advice and built the lodge, restaurant, night-
club, hotel accommodations, swimming pool, tennis
courts, golf courses, country club, spa, and town houses
in a cluster together on the Blanco, so that the rest of the
ranch remained as it had always been, free of development. Caleb's original ranch house and garage, where
Jenny and Blade now lived, were located on the north-
ern corner of the ranch four miles from the resort.
These buildings, set deep in the dark shade of juniper
and oaks, were as secluded as ever.

Blade was glad of that; he was a man who liked wide,
open spaces away from people. He'd learned early that
people could crowd you when they didn't even have a
mind to, and when they had a mind to, they could make
life hell.

It was a mile walk through the thick juniper and scrub
brush from the ranch house down to the cemetery, but
Blade didn't mind. He wanted to walk the land, to get
the feel of it under his boots again. He was careful of
the prickly cactus as he stomped over the flat limestone
rocks amid the scarlet clusters of Indian paintbrush,
pink batches of primroses, and the masses of bluebonnets.

He loved spring in the hill country. It was the most
beautiful time of the year, and it would always be special to him because it was the season when he'd made

love to Jenny that once. As a boy, he'd never thought much about all the flowers that covered the hill country every spring—until that afternoon. But when he'd lain with her slim, warm body crushed beneath his, he'd noticed how beautiful the blossoms were next to her face, how sweet they smelled, how fragile and lovely they were. She was like that, too—sweet, fragile, and lovely. After that the wild flowers had always made him think of her.

He startled an armadillo rooting among the rocks, and a white-tailed deer flew ahead of him as the land sloped down to the river. The cemetery was nestled in the dense shade beneath a grove of ancient live oaks with the river rustling alongside. The grave sites were cool even on the hottest afternoons.

Blade paused at Dean's grave and then walked slowly over to Caleb's. He stared for a long time at the simple cross with Caleb's name engraved upon it.

Some men stood tall, and Caleb had been such a man. A terrible sadness settled over Blade as he thought of the heart attack that had taken Caleb so swiftly eight years before. There hadn't been time to say good-bye, and Blade had never been able to cry over the loss of the only man he'd ever loved. The grief he felt still lay heavy in his heart. Blade owed Caleb a debt he could never repay, and he felt it keenly as he remembered the man who'd adopted him.

Caleb had built the ranch from the little piece of land his own father had left him during the Depression. He'd added to it by ten-acre sections in the beginning, when the land had been cheap. The ranch had meant so much to Caleb; it had been his life's work. And now if Jenny, out of loyalty to Dean's memory, were allowed to follow the foolhardy course of selling acreage to pay the resort's debts, the ranch would dwindle to nothing in a tenth of the time it had taken Caleb to amass it.

"Building's hard, son, wrecking's easy." That's what Caleb had always said to Blade when he was in one of his rare talkative moods.

Caleb had been a builder, and his son Dean a dreamer. Blade was a practical man who played the hand life dealt him, the kind of man who could turn his brother's dream into a reality—because he had to.

Blade had come home, not only for himself, but because he'd at last seen a way to repay that old debt. He would save the ranch for Caleb's grandchild, even if it meant going against Jenny, the woman he had always loved.

"Blade." Behind him, Jenny's voice was soft and respectful. "I thought I might find you out here."

He turned, and there was the shyness in her face that had always appealed to him. She cast her eyes down as if she felt awkward and unsure about having come out to look for him. He liked the red sweater with its row of little white buttons and the skin-tight jeans she wore, and it took all his willpower to drag his gaze from the shapely outline of her slim body.

"I'm sorry about last night, about the way I acted," she said, still with that shy note in her voice. "I'm afraid it wasn't much of a homecoming."

He smiled, thinking how nice of her it was to apologize. She looked so pretty, even if her hair was pinned up in that prim little bun. "I guess it was a better homecoming than I deserved," he said. What would she think if he did what he wanted to, if he went to her and pulled the pins from her hair so that it cascaded over her shoulders the way he liked it to, if he wound the gleaming strands through his fingers before he kissed her slowly on the mouth?

"I'd like to invite you to breakfast," she said. "It would save you from having to go into town."

"Now there's a real peace offering. I'd like that, Jenny. I'd like that very much."

"I took the jeep. Do you want a ride back to the house?"

He nodded, and followed her as she leaped agilely over the rocks down the face of the cliff to where the jeep was parked on the road. He couldn't help thinking how cute and rounded her hips were for so slim a woman.

He went around to the driver's side to open the door for her. He was conscious of her body, so close to his. He hesitated, towering over her. She seemed like such a little thing. Their eyes met, and neither could stop looking at the other.

"How've you been, Jenny," he asked gently, "since Dean died?"

For some reason the way he was looking at her, his manner so easy, his voice kind, brought back in a poignant rush all that she'd lost: Dean, the dreams of their youth, and her illusions about the kind of person she was.

Jenny felt like an idiot bursting into tears out on the road with the warm sun beating down upon them, but once she started, she couldn't seem to stop. All the pain she'd held inside her for so long began to flow out of her.

"Oh, Blade, it's been awful. I've been so lonely. And I haven't known what to do. Half the time I do everything wrong. I depended on Dean for everything, and since he's died, I haven't known what to do with myself. It's like I wasn't ever living for myself. I was living *his* life. And I feel like such a fool right now, bawling like this, when all you did was ask me a simple question. You don't want to hear about my problems." She sobbed more forlornly than ever, thinking how ridiculous it was that she felt so close to this man who'd been away so long.

Without thinking, Blade drew her into the hard circle of his arms. It was painfully obvious that she still loved Dean. But Blade wanted to hold her. He'd been aching to ever since he'd come back to Zachery Falls.

"There, there. Shh. I'm the fool. I should have known better than to ask you a stupid question like that. I ought to know what it's like to hurt so much inside that you're afraid to let it out for fear it'll consume you. I hurt so long myself I didn't know there was any other way you could feel. But maybe it's better for you to talk about it than to hold it all inside. I hate it when you cry, but if it'll make you feel better, you can cry all day for all I care." He stroked her hair. "Yes, Jenny, for you I'll just stand out here forever if that's what it takes. I'll even ignore my grumbling stomach and forget your sweet promise to cook my breakfast when I'm about half-starved," he said, trying to tease her out of her mood.

She knew what he was doing. "I'm trying to stop," she choked helplessly, but the tears kept flowing.

Gently he traced the trail of a tear down her soft cheek with one of his fingertips.

"That bad? Well, Dean was quite a guy. The whole town loved him. He had a good life. I think he had everything a man could need to be happy. He had you."

That made Jenny think of how she'd wronged Dean by yearning to be in another man's arms, and she continued weeping.

"You're probably upset because I came back," Blade said. "This is all my fault. I shouldn't have surprised you like that last night. I should have realized what a shock it would be."

"Oh, no!" she blurted, too distraught to deceive him. "I wanted you to come to the ranch. I felt awful when you didn't. I kept wondering where you were those two days when you didn't come, and they said you were with Susan Harper." Then, realizing what she'd admitted, she turned as scarlet as the Indian paintbrush blooming in bold, bright tufts at her feet.

If he didn't know better, he'd have thought she was jealous. But a woman like Jenny had no reason to be jealous of someone like Susan Harper, so he discarded that notion instantly. But there was pain in Jenny's face, and he knew he was responsible for it.

Suddenly she surprised him. "I'm glad you're back, Blade," she said passionately, and threw her arms around his neck. She pressed her body against his and hugged him tightly. "I don't feel so alone anymore."

He felt her breasts rising and falling against his chest, her hands caressing his neck, touching the tendrils of gold that curled against the collar of his shirt, and he was terribly aware of her as a woman. She smelled so sweet, as if she'd just bathed. Her body fit his perfectly, and it made him remember that time he'd lain with her in the grasses beside Cypress Creek. The desire that rose in him seemed to be an almost unconquerable force, and the perspiration that broke out on his brow felt cold in the chilled air. He clenched his fists so tightly his nails dug into his palms.

It took all his willpower not to lower his mouth and taste the sweetness of her lips, but he knew that if he did, he wouldn't want to stop there. He wanted her. It seemed to him that he had longed for her for a lifetime. But a woman like Jenny wasn't anything like Susan. Jenny had thrown her arms around him because she wanted to be comforted, not because she wanted his hands all over her. She was used to nice men, like Dean and Mike Kilpatrick. It was living hell to try to be a gentleman, Blade thought. Lord knew he didn't have much experience in that role. But this moment with her was too special to ruin, and he would ruin it if he let his needs take over. For the first time in their long acquaintance she'd come to him as an adult seeking friendship and understanding. And damn, if it killed him, that's what he would give her.

Blade knew she didn't want his lovemaking. How would she react if she knew that her hips pressing against his loins made him feel wild enough to rip her clothes aside and carry her into the deepest part of the woods? He only knew how he would feel when her trust turned to disgust after he did that. He knew too well what it was to be treated as if he were dirt, and he hated that feeling. He didn't think he could stand it from Jenny.

So he stood leaning back against the jeep with her body pressing close, her long slim legs touching his, her breasts crushed against him, and he went on holding her until her sobs quieted. Even after that, when she didn't pull away, he held her, and his body was wracked with the delicious torture of his need. He felt torn apart by his conflicting desires, his physical arousal fighting with his wish to be the kind of man she wanted.

At last she tilted her head up, and her expression was shyly embarrassed. "I feel much better. Maybe all I needed was just to have a good cry."

Even with tears streaking her cheeks she was beautiful. Several of the buttons on her sweater had come undone, and he could see beneath the neckline. The bra she was wearing was transparent, and he saw the creamy, swollen smoothness of her breasts and the darkened tips of her nipples. He wanted to touch her, to caress her, to lower his mouth and lick the roseate tips of her breasts until they hardened. He wanted that badly.

"Thank you, Blade, for being so kind." Her face was luminous in its innocence.

"You're welcome, Jenny," he managed in a voice as dry as dust. Gently he disengaged her body from his.

Then he helped her into the jeep and walked around the back and swung himself inside next to her.

It was hell being a gentleman.

Odd, how tiny the kitchen seemed with Blade filling it, Jenny thought. His long legs were sprawled beneath the table as he drank his coffee and read the paper. Maria was giving Cathy her bath, and the child's treble shouts could be heard in the background. She wanted to go see her Uncle Blade again.

When Blade had first come inside the house, he'd gone to Cathy's room, and the child, who was usually so shy with strangers, had thrown herself headlong into his arms, thumb plugged into her grinning mouth.

"You're a mighty big girl to be sucking your thumb so voraciously." He'd laughed.

Jenny had not laughed at that. Did even men like Blade Taylor think that all two-year-olds should be mature adults?

"Thumb," Cathy had cooed proudly, pulling it from her mouth and exhibiting it to him. He'd laughed again.

"You remind me of your grandpa, girl, with your dimples. And Caleb always was one to be proud of anything he did even when it wasn't so much. He'd have given anything to have known you, you know." He'd kissed her golden curls.

They'd played a while longer, the child and the man, before Maria had taken Cathy for fear that Blade's patience would wear thin. He was such a masculine man. It was amazing how gentle and patient he could be with a baby, Jenny thought.

She felt both excited and strange having him back. He was different, somehow. Surer of himself, and easier to be around. She didn't have the feeling that he might erupt at any moment the way he had when he was younger, though, come to think of it, he'd never erupted with her after that time in the first grade when she'd tried to give him a sandwich and unintentionally offended his pride. He'd always been nice to her.

Jenny tried to concentrate on the scrambled eggs and biscuits she was cooking, but her mind crept back to the wonder she'd felt when Blade was holding her. She'd never felt quite like that with Dean, even after ten years of marriage. She'd poured out her troubles to Blade, and his warmth and understanding had lifted them from her. Dean had always come to her with his problems, but he had had no time for hers. Jenny felt so close to Blade now, in some strange unfathomable way, closer than she'd ever felt to anyone.

They ate in silence, or at least they did after Cathy had finished her breakfast and toddled outside with Maria to play with her puppy. It was an easy, companionable silence. When the dishes had been cleared away and loaded into the dishwasher, they sat back down at the table, sharing sections of the newspaper, drinking their coffee.

At last Blade set the paper aside. "Jenny, I was wondering if you had the time to spend the day with me."

Her heart leaped at that simple invitation as her eyes met the dazzling blue of his. He had the most beautiful eyes, she thought, too beautiful for a man, especially a man as rugged as Blade. They were such a startling, vivid color and fringed with thick dark brown lashes. There was a warmth in them that made her go hot all over.

"I haven't been able to get my old motorcycle started, and even when I do, I want something more practical to drive. So I've decided to go into Austin and buy a truck. I was hoping you'd go with me. We've been in-laws for ten years, and I don't think we've ever really talked. Maybe it's about time we did."

This from Blade Taylor, whom everyone said had no use for small talk with women? Blade, who used women for only one thing? She knew the truth of that, for hadn't he used her, too, that once? The shameful thing was that she hadn't minded.

She was as thrilled as a child, but she fought to keep her excitement out of her voice. She knew she should say no, feeling about him as she did, but of course she didn't.

"Why, Blade, I'd love to."

*   *   *

They had a wonderful time in Austin. Blade purchased a Ford Bronco after an hour's haggling with an obnoxious salesman, and the truck was to be delivered to the resort the next day. Blade bought some new clothes in a men's store, and it made Jenny feel all funny inside when she saw how handsome he was in everything he put on. He was so lean and virile, and the years had intensified his sultry sex appeal.

Jenny had packed sandwiches and a quilt, and on their way back to Zachery Falls they drove out toward South Lamar to eat in Zilker Park on the high, grass-covered bank beside the Colorado River. In the park, sunshine filtered through the thick leaves overhead and sparkled on the water. Lovers wrapped in each other's arms lay on blankets beneath trees. Children were paddle-boating amidst a swarm of ducks. Couples canoed on the dark green river, their paddles barely stirring the languid water. A few hardy swimmers were doing laps down the length of Barton Springs, but the water was too cold for most, fed as it was by underground springs. The natural limestone pool was icy even on the hottest summer days.

When they finished with their picnic, Blade and Jenny lay beside each other, watching the clouds float by overhead.

"It was sweet of you to come with me today," Blade said. "I really appreciate it. You really gave that Ford guy a hard time at the end." He chuckled, remembering the way she'd stormed at the little man for the outrageous promises he'd made, demanding that he put them in writing.

"I just didn't like the way he was trying to take advantage of you."

"You always were one to fight other people's battles. I guess that comes from being a preacher's daughter." He smiled at her, but a trace of his old cynicism had crept into his tone. "But then, I wouldn't know much about that, would I? I'd always had too many battles of my own to fight to ever have the time to defend someone else. Sweet, sweet Jenny. We're about as different as two people can be." There was something almost angry in his voice when he said that.

Jenny hadn't come with him because she was sweet or noble, and as the day had passed, her reason for going along had preyed heavily on her mind. Sometimes she thought she was every bit as bad as he. Every time she looked at him, a flutter of excitement swept over her. Right now her eyes were tracing the broadness of his shoulders, the contours of his chest and stomach, the lines of his narrow waist—and her thoughts were not those of a lady.

She was marveling at the animal magnificence of his male body. This longing to touch him and for him to touch her was a new kind of torment. It had never been like this when she was with Dean, and she was at a loss to understand the terrible power of her feelings for Blade. She knew she should be thankful for this new friendliness with him, but she felt strangely restless. The devil within her was remembering the old, smoldering Blade, and it was difficult, so difficult, to feel thankful for mere friendliness when what she really wanted was something much different.

Suddenly she almost wished she were Susan Harper. She knew Blade would be different with Susan. He wouldn't lay here plucking at blades of grass and watching the clouds float by with his handsome face so cool and impassive. He would pull her beneath him, and he would kiss her with hot, possessive lips, and she would kiss him back, without shame. He would suggest a motel room, and she would say yes without a shadow of guilt.

Jenny felt warm suddenly, despite the cool spring air, at the mere thought of Blade's lips searing her flesh, at the thought of what he would do to her in the privacy of a motel room. She remembered how he'd kissed her before, how his mouth had kissed her everywhere, in secret, shamefully intimate places, learning her with his mouth as Dean never had.

It was wicked, the way she remembered it all so clearly. Because Blade was so near, and she could feel the warmth of him and catch the scent of him, the memory of that long-ago afternoon when he had made love to her came back to her with startling, poignant force. And all the time she lay remembering the wild, shameful glory of his loving, Blade went on infuriatingly plucking those blades of grass, deliberately ignoring her.

Jenny remembered how he had kissed her, his mouth hard and demanding until she'd opened her lips and accepted his tongue. Slowly, he had taught her the lure of passion, the song of the siren, with those long, wanton kisses on that drowsy spring afternoon when he'd awakened her innocent, untutored body to the splendor it had been designed for.

He'd undressed her and kissed every bit of bare feminine flesh he exposed, telling her how beautiful she was, exciting her as much with his words as with his lips. His hands had moved over her so gently that she'd marveled at the tenderness of the wild, untamed Blade Taylor.

How could he touch a woman thus, so that she shivered from the mere brush of a calloused fingertip? His lips had traveled to all the places his hands explored, trailing along the velvet skin of her throat, his mouth nibbling lower to the rounded tops of her breasts, and drifting lower still, pushing her hands aside and murmuring softly, "Leave me be, Jenny. There's no shame in being a woman. You're so beautiful." And she'd let him, and gloried in the letting.

Thinking of him and the way he'd loved her once, Jenny fell asleep beside Blade. The air was cool, and he smiled down at her beautiful, tranquil face. She was so innocently trusting. He removed his suede jacket and covered her slim shoulders with it.

In her sleep she murmured his name with a tenderness that startled him, and she moved closer to him, seeking the warmth of his body as she cuddled more closely against him, pressing her breasts and hips to him, draping her arm over his waist.

Lord, why had she done that? How was a man to stay sane when he was inflamed by her merest gesture? He groaned inwardly when he felt the button-tips of her nipples through her sweater. His body hardened, but he didn't move away for fear of awakening her.

He couldn't resist caressing her, removing the pins from her hair and letting it fall across his arm where it gleamed in the sun like rich dark chocolate. He buried his face in the soft-smelling thickness even though it was a special kind of torture to do so. He moved his hand along her back, tracing the slim, soft line of her body down to the swelling of her hips. When she stirred, and he thought she might awaken, he let his hand fall away.

He looked at her, savoring the beauty of her, the nearness of her.

They lay in each other's arms, and at last Blade fell
asleep too, with his arms wrapped tightly around the
woman he loved.

Four

The kiddie train, loaded with laughing, squealing youngsters, whistled as it chugged past on its track near the tree in Zilker Park where Jenny and Blade lay, startling them. They awoke tangled in each other's arms and legs. Jenny was amazed that her hair had come loose from its knot and spilled in brown waves over Blade's shoulders. Several buttons on her red sweater had come undone again, and the shadowy indentation between her breasts was exposed.

What must he think? She flushed and felt embarrassed as she sat up, hastily pulling her body from his. Everywhere he touched her his skin scorched hers, filling her with wanton, pleasurable sensations that were wrong, under the circumstances.

She couldn't look at him as her fingers fumbled with the buttons of her sweater, and he read in her embar-

rassment disgust at having awakened and found herself
in his arms.

Nothing had changed, he thought bitterly, the easiness he'd felt toward her suddenly leaving him. She was
just like all the other nice women in Zachery Falls, who
still thought he was filth and that they were too good to
be touched by dirt like Blade Taylor. His stomach
tightened with that old angry feeling he thought he'd
put behind him when he'd left Zachery Falls ten years
ago, and he jumped to his feet, his face so cold and dark
that it made her want to cry as he began gathering their
picnic things and throwing them into the basket.

They rode back to Zachery Falls in silence, each of
them locked in their own private misery, yet each
acutely conscious of the other. The brown hills whipped
by as Blade drove, but neither saw them. He stopped
only once, to buy a package of cigarettes at a drive-in
grocery. She stayed in the jeep and chewed a fingernail
until it was ragged and ugly and bleeding.

Blade had told her that he was trying to quit smoking, and the fact that he smoked now told her how angry he was. She stared at his face, trying to understand,
but his chiseled features were as unreadable as a carved
statue's. This was the inexplicably volatile Blade she
remembered from the past, and she was at a loss to
know what she had done to infuriate him.

Neither of them spoke until Blade roared past the
entrance to Woodlands Hideaway without turning in.

Then, in a feeble voice she dared. "Blade, that
was—"

"We're not going home just yet," he said, his voice
low with suppressed anger.

"But why? Where are you taking me?"

"We have an appointment at Mike Kilpatrick's."

"On Saturday?"

"Mike told me he'd be in his office all afternoon, catching up on some work."

"But you didn't say anything about an appointment and neither did Mike."

"I asked him not to."

"You did what? Blade, what is going on? What's the matter with you?"

"You'll find out. Kilpatrick is being handsomely paid to explain all the legalities to you."

"But why won't you tell me yourself?"

"Because I don't feel like talking at the moment, if you don't mind."

She did mind, but he didn't say another word for the rest of the drive.

Once they alighted from the jeep they had to walk up a ramp and across a sidewalk to get to the law offices. Blade's face was still dark with the anger that ate at him on the inside and made him look fierce and dangerous on the outside. On their way to Mike's they passed several people they both knew. Katey Scudder stared at Blade with wide eyes and scarcely spoke to Jenny. Margaret Harris drew herself up haughtily and wouldn't even look at either of them. No one had ever cut Jenny dead in Zachery Falls before, but that was how they had always treated Blade.

Jenny saw that Blade's mouth was twisted in an even tighter line than before. He was walking so fast that she had to run to keep up with him, and she realized that he was not as indifferent to people disliking him as he had always pretended. All his old anger toward everyone had been a defense. Suddenly Jenny was furious that they felt they could treat him like that. How could they so self-righteously treat another human being as though he were dirt? Blade wasn't trash. He hadn't ever been. He'd just been a poor boy who was unfortunate enough to have been born to abusive parents—and the townspeople had abused him as well. He'd always deserved better. No wonder he'd acted so tough when he'd been younger.

It rubbed Blade's nerves raw when Mike came forward and took Jenny's hand in his as if it were his right and kissed her lightly on the cheek. He hated the way she accepted Kilpatrick's affection with a smile instead of flushing darkly as she had when she'd awakened in his own arms all mussed and deliciously sexy-looking. How he had wanted her then, before he'd realized what her feelings were. Then he'd gotten so angry he'd felt like smashing everything in sight. It was hell wanting someone who didn't want you.

Mike leaned across his desk and nervously handed a crisp set of legal papers to Jenny.

"But this is Caleb's will, and the papers for incorporating the resort. Why..." Jenny began.

"I'm giving you these papers so that you can read them at your leisure," Mike said slowly. "But if you'd like I'll briefly summarize the more pertinent facts for you. I've always felt that you should have known them, anyway."

What in heaven's name was going on? Why had Blade brought her here? And what did he have to do with any of the legalities involving the resort?

Blade sat silently beside her, his long legs crossed negligently as he leaned back and lit a cigarette. Even so, there was a tension in him, in Mike, and in the room.

"I don't understand the meaning of Blade's presence. Why do you feel it necessary to explain something involving my property in front of Blade?"

Mike and Blade looked at one another for a long, uncomfortable moment, but neither spoke. At last Mike began, and it was obvious he dreaded saying what he had to say.

"For one thing, Jenny, the property isn't just yours."

"What?"

"It belongs to Blade, too. Eight years ago Caleb left half of his estate, including half the ranch, to Blade. When Dean and I drew up the incorporation papers, Blade was a full partner."

"That can't be true."

"It is. I wanted to tell you when Dean died. The information was recorded in several legal documents that are in your possession."

"I never read them."

"I knew you didn't, and I tried to persuade Blade to tell you about it himself. Blade said he didn't want to upset you at the time. He said you had enough to make you unhappy without any additional problems. Earlier, both Blade and Dean had told me not to inform you about this unless it became absolutely necessary, and when Dean died, I thought it was necessary that you be told. But Blade insisted on sticking to the old promise he'd made Dean."

"What promise?"

"When Dean built the resort, he and Blade made a deal. Dean would manage the ranch and resort and send Blade's share of the profits to him. Blade promised he would never interfere unless he felt that he needed to. Unfortunately, Jenny, he feels that time has come. The loans that I've advanced you to keep Woodlands Hideaway afloat without the sale of acreage this last year have come from Blade. He's concerned about the management of Woodlands Hideaway. He's come home to take over.''

Jenny went white with shock, and she stared hard at both men, feeling bitterly confused. Dean had deliberately withheld this very vital piece of information from her, and Mike had known all along. For the two years since Dean's death, Mike had known, and still he hadn't told her that Blade owned half the ranch.

She was furious at both of them. They had treated her like a child.

She thought of how foolishly she'd behaved since Blade's return. She'd longed to see Blade even though she'd been afraid to. And when he'd moved in at the ranch she'd stupidly jumped to the conclusion that he must have cared in some way about Cathy and herself.

But Blade hadn't come back to live at the ranch out of any feelings for Caleb or Dean or for herself. He'd come back because of money. For ten years he'd stayed away, and as long as the ranch had remained profitable, it was obvious that he'd never had the slightest intention of returning. Doubtless he preferred the crude sports the townspeople accused him of—drinking and womanizing. He had no interest in working the ranch or running the resort as long as there was someone else to do it for him. At that moment, Jenny was mad enough to believe anything of him.

Blade was after money. That was the worst thing of all. All day she'd been so thrilled to be with him. Remembering the way she'd lain beside him in the park dreaming of the time he'd made love to her made her feel like a lovesick idiot. Why had she thought he might have cared about her? Why had she so stupidly allowed herself to idealize his motives?

Too, she'd behaved like a fool on the road this morning, crying all over him about her unhappiness. That feeling of closeness had been without foundation. Why did he care? He was after the money, that was all.

She was madder at herself than she was at anyone else, but of course it was much more satisfying to vent her fury on Blade. "What makes you think you can run Woodlands Hideaway any better than I can, or that I'll let you?" She lashed out at him.

"I can hardly do worse." Blade's blue gaze was cool and steady as he regarded her. "As I see it, it's either run it better or sell out. At the debt we're carrying, we can't afford to continue with the monthly losses we've been sustaining. I've done some research and I've decided to hire a resort management company I'm favorably impressed with, Nichols Inc. I've met with Bob Nichols in Tennessee, and he's turned around resorts that have been in worse shape than Woodlands Hideaway. He's very enthusiastic about bringing his team out."

"You decided to hire this Bob Nichols without even consulting me?"

"That's right."

"And what if I'm against it?"

"You don't have any choice. I've got more money riding on Woodlands Hideaway than you do. In the last fourteen months you've accepted more than $100,000 from me in loans to keep the resort afloat. If you read the notes you signed, you'll understand the power I now have, power that you have given me."

"I can't believe that you—"

"Believe it. Jenny, you're a careless businesswoman. You have only yourself to blame if any of this comes as a surprise to you."

"Blade Taylor, you've always been hard. Maybe everybody in Zachery Falls was right about you all along," she cried, knowing that she was being unfair, but too angry to care.

He shrugged, but the dark look that she hated was there on his face. "Maybe." Then he got up and turned to stalk out the door.

"Blade, I can't believe you're going to walk roughshod over me like this."

"If that's what you want to call it, you can believe it. As I see it, all I've done is hire a professional with twenty years of experience in the business. Nichols owns hotels of his own. He knows what he's doing, and you obviously don't. Unlike you, I'm willing to admit that I don't either, though I have every intention of learning. If you care to join me, you're welcome to come along for the ride. If not—" He hesitated, and the faintest hint of the devilish smile she found so disarming when they weren't angry at one another curved his sensual mouth. Only now, in her anger, she thought it derisive. "If not, I guess you could always stay home and take up a hobby. Why don't you give thumbpainting a try? From what I hear, a lot of people around Zachery Falls feel that that wouldn't be such a bad idea."

At that last she went red with fury. She started to say something, but all she could do was stutter crazily.

Blade swung the door open and walked out of the office just as Mike pulled Jenny into his arms and began to speak soothingly to her. But Blade had seen Kilpatrick embrace Jenny, and the knowledge that he was leaving them alone together burned through him as painfully as a tongue of fire as he strode down the long hall to the front of the building.

That old feeling of being shut out that he'd always had whenever he'd seen Dean and Jenny together was upon him, and he knew he had to get out of Zachery Falls fast before he did something he would regret.

For two days and two nights Blade did not return to the ranch. Jenny told herself that she was furious with him, that she hated him for the way he had so callously treated her, that she was indifferent to where he was and what he was doing. She accepted delivery on his Ford Bronco when it arrived only because it would have been spiteful not to. She worked at the resort as she always had, not mentioning to the employees that there were soon to be massive changes in management.

Despite her determination to be indifferent to Blade, every time she returned to the house from her office she couldn't help looking over at the garage to see if the Bronco was where she had left it, or to see if a light was on in his apartment. She told herself when she did these things that it was only human to be curious. It wasn't that she really cared.

Liar, a wiser voice whispered.

On the third night of his absence she was roused from her sleep by a loud series of noises outside. Heidi and her pup were barking, and something heavy seemed to be thudding upon the ground in the backyard.

Throwing on her robe, she crept to the back door and looked out. The light was on in Blade's apartment. Then she saw the shadow of a man by the doghouse. He was hacking clumsily at something on the ground, and then he stopped, leaning heavily on a hoe. She heard Heidi's whine and that of her pup and then the low croon of Blade's voice as he bent to pet the dogs.

She threw open the door and the moonlight slanted down upon her, illuminating the shape of her body through her thin negligee and peignoir.

"Jenny, what the hell do you think you're doing, coming out here like that?" Blade muttered, his eyes moving over her.

"Maybe I should ask you the same thing," she replied undaunted, stepping onto the porch.

He was roughing Heidi behind her shaggy ear the way she liked to be petted. How was it that Blade Taylor knew so much about touching animals and women the way they enjoyed being touched? It was crazy how happy she felt that he was back.

"I heard the dogs carrying on, and I came over to see what the matter was," he explained.

His voice sounded funny, slurred. Uneasily she wondered if he'd been drinking.

"And?" she asked coolly.

"Just a little old rattlesnake."

"Just! In my backyard?" Horrified, Jenny rushed down the steps to investigate the inert coil beside the doghouse. Her nightclothes fluttered against her body, outlining the shape of her breasts, the slimness of her waist, and the length of her legs.

"My aim wasn't too good. I'm afraid I hacked up a few of your flowers before I killed him."

"Oh, I don't care!" she began passionately—then she smelled the liquor on his breath. "Blade, you've been drinking."

"It's true I haven't been in Sunday School. But then I'm afraid I've never laid claim to being the gentleman of your dreams. I'm not a Kilpatrick or a Dean." He laughed softly, and the rich sound of it in the darkness made her feel oddly excited.

"That's nothing to be so proud of."

"Who said I was proud of it?"

"Where have you been? With Susan Harper?" What had made her ask that last?

"You've got Susan on the brain, girl." He stepped closer, and there was that aura of wild danger about him that she remembered so well. His bold eyes raked her up and down, and she realized she should never have come out in the darkness with him. "As a matter of fact, I've been in Tennessee, meeting with Bob Nichols. He came back to Zachery with me, so we can begin work right away."

"Oh."

"It's plain to see you still think the worst of me, like everybody else in Zachery Falls. Everyone thinks that all I want is an easy woman and something to drink. Well maybe it's about time I lived up to your expectations. Or lived down to them, as the case may be. There can be fun in that kind of living, Jenny. Maybe it's time you learned that there's a hell of a lot more to life than church socials." Again there was that soft male laugh as he came toward her, still looking her up and down with hot eyes. "Don't you know it's dangerous to come out in the dark alone with a man like me when I'm half drunk and feeling wild?"

Involuntarily she backed toward the house. But despite her fear, she felt drawn to him. She felt like moving into his arms, instead of away from them. She wanted to be crushed against the hard length of him, to feel her mouth consumed by the heat of his.

She didn't know that her face had gone soft with desire.

"Jenny," he rasped, "you'd better go back into the house before it's too late."

Oh, would he never learn that she was as wicked as he? Perhaps that was at the bottom of this craving she had. Perhaps, just perhaps, it was time she taught him. She didn't budge an inch, fascinated as she was by that untamed aura of maleness that clung to him, yearning for the magic of his touch. She stood looking at him with her heart in her eyes.

"Girl, you don't know what you're doing."

Oh, she knew.

"You're beautiful," he breathed in a voice that was hoarse and strange.

"Blade," she said shakily as his arms slid around her beneath the filmy robe to caress the bare warmth of her flesh. His languid stroking sent shivers through her, and she felt as if there were a dizzying hollow in the pit of her stomach. "Oh, Blade."

The stars were brilliant in the ink black sky, and the cool night air was fragrant with the scent of wild flowers.

He could scarcely believe that she'd come to him like this. A wild joy flowed through him, and his hands tightened around her slim waist. He lifted her up and twirled her around in the sweet darkness. Her hair came loose and swirled down against his face. Her night-clothes floated like gossamer veils. She was laughing, and so was he.

Very slowly, he brought her back down to earth, letting the lithe firmness of her body slide erotically against his so that she could not help but learn the state of his arousal.

She stared at him, feeling suddenly shy and awkward, not being as experienced in these things as he. Her uncertainty grew, and she tried to pull away, wanting to run from the danger of him. But he held her fast, his mouth seeking hers.

He kissed her long and deeply, his tongue invading her mouth, his male body pressing close. His hands caressed her breasts as he molded her against him. When he released her at last, she stumbled backward, looking at him. In the moonlight his face was dark with passion, and his blue eyes held a wild glitter.

He was a stranger to her.

"Blade, I shouldn't. We shouldn't."

"Oh, but we should."

"No!" She took a step backward.

He didn't come after her because he knew that she would run if he did. He could easily take her by force. But he didn't think he'd have to.

"What a tease you are, Jenny Zachery," he said, but there was no anger in his voice. "To come out here like this and tempt me from the path of virtue—not that I've ever been one who minded being tempted from that path. And then when I'm all hot and bothered, you pull the temptation away." His low chuckle mocked himself as well as her. "You know, sometimes I think you're not as different from the Susan Harpers of the world as you like to pretend." At her look of shock, he said, "And that's not such a bad thing, either."

"I'm afraid, Blade."

"Why should you be afraid of being a woman?"

"I don't know. I guess I've always been afraid—of being *me*," she admitted.

"Maybe it's time you stopped."

"Dean—"

Dean! Always Dean! Blade didn't think he could stand it if she talked about Dean at that moment. Was he always to be there, between them, even when he was dead?

"I don't want to hear about how you love Dean, damn it," he growled, reaching for her.

The anger she saw in him reminded her of her fear, and she ran toward the house, eluding him, stumbling up the stairs. He caught her around the waist just before she reached the door and pulled her fiercely against himself. His mouth came down on hers hard, frightening in its demand. He pushed her back against the wall, imprisoning her with his body, and he kissed her again and again in a series of drugging kisses that left her limp and weak and clinging to him. Hot tremors of exquisite longing traced through her.

"Maria's inside, asleep in the house," she warned when at last he released her lips so that his mouth could nuzzle the softness of her throat. "I'll scream—"

"There won't be any screaming tonight, Jenny, girl. Only loving," he murmured with a sexy chuckle. Then his mouth smothered the cry she would have uttered, so that it became no more than a helpless gurgle in her throat.

His hands moved through her hair, caressing the tumbling masses that fell about her shoulders.

"Jenny... Jenny. My God, Jenny, you're so beautiful, and I've wanted you so badly, so long, I thought I'd die with the wanting." His eyes were smoldering with passion as he lifted her into his arms, carrying her effortlessly down the stairs and across the backyard toward his apartment. He was panting slightly when he reached the top of the stairs and kicked his bedroom door open with his boot.

Inside the small, immaculate room he carried her to the bed and laid her upon it, following her down. He kissed her, and his hands moved over her body in a slow, expert way that inflamed her every nerve ending. She was thoroughly, breathlessly aroused when he finally loosened the ribbons that fastened her robe and slid it from her shoulders.

The lamp near the desk was on, and she said faintly, "Blade, the light. Turn it off."

"I want to see you."

"But—"

"I think you're beautiful. There's nothing to be ashamed of."

Dean had always made love to her in the darkness because of her shyness, and he'd never seemed to mind.

Blade removed her nightgown, and then he buried his lips against her navel, kissing her there with his tongue until wavelets of desire coursed through her everywhere from that erogenous spot. She placed her hands in his golden hair and held him close. It seemed that she'd always wanted this, as far back as she could remember. Only she'd never, never wanted to admit it.

At last he stood up and she watched, fascinated, as he undressed. Bronzed fingers started at the bottom of his blue shirt and unfastened the buttons one by one. He stripped off his shirt, and she marveled at the play of tanned muscles as he leaned over and hung the garment over the back of a chair. Slowly his fingers undid his belt buckle, and he slid his jeans off. In another moment he was naked. He looked like a Greek god. He was so beautiful, and she was wantonly thrilled that he was so obviously virile and all male, and so terribly, magnificently in need of a woman. She wanted to touch him there, but she felt afraid and shy at the same time.

When he came to her again his hands were shaking, so powerful was his desire. He was trembling all over.

He lay on top of her, his body molded to her soft length, and he kissed her lips in that gentle and yet passionate way that could stir her soul.

Just as his hands were exploring Jenny, learning her readiness, the screen door of the ranch house slammed shut directly beneath them. The porch light flared, and Maria's anxious voice floated to them in the darkness. The thrilling sensations evoked within Jenny by Blade's touch were abruptly shattered.

"Mrs. Zachery!" came Maria's insistent cry.

They froze in one another's arms, each of them listening, Blade in frustration and Jenny in horror. They heard the sound of Maria's house slippers shuffling along the porch. Jenny stared out the window and watched the bobbing wand of light as the woman searched the darkness. Then Maria disappeared around the back of the house. Soon she would come to the garage, and perhaps she would even come upstairs.

"Blade, I can't let her find me like this with you," Jenny began desperately as she groped for her nightgown and robe.

"No, of course not."

His voice was low and cynical, and it hurt her somehow. His hands loosened upon her soft, warm body, and though she felt empty and lost, she left him. He made no move to stop her as she hastily dressed.

"I—I hope you can understand," Jenny said, buttoning her robe.

"Oh, I understand."

His face was dark and mocking, and Jenny thought that his broad grin was every bit as hateful as his cynical tone. He began to laugh softly.

"No, you don't," she said miserably and then she ran out the door into the sheltering darkness.

As she entered the backyard she called quietly to her maid. "You're making enough noise to wake the dead, Maria."

"So there you are." The dark eyes in the brown face were speculative.

"There was a rattlesnake in the backyard. I was going to put the hoe in the garage."

"Oh." Maria was only half-believing, perhaps because the hoe was still leaning against the doghouse.

"You can see for yourself. Look on the ground beside the doghouse," Jenny said coldly as she swept past the other woman and went inside.

When she was safely inside her bedroom, Jenny's thoughts returned to Blade. She wondered what he was thinking. He hadn't liked her leaving him.

But she had liked it no better than he. She'd wanted him for so long. Even now her blood ran hot at the thought of his touch, his kisses. His passion had inflamed all the feelings that had lain dormant within her, intensifying them. The shattering fulfillment she'd known only once had been tantalizingly within reach only minutes ago. Now all that was lost to her, and it was more painful than ever that she had to sleep in her cold bed where she felt so achingly alone.

Blade couldn't sleep either. Instead, he dressed and stepped out into the darkness. For a long time he stood in the shadows of an oak tree, watching the house, wanting Jenny so much that it hurt. Heidi came to him to have her ears scratched.

Blade stooped and petted the dog. "At least you're getting what you want, girl," he said gently. He stared at Jenny's darkened window again.

It was no use wanting what he couldn't have, he told himself harshly.

Jenny wanted him the same way she'd wanted him when she was a girl, and she was ashamed of the wanting. She didn't want anyone to know how she felt. Not that he blamed her.

But he didn't like it, either, and the hurt she'd inflicted swelled into a fierce, dark anger against her. If it hadn't been for his desire to do right by Caleb and his granddaughter, Blade would have left Zachery Falls forever that night. Instead, he decided to go to the resort bar and see if Bob Nichols was still there.

Five

When Jenny awoke, she felt just as exhausted as she had when she'd gone to bed. She was numb with the pain of wanting and denying that she wanted. If only she'd had the courage to give herself to Blade. But he hadn't really wanted her. He'd only been drinking, and she'd been available. She should be glad that Maria had come outside and saved her from herself.

But she wasn't glad, and that was wrong. But then, everything she was thinking and doing these days was wrong. What was happening to her? To her morals? To her sense of values?

It was wrong for her to take such pleasure in the arms of a man when love words had never been spoken between them, and probably never would be. When, indeed, she knew that Blade didn't love her, not the way Dean had loved her, in the noble, respectable, sensible way that led to a conventional marriage and two lives joined together. When she even doubted that he could really love a woman, let alone marry one and live respectably. But Blade needed her in a way that Dean never had, and somehow, although it was against everything she believed in to yearn to sleep with a man she wasn't married to, she was excited by the way Blade wanted her with that all-consuming passion. It was exciting to think of him desiring her and not just respecting her for all her virtuous qualities, the way everyone else did.

But then, why *would* he respect her, knowing her in the way that he did? A tiny voice nagged at her. What would everyone else think if they learned the truth about her?

It was the hypocrite in Jenny who wanted everyone in Zachery Falls to go on thinking well of her; it was the hypocrite who had made her run from Blade's lovemaking at the first sound of Maria's voice. It would never, never do for the Widow Zachery to be found in bed with Blade Taylor. But the woman in Jenny yearned—and knew it was wrong to yearn.

The sunlight flooding Blade's room spilled its white brilliance into his face. He groaned as he grew aware of a terrible pain that seemed to split his head in two. He sat bolt upright, and the pain pounded through him more strongly than before.

"Damn, what the hell—" But the feeling was not all that unfamiliar, although in recent years he hadn't had cause to suffer from it often.

Blade remembered the whiskey he'd consumed in the resort bar with Bob Nichols; then he remembered Jenny, and the way her face had looked, beautiful and soft with desire.

Staring at his rumpled pillow, he buried his face in his hands. What had he almost done?

But he knew what he'd done, and as he dragged himself out of bed and walked toward the shower, he was swamped by the most terrible feelings of remorse he'd ever known. He'd almost taken what a woman like Jenny would never have willingly given him. He remembered how she'd run from him, how she'd tried to scream on the porch, how quickly she'd left him when she'd heard Maria, and those blurred memories made him feel worse.

He stepped into the shower, feeling queasy as he forced himself to endure the splintering chill of the water spraying down upon him. How would he ever face her? Like a coward, he knew that he couldn't, not right now. So he dressed hurriedly and went down to the restaurant to have breakfast with Bob Nichols.

From the house, Jenny heard Blade's Bronco on the road, and she rushed to the window only to see him drive away. Filled with a wrenching sadness, she watched until the plume of dust that had billowed behind the truck settled once more on the road.

Did he despise her now, for what she had done? She wanted to die of shame for letting him know how she wanted him, and also what a hypocrite she was, at the same time. But, of course, she could not. Cathy began to cry, and Jenny left the window to see what was the matter.

After breakfast Jenny dressed in a long-sleeved gray cotton dress that was as demure as a puritan's garb. She pinned her hair in a prim knot at the nape of her neck and stared at herself hard in the full-length mirror in her bedroom. There were no telltale ravages of passion ev-

ident upon her smooth alabaster skin. Satisfied, she left
for her office.

Blade's Bronco was parked in front of the resort's
lodge, but she didn't see him that morning, though she
remained nervous and expectant in anticipation that she
might. When she finished writing the innumerable promotion letters she went down to the restaurant for
lunch. She was already inside the dining room when she
heard the sound of Blade's laughter. There was no way
she could bolt from the room like a startled goose flap-
ping for cover, so, feeling mortified, she headed to a
nearby table and sank down in a chair with her back to
the place where Blade was sitting with several men. She
gave her order to the waiter and tried to ignore the un-
easiness she felt at being near Blade.

The carpet in the restaurant was thick and soft, so she
didn't hear Blade's tread as he approached.

"Jenny—" Blade's soft, deep voice came to her from
behind.

It was difficult to raise her eyes to his.

His face was dark and remote. There was a bleak-
ness in his eyes that tugged at her heart. Suddenly she
longed for the easiness that had been between them the
day they'd gone to Austin. Had she lost even that because of last night?

"I was hoping you would join us. I'd like for you to
meet Bob Nichols and the men he's brought with him
from Tennessee," Blade said.

No words of tenderness. No indication that there had
ever been anything between them. Jenny's stomach
clenched into a knot as tightly wound as that of her hair.
She wanted to cry, to nurse her hurt in private, but of
course that was impossible under the circumstances. She
couldn't very well refuse him, so she nodded mutely,

wishing all the while that she could sink into the middle of the earth or some other place equally far removed from Blade Taylor.

She did not know of the pain that her silence and the dull unhappiness in her face brought him, nor of the control in him that prevented his going down on his knees and begging her forgiveness. Never had he loved her more than now, when he thought he'd lost even her friendly regard.

When his hand touched the back of her waist as he escorted her to his table, she was terribly aware of it, and she flinched away from his fingers. She didn't see the darkness that came to his eyes when he felt her reaction.

Bob Nichols was silver-haired and fatherly, a man well into his sixties. He reminded Jenny of Caleb, and she wondered if that was why Blade thought so highly of him. Throughout lunch his conversation was filled with practical suggestions for immediate changes and expenditures. He had a three-phase scheme for making the resort profitable. To her surprise, Jenny found that she felt only relief as she listened to Blade and the men talk. Her original resistance to the situation melted away as she listened to Bob's commonsense solutions to problems that had seemed to her insoluble. It seemed to her that Blade had lifted a horrendous burden from her shoulders by coming home and hiring Bob, and when she remembered the way she had treated him in Mike's office, she felt truly ashamed. She'd been so ignorant, so frightfully ignorant. She'd lashed out and said things she should never have said.

It pleased her when Bob complimented a few of the areas where she'd actually done the right things. To her astonishment, she realized that she was actually looking forward to all the changes that were going to be made. Of course, they would not be easily implemented. The staff would balk and want to cling to the old, comfortable ways. But as she left the table, she felt positive that they would at least make a start in setting things right.

In the week that followed, things did not improve between herself and Blade. He avoided her. During the days when she was in the office, he stayed away from that part of the resort. During the evenings he didn't come home until long after she had gone to bed. She would lie in bed, wondering where he was, torturing herself with visions of him in Susan's bed.

When he chanced upon her at the lodge or anywhere else in the resort, he was stiff and uncomfortable in her presence. He would quickly find some excuse to leave and see to something else if it became obvious that she had to stay where he was for a while. She was relieved when he left because his coldness hurt her so.

It killed her, the way he wanted nothing to do with her, the way he stayed away as if he couldn't stand the sight of her. Nevertheless, every night she cried herself to sleep after she heard his truck drive up and his footsteps on the stairs.

How she longed for him to come home earlier, to walk up the front porch, knock on the door, invite himself inside. She envisioned him lifting Cathy high above his shoulders while she squealed with delight. Then later, when the child was content to play by herself, Jenny imagined Blade coming close and folding her in his arms and holding her tightly against him. They would laugh and talk quietly and share things, the special secret things that only lovers share. All the pain that had been locked within her for so long would dissolve and flow out of her, and she would love and be loved.

But, of course, Blade was not that sort of man, and he did none of those things. He went on avoiding her, and she went on longing for him, her spirit crushed by her secret sorrow. Hopelessly she wondered if time would ease the hurt so that she could learn to stand his indifference. All she knew was that when Blade Taylor had come home, he'd turned her world upside down, and she no longer knew how to live.

Blade worked hard in the month that followed, harder than Jenny, harder than Bob Nichols, harder than anyone at Woodlands Hideaway. Jenny watched him, admiring the way he worked undaunted despite the innumerable setbacks and all the complexities he had yet to learn about the business.

He took inventories of every guest room and every town house in the hotel rental pool. He read ten years' worth of income tax returns, poured over account books, went through every piece of paper in every filing cabinet, spent long hours talking to the employees and to the town house owners.

She couldn't have known that it was his longing for her that drove him to work until he could collapse in bed in a state of exhaustion. Even when he didn't get to bed until midnight and he'd been up since dawn, he sometimes lay awake, haunted by her. Every time he chanced upon her at the resort he drank in the startling beauty of her. He could not stop himself from mentally stripping the clothes from her body and remembering the voluptuous femininity that had so aroused him, even when these visions brought him sharp pain. Yet he was careful to hide his feelings, for her sake, re-

minding himself that Kilpatrick and Dean were the sort
of men she could want without shame.

For Jenny the days passed listlessly, hopelessly.

One bright Friday morning in May, Carol Thompson, the head of housekeeping, came into Jenny's office with the news that two television sets had been stolen from Town House 34. Jenny pulled out the file on the town house only to discover that those sets were brand new; only a month before, two sets had been stolen from that very same town house. Jenny was about to pick up the phone and call the owner when she decided to go to Blade first.

His secretary ushered her into his office and then left, closing the door behind her. They were alone. Blade was on the phone, but he nodded to Jenny to sit down.

Her heart tripped with an odd little pang at the sight of him. This was the first time in over a month that they'd been alone together. She relished the chance to look at him. His skin was browner from the hot Texas sun; the golden hair that tumbled over his brow so rakishly had grown longer. She was achingly aware of the size of him, of the broadness of his shoulders, and of his hard muscular body, as well as of the deep yearning that lay within her to go into his arms and become a part of him.

He was so handsome. She knew he could have any woman he wanted, even one of those in town who professed to despise him. Jenny had to fight against the sickening sensation of jealousy as she wondered for the millionth time about the women he must surely be seeing.

"What is it, Jenny?" Blade asked at last after he'd hung up the phone. His vivid eyes met hers with a little of their old intensity. She was more aware than ever of his animal magnetism, and she flushed at the wanton thoughts that went through her head.

"I hate to bother you with this," she began hesitantly.

"Don't you know by now that you're never a bother?" he said, his tone almost as easy as it had been before that night of passion and hypocrisy.

"Blade, two more television sets have been taken out of Town House 34."

"Two more? Did you know that we've lost eighteen color sets from the town houses alone in the last two months?"

"I knew we'd lost some, but until Carol came to my office this morning—"

"*Some!*" Blade rose from his chair, jamming his hands deep into his pockets, and went to stare out the window that overlooked the pool and tennis courts. "The town house owners are up in arms, and I don't blame them. Those television sets cost nearly five hundred dollars apiece."

"But, Blade, there doesn't seem to be anything we can do." She spoke hesitantly.

He looked at her, his blue eyes sharp. "I think there is."

"What?"

"Wait and you'll see," he returned cryptically. Since she could think of no excuse to remain in his office, she got up to leave. He followed her. She was at the door when his voice stopped her.

"Jenny—"

She turned and her eyes met blue ones that were brilliant with an emotion she couldn't define. Her pulse thudded with sudden pleasure. Surely he couldn't look at her like that if he didn't feel something for her.

"I was wondering—" He hesitated.

"Yes, Blade?" She tilted her face inquiringly, scarcely daring to hope.

"I was wondering if you could help me with something."

"Of course."

"One of the employees can't make the resort hayride tonight, and we don't have anyone else to drive the tractor or host the dance. I offered to take his place, but I've never done it before. I was wondering if you would mind helping me."

It was only business. It wasn't as if he were asking her for a real date, as if he wanted to be with her for herself alone, but Jenny felt thrilled nevertheless. She blushed, radiant.

"Why, yes, Blade. I'd be happy to, that is if Maria doesn't have plans to go out." Jenny said that last just so she wouldn't sound too eager.

It was a perfect evening for a hayride. The sun was sinking in a haze of pink gold, and the full moon was yellow as it came up on the opposite horizon. The air smelled of sweet budding flowers and tart, fragrant juniper.

Adults and children clambered, laughing, into the wagon after Jenny collected their tickets and passed out their name tags. Though Blade had scarcely spoken to her since she'd arrived, his smile of greeting had left her as breathless and as excited as though she were a young girl with her first crush. Indeed, she felt young, giddily, delightfully young, as she'd never felt when she'd actually been young.

When the wagon was loaded and Jenny had finished listing the safety rules, she was about to take her place in the hay with the guests, but Blade came to her. She felt the light, possessive pressure of his fingers at her elbow, and her heart leaped at his touch.

"I need you to ride up front with me, Jenny, if you don't mind. To show me the way," he explained in that low voice that set off vibrations deep within her.

She nodded, feeling weak with joy at his invitation.

Odd, Blade saying that, when he'd grown up on Zachery Ranch, and still knew every inch of it better than any living human being. She was too thrilled to question him, however, too radiantly happy when he helped her up on the seat beside him to say anything that might cause him to change his mind.

They rode in silence, each wishing the other would speak, until at last Jenny did.

"This makes me remember how it was when we were kids," she said softly. "Do you remember Caleb always letting Dad bring the church youth group out here for our annual hayrides?"

Blade remembered only too well. He remembered how alone, how shut out he'd felt when he'd watched all the kids pile into the hay. He remembered the way they'd teased each other and acted silly, their manner so young and carefree in a way he'd never been young. Some secret part of him had longed to be one of them, however much he'd tried to deny it. Hell, sometimes Blade thought he'd been born grown up. Or was it just that Jamie's beating him and neglecting him had done that?

Blade said nothing, not wanting to remind Jenny of the chasm that had always separated them.

"We used to sing songs and kiss, and giggle about it all. Why is it that songs always sound the best when you're outside, when you're young and caught up in the excitement of what seems like an adventure?''

Blade didn't know quite what she was talking about, but he liked the sound of her voice in the darkness and the pleasant sensation of her nearness.

"Blade, how come you'd never go with us back then? Dad always begged you to, and remember that time I asked you, too? But you wouldn't come that night, either."

Blade remembered how she'd come up to the ranch house especially to ask him. That had been before he'd moved into the apartment above the garage. Jenny had always been nice to him. He'd been showering when he'd heard the door, and he'd answered it wearing only a pair of jeans. When he'd seen Jenny standing there in the soft light of the porch, looking so pretty in her dress of gingham and ruffles, his heart had seemed to stop and then start up again in a fierce rush of youthful, painful excitement. He'd been about to duck back inside after his shirt. It had seemed too intimate, too dangerous somehow, standing half dressed when they were alone at the house. But she'd called him back in that shy, sweet way of hers that he could never resist.

"Please don't go, Blade."

"I was only going after my shirt," he'd said gruffly.

She'd spoken softly. "I like you like that. I think you're beautiful, you know."

Then she'd turned red at her boldness, and that made her seem even prettier to him. And it made what she'd said even sexier, somehow. Imagine a girl like Jenny Wakefield liking to look at him and being scared of those feelings, but brave enough, nevertheless, to speak her mind. He'd noticed how she went on looking at him despite her shyness. He'd liked the feel of those hot green eyes too much, and it was that night that he'd first begun to think he couldn't live if he couldn't have her.

"I only came up to tell you all the kids are down at the barn, ready for the hayride," she said. "Won't you come, too? You never have, you know, and this is our senior year and your last chance."

"You should leave me alone, preacher's daughter." The thrill he felt at her asking him made his voice sound rough, and he had to make an effort to conceal his feelings. "Don't you know what everyone says about me?"

"I know. But I don't believe half of it."

"Maybe you should."

"Maybe." She batted her lashes in that shy way of hers that charmed him. "And maybe not. Maybe you're not half so tough and mean as everybody says. If you're so mean, Blade Taylor, why do you go out when it's freezing and help cows with their birthings? Why did you tend that sick calf day and night for three weeks straight, 'til Caleb made you stop because you got sick yourself? Why are you afraid to stand out here in front of me without your shirt? No, I don't think you're mean and tough. I think you're shy and scared. You're a coward, same as me."

"I'm no coward!" he'd yelled down at her through the screen, but inside he knew she was right. He was scared of not fitting in with people, of the other kids and what they said when his back was turned. And she was right about his shirt, too. He'd wanted it because it seemed safer somehow to be around her with the barrier of all his clothes between them, and he respected her more than any girl he knew. He was uncomfortable with her knowledge of him; it was an invasion of his inner self.

Without thinking, he'd shoved the screen door open angrily, and he'd stepped out onto the porch.

"You shouldn't have come up here, preacher's daughter," he said mockingly. "'Cause you're wrong about me. I'm not like your friends at the barn."

"I know."

Her voice was sweet and soft and sexy. Suddenly all his anger was gone and in its place was that powerful emotion he felt for her that was always just beneath the surface, the emotion he'd always fought to hide.

She didn't try to run when he pulled her into his arms and crushed her slim body between the porch pillar and his own young, muscular frame. She smelled of rose water and other delicious feminine fragrances, and he'd groaned as his need for her rose within him. It was hell being male and young and wanting so badly a girl who was innocent and virginal.

"This is crazy, you know, a guy like me wanting a girl like you. But I do. I always have."

He felt like a fool, pouring his heart out to her. He was as corny as any soap opera character. Tough Blade Taylor. He never said things like that to a girl.

But Jenny was different. She had always been so special to him.

He stared at her and was dazzled by her youthful beauty. Her pale skin was aglow, and the silken masses of her brown hair framed the loveliness of her face. She was exquisite, small and gracefully slender, with rounded, firm breasts that swelled temptingly against her dress. He felt them rise and fall slowly against his bare chest with her every breath. Oh, she was sweet, sweet torture, but he couldn't let her go.

His arms were around her narrow waist, and he lifted her from the porch floor, bringing her hard against his strong body. He bent his head and kissed her full on the lips. He explored her soft, surprised mouth without any hurry even though his entire body was suffused with surging desire.

He knew enough about women to know that Jenny, for all her innocence and purity, was more hotly responsive than any girl he'd ever kissed. Her lips were trembling beneath his. There was that magic of touching and being touched by the other between them, that rarity of bonding that exists between a man and the right woman.

"Open your mouth," he instructed.

She moaned, then obeyed so that his tongue could thrust deeply inside.

When one of his hands slid to her breast, she held herself very still, like a frightened fawn, and then ever so tentatively she leaned into the cup of his fingers as if she wanted the intimacy of his hands on her body more than she wanted anything. She was breathless from his kisses, from his holding and caressing her, and he felt her fingertips in his hair. She felt her other palm running wonderingly across the expanse of his broad shoulders. At last she pulled away, as if the touch of him was too exquisite to endure. Though his every instinct cried out to him to stop her, he loosened his hold.

"Oh, Blade, Blade—" She sighed, her sweet voice whispery and passionate, her green eyes darkly afire.

She did a strange thing then. She placed one of her small hands on either side of his face, framing it as if it were very dear to her, as if she truly loved him. Though it was a powerful eroticism, her caressing him like that with such tenderness, he did not kiss her again or press her close as he wanted to.

"Blade, if you're bad, then what am I? I shouldn't be here like this. I should hate it when you kiss me, loving Dean as I do. He's asked me to marry him as soon as we graduate, and I'm going to. But why do I keep thinking of you? Why does it make me feel so strange just to look at you? So you see, Blade Taylor, I know all about being bad, 'cause I'm just as bad as you."

She'd begun to cry then, just as Dean came around from the back of the house. Dean took one look at his shirtless brother and his girlfriend in tears and caught the passionate undercurrents of the scene. Not understanding them, his mind leaped to the nastiest possible conclusion.

"Did he try to hurt you, Jenny? Or treat you like one of his girls?" Dean hollered. "Because if he did, I'll—"

Jenny instantly rallied and stepped between them. "No, of course not, Dean."

"It'd be just like him!"

"What the hell have you ever known about me, Dean Zachery?" Blade cried, stung by his brother's accusation, and by the strange jealousy that Dean's protective arms around Jenny provoked.

"It's all my fault, Dean," Jenny said quietly. "I came up here to invite him on the hayride, and he said—"

"What did you do a fool thing like that for?" Dean demanded, suddenly angry at Jenny. "Haven't I told you often enough what he's like?"

At that Blade jumped toward his brother with clenched fists, but before he reached him, Jenny's hand came up, touching his bare arm ever so lightly, her green eyes huge and pleading when they met his.

"Please, Blade, don't fight him. He's just mad, and so are you. I can't bear to be the cause of trouble between you."

Funny, how her soft plea had taken all the anger out of him. "All right," he replied gruffly, and without a word he'd gone back inside the house, though it hurt like hell, leaving her like that with Dean. Later, he imagined her buried deep in a pile of hay with Dean kissing her in all the soft, sweet places Blade had wanted to explore with his lips, and that had hurt even more.

Blade had gone out that night, but none of the girls he'd found and none of the wild things they'd done to pleasure him had made him forget the way a preacher's daughter had told him that she liked him without a shirt, that she liked him holding her and kissing her, and thought she was bad because she did.

It was then that his desire for her had started to consume him like the slow smoldering of a spark before it bursts into flame. He was that spark, ready to burst. It was then that he began to seek her out so that she would talk to him in her shy, sweet way, so he could feel the heat of her gaze as she watched him when she thought he didn't notice. Not long afterward she'd ridden over on horseback to Zachery Ranch, claiming that she was looking for Dean, though Blade was practically certain he'd heard Dean tell her over the phone he would be in Austin all that day.

Blade had offered to ride with her part of the way home across the Zachery land. Deliberately, he'd suggested that they stop to talk beneath the shade by Cypress Creek, and all too soon he'd taken her into his arms and kissed her in a slow, hot way that aroused them both and showed them the scorching power of the youthful desire that was between them.

They'd made love that afternoon, and she'd cried afterward, making him feel terrible for what he'd done. Maybe if she hadn't cried and acted so frightened and ashamed of herself, he wouldn't have felt so awful. But he'd felt ashamed, too. Imagine tough Blade Taylor's conscience hurting because he'd taken a girl who'd been as willing as any he'd ever had.

After that he'd stayed out of her way, hating himself for his monstrous selfishness, for taking her that way when she really loved Dean.

"You're very quiet tonight, Blade," Jenny said softly, bringing him back to the present, back to the roar of the tractor and the laughter and singing of the hotel guests in the hay wagon that rumbled behind them, but most of all back to her gentle presence beside him.

"I was thinking back to when we were kids," was all he said.

Things hadn't changed. Not really. He wondered if they ever would.

Blade slanted a sidelong glance at Jenny. She seemed just as unreachable as ever, and his wanting her was still the same.

What in the hell was he going to do about it?

Six

Blade drove on, and Jenny noted that not once did he ask her for directions as the tractor jolted down the road in the velvet, star-brightened darkness. When they reached the wide grassy spot by the creek where the barbecue cookout and dance were to be held, Jenny saw that, as always, lanterns had been hung in the low branches of the oaks above the wooden and concrete platform that was used as a dance floor. Resort workers were bustling around the barbecue pits. Long tables swathed in red-and-white-checkered tablecloths had been placed near the creek and bandstand. Almost immediately the band began to play familiar country-and-western music, and the guests began to sing along enthusiastically.

Blade helped Jenny down, and without a word to each other they went to work. Jenny gave directions to the guests, pointing the way to the rest rooms and the bar and to the tables of hors d'oeuvres.

As the party progressed, and Blade continued to avoid her, Jenny's spirits sank. It seemed to her that nothing had changed between them, that Blade hadn't wanted her with him tonight after all. She'd been foolish to hope.

It hurt the way all the female guests between the ages of eight and eighty flocked around Blade, but what hurt the most was the way he seemed to enjoy their attentions. He laughed and joked with every woman—every woman except her. At the moment he was dancing beneath the trees with a pretty girl named Louise, who couldn't have been a day over twenty. Her raven head rested dreamily on Blade's shoulder, and her eyes were closed.

Jenny shuddered with the painful throb of her jealousy and decided it was foolish and masochistic to watch them. She decided to try and find something to occupy herself. As she turned to go to the buffet line, she found herself facing Ross Jackson, a wealthy hotel guest from San Antonio. He was middle-aged and a little overweight, but oddly charismatic nonetheless.

He grinned broadly. "You're just the little lady I was looking for. Would you like to dance, Mrs. Zachery?"

Usually Jenny avoided dancing with the resort guests, but as she slanted her eyes toward the couple beneath the trees, the pain she felt at the sight made her say lightly, "Why, I'd like that, Ross, very much."

Ross was a big talker, and he continued to talk even while he danced.

"I'm mighty impressed with your resort, little lady. Mighty impressed. So impressed, in fact, that I'm very tempted to invest in a couple of lots and that town house that's up for resale."

"Why, thank you, Ross."

"That Blade Taylor seems to have a level head on his shoulders, despite what a few people say."

Jenny tensed at the mention of Blade and at the hint that he was being criticized in town. Would the gossiping about Blade never cease? When would people learn that he was just ordinary, like everybody else?

"He's very capable and very hardworking, and he always has been," Jenny said in Blade's defense. "No matter what people say."

"That's the way he struck me—but when I was in town that's not what I heard. Folks are mad about him popping up, claiming half of what's yours and your child's."

"It's none of their business, Ross," Jenny said grimly.

"You're mighty quick to defend him," Ross said perceptively. "Mighty quick. I wonder—"

"Don't! He's my brother-in-law! That's all. And my partner. I don't like the way people around here always talk about other people's business. Once they start on someone they never seem to stop. They've been talking about Blade since the day he was born."

"I guess that's the way with most small towns, in Texas, anyway. But, little lady, if I were you and I didn't like people talking, I'd at least make him move out of that garage apartment, and quick. People are talking about that, you know."

"What?"

Ross's expression was gentle. "Well, what would you expect in a town like this? They're talking about him living out there all alone with you."

Jenny flushed with anger, not at Ross, but at the thought of the malicious gossip going on behind her back. She was remembering the speculative glances she'd received of late. Until this moment she hadn't thought much about it.

Fortunately, the music ended. Jenny was so upset she couldn't have danced another step. In fact, she was so upset that she had to go off by herself for a minute before she could face people again.

When Ross left her she didn't return to the party. Instead, she walked along the path beside the creek until it meandered into a steep, wide bank near some smooth rocks. She sat down on a rock and stared unseeingly at the silvery water as it rippled in a glistening cascade over a man-made dam.

Why were people so cruel? Why did they want to think the worst of Blade, and now of her?

But it *was* true in a way, what they were saying, a tiny little voice whispered.

Not anymore. Not anymore. Blade hadn't even looked at her in weeks. And that was more painful and humiliating than anything. More painful even than the gossip.

In the darkness she didn't see Blade's careful approach. The gurgling of the creek and the whine of violins in the distance concealed the sound of his footsteps on the rocky path.

Blade's voice came to her, hushed and vibrant and achingly masculine.

"Jenny—"

Her heart began to pound jerkily. She hadn't wanted him to find her like this. Still, she couldn't stop herself from responding to his gentleness.

"Over here," she replied dully.

"You okay?"

"Sure."

"You don't sound it. Did Ross make a pass at you? Because if he did—"

"Don't be ridiculous. All he said was that he was impressed by what you've done here since you've come back. He's thinking of investing in a lot or two and a town house."

"Jenny, that's wonderful. I don't need to tell you how much we need the capital we'd realize from a sale like that."

Blade moved closer, and then she could see him in the moonlight. His hair was silver fire as it tumbled against his dark face. He was so tall, so magnificently lean and broad-shouldered. As always she felt excited just at being alone with him, and she ached for his arms to close around her, for his body to press into hers so that she could feel the warm, muscular power of him. But all he thought about these days was the resort and making money, she remembered with a flash of resentment. He avoided her and sought other women like Louise, the girl he'd been dancing with.

"Yes. It's just great," Jenny said flatly, turning away from him.

"What happened, then, to upset you?" Blade persisted.

"Would you just go away and leave me alone?"

"No."

His voice was right behind her now, and the sympathy in it made her heart rush.

His fingers closed gently upon her shoulders, and the thrill she felt at his touch was almost painful.

"Jenny—"

Why was it that just the way he said her name could make her feel so pleasantly warm, so sexily female?

"Girl, is it impossible for us to talk?"

"That's what they say about you, isn't it?" she lashed out irrationally. "That you can't talk to a woman. That you can only use her in a physical way."

"Where in the hell is all this coming from?" he demanded, the first trace of anger entering his low tone.

"Just go back to the party."

"You're gonna tell me what's wrong because I'm not leaving 'til you do." His fingertips played with her hair, and she felt herself going as soft as mush at his nearness.

She whirled, angered at both herself and him for the ease of her responsiveness to him, angered still more when she remembered the way he'd danced with the other girl. "All right, since you insist. Ross said people in town were talking about you and me, about us living out here alone together. And I don't like it!"

He went white in the moonlight, his tanned face as pale and sickly as bleached bone, and that shuttered look that she hated was in his eyes.

"So that's it." His voice was no longer soft, but harsh and filled with anger. His fingers tightened on her arms. "Things never change, do they?"

"I don't suppose they do. Not around here, anyway," she replied in a low, dreary voice.

"It must be awful for you, your name being linked with mine. You told me the first night I came out here that you didn't want me living on the ranch because people would talk."

Had she said that? His voice sounded so odd, almost as though he were hurt. Had she hurt him by saying that? Did he care for her after all?

"Blade, sometimes I say things I don't mean."

"Or maybe you do mean them. Beneath the surface maybe you're just like everybody else in Zachery Falls, ready to think the worst of me, ready to think that I'm so depraved I can't keep my hands off a decent woman even if she happens to be my sister-in-law. Sometimes I think I'm a damned fool for coming back here and working my guts out to save the ranch for you and Cathy."

She turned to him in wonder, and her eyes met the glittering darkness of his.

"Blade, is that why you came back—to help me?"

"I thought you believed the gossip about me," he ground out fiercely as he dragged her into his arms, pulling her against his body. "That I don't do anything for anybody except myself, that I came back to take the ranch and maybe use you for a while in the bargain. The hell with them," he said bitterly. "The hell with everyone in Zachery Falls! I'm sick of them turning my life inside out and making me into what I'm not." His hands moved over her in angry possession. "You're mine. You've always been mine. They're right, you know, in a way. I came back because I wanted you. I came back to take what's always been mine. Maybe it's time I did."

The sensual curve of his mouth was cruel and terrifying as he bent closer.

"Blade, don't." She wanted him, but not like this, not when he was angry and determined to be deliberately hateful. She reached up to place her hand placatingly on his chest.

"Why the hell not?" He seized her hand in his and brought it roughly to his mouth, kissing her wrist with passionate anger until she trembled from the touch of his lips. She knew that he felt the leap of her pulse beneath his mouth. "And what would people say if they knew the whole truth?" he began, his velvet voice very male and cynical. "If they knew how you tempted me with your kisses and your wildness? If they knew how you teased me and then hid behind your damnable ladylike virtue and hypocrisy? If they knew that you wanted the man they all despise and that you were too cowardly to own up to the wanting?"

"Blade—"

"Shut up, Jenny. Maybe people are right after all. Maybe a man like me can't put things into words with a woman. Maybe a man like me has no use for talking at all, no use for anything but taking and using a woman the way she was made to be used. You're a woman, Jenny Zachery, for all your attempts to pretend otherwise. Maybe it's time I made you *my* woman."

Blade's arms crushed her slim body hard against his own. His mouth claimed hers at last with a kind of wild, desperate urgency. For a month he'd left her alone because he'd thought that was what she wanted, and he'd had no other women, though there had been plenty who had chased after him. What Jenny had said about hating to hear her name linked with his enraged him. He was filled with frustrated desire, filled with anger that he couldn't have her, that no matter what he did to please her she was determined to humble him. He kissed her again and again with hard, bruising lips, not caring if he hurt her, if he shamed her. Did *she* care when she shamed him with her insults?

Jenny braced her hands against his chest and shoved at him furiously, but her efforts were insignificant against his superior strength.

He laughed softly in the darkness. "Girl, don't you know that your fighting me is only adding to my pleasure?" he murmured as he felt her soft hips squirm against his hardened body.

"How dare you be so insolent?" she cried.

"And why shouldn't I dare, being the man I am? Especially after the way you've teased me with your soft beauty and your hot eyes and your damnable virtue. If you were anyone else I would have taken you by now."

His arms were like iron bands imprisoning her. He forced her mouth to open and admit his tongue so that it could mate with hers. Again and again Blade forced Jenny to accept the bold intimacy of his mouth, the wanton caresses of his hands as they slid over her. His fingers unbuttoned her blouse and slid the edges aside so that his hands could knead the soft flesh of her breasts.

Jenny felt as though she would faint with desire as his mouth continued its assault upon her lips and throat with long, flaming kisses, his tongue flicking along the base of her earlobe. He pushed her blouse down over her arms and it fell to the ground. He held her bra beneath her breasts so that it cupped them into rounded globes that sprang enticingly forward, their pink nipples so temptingly succulent he could not long resist lowering his mouth to feast upon them.

"Don't. Oh, Blade, don't!" she cried as his lips came nearer, but when he nuzzled his head gently between her breasts, the pleasure was almost more than Jenny could stand. She moaned and buried her hands in his rich golden hair as she felt his tongue slide in a rough caress against the tips of her breasts, stroking them, licking them until spasms of longing made her forget all save the raw quivering of her skin beneath his tongue and the warm whisper of his ragged breath as it fell upon her flesh. His fierce wild anger burned through her as passionately and as primitively as did his desire, and everything he did dissolved her pious resolve to fight him.

She shouldn't let him do these things when there was no love between them, when it seemed almost that he hated her. But she scarcely knew who she was or who he was, so lost was she in this new, strange world of swaying rapture. She only knew that she ached for his touch and for his kisses, that she reveled in the savage hunger he had for her.

At last he lifted his mouth from her body. Bereft at the loss of his warmth, she stumbled backward against a huge rock. He was shaking and breathing hard, but he made no move to touch her again. It was as if he knew that if he did, he would not be able to stop himself from taking her.

"Do you know what it does to me to want you and to know you don't think I'm good enough for you? This may surprise you, Jenny Zachery, but loving you would be no good for me either, with you despising yourself and me for what's always been between us." He ran his hands wearily through his golden hair in an agitated motion. "Nothing's changed since you slept with me ten years ago and then married Dean because you thought I was trash."

"But that's not why I married Dean."

"The hell it isn't. You may want me in bed, but out of it you want a man like Dean or Kilpatrick at your side. I'm good enough for a secret affair but not good enough to be seen with. Oh, I know my place, Jenny girl. It's a wound that's raw and burns like hellfire deep inside me. You hate the way you feel about me, and that makes me feel worse than anything anyone else in Zachery Falls could ever say or do.''

With that, he turned and left her staring after him feeling more terribly forlorn than she'd ever felt in her life.

Stooping, she reached for her blouse to cover herself. She was on fire from the wondrous feelings his touch had aroused, yet he actually believed that she scorned his touch, that she thought him beneath her.

Oh, but he was wrong. That wasn't how she felt at all, but would he ever give her the chance to tell him? And would he believe her if she did?

Seven

Blade returned to the ranch house and stormed up the stairs to his apartment. He arrived home long before Jenny, because after he'd left her she had put herself back together and rejoined the party as if nothing out of the ordinary had happened, as if she weren't upset in the least.

Was she so icy, so untouchable? Her calm was unendurable when his own emotions were in such chaotic fury.

He had asked one of the waiters to drive the tractor back, because after his outburst with Jenny in the woods, Blade knew he was incapable of suffering through the rest of the cookout with the women joking lightly and teasing him, with the music and dancing. But most of all it was Jenny's presence that drove him to seek the sanctuary of his spartan room while he was plunged into his own private hell.

Damnation! How was it that a woman could crawl under a man's skin and cling there for all eternity? There was no losing her, no fighting her. It seemed he'd always been shackled to her. Even when he kissed her in frustration and fury, she could make his blood boil with desire as other women far more beautiful and willing could not. What was it Jenny had? It shook him to the core of his being, this blind, insane wanting. But then, Jenny had always been able to do that to him. Only to-night he hated her for it, and he hated himself as well for the need that consumed him.

He wished he were back in the marines, a million miles from Zachery Falls and Jenny. But then the memories came flooding back, memories of dirt and flies and the incessant roar of artillery, the stench of oil burning, the feel of a tiny body limp in his arms—all these things came flooding back with shattering force, and as always he deliberately shut the war and all its horror out. He did not wish to be back there at all. He wanted to be home and at peace.

And what he wanted most of all was Jenny beneath him in his bed. He wanted her naked body clinging to his, her silken brown hair rippling across his pillow and entwined in his fingers, the scents of their bodies mingled, the essence of his manhood plunged deep within her. He wanted to hear her whisper love words and moan with passion as she writhed and twisted in his arms. He wanted her to need him as he needed her. He imagined her begging him for the pleasure he could give her, pleading for the ecstasy of his lovemaking, and feeling unashamed about his loving her.

He suppressed the tantalizing vision because it made his blood rise again with desire that would never be satisfied. What a joke it all was, really. Blade laughed bitterly, mocking himself. How everyone in Zachery Falls would laugh if they knew the truth: that tough Blade Taylor, who'd always had a way with women, was pining after a preacher's daughter he couldn't have. It was only what he so richly deserved for all his badness, they would have said, and maybe it was.

Blade pushed open the door and stepped inside. The room smelled of cigarette smoke and a rich, stifling perfume that was all too familiar to him. The tip of a cigarette glowed in the darkness near his bed.

"I thought you'd never come home," Susan purred throatily. "I've been waiting for you, Blade."

"So I see," came his dry reply. "I didn't notice your car."

"It's out back, behind the garage. I didn't want to block the drive. Besides, I wanted to surprise you."

"Well, you certainly did."

"Cigarette?"

"Don't mind if I do."

He went over to the bed, knelt, and struck a match. In the light of the flame their eyes met, and hers were heavy with invitation and desire. The dress she wore was low cut, and had a slit that exposed one thigh. She curved her leg, and his hot gaze slid down the length of it as he stood up again.

Oh, Lord, he thought wearily.

"You haven't called me, Blade. Not in a long time."

Blade had never liked being chased, but then, women like Susan never understood that sort of reticence in a man. "I've been busy," he said mildly.

"Who'd ever have thought Caleb would have left part of the ranch to you in his will? Why didn't you come back to stay after he died, Blade?"

"There wasn't any reason to. Dean was here, taking care of things."

"So you're a rich man. Funny how things work out."

"Life's a joke, all right," Blade agreed in a lazy voice, dragging deeply on his cigarette. "And mine more than most." Only he didn't feel like laughing. Not at the moment, anyway.

"Aren't you even just a little bit glad I came all the way out here to see you tonight, Blade?" she asked ever so silkily, seeking to draw his attention back to herself. "I've been missing you."

She reached out and laid a hand on his sleeve, and he felt the imprint of her soft fingers burn his arm. He stared at the slender hand clutching him, surprised at his lack of response.

His need for Jenny was still a hot, churning force inside him, and Susan's invitation couldn't have been more blatant. Susan was beautiful, ripe and blond and lush, more beautiful than Jenny, really. He knew too well the pleasure Susan could give him, but he did not want her. His gaze wandered again over her sexily exposed leg.

Susan *was* lovely. But Blade, for all his need of a woman, felt only a deep reluctance toward Susan. Because despite his anger toward Jenny, it was Jenny he loved, Jenny he wanted. And he didn't want Jenny finding Susan here in his room.

"Susan," he began gently. He had no wish to hurt her.

He sat down on the bed beside her to explain again what he'd told her that first afternoon, that they could only be friends. But she misinterpreted his coming to her, and she swayed toward him, her arms encircling his broad shoulders. Before he could say or do anything to stop her, she'd leaned forward and kissed him.

Jenny parked in front of the house and sat in the darkness for a long while, trying to get up the nerve to go over to Blade's room. There would never be an easier time to face him than now, she supposed. She glanced up at his window and saw a faint glimmer of light behind the shade. His Bronco was in the drive.

She had to convince him that he was wrong about her, and explain that she'd been wrong as well. She hadn't known how he'd felt, and because she hadn't known, she'd unwittingly hurt him. She had to make him understand that she didn't think of him the way he thought she did; it was her own feelings that confused her and made her feel guilty, not his bad reputation. She'd never believed in that, anyway.

As she climbed the narrow stairs, her heart beat faster with fear at the thought of facing him. He had been so formidably angry at the cookout. She felt anguished at the thought that he might never forgive her for what she'd done.

His door was ajar, and she peered inside uncertainly, feeling shy and more afraid than ever. The hand she lifted to push the door open farther froze in midair. What she saw in the dim light made her blood run cold.

Everything seemed to blacken like burning paper crinkling in a dark fire, and for an instant, she thought she would faint. She couldn't tear her eyes from the sight of Blade and Susan on the bed, kissing. Jenny saw Susan's arms twined around Blade's broad back, and the long curve of her naked leg. They were still dressed, but it took no imagination to know where a kiss between a man like Blade Taylor and a woman like Susan Harper would inevitably lead.

Somehow Jenny managed to stumble backward in silence. She felt sick with confusion, jealousy, and betrayal. It seemed unbelievable to Jenny that Blade had made love to her so passionately in the woods and then gone to Susan as if his feelings for her meant nothing. Oh, how could he? How could he?

So, everybody was right about him. Any woman would do for him as long as she could be had easily. Only a fool would go and fall in love with a man like him—because all Blade would do was break such a woman's heart.

Was she in love with him? Jenny squashed that idea at once. Of course she wasn't. Love was a noble emotion, not the surging of meaningless passion that she felt for Blade. But the anguish she felt was as real as if she were truly in love.

Tears blinded Jenny as she ran to the house and shut herself inside her own room. How naive she was to have believed in Blade even for a moment, to have believed that there was anything fine and noble in his coming back and helping her with the ranch. What a laugh. The worst was that even after finding Susan in his arms, Jenny still wanted him with that same aching need, and it was even stronger than before.

A sound on the stair made Blade remember himself, and he finally managed to disengage Susan's arms. Pushing her away, he stood up.

"You'd better go, Susan," was all he said.

"Go?" She stared at him incredulously and slid her leg along the bed to bring his attention to it.

"There can't ever be anything between us," he said hoarsely, thinking himself insane for not making love to Susan when he was in such acute need of a woman.

"Blade, you can't mean that."

"But I do. I told you before I only wanted to be friends."

"I know, but—"

"Believe me, Susan, you deserve someone who can love you. And I can't. You ought to try and work things out with Bill."

"I don't want Bill, if I can have you. Is there someone else?" When he said nothing, she spoke slyly. "It's true what they're saying in town, isn't it? That it's Jenny Zachery you want. And maybe you've already had her."

"Don't talk about her," he snapped, admitting nothing, but his fierce anger told Susan she'd hit upon the truth.

"So it *is* Jenny!" Susan jumped up angrily. "You think you're too good for me now, don't you? Because I have a traveling job and kids I see every other weekend. Isn't that a laugh, Blade Taylor thinking he's better than Susan Harper!"

"I think you'd better be going, Susan."

"What can you possibly see in a woman as spineless as Jenny Zachery? She doesn't even know what to do with a man like Mike Kilpatrick, much less a full-blooded male like you. Well, I feel sorry for you, Blade Taylor," Susan finished spitefully, "the way you've always hated all the goody-goody gossips of Zachery Falls, because she's the worst of the lot. I'll bet she despises you and always will."

"I think you've said more than enough," Blade said grimly.

From the bleak look on his handsome face, Susan took cruel satisfaction in the belief that she had. Then she walked out and banged the door shut behind her.

The rest of the weekend passed dismally for Jenny. She had accepted a date with Mike to go to the town's annual dance. Mike was as nice as always, but being with him and realizing how empty she felt away from Blade only made Jenny feel worse than ever. She noticed for the first time that people were staring at her, newly curious about her because of Blade, but only one person was bold enough to say anything. Cindy Ruthers was a sly, plump girl with an envious, gossipy nature, and she waited until Mike was at the bar with the men, leaving Jenny alone.

"Didn't expect to see you with Mike ever again," Cindy said, her voice furtive and eager as she walked up to Jenny.

Cindy had never been one of Jenny's friends, and Jenny turned on her defensively. "Why not?"

"Well, you know folks are saying that you and Blade—"

"You shouldn't pay attention to gossip," Jenny snapped.

"It's hard for a girl not to listen when the talk's about a man like Blade. But then you'd be one to know what I mean."

"I don't like gossip, and it's not true. Blade's not bad."

"I wasn't saying he was." Beneath the crop of frizzy ringlets that seemed to sprout from her forehead, Cindy's black eyes were bright and avid.

"Then what are you saying, Cindy Ruthers?"

"I was only wondering what it's like, you and he out there all alone when he's always been one for the women."

"Since you know so much, you should realize that Blade has no need to make up to a stick like me when he could have any woman, especially when all the other women in town are so much more interested in him than I am."

"Oh, I wouldn't be so sure of that," Cindy said.

"We're business partners, Blade and I. That's all, and he has as much right to live on the ranch as I do. As for being alone with him, I practically never see him. He works all the time. And Maria lives in the house with me and Cathy, and then there's everyone else at the resort."

Cindy looked at her, and her sharp black eyes were round with disbelief. "Well, Jenny, all it takes is a match to make a stick catch fire, and Blade Taylor's pure dynamite." And with that she walked away, leaving Jenny alone once more.

Jenny went to church on Sunday morning. After the service she ate lunch with Mike and his friends at the Bluebonnet Café. That afternoon she drove into San Antonio and took Cathy to the zoo. All weekend she tried not to think of Blade, but the memory of seeing him with Susan was a constant torment.

Jenny saw little of Blade during the week that followed, although she was deeply aware of him when she did. He seemed as determined to avoid her as she was to avoid him. For that at least she should have been thankful, but of course she wasn't. She kept wondering where he was and who he was with, and despite her determination to hate him, she longed to see him.

* * *

The next Saturday afternoon, before she was to get ready for yet another date with Mike, she saw a double horse trailer parked near the barn. When she went to investigate, she found Blade slowly leading a black thoroughbred stallion with the look of the devil in his eyes down the length of the corral.

"Blade, what are you doing?" she asked in surprise as she stepped inside the corral and watched him struggle with the horse, talking soothingly all the while. She watched with fascination the ripple of muscles along Blade's broad back, as well.

They were magnificent, the horse and the man, two splendid male specimens, each as wild and determined to have his way as the other. Each was a challenge to the other.

"Keep clear of Mac, Jenny. He's half wild from not having been ridden in over a year. I bought him and a mare at that cattle sale I went to two weeks ago. They've just been delivered. You'll enjoy the mare—Red, they called her—but I'll have to tame Mac—if that's even possible—before I can ride him."

"Mac. That's a strange name for a horse."

"He's a strange horse, and not noted for the most pleasant of dispositions."

"But Mac?"

"It stands for Machiavelli. You may remember that a few hundred years ago there was a certain unscrupulously cunning and rather deceptive Italian statesman—"

"Oh, dear."

"Mac has more in common with that individual than his name, I'm afraid."

He ignored Jenny after that and concentrated on the horse, talking gently, stroking the sleek black neck. Blade knew horses as well as he knew women, and if Mac could be gentled, he was the man who could do it. As she watched him work with the horse, Jenny forgot for a moment her fierce rage and her feelings of humiliation over his involvement with Susan, and longed for him to speak as softly and to touch her as gently as he caressed the horse. But he continued to ignore her, until finally she remembered that she wanted to set her hair before her date with Mike.

As she was leaving the corral she accidentally brushed against three long boards that were leaning against the fence. The lumber had been stacked there carelessly by Chuck, who had been planning to use the boards to patch a hole in the barn wall. The heavy boards crashed to the ground in a thunderous clatter, and Jenny jumped aside so they would not strike her.

From behind her she heard Mac's wild scream as he broke loose from Blade.

"Jenny, watch out!" Blade cried hoarsely.

She whirled in time to see Blade lunge in front of the horse to save her from being trampled. Hooves thudded heavily against flesh and earth and because of Blade's quick action the horse swerved, narrowly missing Jenny before he sprang forward and galloped past her out of the gate that she had opened.

Jenny gave no thought to the horse, but rushed over to where Blade lay on the ground. He sat up slowly, his mouth a thin, tight line that told her he was in pain. A trickle of blood ran the length of his cheek.

She knelt beside him in the dirt, touching his bruised and bloodied cheek with her fingertips.

"Blade, are you all right?" She was white and ill at the thought of how close he'd come to being ground into bloody pulp by the savage hooves. "Oh, Blade—"

"'All right,' is not exactly the way I'd describe how I'm feeling at the moment," he said a bit ruefully, rubbing his cheek. But he looked at her, and his blue eyes were as startlingly vivid as ever as he attempted one of his jaunty smiles.

His hand closed over hers tightly, and his expression was both fierce and gentle at the same time.

"That was close," he said, his grip tightening on her hand as if to assure himself of her safety. "Too damn close." She felt his hand shaking in hers, but she didn't know of the fear that tore at him inside when he thought of her being injured. "Stay away from the barn for now, until that demon is tamed," he said in abrupt dismissal.

He rose and helped her up as well. Then he moved past her, his strides long and easy, despite his aches and pains. She didn't know that he was leaving because his feelings for her were so intense that they were barely under control.

"Blade—"

He turned, and the sunshine was brilliant in his golden hair. She noted the bruise on his cheek and the dark stain on his shirt where the horse had knocked him to the ground. He could have been killed because of her. Blade killed! At the thought a feeling as dark as death itself wrenched her heart, and she realized how utterly lost she would feel if anything happened to him.

"You're not going after the stallion," she said desperately.

"I damn sure am."

"Please, Blade, you might get hurt."

The sympathy in her voice upset him, because any passion from her reminded him of the feelings she had for him that she did not want to have. His own emotions were raw and too near the surface, and he could not keep the anger out of his low tone.

"And why would you care about that, Jenny? Why aren't you inside getting ready for your date with Kilpatrick? I thought he was the type to arouse your womanly concern while I only arouse feelings you're ashamed of."

"How did you know about my date with Mike?" she asked weakly. His rough tone hurt her.

"Word travels fast around here. Or did you forget that there are no secrets in Zachery Falls? Maybe I should date someone myself, so people won't link us together. Why I haven't gotten involved with another woman since I came to live out here is beyond me."

"But you are!" she wanted to cry out, thinking of Susan. So he was a liar as well as a womanizer; doubtless he was several other equally detestable things as well.

"I guess it's the wisest thing," Blade continued, "your going out with Kilpatrick. Maybe it'll hush the talk about us, and you'll be able to hold up your head in town again." He smiled derisively. "Maybe, just maybe, you'll wash away the taint of your association with me."

Jenny was remembering how she'd felt when she'd seen him kissing Susan, and suddenly she was filled anew with hurt and resentment toward him. How could he chase women so casually? It was infuriating and humiliating to care so much for a man who cared nothing for her. Suddenly the need to hurt him as he had hurt her overwhelmed her.

"Yes," she agreed passionately. "I hope it will wash away the taint of you, Blade Taylor. Any woman would be proud to be seen with a man like Mike. He's a gentleman. He respects me. Whereas you . . . all you know how to do is drag a woman down to your own level until she has no self-respect or pride left."

Blade stood very still, and he looked at her for a long time as the breeze ruffled his golden hair. There was a taut intensity about him that unnerved her and made her feel ashamed of what she'd said. It did no good to think that he had driven her to say it because he'd made love to her that night and then been with Susan such a short time later. Suddenly Jenny felt afraid as Blade stalked toward her. The stillness was gone from his face and in its place was an angry violence.

Jenny stumbled as she tried to back away from him, but Blade caught her, yanking her against him.

"Wash this away if you can," he muttered as he brought his mouth down hard upon hers and forced the curves of her body to melt against his male contours. She felt the hard muscles of his thighs against her body, the power of his chest crushing her breasts. His lips were hot and familiar, his embrace deliberately insolent, but everything he did stirred a warm tide of delirious feeling that both bewildered and frightened her. She went limp, unresisting, as thrilling quivers coursed through her, and she forgot everything but Blade and his hands and mouth moving over her.

As always his lovemaking brought a familiar blaze of hunger to them both, even though she knew he was using her, demeaning her. He kissed her with slow, hot lips, and she shivered despite the warmth of the day. He arched her body against his own, and his mouth traveled down her throat to the hollow between her breasts.

His lips were like raw flames flicking her insides until she was molten with arousal. She moaned in surrender, and more than anything she longed for him to lift her into his arms and carry her to some private place and make love to her. She thought of the hayloft in the barn, plump and soft with fresh hay. But he didn't do that.

Very slowly he released her and pushed her away, but passion was throbbing in them both. His desire made him even angrier at himself and at her, while hers deepened her feelings of humiliation, because she believed she meant no more to him than Susan Harper did, and maybe not as much.

"I hate you," she said in a low voice choked with pain. "I won't be treated like one of your cheap women!"

"Won't you? You asked for that, you know. What in the hell did you think you were doing?" he demanded. "Coming out here, watching me all afternoon? Why the hell don't you stay away from me if you despise me? If you don't want my kisses? If you don't want me? I damn sure try to keep clear of you. Why don't you chase after Kilpatrick if he's the man you really want?"

Hurt, she was defiant. "That's exactly what I intend to do."

"And do *his* kisses make you feel like fainting? I could have taken you now, and you know it. As easily as I've ever taken any woman. More easily than some."

It galled her to hear the truth about herself put in such blunt terms, and she hated him for it. "There's no reason to compare yourself to Mike. You and he aren't in the same league at all. Mike's a gentleman," she replied, huffily as if that said everything.

Blade's lips curled. "So you've said, but I'm surprised that a girl of your unbridled, passionate nature doesn't find that a bit of a bore."

"How did you kn—" She caught herself in the nick of time. "You don't know me at all. Not really."

"Don't I?" His gaze was hot and impertinent, his smile knowing, and she realized that he was remembering that long ago afternoon he'd made love to her, when he'd explored every part of her with his mouth and tongue. "And I thought I knew you as well as any man," he said with a smile. Then he shrugged. "But nice as it is discussing some of my most cherished memories of you, I guess I'd better go after Mac before he gallops over the county line."

He was leaving. Dismissing her as though she were of no consequence. The desire to have the last word swelled within her breast.

"Blade Taylor, if you're stubborn enough to go after that horse, I hope he tramples you into the ground and makes raw meat of you," she cried, still furious.

He merely smiled sardonically. "How nice. And to think all these visions of homicide and gore come from the sweet, pure lips of a preacher's daughter."

"I hope you break your fool neck! I hope it snaps like a twig!"

He laughed curtly.

"I do!"

"Oh, I believe you, but you can save your insults, Jenny." His voice was silky. "You know, a man can only die once."

"Well, that's certainly a pity in your case."

"So I've been told," came his dry reply.

He grinned as she stormed past him toward the house. "Cheer up," he called. "This may be your lucky day. I may indeed be trampled into the dust by that four-legged beast. You can come to my funeral. That should really be a jolly event for you and everybody else in Zachery Falls. A pity I won't be there to enjoy making all of you so happy." She heard his laughter following her and quickened her pace.

All too soon she regretted her anger and her insults, but it was too late to apologize. He'd left immediately to search for Mac. As the hours dragged by and he did not return, she began to fret. Maybe a stray hoof had bashed him in the head and he was lying unconscious in a pasture somewhere. The thought made her tense and fearful, but when she considered going to look for him, she reminded herself of how ridiculous it was of her to care, and how humiliated she would feel if he wasn't hurt and he discovered her concern for him.

Oh, he was abominable, and she wished that he'd never come back. Her awareness of him was consuming her. She didn't know how to think anymore. She couldn't even act naturally. It was not her habit to be quarrelsome with anyone; why then did she quarrel with Blade?

Hours later, when Mike was driving her to the party, she saw Blade in the distance, a lonely, broadshouldered figure silhouetted against a bloodred horizon. He was leading the powerful Mac homeward. Deep relief washed through her at the knowledge that he was all right. It wasn't really so much that she cared about Blade that made her glad to see him safe, she told herself quickly. It was just that she would have felt guilty if she'd driven him to serious injury because she'd made him mad.

Jenny did not see Blade again for the rest of the weekend, and she knew that it was deliberate on his part. But she thought of him, and she wondered whose lips he kissed in the sultry darkness, whose body he pressed beneath his against some soft mattress. And when she thought about it, she felt like dying.

On Monday morning Jenny's stomach twisted with dread at the prospect of going to work and seeing Blade on a casual basis throughout the day. So she did the cowardly thing; she called in and said she was sick.

At ten o'clock, Jenny was outside playing with Cathy and Heidi in the backyard when she saw Blade's Bronco on the road, heading for the house. A sudden vision of him wrapped in Susan's arms momentarily engulfed her in pain. Then she forced herself to pick up the stuffed bear that Cathy had deliberately dropped in her favorite game of ut-oh. Absently Jenny handed the bear to the little girl, but her attention was riveted to the sound of the truck in the drive.

Blade strode around the corner of the house. His handsome face was dark with concern, but then his look of worry died, and he smiled at the sight of her playing with the golden-haired child. The anger he'd displayed on Saturday afternoon seemed to have vanished. Doubtless, Jenny tortured herself grimly, he'd lost it in the pleasure he'd found in another woman's arms.

Cathy ran from her mother and tumbled into Blade's strong brown arms, and Jenny almost envied her own daughter for the easiness she shared with her uncle. Blade laughed at the child and dropped her bear onto the ground for her. "Ut-oh," he said gently, and Cathy beamed at him before she stooped to retrieve the toy.

Over Cathy's curls, Blade spoke in a low voice to Jenny. "I thought you were sick."

Had he really been so concerned that he'd driven all the way back to the house to see about her? Jenny pushed that sudden, hopeful thought aside. Why was she always determined to see everything he did in such an eternally romantic light? Would she always be such a fool where one man with a rowdy fall of gold hair and a devilish grin and a terrible reputation was concerned?

"I didn't feel like working," she replied stiffly. "But since when is what I do any of your business?"

The light in his eyes died, and she hated the way he looked at her.

"I don't suppose it is," he said slowly. "I'm disappointed in you, though. Not that I haven't always known you were less than perfect. There's your temper, of course, and then there's—" His hot blue gaze slid over her with the look of a man who knew a wanton when he saw one, despite her false pretenses, and Jenny flushed with shame. "Well, suffice it to say that I'm well aware of many of your weaknesses, but this is a new one on me. I never realized you were a quitter."

Jenny compressed her lips in fury. She longed to upbraid him for his insolent glance and insinuations, but how could she, without seeming to be one to protest too much? "The hit dog hollers," her father had always said. "I'm *not* a quitter," she grumbled at last.

He stared at her in frank disbelief. "I don't blame you, though, for quitting. Not really. The resort is in a real mess. Sometimes I feel like giving up myself." He dropped the bear again and Cathy cooed with delight as she toddled after it.

"I'm not giving up!" she cried. "Can't you understand?"

"Oh, so you've decided to take my advice and that of everyone else in Zachery Falls and stay home and persuade this little minx to give up her thumb." He ruffled Cathy's curls and then lifted her high in his arms, teddy bear and all. "I see she's got it in her mouth as usual."

"Thumb, Uncle Blade!" Cathy squealed proudly.

"The hell you say!" Jenny exclaimed. "She's barely two, and she'll stop by herself when she has a mind to. I'm going to work right now."

"I thought you would, when I said that." He was laughing softly, and his laughter made her more furious than anything.

As Jenny drove in to work she knew that she had been tricked. He'd come out to the house and when he'd found her well, he'd goaded her into returning to work despite the fact that it was the last thing she wanted to do. He was insufferable.

Still, deep in that most secret place in her heart, Jenny was glad that he'd cared enough to come after her.

Eight

"**M**r. Taylor would like to see you in his office, Mrs. Zachery," Lilly said with a knowing smile that infuriated Jenny.

"All right," Jenny snapped. This was the fifteenth time she'd been summoned to Blade's office today, or that he'd come to hers on some bit of nonsense. She'd scarcely been able to get a thing done because of all the interruptions.

As she got up from her desk, Jenny was aware of Lilly watching her with a faintly disrespectful look of speculation. It was a look that everyone in Zachery Falls had these days when they glanced at her, even Mike.

Ever since that Monday morning when Blade had come to the ranch house and goaded her into returning to work, his attitude toward her had been blatantly different. Instead of avoiding her, he had begun to deliberately seek her out.

When he inspected the town houses, he insisted that she accompany him. After all, wasn't she his partner? Sometimes they would be alone together inside a town house for more than an hour while he made notes about one thing or another. All that time she would be thinking of the gossip that their being alone together would surely cause, because the maids would watch them go inside and wait to see when they came back out, as well.

Jenny wanted to say something to Blade, but somehow it was too embarrassing a subject to broach with him, especially when he did seem to be working so conscientiously to improve the resort. She could scarcely fault him for his enthusiasm for work that was benefiting so many people—including herself. Not when his efforts were beginning to pay off so handsomely. The monthly gross was steadily and rapidly rising. The resort itself hummed like a well-managed factory, and Blade was the cause of that hum. The staff was happier than they had ever been, and the resort guests constantly praised everything.

But why did he demand that she be with him constantly? Whenever Blade drove into Austin or San Antonio on resort business he invited her to accompany him, saying that he hated to make important decisions without her advice. When she tried to refuse such invitations, he would press her unmercifully until she accepted. Of course that was never too difficult for him, because she wanted to go with him despite the fact that it made people question their relationship.

The telephone line between their offices buzzed continually when they were both at the resort. It seemed that Blade could no longer make the most inconsequential decision without first seeking her opinion. What irritated her the most was the fact that his attention and friendliness thrilled her, when she knew it all meant nothing to him.

In the evenings he came up to the ranch house on the pretense of working with her on various resort projects, but in reality he did little work. He talked to her and he played with Cathy, and all the while Jenny was aware of Maria watching them with a knowing smile on her face, the same smile that everyone in Zachery Falls wore these days when they saw her with Blade.

Blade took her horseback riding as well, to inspect the ranch, he said. But just what he was inspecting she was never sure. Mac was still half wild, and it frightened her when Blade insisted upon riding him.

They rode everywhere together, and were sometimes gone for hours on Saturday or Sunday afternoons. Occasionally they rode to the cemetery. Once he took her to the cabin that he and Caleb and Dean had used whenever they'd gone hunting on the most remote and wildest section of the ranch. To her surprise, it was clean and neatly furnished, and Blade admitted that he'd used it more than once since he'd come back when he'd felt the need to get off by himself. To her amazement, she learned that that was where he'd spent his first few nights in town before he'd moved into the apartment over the garage. Jenny could not help remembering all the times she'd believed he was with a woman. Had he really been at the cabin seeking solitude?

Blade had not touched Jenny physically since that afternoon in the corral, but every time he looked at her there was a hot light in his eyes that he no longer made any effort to conceal from her or anyone else. He watched her constantly. He seemed to be waiting for something, but she didn't know what. She only knew that she felt nervous herself, and that this change in him made her feel strangely expectant.

Once when they were in town together, Susan drove by in her red Porsche, but when she saw Blade with Jenny, she looked the other way and didn't return his wave.

Jenny wondered about that. She even asked Blade about it.

"Aren't you speaking to Susan these days?"

"I'm speaking. Apparently she's not," he returned indifferently, as though the subject of Susan held not the slightest interest for him.

"I hear she's dating her ex-husband again."

"I hope they get back together, for their children's sake, and for Susan's too," Blade said easily, without a trace of jealously. "You know, she only sees her kids every other weekend. Children need more mothering than that."

"But I thought you two—"

Blue eyes slanted toward Jenny. "You thought wrong."

"Everybody said—"

"Everybody in this town would do a hell of a lot better if they would start minding their own business instead of mine."

Something in Blade's voice told Jenny that the subject of Susan Harper was closed. Jenny wished she could forget the way he'd passionately kissed Susan that night on his bed as easily as he apparently could, but the memory of that naked leg and their wanton embrace stayed in her mind, haunting her, bringing her endless pain. It prevented her from believing that Blade could ever really love one woman. Had he not passionately proclaimed his need for Jenny and then taken Susan into his arms the very same night? And now he had abandoned Susan as well. It was apparent that, for all his charismatic appeal and overwhelming maleness, he lacked the ability to love and be true to one woman. But she'd always known that, and Jenny reminded herself that she didn't love Blade, however appealing she found him physically. Why should his inability to be faithful trouble her so, when her own feelings for him were equally shallow?

In short, she was more confused than ever about Blade as she walked briskly down the hall to his office to answer this latest interruption of her day. Her cheeks were crimson in irritation, and Chuck grinned knowingly as she passed him, misinterpreting completely the reason for her color. Chuck's smile only made her more angry at Blade because it was his fault that people now thought the worst of her.

As she strode into Blade's office she was determined to tell him that she couldn't get a thing done when he constantly interrupted her. Her hot words died in her throat the minute she saw that he was not alone. His office was crowded with law officers, and the atmosphere was tense.

Blade, who'd been sitting behind his desk with an air of lazy unconcern, stood up, and came toward her to escort her inside. Everyone in the room was as conscious as she of the brown hand resting possessively at the back of her waist and the warm white smile that was meant only for her.

"Gentlemen, sheriff," Blade said easily, his hand still upon Jenny's waist. "I'm sure you all know my partner, Jenny." Blade's blue gaze was deliberately bold and intimate as he glanced toward her again.

Blade never called her Mrs. Zachery any more in front of people, as he had for so long, and there was no mistake in anyone's mind that Blade Taylor was seriously interested in her as a woman.

Everyone nodded and smiled at Jenny—that is, everyone except a frail-looking boy of about eighteen who was handcuffed and seated beside Sheriff Blunzer. He sat slumped in his chair with his black eyes downcast, but occasionally he looked up, tossing his head so that his long black hair didn't tumble over his eyes, as he glared around the room with hatred.

"Blade, what's going on? Why is that boy—"

"We've solved the mystery of the stolen television sets," Blade explained succinctly. "I've spent several weekends and nights inside vacant town houses, trying to catch the thief, and last night it paid off. I caught Rick here letting himself into Town House 48 and unhooking the cable of a television set. He finally admitted to me that he stole a set of town house keys from one of the maids he's been dating, and he's been stealing television sets one by one on Sunday afternoons, whenever he and his family needed the money."

The boy stared angrily at Blade and then at Jenny as if he resented being talked about.

"We have enough hard evidence to put him in prison for years, ma'am," Sheriff Blunzer said importantly, "if only you'll agree to press charges."

"Of course I'll agree, if that's what Mr. Taylor wants to do."

Jenny stared at the boy. It was horrible to think of one so young having to go to prison.

"That's just the problem," Blunzer said. "That's not what Mr. Taylor wants to do. I can't get him to press charges."

"What?" Jenny looked up at Blade in surprise.

"Jenny," Blade began, "I've talked to the boy, and to his mother. Their situation really is quite desperate. There are five children in the family. The father drinks. This boy, Rick, has been the sole support of the family for two years, ever since he dropped out of school to go to work. Four months ago he lost his job, and he hasn't been able to get another one. His mother's been sick."

"But surely there are agencies that can help... money..."

"It wasn't enough. I want to pay the town house owners myself for the television sets, and personally take custody of the boy. I'll hire him and take a small amount out of his salary each week against the price of the stolen sets."

Jenny stared at the angry, defiant boy, filled with doubt at the wisdom of Blade's assuming responsibility for him. What if he hurt someone? A hotel guest? Cathy? At the very least, he'd probably steal from them again.

"Blade, are you sure this is what you want to do?"

Blade glanced at the boy, and his blue eyes were filled with a look of profound compassion and empathy. "I'm very sure," he said at last.

Sheriff Blunzer snorted. "You'll be sorry, Mr. Taylor. You don't know what you're doing. His dad's a drunk. His mother's a liar. This boy's a thief. He'll likely turn out to be as trashy as his folks."

The boy tried to lunge out of his chair like a wild animal, but two deputies restrained him.

Blade stared thoughtfully at the sheriff and at the fierce, proud anger of the boy for a long moment. "You called him trash. In case you don't remember, sheriff, that's what everyone has always labeled me."

* * *

An hour later, Blade, Jenny, and Rick were alone in Blade's office. Rick was rubbing wrists that were finally free of manacles and staring at the floor.

"Why'd you do it, Taylor?" Rick muttered in a voice that was scarcely audible.

"Maybe I want to give you a chance to prove you're not what Blunzer says."

"I don't want your charity."

"It's not exactly charity," Blade said mildly. "You might say that I'm repaying an old debt."

"You don't owe me nothin', 'cause I never did nothin' for nobody, especially not for you."

"It's not the kind of debt you repay to the person you owe. Besides, the man I owe is dead."

"I could run, Taylor, you know that. Or steal you blind, if I had a mind to," Rick said angrily.

"You'd be cutting your own throat and that of your family, and I'd see that you're caught, Rick, because you're my responsibility now. And I take my responsibilities seriously. I don't like people stealing from me. Not you. Not anybody. If you're smart, you won't even think about stealing again. You'll work and prove to me and everybody else around here that you're made of something better than they think you are. Or maybe you *are* what Blunzer thinks."

"I'm not!"

"That won't be easy to prove. From what I hear, people around here are pretty set against you."

"I'll prove it."

"What kind of job would you like?" Blade asked, changing the subject. "You'll start at the bottom, of course, but we've got all sorts of jobs around here."

There was a long pause. At last Rick spoke, and there
was less anger in his voice than before. "I've always had
a way with horses, Mr. Taylor."

Blade smiled. "Have you now? Then that's settled.
Report to the stables in the morning. Eight o'clock
sharp. For now, go home and tell your mother about
our agreement."

"You mean I'm free to go?"

Rick looked up and Blade smiled.

"There's one thing you need to learn about me,
Johnson. I don't like repeating myself. Now get out of
here."

Rick scrambled out of the room.

Jenny turned to Blade and their eyes met. It was
strange, how incredibly wonderful she felt.

"Blade, that was very kind of you, trying to do
something for that boy."

He merely shrugged. Then he grinned at her, and
there was a hint of mischief in his eyes. "It was nothing, really. Chalk it up as my good deed for the day.
And put it on the same mental blackboard where you're
always listing my bad deeds, okay?"

"None of the more virtuous citizens of Zachery Falls
would have put themselves to such an expense for a
stranger, or considered taking such a risk," she said.

"Then maybe they aren't so virtuous as they think
they are. It would never occur to them that there's good
in someone even after he's made a mistake or two—like
Rick Johnson. Not that I care what they think anymore."

She reached out and took Blade's hand. With anyone else it might have been no more than a meaningless, friendly gesture, but as always between them there
was the spark of something else in their lightest touch.

His arms came around her in sudden passion. His expression was intense; his lips hovered inches above hers, and Jenny felt oddly breathless as he lowered his mouth, capturing hers in a kiss that was hungry with frustration because he had not kissed her or held her in weeks.

He realized at once that it was unwise to kiss her. It was contrary to his plan, but the expression on her face had been too soft and beautiful to resist. It was heaven to feel her soft lips under his without any anger or shame between them. Her arms encircled his waist, and she pressed herself against him as if her need was as blind and overwhelming as his, as if this time she couldn't deny the rising tide of desire in herself.

Blade deepened the kiss. His tongue curled inside her mouth, touching the tip of hers. His loins felt as hot as melting wax as she eagerly returned his kisses. It satisfied something deep within him to know that she wanted him as desperately as he wanted her, despite all her protests.

She offered herself to him without restraint. Tiny moans of pleasure and excitement escaped her lips. All her innate sensuality was aroused, and the feel of her slim body against his own, the body that had haunted his dreams, drove him insane with a fierce desire to possess her. Her body was his for the moment: the taut breasts, the long legs, the sweet hips.

Neither spoke; their responses were wordless and instinctive. Though there were no avowals of love because each was too proud to betray himself aloud, the intensity of their feelings was revealed in every caress, in every kiss.

Blade longed to be alone with her, in some remote, private place. God, it had been so long since he'd had a woman. His loins were on fire.

Suddenly Blade's secretary burst through the door, and the intimate moment was shattered.

"Oh, I'm sorry," Nancy exclaimed, in blushing confusion. "I thought you were alone, Mr. Taylor."

Blade's arms dropped slowly away, and Jenny flushed in mortification to have been discovered kissing him. She felt weak, dazed. How could Blade look so calm? He looked as if he didn't mind the interruption in the least, while she felt ravaged. She didn't notice that his hands were knotted into hard fists against his thighs.

"What is it, Nancy?" he asked smoothly.

"There's a Mr. Thomas to see you, Mr. Taylor, about the possibility of using Woodlands Hideaway as a conference site for his computer seminar."

"Oh, yes. I'm afraid that appointment completely slipped my mind."

Nancy flushed prettily as she darted a glance at Jenny, who was frantically pinning her hair back into its normally tidy bun.

"Show him in, after Jenny leaves. She and I have not quite finished our... er... our business discussion," Blade said with a bold smile.

The door clicked softly as Nancy exited.

Jenny whirled on him. "How could you?"

He grinned. "How could I what?"

"Act like nothing was wrong!"

"Nothing is."

His casual attitude infuriated her even more. "Nothing except that my reputation is in shreds."

"It already was, or hadn't you noticed?"

"You mean you knew all along that your behavior was making people believe that you and I are lovers?"

"This should finally prove how little a person has to do in this town to be labeled 'bad.'"

"But I've done nothing wrong."

His smile was devilish. "Exactly."

"You're a rogue."

"I've been told that before."

"And you don't care?"

"Maybe I learned a long time ago, Jenny, that I can't help what people say about me."

"You've never even tried to change."

"Maybe I'm satisfied with the person I am. Why should I change just because a lot of meddling busybodies think I should?"

"My reputation is in shreds because of you, and you stand there grinning, acting like you've done something to be proud of. You don't care what you've done to me."

"No, as a matter of fact, I don't. I've lived with a bad reputation for years. Now that you've lost yours, there's less to keep us apart. The bridge between your virtue and my sin is gone, and you're on my side of the river now, girl. Who knows, maybe you'll learn to enjoy the freedom you'll gain from the loss of that reputation you think so precious. For one thing, now you can share my bed without worrying what everyone thinks. They already think the worst."

"You planned this!"

"Hell, Jenny, you were never the girl they thought in the first place, were you? So staid and everlastingly proper, so faithful to my brother, Dean?" Her cheeks flamed at the knowledge in his eyes. "Why don't you try being yourself for a change? You may find that's a better way to live than worrying about what other people think all the time."

"I hate you, Blade Taylor. You've deliberately ruined my life."

"Oh, I wasn't trying to ruin it."

"Well, you have."

"Are you so sure? Tell me that again tonight, after we—"

She was too angry to allow him to finish. "For your information, I'm through with you for good. I have no intention of letting you touch me again, tonight or any other night."

"Then I'll have to change your mind about that, won't I?"

"You—" She choked back her words, realizing there was absolutely nothing she could say to take him down a notch.

He merely smiled as she stormed out the door, but there was a wealth of promise in his bold blue eyes.

That evening Mike dropped by the ranch house unexpectedly. When Jenny opened the front door, the sinking sun was golden on the hills. Maria had taken Cathy to the stables to watch Blade while he was exercising Mac.

"Why, Mike, it's so nice to see you," Jenny said, coming out onto the porch. "Can you stay for a while? Would you like a cool drink? We could sit out on the swing and talk. You know we haven't done that in ages." In the back of her mind was the cowardly notion of using Mike as a shield to hide behind when Blade made his inevitable return to the house.

"This isn't exactly a social call."

She hadn't thought it was.

"I want to talk to you, Jenny, about the rumors concerning you and Blade Taylor."

Jenny stiffened as she led him to the swing. "I don't care to discuss that subject with you or anyone else. I haven't done anything wrong, and I'm not in the mood to defend myself."

"I never thought for a minute that you had. But it's an outrage the way Taylor's dragging your reputation through the gutter just by constantly hanging around you and looking at you the way he always looks at his women. He knows what everyone thinks of him around here, and if he were a gentleman, he'd stay clear of you. It's bad enough him coming back and taking what should have been yours and Cathy's, not to mention him freeing criminals so they can run loose."

"What's an outrage is the way people talk about others even when they have no cause," Jenny said heatedly, sidestepping the subject of Blade. It was curious the way it irritated her to hear Mike speak ill of Blade, even when she herself was furious with him.

"I've decided there's only one solution to this problem that will shut people up once and for all," Mike said.

"And what's that?" Jenny asked, perplexed by his softening tone and the warm light in his eyes.

"It's time you got married."

From the darkness behind them came Blade's deep voice as he rode up on Mac.

"My feelings exactly, Kilpatrick. Marry me, Jenny. I'm more than willing to make an honest woman of you."

"I didn't mean that she should marry you, you fool! I meant me," Mike shouted, bolting out of the swing toward Blade.

Mac reared at the sudden movement, and Blade spoke soothingly. "Easy there, boy. Don't go getting skittish on me." To Mike he said, "Kilpatrick, I'll thank you to take your seat again and not go spooking Mac.

And as for you marrying Jenny—it's my name hers is linked with, not yours. What would people say, anyhow, about you marrying one of Blade Taylor's women?''

Mike looked as green around the gills as a gasping fish as he sank back onto the swing. Jenny was every bit as angry as Mike was at Blade. How could he make a joke of asking her to marry him and insult her so odiously at the same time? It was obvious he didn't really care about her or he wouldn't speak that way. She clenched her teeth and glared at Blade, hating him most of all for the rippling excitement his teasing remark about matrimony stirred deep within her.

''I wouldn't marry you if you were the last man on earth, Blade Taylor. The very last man!''

''Of course she wouldn't. No virtuous, self-respecting woman would want you, Taylor. Not in this town,'' Mike interjected smugly, sure of himself on that subject.

Blade laughed down at them both. ''This one does,'' he said pointedly, looking at Jenny. ''Tell him, girl. Tell him it's me you want and not him. That it's always been me, even if it's not marriage you want. Tell him that you're my woman.''

''You're a liar, Blade Taylor,'' she cried.

''I'm a lot of things, and not all of them good. But a liar I'm not, as you well know. Tell him, girl, what's between you and me, what's been between us these past ten years, even before you married Dean. Or are you such a tease that you want him eating his heart out over you for the rest of his life?''

Mike turned to Jenny in confusion. ''What's he talking about? There's nothing between you two. You always loved Dean.''

Jenny clasped her hands over her mouth and gave a strangled gasp. All she had to do was deny what Blade said. Mike would never take Blade's word against hers. "Mike—" she began, but suddenly she was too choked to speak.

"Tell me Taylor's lying," Mike demanded. His eyes pierced hers.

Something broke inside her, and she just didn't care anymore what people thought of her. She couldn't lie to Mike. She was through trying to live up to the false image of perfection everyone had of her.

"Mike, I—I can't," she admitted at last, "because... it's true."

"What?"

"You heard her, Kilpatrick. Now if you don't mind, I'd like a word alone with my... er... fiancée."

Mike looked venomously at Blade and then stomped down the steps and rushed toward his Cadillac. Jenny hesitated and then ran after him, determined to explain, but when she reached the drive it was choked with dust and exhaust and lit with the red twinkle of disappearing taillights.

"Mike—" She called after him, but he didn't hear. And had he heard, he would not have stopped.

She whirled to run back to the safety of the house, where she could nurse her bruised pride and angry hurt, but she found Blade, magnificently astride the prancing Mac, directly in her path.

Never had Blade seemed more terrifyingly handsome than he did now in the purple twilight. His hair was a shower of gold falling rakishly across his tanned forehead. The first three buttons of his shirt were unfastened, revealing his bronzed chest; his jeans snugly molded his powerful thighs. But it was the look in his

eyes that alarmed her. They were dark and yet startlingly vivid, blatantly communicating his sexual desire. Never had he seemed more ruthless or more
masculine, and suddenly she was frightened. Nevertheless, she squared her shoulders and said bravely, "Get
out of my way and let me pass, Blade Taylor."

He merely laughed, and it was a vibrant, sexy sound.
"So you can go inside and sulk? Not on your life."

Jenny hesitated. She was uncomfortably aware of the
growing darkness, and of the fact that Maria and Cathy
had not yet returned to the house.

"Where's Cathy?" she demanded, sensing the presence of some unnamed, primeval danger.

"There's a children's movie at the lodge, and I sent
her to the resort with Maria—so you and I could be
alone." His voice was low and husky, and something in
its timbre made her feel hot and quivery inside.

Alone. The word repeated itself in her mind, sending
out signals of raw, searing danger.

"Without my permission?" she gasped weakly,
stalling in a vain effort to divert him.

Blade grinned at that, real amusement dancing in his
bold blue eyes. "That's right, Jenny. You and I have a
lot to discuss, and I don't want to be distracted by your
little angel."

"I'm through talking to you, Blade Taylor!" she
cried.

He chuckled. "That, my darling, may be the best idea
you've had tonight."

Blade leaned forward and made a clicking sound with
his teeth against Mac's flattened ear, and Jenny saw his
heels press lightly into his mount as he reined the horse
toward her. As his eyes slid over her body, she knew
what he wanted, what he intended. There had always

been a barely leashed wildness about him, and tonight he wore the look of a man who would take what he wanted with no thought of the consequences.

Without thinking, she began to run from him.

In her jeans and sneakers she was more agile than usual, and she ran with the fleet swiftness of a terrified deer, racing away from the house toward a thick stand of oak and juniper. If only Blade hadn't been between her and the house, she could have gotten inside and locked him out. But what good would that have done? she thought desperately. He knew she was alone. He could easily get inside and overpower her.

Branches tore her hair loose from its bun and it streamed down her back. Still, she ran deeper and deeper into the woods until it was so dark she could scarcely see. She stumbled and fell and picked herself up again. The last rays of the sun were like glimmering ribbons of fire as they filtered among the trees. Behind her she could hear the clatter of Mac's hooves on the loose rocks, and the echo of Blade's hushed laughter.

He was enjoying himself, the devil!

She was right, but she didn't know how much her slim, fleeing form tantalized Blade as she ran before him, how he deliberately held the horse back so that he could watch her slender body dart to and fro between the trees, her long, dark mane swinging wildly about her shoulders. She was as beautiful to him as a wood nymph, with her narrow back, her curving hips, and her long, graceful legs. Every so often a shaft of fire illuminated the exquisite loveliness of her. She was as rare and precious as a blazing jewel, and he was determined to possess her.

At last Blade, longing for the feel of her body crushed to his, grew tired of the game and dug his heels into Mac so that the horse spurted into a mad gallop through the trees after her. Catching up to her, he leaned over and captured her, one arm tightly wrapped around her waist, bringing her up beside him. The warmth of her against him set Blade on fire.

Jenny writhed in his arms, and Mac reared wildly in surprise, frightening her even more than Blade did.

"Quit fighting, girl, or this horse will bolt, and it'll be the end of us all."

The will to fight left her, her fear of the uncontrollable horse subduing her. Besides, she was too exhausted and breathless to resist the fierce strength of the man whose arms bound her so tightly against himself. As Mac galloped into the darkening twilight, away from the house, across the rough acreage of cactus and brush and oak, away from every trace of civilization to the most remote part of the ranch, the man and the woman grew aware of the erotic pleasures of riding the plunging steed together.

Jenny's hips were pressed closely into Blade's loins, and every thudding movement rocked them together until the slightest touch seared their bodies like a flame. Blade's hands moved over her as they rode, unfastening her blouse despite her feeble attempts to thwart him, so that it was warm bare flesh that he touched with his callused fingers.

She felt his lips move hungrily beneath her streaming hair even as his hands caressed the swelling globes of her breasts. She knew she should struggle harder, that she should scream, but Blade's touch, coupled with her fear of the horse, had temporarily lulled her will to fight. Dimly, she knew she shouldn't let Blade have his way with her so easily, but even as she thought of fighting him, some part of her reveled in this moment that was as wildly glorious as her most passionate dreams about him, and she was weak with shame and delight.

The man and woman raced deeper and deeper into the black night, into a world that was primal and dark with danger and swirling passion.

Nine

When Blade finally halted the snorting Mac, Jenny saw the shadowy outlines of his hunting cabin in the dim light. Blade dismounted first and tied the reins to a low tree limb. Then he lifted Jenny from the horse, pulling her close to him so that her body slid against his all the way down, stirring his male senses until they screamed to possess her. To Jenny his action was familiar and insolent, and it awakened her to the reality of her situation.

As soon as her feet touched the ground she tried to run, but Blade pulled her into his arms and kissed her hard, his mouth forcing hers open to admit his tongue. He kissed her again and again with a fierce, savage hunger while she struggled in vain. At first his kisses were harsh and angry because she fought him, but after a while, as her resistance faltered, his mouth gentled upon hers until at last the kisses he rained upon her pouting, bruised lips were infinitely tender. Finally he dragged his lips from the sweet, wanton delight of her mouth, but he went on holding her, his whole body trembling.

"Do you know what it did to me, seeing you with Mike tonight?" he admitted roughly, shaking lips pressed into her hair, in a voice that vibrated through every part of her being. "To think of you married to him? Of you lying with him in his bed? Of him owning you the way Dean did?" Blade's grip tightened on her slim shoulders from the torture his thoughts aroused. "For months I've wanted you, Jenny. I can't bear the thought of losing you to him the way I lost you to Dean. Just as I don't think I can live if you don't let me have you tonight."

"Why are you giving me a choice now?" Her voice was light and breathless. "I thought you were carrying me off to—"

"Rape you," he finished. There was bitter shame in his low words.

"Yes."

She could feel the violent pounding of his heart beneath her ear.

"I've never yet taken a woman who didn't come to me willingly. I guess tonight is as close as I've ever come. But you can go back to the house, Jenny, if you want to. I won't stop you."

He held her locked against his hard thighs, and she sensed what his agony would be if she demanded that he release her. He was giving her back the thing she had fought for so desperately when she'd run from him in the woods—her freedom of choice. She had only to say, "Take me back," and he would. But for some strange reason she said nothing, even though to delay only added to her danger. At any moment he might lose control again and change his mind.

She stared up at him in silence, tormented by the chaos of her emotions just as he was tormented by his. She wanted him even though she thought the wanting was wrong without commitment. Now that he was being serious, he'd made no mention of marriage, only of passion. But she was not made for the easy kind of loving Blade accepted as the normal pattern between a man and a woman.

Gently, Blade bent his gold head to hers again, and his hands spanned her tiny waist. He seemed so big and so magnificently powerful against her smaller, feminine body. He was so virile. Everything about him thrilled her, his hands on her waist, his lips in her hair, his throbbing, barely leashed male passion.

"Jenny girl," he began softly, caressingly. "These past few months have been a living hell for me. I know I've never been half good enough to deserve a woman like you, but I've always wanted you. I couldn't stand you thinking of me the way everyone in town always has, feeling that I'm no good, that any intimacy with me would be like wallowing in filth, that my touch would taint you."

"I never thought that, Blade," she said quietly.

"You said it, that day at the corral."

"That was because you'd made me mad by goading me about Mike, and by saying you were going to date another woman. I was jealous and hurt."

"I haven't looked at another woman since I moved back to the ranch, Jenny."

"But what about Susan Harper?" Jenny blurted out.

"Susan again? Girl, when are you going to give up on that? I don't care about her. What makes you think I do?"

"Blade, I—"

Blade heard the trembling hurt in her voice. "Jenny, Susan has never been important to me, and I don't matter to her, either. Didn't you yourself say she was back with her ex-husband?"

Jenny hovered on the verge of admitting she'd seen Susan in his room, but what was the use? Obviously that had meant nothing more to Blade than the satisfaction of a passing need. Sadly, Jenny realized that he probably saw his desire for her in the same light, and she hesitated.

"Blade, I don't know what to do. We're so different, you and I. We don't think alike about a lot of very important things. We don't share the same values."

"Yes, I suppose we are different in a lot of ways, but I value *you*, Jenny. Maybe that's more important than anything else between a man and a woman."

Could he value her for anything more than her body? she wondered, and her heart ached with the fear that he couldn't.

His voice went on in the soft darkness. "I've told myself it was crazy, my wanting you when I wasn't the kind of man you wanted or deserved. I tried to put you out of my mind, to think of the resort, to think of anything, Jenny, except you. Still, there were times I thought I wouldn't be able to stop myself from coming to your room and forcing you to give me what I wanted because I needed you so much. That made me feel low, as if I were no better than an animal, with no control. I couldn't stand watching you at the resort, so I tried to avoid you. But you were always around, so serene, so untouched, so unreachable. Girl, you drive me crazy, you're so beautiful. So I went on wanting you, dreaming of taking you. Sometimes I thought that if I did force you, I could make you accept me and forget Mike and Dean and whoever else might be in your thoughts. But I can't force you, Jenny. I don't ever want to hurt you. I'm sorry I scared you tonight, chasing you. There was a demon riding me when I saw you like that with Mike.''

Something inside Jenny surrendered, and she knew with sudden, painful insight that she loved Blade, that she had always loved him. That she had always been afraid of loving him. She'd even married his brother because she was so afraid of her feelings. It was not anything bad within Blade that she'd feared; rather, it was his power to unleash a heart that she'd bound so tightly with her prudishness and hypocrisy. She was afraid of real love, of the giving up to another of herself, of the terrible risk involved. And now, even though she was more afraid than ever, she knew that if she didn't risk everything for this man, even the values of a lifetime, she risked her very life itself. Maybe she and Blade didn't want the same things or see life from the same slant. Maybe she couldn't bind him with the conventional ropes of marriage and eternal fidelity, but she would never know what they could share together if she didn't take a chance and meet him halfway.

In that blinding instant she decided to give herself to Blade on his terms, to demand nothing from him in return, no matter what the inevitable cost to herself.

''There's no one in my thoughts except you, Blade Taylor,'' she admitted shyly, tears of happiness and love shining in her eyes. ''And you've already ruined my reputation now, haven't you? Maybe it's high time I earned my black name."

He smiled at her as he read her meaning, a slow, crookedly charming smile that brightened her heart, and then he placed a large hand on either side of her face and kissed her long and deeply and very tenderly.

She broke away and murmured, "I'm beginning to think there's some truth in what you said this afternoon. There may be great pleasure in living up to my wicked reputation."

"Wanton!" he murmured in that silky voice of his that could make shivers trace through her. He laughed as he lifted her into his arms. "There'll be great pleasure, my love. I promise you."

He lifted her into his arms and carried her into the cabin, laying her upon the bed and following her down.

"Jenny, my darling Jenny."

Months of frustration and pain spilled out of him as his lips lowered to hers in a light, undemanding kiss that belied the intensity of his desire, a gentle kiss that made her moan softly, longing for him to deepen it. But he was determined to take her slowly, to arouse her fully before he assuaged his own all-consuming need.

With expert ease he undressed her, unbuttoning her blouse with fingers that brushed her bare flesh, unfastening her jeans, sliding the garments from her creamy skin until she lay gleaming and naked in the streaming moonlight. She was as beautiful as she'd been in his dreams, green eyes passionately afire. It seemed to him that he'd wanted her for all eternity.

He stripped, shedding his boots first with a clatter upon the plank floor and then his shirt. He was bronzed and naked when he came to her and wrapped his arms around her again, positioning her beneath him, their bodies molten everywhere they touched, flesh upon flesh, man upon woman. He groaned with pleasure at the rounded softness of her belly and the long smoothness of her legs against his hard, muscled length.

"Open your mouth to me," he said huskily. "I want to taste you."

She let his tongue slide inside, and he kissed her deeply, intimately, savoring the wet, sweet warmth of her mouth.

His mouth glided down the pale column of her throat, kissing her beneath her ears, along the delicate line of her jaw, hesitating at the base of her throat, his lips lingering upon her madly beating pulse. Then his golden head moved lower and she felt his teeth and tongue gently playing across her nipples.

Her fingers wound into the thick, bright fall of his hair, and she brought his face back to hers so that he kissed her again on the mouth. His fierce kisses enflamed her, and she sighed, clinging to him, aching for him.

But he went on caressing her and kissing her until she thought she would burst with desire. At last she felt his hand move between her legs, and he touched her, the gentle, stroking motion of his fingers sliding over her, manipulating soft flesh into heated arousal, his fingertips teasing at first, and then evoking exquisite quivers of sensation that built until she thought she would die if he didn't take her.

She arched her body against his, moving her hips against the thrilling pleasure of his hand, but it was not his hand that she wanted.

"Love me, Blade . . . I can't stand it anymore if you don't. Quickly. Please. Oh . . . quickly."

Her passionate demand, whispered hotly against his ear, excited him more than anything, and he took his hand away and swept her beneath him, fitting her body to his, entering her carefully and moving slowly and rhythmically at first, until his passion consumed him and he could hold back no longer, he could only give vent to the raging force that drove him. Her body was splendor, sweet, savage, shattering splendor that drew him out of himself until he shuddered deep within her. Only vaguely was he aware of the way she clung to him desperately, her fulfillment a tremor that seemed to go on and on even after his own body stopped shaking.

Afterward, he did not release her, but went on holding her, her head cradled in the crook of his arm, her hair spilling in silken waves upon the pillow. One of her hands lay upon his stomach, the other lightly caressed his jaw. Their faces were so close that she felt his warm breath stir against her skin as he stared deeply, lovingly into her eyes. She felt that she belonged to him utterly, even if he could never belong utterly to her.

Despite her doubts about the future and about Blade's ability to love her as deeply as she loved him, Jenny had never been more blissfully happy. She'd never known the passion of this night in ten years of marriage, yet for once she was able to think of Dean without guilt. He belonged to the past, and she'd been as good a wife to him as she could be. Now she loved Blade.

She knew Blade lacked Dean's faithful nature, but perhaps it was selfish to ask for lasting love when Blade could satisfy her so gloriously, so completely. For the moment what they had together made all other needs seem trivial.

"I love you, Jenny," he murmured in a strange, broken voice.

She didn't know that he'd never said those words to a woman before, and though she was thrilled, she wondered what he really meant by them. Did he say that to every woman who pleased him in bed? That thought brought her both pain and pleasure, pain to think of other women sleeping with Blade, pleasure because she knew she had made him physically happy.

His hand drifted over her body, across her breasts to her stomach. "You could have a child," he said, "if we aren't more careful. I wanted you so much, I didn't think. I'm sorry, Jenny."

His words unwittingly brought more pain because they reminded her that he was not the kind of man who would make such a commitment to a woman. She wanted his child. She wanted *him*. She wanted marriage and a lifetime together, while he wanted none of those things. Was life really so simple for him? she wondered. She supposed that it was.

A sweet, aching sadness engulfed her, making her feel lost and afraid, and she pressed her face into his chest for comfort as she began to cry for all the things she wanted and could never share with him. Blade's arms tightened around her, her tears wracking him with torture and guilt. She had cried that first time so long ago, and two days later she'd married Dean. What had he done to make her cry, when all he wanted was to make her happy? Blade wondered.

"Don't cry, Jenny. I can't stand it when you cry."

He searched and found her lips and kissed her with all the passion in his being, and she returned his kisses, seeking the numbing comfort his lovemaking could give her, enflaming him again with her fierce caresses and the provocative movement of her body rubbing against his, until once more desire seared them and swept them in its burning tide.

In the splendor of his loving she forgot, but only for the moment, all that she could never have.

Six weeks passed, six sensual weeks of passion and the questing for fulfillment. During the days when Blade and Jenny worked at the resort, when each knew the other was near but they couldn't be together, a fever burned in both of them. Neither could wait for the evenings when they could be alone, those hours after Maria put Cathy to sleep and went to bed herself. Then Jenny would slip out of the house and go to Blade's room. He would be waiting for her, as eager and filled with desire as she. She would run to him, and they would melt into one another's arms, clinging, kissing, seeking the glory that only one could give the other.

Sometimes he would draw her down on the bed, covering her breasts with his hands, softly massaging her, sliding his hands over her body even before he undressed her. Sometimes when they were naked he lay back and pulled her down on top of him, easing her body onto his, encouraging her to make love to him. Straddling him, she would move slowly at first, watching his face, exulting in the passion she aroused in him. His fingers would trace lightly back and forth along her spine or move up across her belly to cup her breasts.

Blade was a passionate man, and he made love to her with a completeness she had never known before. For Blade, touching Jenny and being with her was his heaven upon earth. She was the mate of his soul, and his physical love for her was sacred. Sometimes he was wild, sometimes gentle, but every time they were together he made her feel she was the only woman on earth who could arouse him thus. He made her feel infinitely precious. Her love deepened, and she fell more and more under his spell, until it seemed to Jenny that there was no part of her that did not belong to Blade.

He had no inhibitions, and with him she shed the modesty of a lifetime as he taught her the wonders of love. He pleasured her with his lips and tongue, overriding her initial protests, encouraging her to make love to him in the same way, until soon she found she gloried in this kind of loving as much as he. Sometimes they rode their horses far out over the ranch, and he would find some beautiful, deserted bower for their love. Once, when they were hot and dirty from a long ride, he playfully pulled her into the creek fully dressed. The sight of her blouse clinging to her thrusting breasts made him forget his playfulness, and he made love to her in the middle of that scorching spring day as they stood there together, wet mouths fused. He held her closely, plunging deep within her body, while the cool green waters of the creek curled around their legs. Afterward they swam and laughed and made love again.

Blade awakened fully the earthly sensuality in her nature that she had struggled so long to suppress, and Jenny lived those weeks in a daze of happiness. It was only when she was not with him that she doubted his love.

One night, after they'd made love, she asked him about the scars crisscrossing his lower back and thighs.

He frowned, and she felt a sudden, inexplicable tension in his body before he rolled from her and crossed his arms over his chest. For a while he stared in silence at the ceiling, and she didn't know if he was going to answer her. He looked so bleak. When he finally spoke, his voice was so low she could scarcely hear him, the sound seeming to be dragged out of him.

"I was wounded in Lebanon."

Tentatively, she reached out and touched the ridged flesh on his legs, and he winced at her light touch.

"How?" she whispered.

"It's not something I've ever been able to talk about—with anyone."

"Please tell me. Maybe it would make it easier for you if you shared it."

"I don't want to burden you with my pain, Jenny."

She saw an anguish in his eyes that was past her comprehension. "But I want to know."

"No, you don't. Not really," he replied quietly. "You only say that because you don't understand." For an instant his expression softened. "How can anyone understand the insanity of war? You just live through it if you have to."

"It's over," she said gently.

"For me, maybe. For those left—" He shuddered. "It was hell over there, like I've never been through before or since. I guess it still is."

Jenny could feel him trembling, and she caressed him, seeking to comfort him.

"Just tell me a part of it, Blade."

He attempted to, in a remote voice that didn't sound at all like his own. "I tried to save an Arab kid who had been hit by shrapnel, but he died in my arms." He stopped. For a moment he was too shaken to go on. "Maybe it was better that he did, poor kid, because he was cut to shreds. I was shot trying to rescue him. Damn it, Jenny, he died because of what we did—maybe even because of me."

"Not because of you, Blade. Never because of you."

A cold sweat broke out on Blade's forehead as he re-lived that day. He remembered it all, the ceaseless, ear-shattering explosions, the stench of burning oil, the black curls of smoke above orange flames, the heat, the perpetual buzz of flies, the choking dust in the streets every time a jeep or tank zoomed past. The child had been hit in the street, and Blade had braved enemy crossfire in his vain attempt to save him. He'd scooped the child from the rubble, cradling that helpless bundle in his arms as he ran for cover. Three bullets had ripped into Blade just a second before he reached safety. In searing pain, he'd had to crawl the last few feet to reach the American lines. He'd handed the child to a soldier and then pitched forward into the dirt and his own blood. Mercifully, he hadn't regained consciousness for two days. He'd almost died, and he'd been given a medal for that act of heroism, though he never spoke of it. He couldn't speak of it now, not even to Jenny. The horror of combat was something that was locked deep inside him.

"I can't talk about it. Don't ask me any more."

Blade's blue eyes were stark and empty. He never voluntarily brought up his time in the marines, and af-ter his attempt to answer he lapsed into silence, trying to put the hellish images out of his mind. He wanted only to protect Jenny from the terror and hell he'd ex-perienced.

But Jenny wanted to draw him out. She knew that his life had not been smooth and protected, as hers had been. If they were ever to understand each other she re-alized she was going to have to force him to reveal him-self.

"This scar on your leg looks different from the others," she persisted, indicating a jagged line on his tanned thigh. "It's not so raw and new-looking."

Her hand touched the length of wrinkled skin. He'd never told anyone the truth about that scar, but that memory was the bitterest of all. Strangely, he could speak of it now, though. It seemed almost as if it had happened in another lifetime.

His voice was dry and hard when he spoke. "That's where my father, not Caleb, but Jamie, laid me open with his screwdriver when he was drunk and I jumped between him and my mother—before she ran away and left us. He was crazy that night. He would have sliced me to ribbons if I hadn't run off and stayed away for three days. I was eight years old. He worked my mother over real good that night."

He stopped, gripped with tension. Now she would recoil and think him little better than an animal. What did a gentle woman like Jenny know of the sordid ugliness of life or the hellish bloodline that frowned in his veins?

"Oh, Blade, Blade, how terrible it all must have been for you." Her fingers were lightly caressing his scar as if to comfort him. "Where did you go when you ran away?" Her heart went out to that poor lost child.

"Caleb found me sleeping under a bridge, half frozen, and he took me in until my old man came after me."

Jenny was too horrified to speak; she lay in rigid silence as she pondered the pain of his childhood. At last she said, "I don't think I've ever appreciated my own childhood until right now. My family was strict, but loving. They never deliberately hurt one another. I still miss both my parents. You probably don't remember, but you wrote me a letter when they died in that car wreck not long after Caleb's death. It meant a lot to me, Blade, your writing when I felt so awful about them."

"I wrote because you were always special to me, even back then, Jenny," he said softly, pushing a strand of hair back over her ear. That was as close as he could come to admitting the depth of his love for her; he was still afraid that in the end she would reject him. Blade had been based in Japan when he'd heard about her parents. He'd known she was hurting, and he'd wanted to be with her to share her pain, but he couldn't get leave. How he'd envied Dean. Blade had thought of Jenny constantly, knowing she was going through a difficult period. "It wasn't enough, my writing. I should have come home."

"Dean was there," she said quietly. "I guess there wasn't much anyone could have done."

"Yes," he said, frowning, her mention of Dean reminding him that she'd had no need of him as long as Dean had been alive. Blade wished with all his heart that he was more like Dean or Kilpatrick; this conversation about their backgrounds had made him realize again how different Jenny and he really were. Could a woman like her ever be happy with a man like him?

Because he couldn't say the things he wanted to, he pulled her into his arms and showed her, in the only way he knew how, how much he loved her. Within moments her mood was as passionate as his, and she was breathless and throbbing with desire when he pulled away.

"Blade, w-why are you stopping?"

He smiled at her eagerness as he gathered her once more into his arms and bent his brow to hers with affectionate playfulness so that they touched, brow to

brow, nose to nose. "The other night, didn't you admit that you'd wanted to make love in the hayloft the
day I kissed you in the corral?"

She nodded, and her eyes were sparkling as he lifted
her effortlessly and strode toward the door. "Blade,
don't you think we should take a quilt?"

He set her down. "And I thought you were too
breathless and passionate for such practical considerations."

"Forget the quilt then," she said.

"Not on your life." He picked up a blanket and took
her hand in his, leading her out the door. "I want to
indulge your fantasy, girl, not cope with scratches from
that prickly hay for the next year."

They ran toward the barn, laughing in the moonlight
like children. When at last they reached the loft and
spread the blanket down upon a bed of hay, Blade stood
very still and held out his hand. She went eagerly into
his arms, abandoning herself to the physical pleasure of
his lips and tongue and thrusting male body until he
made her his in a searing blaze of passion that left them
dazed anew with the wonder of their love.

After that, there was a new, unspoken closeness between them. Blade spent time with Cathy and seemed to
enjoy the antics of the two-year-old. He even tried to
convince Cathy to give up her thumb, but he got no
futher than Jenny had, and Jenny teased him unmercifully about his failure. It wasn't that Cathy didn't take
great interest in his attempts to make her stop sucking
her thumb, because she did. She would run to him and
say, with a dimple and a giggle, holding a bottle of
thumb-paint proudly, "Paint, Uncle Blade. Paint
Cathy's thumb."

He would laugh and then try to be stern. "Okay, I'll paint it, you little rascal, but that means you're not supposed to suck it after I do. And I don't want to hear you sneaking into the bathroom and washing it off like you did yesterday. You're a big girl now. Big girls don't suck their thumbs."

Cathy would only nod brightly while he painted both thumbs. "Some big girls do, Uncle Blade."

He would laugh as he talked to her, and Jenny would laugh at them both. It was never long before Cathy found some pretext to wash her hands, and her thumb would be back in her mouth as usual.

"Hell, Jenny, she even sucks her thumb when she's asleep. Didn't you say you bought a book on this subject? I think it's time one of us read it."

"Maybe it's time you listened to me for a change, darling. She'll give up her thumb when she's ready."

"You know, that advice is sounding more sensible every time I hear it. I wonder why I didn't think of it myself."

Jenny would have been very happy if she thought Blade truly loved her as she loved him, but the more deeply she fell in love with him, the more terrible it seemed to her that he couldn't love a woman with his heart and soul, that he didn't want to make the commitment of marriage. Jenny was increasingly aware of the town's growing speculation about them as a couple; though Blade now took great care to be discreet, one look at Jenny's radiant face when her eyes met his told all. And no matter how often she told herself that giving up her virtuous reputation was worth it if she could lie in Blade's arms at night, she was bothered by having an affair with him.

Jenny lay awake many nights, unable to sleep, because deep in her heart she felt it was wrong to sleep with Blade if she wasn't married to him, no matter how beautiful their relationship was. But she said nothing to Blade; she didn't want to push him into a commitment he was uncomfortable making. After his one mention of marriage in front of Mike, Blade had never again brought up the subject.

June came, and with it the blasting, dry heat of a Texas hill country summer. Air conditioners hummed full-time. Guests loitered in the shade and swam in the pool and creek for relief. Jenny consumed huge quantities of ice tea and cold water. Outside, in the middle of the day, the ranch seemed as hot as a furnace. Despite the heat, the resort overflowed with guests, though not as many as Blade said they needed, but the more guests, the more Blade worked.

Despite the depressed state of the Texas hotel business in general, Blade was working terribly hard to make the resort a success. Sometimes he would call Jenny into his office to go over the statistics they were up against.

"Jenny, do you realize that in Houston hotels the occupancy rate averages less than fifty percent—and many of those rooms are filled by discounting, sometimes drastically? Their business still hasn't recovered from all the overbuilding in the industry, the devaluation of the Mexican peso, and the stagnation of the oil business."

"But we're not competing with Houston."

"I'm afraid we are. We can't raise our rates because we have to be able to offer a comparable package to conventions. Woodlands Hideaway doesn't have a location that's as easily accessible as Houston, Dallas, or

San Antonio, so we've got to fight them for every nickel of business.''

Blade began to travel. He had brochures printed. He made contacts with travel agents, promoting Woodlands Hideaway with zeal and determination, but secretly, Jenny wondered if he traveled because he was growing restless. When he was in Zachery Falls he was with her constantly. But more and more he was on the road, and Jenny was afraid that when he was gone he sought the company of other women. Even though he called her every night while he was gone, she couldn't bring herself to fully trust him; she was too unsure of herself as a woman. She didn't know it, but Blade understood her feelings. For all his outward toughness, he was gentle and sensitive toward her, never deliberately inflicting hurt, but this only made her believe more strongly than ever that he was simply showing her consideration by not chasing women in Zachery Falls.

When she was besieged with doubts, she would remember that she'd never been wild and fun-loving like the Susan Harpers of the world. Was it any surprise that a man like Blade, who was not inexperienced with women, would want variety? How could he be satisfied with her?

She made herself miserable when he was gone, but she never told him of her jealousy for fear that would drive him even farther away. Blade sensed that something was wrong, but she denied it when he asked her, though her silence afterward made him worry even more. He thought that she regretted their relationship, and, as always, he believed that he was not good enough for her, that he should go away and leave her so she could marry a man more her type, like Mike Kilpatrick. He remembered how she'd married Dean ten years

ago, and he wondered if she wouldn't be engaged to
Kilpatrick now if he hadn't returned and practically
forced himself upon her.

So they went on, Blade and Jenny, loving each other
yet not understanding the secret unhappinesses locked
in one another's hearts.

Ten

Pregnant! The word had thrummed in Jenny's brain during the hour-long drive from her doctor's office in Austin back to Zachery Falls.

For once Jenny was glad that Blade was out of town on business. She was so upset that she could never have concealed her distress from him.

Standing before the full-length mirror in her bedroom, Jenny slowly took off her clothes, shedding the garments one by one into a heap on the floor. She stared at her nude body, running her hands across her smooth belly. Already her breasts were fuller, her complexion more glowing.

A mixture of wonder, pride, and shame filled her—she was carrying Blade's child. Since that first night, he had taken every precaution to avoid pregnancy. Though he'd never mentioned his reasons, she guessed that a child was the last thing he wanted, and the prospect of telling him that she had conceived sent a shiver of doubt through her. Nonetheless, a part of her was ecstatic. She loved Blade, and she wanted his child.

But the next moment she remembered the difficulty of her situation, and her joy faded. She wasn't married. Blade had never even hinted at that possibility. How could she go on living in Zachery Falls? People would talk. It wouldn't be fair to the baby, nor to Cathy. For the first time Jenny was almost glad that her strict mother and father were not alive; they would be spared this shame.

Jenny sank down on the bed and huddled beneath a blanket, feeling mortified and frightened at the thought of being an unwed mother at this stage of her life. What on earth was she going to do? What would Blade say if she told him? Would he think she was trying to trap him into marriage? Everyone had always said that he wasn't the marrying kind. She didn't want to make him unhappy, but the child was his. She had to tell him. What if he rejected her and the baby? The mere thought brought a crushing sensation of sorrow and the first sting of tears to her eyes. She closed her eyelids tightly so they wouldn't spill. She was afraid that if she let herself cry, she would never stop. Oh, what, what was she going to do?

She'd been heedlessly reckless, selfish and unthinking in her love for Blade. Why hadn't she thought of how this might affect Cathy? But she had. Blade had been careful never to sleep with her in the house. She'd always left him and returned to her own bed, so that Maria would not know that she had slept with him. He never touched her in public.

Oh, why had this happened when they'd been so careful every time but that first night? Pregnancy couldn't possibly be hidden for long, and Jenny knew that her condition would force all the secrets of her heart into the open. She and her baby would be a matter of common, unkind gossip very shortly if she didn't take steps to prevent it.

There was only one thing she could do. She would have to leave for a while, perhaps forever, but first she had to tell Blade.

Blade returned from his business trip that evening, and he was so happy about the three conventions he had booked for the slow winter season that she couldn't bring herself to tell him her news that first night. It was too heavenly to slip into his arms and let him make love to her, to pretend that everything was just the same between them. A week stole past, and then another. Jenny was so afraid that her news would drive Blade away that every hour that she did not tell him seemed to her an hour that she still had him. The thought of telling him became more and more difficult to face. Because she hadn't told him that first night, not telling him now became the easiest course.

Blade was aware that something was wrong, and he was terribly afraid that Jenny was trying to work up the nerve to tell him that it was over between them. So he didn't press her whenever she seemed to be on the verge of confiding in him. Instead, he would shush her and hold her and kiss her until the flame of passion consumed them and there could be no thought of anything other than letting the wildness of their need wash over them.

One hot afternoon when they were out riding Jenny was overcome by nausea. Usually she enjoyed their late-evening rides, but that day they had decided to ride earlier than usual. The heat was stifling; no breeze stirred the leaves or high grasses. Jenny had forgotten her wide-brimmed hat, and the sun baked down upon her. Trickles of sweat ran down her back beneath her cotton blouse as she fought to suppress her queasiness, but her sickness would not be restrained.

"Blade, please, help me down," she cried weakly, her embarrassment and fear nearly as acute as her nausea as her gaze met his.

He dismounted and was beside her in an instant, his tanned face grave with concern.

"What's the matter? Jenny, you look ill. Darling, why didn't you tell me—"

"I—"

Jenny took a deep breath in an attempt to control her mounting sickness as he lifted her from the mare. When her feet touched the ground, she pushed against his arms and ran a little distance away, turning her back to him.

"Don't look!" she gasped. "Please. Don't." Then she bent over, unable to say more.

The spasm was long and painful, but at last, when she was able to lift her head and breathe in the fresh air without feeling ill, she became aware of Blade's critical gaze. She still felt weak and shaky, but the nausea had subsided.

"The sun was so hot," she stammered. "I'm sorry."

His blue eyes were piercing. "Riding doesn't usually make you sick."

"Blade—"

"You're pregnant, aren't you?"

She stared at him bleakly, hopelessly.

"Yes."

"Why didn't you tell me?"

"Because—" His dark look choked off all utterance. It was obvious he wasn't happy about the baby at all. "Blade, I never meant for this to happen."

His expression grew even harder, but his eyes were more brilliant than ever. "And obviously you're none too pleased."

"Blade, that's not how I feel. You don't understand."

"Oh, I understand, but you're much too kind to tell me the truth. I've known something was bothering you for a long time, Jenny." He paused, his expression softening as he regarded her white, troubled face and reminded himself that she was unwell and carrying his child. "But this is hardly the time or place for this discussion. I want to get you out of the sun and back to the house. If I'd known you were pregnant I would never have asked you to ride and risk harming you or the baby."

He led her back to the mare and helped her to mount, but he did not climb back on Mac. Instead he walked, leading both horses slowly, asking Jenny often if she was all right.

Jenny was fine now except for the knot of fear that bound her emotions. Blade was grimly silent between his concerned questions regarding her health, and his silence frightened her.

When they reached the house, Blade helped her down and led the horses to the corral without a word. She watched him go, filled with a black, devastating sorrow at the thought of losing him. She wanted to weep and scream and run after him to beg him not to leave her, but pride stiffened her back and saved her from that last humiliation. Feeling drained, she turned and went slowly into the house.

Blade felt like a man who was dying inside. He loved her, but he knew she could never love him. What woman could—the way he'd been raised? The way he'd lived. He'd tried to change, to live the past down. He'd gone to college and then joined the marines. He thought of the long years of work and sacrifice. Was it all for nothing? It seemed so now. He didn't know how to make Jenny love him; what could he do that he hadn't already done? Jenny only wanted him, in a way he'd wanted all the other women he'd ever known besides her. He understood that kind of wanting well enough, the fire of physical attraction, the fleeting satiation of a sensual need that never touched the soul. Blade was sure Jenny was still ashamed of her feelings for him.

He remembered how she'd loved Dean, how she'd chosen him all those years ago, even after she and Blade had made love. Blade had known then that he loved her, but what woman wouldn't have taken Dean over himself when the whole town believed he was rotten, no matter what he did? What did Blade Taylor know about gentleness and faithfulness, they were saying even now, about being a husband to a woman like Jenny Zachery? Blade knew better than Jenny what was being said behind their backs. He knew that people pitied her, believing that beneath his polished surface he was as bad as ever, that he'd only come back to take her money and to cheat her out of what was rightfully hers, that he was temporarily putting on a damned good act. They were saying that Blade Taylor had always broken the heart of any woman he'd ever gotten close to, and Jenny Zachery would be no different. He'd take her for everything she had and then leave her without even her pride. In that moment, Blade hated himself almost as much as he hated the world.

Blade unsaddled Red and then mounted Mac again. He had to go off and be by himself for a while. Maybe it was time he left Zachery Falls for good. Maybe that was what was best for Jenny in the long run. Maybe a kid was better off not knowing his father if his father was Blade Taylor.

Blade swung himself easily into the saddle. Digging in his heels, he galloped away, past the house, past the window Jenny stood before. He was too filled with pain to even glance her way. Jenny watched him, and her sadness was even greater than his because she had the terrible feeling that he'd left her forever.

Somehow Jenny lived through that long, hot, sultry afternoon in a daze of misery. Everyone had warned her, hadn't they, and now there was no one she could turn to for comfort. She was utterly alone.

"Bad blood will out," the townspeople had always said. Jenny remembered well every evil rumor she'd ever heard about Blade. Could he really be so heartless? Could he abandon her and his child without a backward glance? She remembered the way he'd kissed Susan that night in his room. Were sex and love meaningless to a man like him? Had Blade ever really belonged to her? She'd behaved foolishly, falling in love with a man like him, and now she was only paying the price.

The sun was sinking in a burst of scarlet and gold when Jenny, not wishing to face even Maria and Cathy, decided to walk down by the creek and dangle her feet in the cool water. She had the feeling that she would never see Blade again, so when she whirled at the sound of a snapping twig, it was with surprise that she met the bold blue of his eyes. Blade's expression was fierce and untamed and somehow terrifying, but his voice was oddly gentle.

"Jenny—"

Her eyes misted and she looked away. She didn't want his pity, nor his contempt.

"Blade, you didn't have to come back. You don't owe me anything."

His voice was low and tortured. "I didn't come back because I owed you anything, girl. I was going to run away the way I always ran away every time Jamie beat me when I was a kid, the way I ran away all those years ago after you married Dean. For months I've known I should have left you alone so you could have Kilpatrick. He could have run the resort, maybe better than I can. But the baby changes all that, doesn't it?" he said bitterly. "I've ruined things for you. Kilpatrick would never marry you, now that you're pregnant with Blade Taylor's child. Besides, I couldn't bear it if you married him anyway."

She turned, frowning in puzzlement. What was he saying? What did he mean? He'd said he was planning to leave. Why had he come back then?

"I know I'm the last man in the world for a woman like you. You said that once, didn't you, that if I were the last man in the world you wouldn't marry me?"

Had he actually taken seriously that remark she'd hurled at him in anger?

"Blade—"

"I want to marry you, Jenny, and before you say no—"

"Blade, just because I'm pregnant, that doesn't mean you have to marry me." Her lashes descended over her shimmering eyes. Her heart was breaking, and she was afraid she would cry.

"I know you could never love me the way you loved Dean, but I would be good to you and Cathy and the baby, Jenny. At least I would try. I've always loved this ranch. I feel like it's my home, just as it is yours. Even if you don't love me now, you're attracted to me, and we've proven we can work well together on a day-to-day basis. That's more than a lot of couples have. We'd have the child, of course, and Cathy. And as I see it, if you don't marry me, you'll be in one hell of a mess. I've cost you Kilpatrick, and you need a man to help you with the ranch and the resort. It's too much for you to deal with alone. Besides, you know how people would talk if you didn't marry. I don't want my kid growing up feeling as though he's not as good as the next kid because his real father ran off and left him. I know the pain of that too well to inflict it on my own child."

"But, Blade, it's not a question of my not loving you or not wanting to marry you. *You* don't love *me*. I don't want to force you."

"Don't love you?" He stared at her incredulously. "Don't love you! Are you crazy, girl?" He pulled her into his arms and buried his face in her long, sweet-smelling hair, his fingers digging into her slim shoulders. "I love everything about you. I've always loved you. That's why Dean and I could never get along. I always resented him because he had you. Why do you think I left here? Because I loved you and couldn't stay in Zachery Falls with you married to Dean."

"Blade," Jenny sighed tremulously, all of her pain leaving her at his admission. "Is what you're saying really true? Do you really love me?"

"There's never been anyone but you," he said.

"But you chased all those women."

"Most of that gossip was exaggerated. If I'd had half the women they said I've had, I'd be dead from exhaustion. I chased a few, I guess, but that was only because I couldn't have the one I really wanted." His lips moved in her hair. "Believe me, Jenny, I've never been the man they say I am."

"Blade, I saw you making love to Susan that night after the hayride," she said hesitantly. "That made me think sex didn't mean much to you."

"What?"

"And I've been torturing myself thinking you must be seeing other women when you travel, that you're bored with me."

"I found Susan waiting in my room that night. I'm sorry for that, Jenny, but nothing went on. I shouldn't even have kissed her, but it happened so fast I couldn't avoid it. I never dreamed you saw us. If I'd known, I would have explained to you long before now. I told her that night that she and I could never be anything more than friends. I wanted you that night, not Susan."

"I'd be mighty gullible to fall for a fool story like that, Blade," she said with a smile. "Susan's awfully beautiful, and you were very angry with me."

"Real beauty comes from inside a woman, Jenny. You've always been the most beautiful woman in the world to me. I was mad at you, but not so mad I lost sight of the fact that it wasn't Susan I wanted and that if I took her, I was being unfair to everyone. As for the traveling, Jenny, I've been working. Don't you know yet that *you're* my woman? I don't need anyone but you if I know you're waiting for me. I don't want anyone else."

In that moment Jenny believed him, and she felt aglow with happiness. Blade Taylor loved her—imagine that! He'd always loved her, even when she'd been married to Dean. Deep in her heart she knew that she'd always loved him, too; she just hadn't realized it. Her love for Blade had been the root of her dissatisfaction in her marriage, and no wonder. Poor Dean. If only she'd seen the truth, he could have married someone who was wild about him.

"I've always been scared of loving you, Jenny, of the way it could rip me apart because I couldn't have you. I'm still scared."

"Blade, my darling, I'm just as scared, because I love you, maybe even more than you love me."

He stared at her in amazement, not really believing her. "Don't say it, Jenny, if you don't mean it."

"But I do mean it. I love you."

His arms tightened around her, and they clung to one another as though to a lifeline.

"Jenny girl," he said very tenderly. His lips sought hers in an ever-deepening kiss. At last he released her. "I can't believe you really love me. A woman like you. Who would believe it? Wild Blade Taylor marrying the preacher's daughter. Saint and sinner. You know—" his blue eyes were twinkling "—I'm almost looking forward to all the gossip our marriage is going to cause. For once I won't mind what they say, my love."

"I love you, no matter what anyone says, and I think I have for years," she whispered against his lips. "It was one of those things I locked away inside myself and tried not to think about. But ever since you came back I've wanted you unbearably. You're so strong and kind. You've worked so hard to help me. You're so handsome." She smiled shyly as she traced her fingers along the skin beneath his throat. "I love it when you touch me, when you make love to me."

"And speaking of that," he began hoarsely, his hand sliding over her body in sudden, urgent need. "You know what holding you always does to me? You stir me, girl, without even trying."

"Yes?" She smiled coyly.

"Don't tease me, Jenny," he groaned.

"That was never my intention, love," she murmured, unbuttoning his shirt and burrowing her face against the hard muscles of his chest.

"I thought you were ashamed of having an affair with me," he said, "because you thought I wasn't good enough for you."

"In a way, I was ashamed, not because of that, but because I loved you. I didn't feel right about sleeping with you without marriage. I wanted a future with you, and children. I was afraid you didn't want those things."

"Not want those things, with you?" He stared at her in wonder. "That's all I've ever wanted, to be married to you, to have a real family, to be the father of your children. What else is there in life?"

"Oh, Blade, I'm so happy. I've never been so happy."

"Neither have I, my love."

The look in his eyes sent shivers through her. His own pulse thudded with violent desire as he swept her into his arms and carried her to a place where the grasses were soft and lush and the creek gurgled and splashed beside them.

"Remember that time we made love when we were kids, Jenny?"

"How could I ever forget?"

"After that one time, I wanted you forever, girl."

He pulled her down until they both knelt on the soft earth. Their mouths touched tentatively at first, then their kiss deepened. He moved his mouth on hers, forcing her lips apart, tasting her, possessing her with his tongue.

His breathing was heavy and ragged from their love-play. Wordlessly, they removed their clothes, each watching the other shed every item of apparel until they were both naked. For a long moment they simply looked at each other, and there was a wealth of loving as their eyes met. At last he took her hand and drew her beneath him.

A fire raged in them both. Her body trembled as he kissed her tenderly; her arms went around his neck hesitantly, her fingertips brushing the soft gold hair that curled against his earlobe. His hands glided over her, stroking her breasts, cupping their new fullness, sliding lower over her velvet-soft skin until she was thoroughly roused.

There was a moist ache in her most feminine place. He touched her there, arousing her with his long, lean fingers, probing, caressing, until she was as breathless as he. She was quivering, and her soft flesh felt delicious beneath his fingertips, smooth as silk and warm as melting wax.

He kissed her again upon her lush, half-open lips, his kiss as fierce and burning as his love. She was his. Truly his. Only his. No one would ever take her from him again. This realization sweetened their lovemaking for Blade and heightened his passionate need. Her hands moved over his muscled shoulders and closed tightly around his back so that she could push her body fully against his. He groaned and pressed her farther into the deep grasses, exciting her with the virile loving of his masculine body.

Jenny burned with desire and sensual delight. With her arms laced around his powerful body and her legs entwined wantonly with his, she cried his name again and again, almost begging as their passion carried them to soaring, volcanic heights. Together they exploded, and waves as hotly molten as lava crashed over them as they clung to one another.

"My love, my darling, my wife," he murmured gently.

Her green eyes opened slowly and lifted to his, drowsy with languorous fulfillment and love. "Blade, I'm so happy. No man could ever make me happier. I love you."

He'd waited a lifetime to hear her say those words. As he stared down at her, he took in her voluptuous beauty. Her cheeks were flushed, her lips reddened and full. She wore the look of a sated woman very much in love.

She was his. At last. Only his.

"And I love you, only you," he said tenderly. "I always have, and I always will."

They kissed each other again, their kiss a promise that their love would last forever.

*　*　*　*　*

A Note from Ginna Gray

Is there a woman alive who isn't a sucker for a rebel? I doubt it. They're irresistible, these maverick "bad boys" who thumb their noses at the world and go their own way.

The Gentling is a story about the healing power of love, the story of a woman who has been so wounded, she is terrified of men.

While casting the characters for this tale, I asked myself what sort of man it would take to overcome such intense fear and open this woman's heart to love. The answer was obvious: a determined "do-or-die" rebel.

However, he could not be simply a man who knew what he wanted and refused to take no for an answer, but a rugged man whose masculinity was merely enhanced by his deep capacity for tenderness.

From that first grain of an idea, my hero was born. Every woman should have a "wild one" like Trace Barnett in her life.

The Gentling was my first book, and I am thrilled that Silhouette has chosen to reissue it. I wrote this story in 1982, and the next year it won the Golden Heart Award (given by Romance Writers of America) for the Best Unpublished Traditional Romance. Silhouette bought it immediately, and my career was launched.

I hope, dear readers, that you enjoy this story as much as I enjoyed writing it. Many years have passed, and I have written over twenty books since *The Gentling* was published, but it will always hold a special place in my heart.

Happy reading!

Ginna Gray

THE GENTLING

Ginna Gray

To my father, Roy Conn, in loving memory.
He never once doubted that I could do it.

Chapter One

Katy Donovan listened to the preacher's pious voice drone on and on, her face a stoic mask. Head unbowed, hands thrust deep inside the pockets of her light, all-weather coat, she stood rigid beside her father, only remotely aware of the biting chill in the March wind or the group of subdued people around her. Overhead, a ragged layer of clouds scudded across the east Texas sky, trailing an eerie pattern of fast moving shadows over the graveside mourners.

It had rained earlier, and the air was heavy with the pungent scents of pine and dank, rusty-red earth. From the woods surrounding the cemetery came the raucous cawing of a flock of crows.

"Dear Lord, we commit unto your keeping the soul of your faithful servant, Henry Alan Barnett," the preacher intoned pontifically. "Henry was a good man, Lord, a respected man. Loved by all, hated by none."

Katy stirred, and at once her father's hand tightened on her arm. On the opposite side of the grave, swathed completely in black and looking tragically beautiful, Saundra Barnett gave a soft cry as she clasped her hands together and lowered her blond head dolorously.

Katy watched her for a moment, then averted her eyes and stared across the glistening tombstones into the distance. A gusting breeze tore a strand of long black hair from the severe chignon at her nape and whipped it across her pale features. Absently, Katy tucked it back into place.

Suddenly watery sunshine broke through the clouds and glinted off the silver handles of the casket, drawing Katy's unwilling gaze. Her eyes narrowed as a surge of bitterness rose like bile in her throat.

Damn you, Henry Barnett, she screamed silently. May you burn in hell forever! Katy was shaking with the ferocity of her feelings, her pulse throbbing in her throat. Instantly regretting the crack in her composure, she took several deep breaths and forced every sign of anguish from her face.

The young widow stepped forward and placed her hand on the ornate casket. "The Lord giveth and the Lord taketh away," the preacher's sonorous voice chanted. "Blessed be the name of the Lord." With a sob, Saundra turned and flung herself into the arms of the broad-shouldered man at her side.

A grimace of distaste broke the calm mask of Katy's features as she watched the theatrical display. She hadn't noticed the dark-suited man before, and now she wondered who he was. Saundra's latest lover, perhaps? The instant the thought popped into her head, she dismissed it. Not even Saundra would be that brazen. At the moment Katy couldn't see the man clearly. His head was bent over the petite blonde sobbing against his chest, while his hands moved consolingly over her heaving shoulders.

Then, without warning, he looked up. Deep-set hazel eyes locked with Katy's blue ones, and her heart crashed against her ribcage.

Trace! Good Lord! Trace Barnett had come home!

The burning intensity in that boldly familiar look tied Katy's stomach muscles into a hard knot. Shaken, she tore her eyes away and moved closer to her father, grasping his arm for support. Her knees seemed suddenly to have turned to water.

The preacher's voice droned mercifully to a halt, and his deeply intoned Amen was echoed softly by the cluster of people around the flower-bedecked casket. As he stepped to Saundra's side, Katy turned and began to walk away.

"Katy girl, aren't you going to offer your condolences to the family?"

There was a cold remoteness about her when she turned to face her father, a blankness in the vivid blue eyes that was chilling. "No, Dad. This is as far as I go. I only came to the funeral for your sake."

"Katy, I—" Tom Donovan's voice faltered as a spasm of guilt crossed his craggy features. "I—"

Instantly Katy softened. Placing her hand on his arm, she smiled reassuringly. "Don't worry about it, Dad. I understand. Really I do." She flicked a quick glance in Saundra's direction. "If you want to keep your job at the farm you can't afford to offend the new owner. So go ahead and do whatever you have to. I'll wait for you in the car."

Without another word, she turned and walked away.

* * *

The compact car bounced along the twisting, red-dirt road at a fast clip. Through the bare branches overhead Katy could occasionally glimpse the cerulean sky, with its flotilla of puffy clouds. If today's spell of warm weather held, soon even that would not be possible. Within a few weeks the interlacing branches of oaks, elms, sweetgums and pecans would form a leafy canopy over the road.

As she rounded a curve, Katy spied a robin flitting through the trees at the edge of the road. Reacting instinctively, she eased her foot off the accelerator. The reduced speed allowed her gaze to wander briefly from the narrow country lane, and immediately a contented smile curved her mouth.

Signs of spring were all around. Every bare limb was covered with tiny buds. Among the undergrowth, tender pale green shoots were already visible, pushing up through the newly thawed earth and the layers of dead leaves that blanketed the forest floor. Snowy white drifts of flowering dogwood brightened the deepest shadows of the forest, and the pinkish-lavender blossoms of the redbud trees provided the first, breathtaking splashes of color.

The cool breeze blowing in through the open windows of the car was fragrant with the smell of newly turned earth. Katy reached up with one hand and released the clasp at the nape of her neck. A shake of her head sent her long, raven-black hair tumbling free. She laughed happily as the wind threaded teasing fingers through the thick, luxuriant mass of ebony and swirled it around her shoulders like a black silk cape.

Katy drove the private country road with the easy confidence of long experience. Her father had been the manager of Green Meadows Farm for the past fifteen years, and she knew every twist and turn, every pot hole. The road was the back entrance to the farm. It cut through the surrounding woods, then made a lazy, meandering loop past the scattered cottages of the married workers, before finally ending at the stables behind the Barnetts' big colonial mansion.

The forest thinned, then gave way to an open meadow. To the right, set far off the road, was the small white frame house where Katy had lived since she was a child of six. Braking, she turned in through the open gate. There was a double garage behind the house but Katy stopped the car beside the pickup in the wide drive. There was time enough later to put it away.

As she reached out to turn off the ignition a movement on the porch caught her eye, and she turned her head. Her hand froze in mid-air when she recognized the man standing there in the shadows.

A crawling, tingling sensation ran up over her scalp, making the hairs on her nape bristle. Damn! If only she'd been more alert, she might have seen him. The she could have driven on and stayed away until he had gone. The blue pickup had not given her a clue, since it was one of the half dozen or so owned by Green Meadows Farm and identical to the one her father always drove. Katy stared at the tall, broad-shouldered man and silently berated herself for her carelessness. She had known, intuitively, that he would come.

A vague feeling of unease had nagged at her since seeing Trace yesterday at the funeral, but she had pushed it away. Foolishly she had allowed herself to be mesmerized by the signs of spring, lulled into a false sense of security and well-being. It was one of those soft, unseasonably warm days that completely beguiles the senses, and Katy had fallen so totally under its spell that she had forgotten all about Trace Barnett.

As she switched off the engine he moved out of the shadows and stood on the top step, watching her, tall and lean and infinitely dangerous looking. His stance was casual as he waited for her to join him, one arm propped against the porch post, the other on his hip, but Katy was aware that his eyes never left her.

Taking a deep breath, she composed herself, climbed from the car, and started up the brick path on legs that were suddenly weak and rubbery. Though well aware that she was being subjected to a thorough, masculine appraisal, when Katy looked directly into those penetrating hazel eyes she almost reeled with shock. They gleamed with a frankly sensual interest which he made no effort to conceal. It was only through sheer strength of will that she was able to clamp down on her emotions and quell the cowardly urge to turn and run. Katy recognized the tingling feeling that raced up her spine for exactly what it was—pure, cold, mindless fear.

There was no specific reason for her fear of Trace. It was strictly a gut level feeling. She had known him nearly all her life, and yet, strangely, did not know him at all. He had been the owner's son, and she merely the daughter of the farm manager, and eleven years his junior. For years their lives had run along a parallel plane, existing at the same time, in the same place, with no point of contact between them. Yet she knew, instinctively, that Trace Barnett spelled danger. She had known that much when she had been only seventeen.

The promise of great beauty had become a reality about that time, and she had blossomed, almost overnight, from a gangly, skinny teenager into a breathtakingly lovely young woman. The transformation had not escaped Trace. During that year before he left the farm she had been aware of the long, speculative looks he directed her way. Cautious and reserved by nature, she had never once acknowledged the open invitation in those wicked hazel eyes. At seventeen she had been far too naive to know the reason for those warm, slumberous glances and that small crooked smile that had set her insides to quivering strangely. But she knew now.

Trace had never approached her openly, but had, nevertheless, managed to let her know that he found her very attractive. Though she had pretended not to notice, she had been both excited and frightened by his attention.

That was four years ago. Now all she felt was stark terror. It had gripped her yesterday at the graveside, when she glanced up and found him staring at her, his face alive with male interest. She had known then that if he stayed, this time he would do more than just look.

Katy forced herself to return his steady gaze as she neared the porch. Trace was the first to break eye contact, and she felt a small sense of victory until she realized that he was now conducting a leisurely inspection of her body, from her tousled black hair to the pink toes peeping out of her strappy sandals. The hot, searing look sent fresh tremors through her. Gritting her teeth, Katy took a deep breath and forced herself to speak.

"Hello, Mr. Barnett." Her soft voice was coated with a thin layer of ice.

Trace's eyes lifted slowly, lingering for just a fraction of a second on the full curves of her breasts, before returning to her face. He smiled. "Hello, Katy."

His voice was low and husky, giving the simple greeting the sensuality of a caress, and Katy stiffened, panic streaking through her. Her heart began to beat like a wild thing against her ribs.

What was it about Trace that disturbed her so? During the past four years she had met, and been unaffected by, a number of interested males. Oh, they had made her nervous and uneasy, but she had never allowed any of them to get close enough to stir the deep well of fear locked inside her. Yet Trace could do it with just a look.

At close quarters he was even more overwhelming than he had seemed yesterday when she had only seen him from a distance. Four years had added maturity to his face and intensified his rugged masculinity. He had the hard, chiseled look one associates with an outdoorsman. His nose was straight and well-modeled, his jaw strong. His lips were well-defined and firm, and when he smiled, they revealed strong, even teeth. Bronze skin was stretched taut and smooth over the prominent bones of his face, and there was a network of fine lines that fanned out from the corners of his eyes. His light brown hair was thick and springy, with a tendency to curl against his nape and over the top of his ears. His hazel eyes were deep-set and hooded, topped by thick, light brown brows and surrounded by short, almost white lashes. Trace was a tall, lean man, with broad shoulders, long legs, and narrow hips. And he was, above all, utterly and devastatingly male.

Katy's throat tightened painfully as she looked at him. He exuded an earthy sensuality that unnerved her, a raw, primitive virility that reached out and touched her, and made her skin prickle.

He was smiling at her, his eyes amused, as though he knew she found him disturbing. He was right, she did, though not in the way he probably thought. Katy lowered her gaze, afraid her eyes would give her away. Some men, she knew, were turned on as much by fear as by passion.

Reaching into her bag, she pulled out her house key. "I'm afraid my father is not here at the moment. If you'd like to leave a message for him, I'll see that he gets it as soon as he returns." A quiver shook her voice, but there was no mistaking the dismissal in her words.

Katy knew she was probably being very stupid, talking to him that way. Trace was now her father's employer. Yet she couldn't help herself.

Turning away, she inserted the key into the lock. She could see him out of the corner of her eye. Trace was watching her every move with disconcerting interest. She opened the door just a fraction, then hesitated, expecting him to take the hint and leave, but he didn't move. Katy gritted her teeth and looked back over her shoulder, a tight smile on her face. "In any case, I'll be sure and tell him that you came by."

To her surprise, Trace seemed to find her efforts to be rid of him amusing. Mocking laughter glittered in his eyes as he stepped closer and put his hand on the door. "If you don't mind, I'll wait," he said with the arrogant self-confidence of a man accustomed to getting his own way.

She stared at him for a moment, totally dismayed. Her heart began to pound. Oh, God! She didn't want him here! Couldn't he see that? Hazel eyes locked with hers, challenging, daring her to refuse him. Finally she nodded her head in stiff agreement, her mouth thin. "Of course. You're welcome to come in and wait," she lied.

"Thank you," he said dryly.

He motioned for her to precede him, and Katy stepped inside. Every nerve in her body seemed to jump when she heard the door click shut behind them. With jerky steps she walked across the room and placed her bag on an end table. Turning, she found that Trace had stopped just inside the door.

His stance was loose and casual, feet apart, hands stuck in the back pockets of his jeans. His head was thrown back and his eyes were scanning the room intently, noting the homey furniture, the pictures on the wall, the braided rug—every minute detail.

Katy watched him, puzzled by his interest. His gaze flickered back to her face and he smiled. "Do you know, I've never been in your home before?" He sounded surprised, as though it were something he had only just realized.

"Yes, I know," she replied bluntly. Of course he hadn't. Neither had his father nor his stepmother. The Barnetts were very class-conscious people. They didn't consider a mere employee their social equal. When Henry Barnett had wished to speak to her father, he had sent for him to come up to the big house. He would not have dreamed of lowering himself by going to his farm manager's home.

Katy edged toward the door leading into the hall. "If you'll excuse me for a moment, Mr. Barnett, I'll wash up. Then, if you'd like, I'll make some coffee."

Trace folded his long frame into an armchair and smiled. "Fine. Take your time."

In the bathroom Katy quickly washed her hands and ran a comb through her hair, studiously avoiding her pale reflection in the mirror. When she had restored order to her appearance she stood quietly for a moment and pressed her hand against her fluttering stomach. Finally she took a deep breath and retraced her steps, giving Trace a nervous smile as she walked through the living room.

"I'll just be a moment," she said, and quickly pushed through the kitchen door. When it swung shut behind her she closed her eyes and breathed a deep, shuddering sigh.

Barely knowing what she was doing, Katy automatically spooned ground coffee into the coffeepot's basket and filled the reservoir with water. She turned on the switch and watched distractedly as a thin stream of brown liquid slowly filled the glass pot. Her eyes darted toward the living room.

It was strange that in the end Trace had inherited Green Meadows Farm. Henry Barnett had declared repeatedly, and very forcefully, that he would not leave his maverick son one red cent. After quarreling violently with his father four years ago, Trace had walked out, and the old man had never forgiven him. No one knew exactly what the quarrel had been about but, as usual in a city the size of Tyler, the rumors were plentiful. Regardless of the cause, the split had been a serious one, and Trace had not returned to the farm until yesterday.

Katy recalled that when she was a child it had seemed as though Trace was constantly quarreling with his father over one thing or another. A wild one. That was what her father called him, though he said it with the affectionate tolerance of a man who had found a kindred soul.

For Thomas Patrick Donovan had also been a wild one in his time. A big bear of an Irishman, he had roamed the world footloose and fancy-free, working when he chose, drinking when he felt like it, and brawling just for the sheer fun of it. But Tom Donovan's wild days had come to an abrupt end when he met Kathleen O'Shea. Her delicate beauty and gentle ways had ensnared him as nothing else ever could, binding him to her with silken ties of love. He had, quite simply, adored her. After their marriage he had become a model husband and, a year later, a proud father.

Katy's eyes darted once again toward the living room. The same thing could happen to Trace, she supposed, though it didn't seem likely. She doubted that love for a woman would ever tame Trace Barnett. He still had that look of a maverick, a rebel, one who thumbs his nose at the world and goes his own way.

A great many people were surprised and stunned when Henry Barnett's will was read and it was disclosed that Trace had inherited Green Meadows Farm. Katy smiled wryly to herself. Not the least of whom was Saundra Barnett, Henry's young widow. She had fully expected to inherit everything. How shocked she must have been to learn that she would receive only a modest sum in cash.

The coffee maker gurgled to a stop and Katy placed the glass pot on a tray. After adding two cups, cream, and sugar, she picked it up and pushed through the door.

"Here, let me do that." Trace jumped up and took the tray from her hands and placed it on the low coffee table. To Katy's dismay, instead of returning to the chair, he joined her on the sofa. The nervous, panicky feeling intensified, making the hair on the back of her neck stand on end. Clenching her jaw, she picked up the coffeepot and concentrated fiercely on filling the cups.

"Cream and sugar?"

"No, just black."

Katy handed him the cup, being careful not to touch him.

Apparently very much at ease, Trace leaned back against the sofa and drank his coffee slowly. Katy didn't have to look at him to know he was watching her. She could feel his eyes on her. She added sugar to her coffee and watched the swirling, brown liquid intently as she stirred it.

"Tell me, Katy. What have you been doing these past four years, other than growing incredibly beautiful?" he asked softly.

She looked up, and her stomach gave a sickening little lurch. His eyes glittered with a disturbing intensity as they roamed over her, warm and boldly sensual. It was the same look she had surprised on his face yesterday.

Katy stared down at the cup in her hand and ran one finger slowly around the edge. "For the last year I've been working at a nursery school in Tyler. Before that I took care of my mother."

She felt tears stinging the back of her eyes and quickly looked away. It was still difficult to talk about her lovely, brave mother. They had known since Katy was fourteen that Kathleen Donovan was dying of a slow progressive muscular disease, but that had not made her death any easier to take. For six years, during the time when other girls her age were in open rebellion against their parents, Katy had spent every spare moment with her mother, heartbreakingly aware that she was slowly slipping away.

"I'm sorry about your mother, Katy. I know you were very close to her." Trace's voice broke through her sad thoughts, soft and infinitely gentle.

She looked at him then and saw that there was a genuine compassion in his eyes. Somehow she hadn't expected that from him, and it had a devastating effect on her fragile self-control. Her chest was tight with suppressed emotion and her throat hurt, but Katy knew she had to make some reply. Otherwise she was going to burst into tears. Blinking away the moisture in her eyes, she smiled faintly.

"Thank you, Mr. Barnett. Actually, I'm the one who should be offering condolences. My mother died almost a year ago, but you've only just buried your father."

"Ah, but I can't pretend that my father and I were ever close, and there was certainly no love lost between us." Trace smiled dryly. "Therein lies the difference."

Taken aback, Katy looked down at her hands. Her relationship with her parents had always been a warm, loving one. They were a unit, a family. The cold indifference in Trace's voice when he spoke of his father made her shiver. When the silence ran on she searched her mind desperately for something to say.

The problem was solved for her when Trace said, "Tell me, whatever happened to your plans for college? I seem to recall hearing that you wanted to be a teacher."

Sensing criticism, Katy's head jerked up. "There wasn't any money for college. My mother's illness was very costly. Dad had to borrow just to pay for her therapy and medication, and he's still paying off the loan." She stared at him, her blue eyes defiant. "But whatever the cost, whatever the sacrifice, if it added just one day to her life, it was worth it."

He looked at her tenderly and smiled. "Of course it was."

His soft agreement dissolved the small spurt of defensive anger, and Katy felt foolish for having bristled. Being this close to Trace made her nervous and on edge.

He leaned over and placed his cup on the coffee table. The movement strained the soft cotton shirt tautly across his broad back and shoulders. Katy's eyes were drawn irresistibly to the play of flexing muscles beneath the thin material, and she felt her mouth go suddenly dry. She looked away quickly when he sat back and turned sideways on the sofa, draping his arm along the back. Her stomach muscles clenched into a hard knot. She was vitally aware of his hand, resting just inches away from her shoulder.

"It's a pity though," he mused, as his eyes roamed over her face in open admiration. "You would have made a very good teacher. You're the gentle, quiet type that children take to." He paused and grinned. "And I've always found that children have a great appreciation for beautiful things." Reaching out with one finger, he ran it along the delicate curve of her shoulder, and Katy flinched.

"Don't, please," she pleaded desperately. She closed her eyes and shivered, her hands clenched into tight fists in her lap. Her nerves were screaming. She had known he would touch her. He had come here for that purpose, not to see her father. All his soft concern and interest was just a ruse. He was just like all the rest of his kind—rich, influential men who thought they could take whatever they wanted, with no thought for anyone else. However, being her father's employer, Trace was in a much more powerful position than the others she had met.

She stood up. "I think it would be best if you just left a message for my father, Mr. Barnett. I really have no idea when he'll be home."

Trace smiled and stretched his long legs out in front of him. "Oh, he won't be too long. He went into town to pick up a part for the tractor. He should be back any time now."

Not if he stopped off for a drink, Katy thought sadly. That was something he had been doing regularly since her mother's death. Thomas Donovan was a broken man, shattered into a million pieces. The loss of his beloved Kathleen had been a blow from which he had never truly recovered. It didn't happen often, and he never drank during working hours, but when his pain became too much for him to bear, he occasionally sought relief in the bottom of a whiskey bottle. It hurt her to see him grieving so, and she didn't have the heart to scold him.

Katy turned back to the devastatingly attractive man who sat lazily on the sofa, looking at her with a glint of amusement in his eyes. She twisted her hands nervously. "In that case, I'm afraid I really must start dinner, Mr. Barnett."

"That's all right. I'll keep you company in the kitchen. I like to watch a woman being domestic." He grinned and winked. "It's something you don't see very often these days."

Katy wanted to scream! Was the man totally insensitive? She had all but demanded that he leave, and still he would not budge!

During the last three years she had become adept at fending off predatory males. Her beauty had drawn the interest of most of the eligible men in the area at one time or another. At first they found her cool reserve challenging, but when it became evident that she was simply not interested, was in fact repelled by their advances, they quickly moved on to easier game. The male ego is a fragile thing at best, and a woman's complete lack of interest is too wounding to be endured for long.

Trace Barnett, however, was a different breed of animal, and Katy was slowly and alarmingly becoming convinced that he would not be so easily discouraged.

She stared at him wordlessly for a long moment. His dogged determination was unnerving. This man was dangerous and she knew it, yet she could think of no reason for refusing him. "Very well," she replied tightly, and turned on her heel. A muscle twitched in her jaw as she stalked into the kitchen.

Trying her best to ignore him, Katy opened the refrigerator door and pulled out two thick steaks. After scoring the edges, she sprinkled them with seasoning and placed them in a broiler pan, then set it aside. Trace leaned against the counter, his arms crossed over his chest, watching her. Katy was acutely conscious of his long, lean frame, and its aura of pure maleness. Suddenly the kitchen seemed too small. Her nerves were stretched to breaking point, and when he spoke she jumped, her pulse leaping in alarm.

"So you're still hiding from the world," he said softly. It was a statement, not a question, and it caught her completely unaware.

A puzzled frown knit between her brows. Had she missed something? She didn't have the faintest idea what he was talking about. Turning back to the refrigerator, she began to remove the salad ingredients.

"I'm afraid I don't understand."

"I'm talking about your job. It's typical of you to choose one where you seldom come into contact with adults. Men in particular. You were as skittish as a young deer four years ago, but I thought by now you would have outgrown that." He shook his head, his hazel eyes intent on her face. "If anything, you're even more withdrawn."

Katy took two salad bowls from the cabinet and placed them on the counter. She was trying desperately to keep her expression calm, though her insides were quaking. "I took the job in the nursery because I love children. That was why I wanted to become a teacher. Since that field was closed to me, this was the next best thing."

She had not looked at him while she spoke, but kept her eyes on her hands as they broke the lettuce up into small pieces, very slowly and precisely. He had no idea how nervous he was making her, or how terrified she was of breaking down in front of him. Only her father knew and understood, and he wasn't here.

Trace leaned closer and tilted his head to look into her face. He was smiling that crooked little half smile. His eyes were teasing. "If you love kids so much you should have some of your own. You'd make a wonderful mother, Mary Kathleen Donovan. But first you need to become a wife"—he paused, then added with a wicked grin—"and a lover."

His warm breath caressed her ear as the softly whispered, evocative words stroked over her, and she shivered violently. Katy put down the knife she was using to dice tomatoes and clutched the edge of the counter with both hands. She closed her eyes and fought down the hysterical bubble of fear that rose in her throat. She had to get him out of here, somehow, and she had to do it *now*. Lifting a shaking hand, she ran it over her brow.

"Look, Mr. Barnett, I don't think—"

A car door slammed and Tom Donovan's loud, booming voice carried through the open windows. "Katy, darlin', I'm home. Would you be havin' a hot meal ready for a poor starvin' man?"

Katy's eyes flew open in sheer panic. Her father was drunk or close to it. The thick Irish brogue was a dead giveaway. Under normal circumstances it was hardly noticeable, but when he was drinking or his emotions were aroused, he always lapsed into the lilting speech of his youth.

Her stricken gaze swung toward Trace, her blue eyes pleading for understanding. If her father lost this job, he would have a difficult time finding another at his age. He had been middle-aged when he had finally married and settled down. Though he had been a loyal and trustworthy employee, no one wanted to hire a man in his sixties.

The front door banged shut. Katy dried her hands and rushed past Trace.

Her father was standing just inside the living room, and her heart sank when she saw him. His face was flushed and he was definitely unsteady on his feet. Even his thick mane of white hair was untidy. Quickly, she walked over to him and slipped an arm around his waist.

"Dad, where have you been? Mr. Barnett has been waiting for you." It was as much of a warning as she could give him. Katy could only hope that he was sober enough to understand.

Tom Donovan stiffened. "What?"

"Mr. Barnett is in the kitchen, Dad. He was here when I came home."

"I wanted to go over the work schedule with you," Trace said, as he stepped into the room. He hesitated a moment, his attention captured by the expression on Katy's face. The deep-set hazel eyes narrowed, then slid back to the huge man at her side. He stared at him for several seconds, his gaze hard and probing. Then, at last, he seemed to have reached a decision. Shrugging indifferently, he said, "However, since it's so late, we'll leave it until tomorrow."

Katy went limp with relief.

Tom's expression grew anxious. He was not so far gone that he missed the paleness of his daughter's face or the harried look in her eyes. A silent message passed between them, and Katy smiled tremulously, reassured by his presence. Only he knew what an ordeal it had been for her, being here alone with Trace for all this time.

A worried frown creased his brow. "Are you all right, Katy?" he asked softly.

"Yes, Dad."

Trace scowled and walked further into the room. His hard gaze sliced back and forth between Katy and her father.

"Is there some reason why Katy wouldn't be all right?" he demanded with an angry edge to his voice.

"Well . . . er . . . no." Tom looked distinctly uncomfortable. "It's just that Katy has been . . . unwell lately."

"I see," Trace replied thoughtfully, his hazel eyes raking over her.

Katy held her breath, silently praying that he wouldn't probe further. She couldn't bear that.

Finally, after an interminable period of strained silence, he turned and picked up his hat from the chair, then gave the older man a curt nod. "I'll meet you at the stables first thing in the morning, Tom. Good night."

Katy released her hold on her father. Politeness demanded that she see Trace to the door. She was a step behind him when he paused with his hand on the knob and looked down at her, smiling.

"By the way, Katy darlin'," he murmured softly, giving an excellent imitation of her father's Irish brogue. "My name is Trace. Remember that."

Chapter Two

As Katy lifted the tiny blond mite, chubby arms encircled her neck and the child planted a moist, smacking kiss on her cheek.

"Bye, Miss Katy."

Katy smiled and hugged the warm little body to her for a second. "Good-bye, Millie. I'll see you tomorrow."

Still holding the child close, she opened the passenger door of the waiting car and bent over. She smiled at the woman behind the wheel as she sat the little girl on the seat and fastened the safety belt around her. "Millie has had a very big day, Mrs. Carter. At play period she built a sand castle all by herself."

A ferocious frown darkened the little girl's brow. "Yes. An' that rotten Jeff kicked it down," she complained petulantly.

Both women laughed at the expression of pure fury on the cherubic little face.

"Sorry about that." Katy's grin was rueful. "I'm afraid Jeffrey Bond has a bit of a crush on Millie, and like most four-year-old boys, he had a rather strange way of demonstrating his affection."

"Oh, believe me, Miss Donovan, I know how it goes," Millie's mother replied, still laughing. "Millie is the last of my brood, so I've been through it all before. Love among the pre-school set can sometimes be rather violent."

"Yes, but it all worked out. After he apologized, Jeffrey helped her rebuild her castle, and it was a beauty."

Refusing to be mollified quite so easily, Millie stuck out her bottom lip. "But it wasn't as good as the first one. Jeff don't know how to build a castle." She sniffed disdainfully, turning up her tiny nose and dismissing the little boy's efforts with the haughty superiority of a very young female.

"Well, never mind, angel. Tomorrow you can build another one, and I'll see that Jeff doesn't bother you." Katy smiled at Mrs. Carter and planted another quick kiss on Millie's forehead. "Bye now, sweetheart. I'll see you tomorrow afternoon." Straightening, she closed and locked the passenger door and stepped back. As the car pulled away Millie waved furiously, and Katy laughed and waved back.

She watched until they were out of sight, then turned back to the nursery school entrance. A satisfied smile eased the tiredness from her face.

Katy entered the small office and locked the door behind her. After closing the draperies, she turned and stepped through the door to the right of the desk and walked down the long hall, stopping several times along the way to pick up the stray toys that littered the floor.

By the time she reached the end of the hall her arms were full. The door to the playroom was slightly ajar. Giving it a nudge with her hip, she pushed it open and walked inside, then stopped short at the sight that greeted her.

Her friend and employer, Jane Cawley, was down on her hands and knees, her jean-covered behind stuck up in the air as she wriggled the upper half of her body under one of the large, extremely low tables.

"What on earth are you doing?" Katy laughed openly at her friend's undignified position.

"I'm...trying...to clean up this...gooey...mess," Jane gasped, groping still farther under the table. "There...I've got it!" Grunting with every move, she began to wriggle backward, and Katy laughed harder as Jane crawfished from under the table. When she extricated her head, Jane turned and flopped down on the floor. Her face was beet red. The short, brown hair that normally hugged her face, pixie fashion, was sticking up at all angles. Still panting from her exertions, Jane lowered her gaze to the squashed peanut-butter-and-jelly sandwich in her hand and made a face of utter revulsion. "Yuck! Would you look at this revolting mess."

Jane pushed herself up from the floor and walked over to the sink in the corner, depositing the mangled sandwich in the trash before washing the sticky remains from her fingers. "How I stand the little monsters for eight hours every day, I don't know. I need to have my head examined."

"Oh, come on now. Who are you kidding?" Katy gave her friend a reproving look. "You love every minute of it, and you know it."

"I know, I know," Jane conceded with a rueful grin, as she turned to help Katy with the chairs. "I just have to complain now and then or people really will think I'm crazy. But you're right. I do love taking care of children. I thought I'd go bonkers when my own became teenaged and got involved in so many outside activities that I hardly ever saw them. I was suffering from what is commonly known as the empty nest syndrome. The smartest thing I ever did was to open this nursery school." She smiled at Katy and winked. "And the second smartest thing I ever did was to hire you."

Katy returned her friend's smile but made no comment. Funny how things work out, she mused. She had taken this job out of desperation, and it had turned out to be one of the best things that had ever happened to her. It didn't pay much, but she enjoyed the work, and she absolutely adored each and every one of the pint-sized tyrants. An added bonus was the close friendship that had developed between herself and Jane during the year she had worked at the nursery. Due to her reserved nature and the demands that had been made on her time during her teenage years, Katy had not developed any close friendships, and therefore valued this one all the more.

Jane was a small, vivacious woman in her late thirties. An eternal optimist, she bounced through life thoroughly enjoying each day, intensely interested in everything and everyone. Though she was not particularly pretty, no one ever noticed. She had laughing eyes and an incandescent smile that made you feel good just to be around her. She was a bubbly, outgoing extrovert, the direct opposite of Katy.

When the chairs were stacked, Jane turned toward the kitchen. "Come on. Let's have a cup of coffee and prop our feet up for a few minutes before we leave."

In the kitchen Jane poured out two mugs of coffee and handed one to Katy. Kicking off her shoes, she curled herself into the corner of the battered old couch that occupied one wall and tucked her feet under her. She looked at Katy and patted the adjacent cushion. "Come sit down. I'm dying to know what's going on at the farm. I heard only this morning that Trace has inherited Green Meadows. Is that true?"

Katy almost laughed aloud at the avid curiosity written on Jane's face. She knew she really shouldn't be surprised that news of Henry Barnett's will had already spread. It was next to impossible to keep anything a secret in Tyler. The city had grown to a respectable size, but in many ways had retained its small town attitude. As the richest, most powerful family in that part of Texas, the Barnetts had always been the subject of a great deal of speculation and gossip. The fact that Trace had inherited the farm was bound to start tongues wagging.

Katy sat down on the couch. "Yes. It's true."

"Ooohhh, isn't that delicious!" Jane squealed with delight. "I'll bet that witch, Saundra, is ready to have a stroke. The only reason she married Henry Barnett was to get her greedy little hands on his money. And now she's been left high and dry."

"Not quite. Though she'll have no share in the farm or any of the other family holdings, I believe she inherited a modest amount in cash." Katy took a sip of coffee, then smiled wryly. "Of course, what the Barnetts call a modest amount would probably be a fortune to other people."

"Mmmmm. Is she going to stay on at the farm, do you think?"

"Your guess is as good as mine. I make it a point to stay as far away from the Barnetts as I possibly can."

"Humph! I can't say that I blame you. Henry was a first-class snob, and so is that high-and-mighty alley cat he married," Jane burst out indignantly.

Jane and Saundra Barnett were the same age and had attended school together, but that was the only thing they had in common. Saundra was a brittle, sophisticated woman. She had thoroughly enjoyed the affluence and social position her marriage provided, while making no pretense of caring for her elderly husband. Her frequent, passionate affairs were common knowledge.

In one of her lightning-quick changes of mood, Jane's anger disappeared, and her face lit up with a smile, her eyes twinkling with mischief. "Tell me, is Trace still the gorgeous hunk he was four years ago?"

Katy's eyes grew round in feigned shock. "Why, Jane Cawley! And you a married woman! Whatever would Frank say?" She gave her a stern look and shook her head. "Gorgeous hunk, indeed!"

"I may be married but I'm not blind. And Frank wouldn't care. He knows he's the love of my life," her friend answered pertly. "So come on, tell me about Trace. Is he still as sinfully attractive as he was?"

Katy looked down at the mug of coffee she held in her hand and slowly traced one finger around the rim. She didn't want to talk about Trace. She didn't even want to think about him. It tied her insides up in knots.

"Yes, I suppose you could say that he's attractive...if you like the type."

Jane looked amused. "And just what type is he?"

"Dangerous."

The word slipped out before she thought, and Katy was instantly appalled that she had voiced her feelings aloud.

The blank astonishment on Jane's face slowly faded as she stared at Katy's bent head. She pursed her lips together thoughtfully. "Now that's a very revealing reaction. Don't tell me. Let me guess. Trace made a pass, didn't he?"

Katy looked up and smiled weakly, her cheeks pink. "No. It's not that."

"Then what is it? You don't usually react so violently toward a man. You just look right through most of them, as though they didn't exist."

"Oh, I don't know." Agitated, Katy waved her hand in the air in a vague, frustrated gesture. "It's just that he's so—so..."

"Sexy?" Jane's eyes were dancing as she asked the provocative question.

"Yes. I guess so." The agreement was given begrudgingly. Katy stood up and walked to the sink and rinsed out her cup. Just thinking about Trace made her feel quivery. Turning, she leaned back against the counter and gripped the edge with both hands. Her troubled expression revealed her inner confusion. "I don't know. Maybe it's just my overactive imagination, but he makes me so nervous and jittery. The way he looks at me...the things he says. It gives me this crawly sensation. I get the overpowering feeling he's up to something."

"Oh-ho! And I can just imagine what! Listen, honey. I wouldn't doubt my instincts if I were you. Trace has always had an eye for good-looking women, and I somehow can't see him passing up a gorgeous thing like you, especially since you live practically on his door-step.''

Katy pushed away from the counter and stooped to pick up her purse from beside the couch. ''I'm afraid this is one woman he'll just have to pass up. I want no part of him . . . or any man.''

''Oh, Katy, don't say that,'' Jane replied sadly. ''Marriage with the right person can be wonderful. And, besides, you were born to be a mother. Why, you love every one of the little imps who comes here.''

The words sent a wave of longing through Katy, so strong it was almost a physical pain, but she gritted her teeth and fought it down. ''That's right. I do. And for me, they'll just have to be enough.'' She had aban-doned all hope of having a family of her own three years ago. For her it was impossible. She knew Jane was puzzled by her attitude, but it couldn't be helped. She couldn't explain, not even to her.

''Katy Donovan! I swear, sometimes you make me so mad I could—''

''My, my. Don't tell me you two are having an argu-ment?''

The two women jumped, then laughed as they turned to see Frank Cawley standing propped against the door frame. A pleasant man with average features, he was the calm, pipe-smoking type, and the perfect counterbal-ance for Jane's bouncy, effervescent personality. Out-side of her parents, they were the most ideally suited couple Katy had ever known.

Jane catapulted herself off the couch straight into her husband's arms, giving him a hard kiss on the mouth, which he returned with enthusiasm. ''Hi, darling.'' She sighed happily, leaning back within his embrace.

"Hello, crazy lady." Frank gave her an affectionate squeeze and ruffled her short-cropped hair, then turned his direct gaze on Katy. "Now, tell me, beautiful. Why was this wife of mine lighting into you like a shrew?"

"Oh, it's the same old thing," Jane spat out disgustedly, before Katy could answer. "She absolutely refuses to have anything to do with men, especially Trace Barnett." Spinning around, she planted her hands on her hips and glared. "You know, Katy, you could do a lot worse."

"Honestly, Jane! Even if he *is* interested, which I seriously doubt, you don't really think marriage is what he has in mind, do you? People like the Barnetts don't marry farm workers' daughters."

"Mary Kathleen Donovan! Don't you dare let me hear you say such a stupid thing again! You're just as good as anyone. And a lot better than most. Certainly better than that bitch, Saundra, and she married a Barnett, even if it was that old snob, Henry."

Katy laughed nervously. Her friend's vehemence startled her. "Jane, for heaven's sake! Don't get so upset over nothing. I merely said the man makes me nervous, and now you're screaming at me because I won't marry him." She turned bewildered blue eyes on Frank. "Does she always jump to conclusions like this?"

He grinned. "Always. Especially when she's defending someone she loves. A regular little tigress, that's my Jane."

"Yes, well. Sorry, love. I didn't mean to get so carried away." Jane smiled ruefully. "It's just that you're one of my very favorite people, and I'll not let anyone run you down. Not even you."

"And I have to say, Katy, I think you're wrong about Trace," Frank added softly, as he took his pipe and tobacco pouch from his pocket. He dipped the bowl into the pouch and filled it, carefully tamping down the loose tobacco with his thumb. "When a young woman is as warm and sweet and lovely as you, all other considerations fade in importance."

Katy gave him a bitter smile. She liked Frank. He was a good friend, and one of the few men with whom she felt at ease. But he was still a man. "Well, this is all rather academic, isn't it? I've only talked with the man once since he returned."

On the way home Katy thought about Jane's indignant outburst. She hadn't meant to give the impression that she thought herself inferior to the Barnetts. She didn't. At least not in the ways that mattered. But neither did she fool herself into thinking they were on an equal footing. The Barnetts, and their kind, had a very definite advantage over ordinary people, an advantage they did not hesitate to use—power and influence. Katy had learned, the hard way, that without it you were helpless and vulnerable. She also knew that theirs was a closed society. They socialized only with people within their own circle, and they married only their own kind. And if one of their group was threatened, the other members of the pack closed ranks around them. You didn't stand a chance if you crossed swords with people like the Barnetts.

Katy drove home automatically, her mind occupied with her gloomy reflections. It was not until she turned into the drive that she realized her thoughts had once again strayed to Trace. Stop it! she told herself harshly. Stop thinking about him! The man was becoming an obsession. And why, she didn't know. It had been four days since that evening she had arrived home to find him waiting on the porch.

On the surface, nothing he had done or said that night could be faulted. Not really. Was it all just her imagination? Katy laughed in sudden self-derision. Maybe she was just becoming vain. Had she become so accustomed to fending off men that she automatically assumed every one she met was going to make a pass? Lord, surely she hadn't become as self-absorbed as all that!

No, Katy assured herself firmly as she climbed from the car. That look in his eyes, and the silky, sensuous tone of his voice when he spoke to her hadn't been a product of her imagination. But now that she'd had time to think about it, she realized his flirtatious manner probably didn't mean a thing. She had forgotten, for a while, that Trace and his crowd played by a different set of rules. It was probably second nature to him to flirt with every passably attractive woman he met. It was instinctive, an automatic reflex. It meant no more to him than blinking. Once he had walked out the door, he had probably forgotten all about her. Fool that she was, she'd spent the last four days worrying and fretting over how she was going to discourage him without jeopardizing her father's job, when if she'd just given it a little serious thought, she would have realized that the whole thing was ludicrous.

Katy unlocked the front door and stepped inside, then leaned back against the panel and closed her eyes. So why wouldn't this crawly feeling go away? a tiny voice whispered.

When her father's truck pulled into the drive Katy was standing at the sink, peeling potatoes. The sleeves of her blue and red plaid shirt were rolled up to her elbows, revealing the delicate bones of her wrists and forearms. Faded jeans hugged her hips and thighs like a soft second skin. Her raven-black hair was sleeked away from her face and held at her nape by a tortoise-shell clasp.

The front screen door banged against its frame. Katy didn't even look up. "Hi, Dad. I'm out here in the kitchen," she called over her shoulder.

"Whatever you're cooking smells delicious." Tom poked his head inside the kitchen door and smiled coaxingly. "I hope it will stretch to three. I invited Trace home to share our dinner."

It took a moment for his words to soak in. When they did, Katy turned slowly, her eyes wide with shock. She stared at her father, unable to believe what she'd heard. Then her gaze slid past him and collided with a pair of glinting hazel-green eyes, and the color slowly drained from her face.

A mocking, half smile played around one corner of Trace's mouth. His amused expression told her he was well aware of her dilemma.

"I hope this isn't an inconvenience, Katy. If it is, please feel free to say so." His tone was very polite, very proper, but Katy knew he was taunting her. Trace was quite obviously enjoying her discomfort.

"Nonsense, nonsense," her father cut in. Sniffing appreciatively, he stepped over to the stove and inspected the bubbling pots. "Katy is frying chicken, and she always cooks twice what we need. Now, come on. It's all settled." He motioned for Trace to follow as he started toward the door. "I'll show you where you can wash up, then I'll fix us a drink before dinner."

Katy stared at the two broad, retreating backs. How could he do this? How *could* he? Her father knew how she felt! But more important, he knew perfectly well that a man in his position simply did not invite someone like Trace home for dinner. Why, old Henry would have had apoplexy had he even suggested such a thing!

The small table set beneath the back window drew her eyes, and she groaned. She didn't suppose Trace had ever eaten in a kitchen in his life. Flooded with a feeling of helplessness and frustrated anger, Katy jerked open a cabinet and snatched a plate from the stack. She rummaged through the cutlery drawer for the proper utensils, then marched across the room and banged the items down on the table. Well, if he intends to eat here, he'll have to, she thought angrily. They didn't even have a dining room!

When Trace reappeared, Katy was standing at the stove, gently turning each piece of chicken, exposing the golden brown crust that had already formed on one side. She kept her eyes on the bubbling oil.

"I'm sorry, Mr. Barnett, if my father's invitation put you in an awkward position or embarrassed you in any way," she stated stiffly.

There was a short pause before Trace replied. "I'm neither embarrassed nor did I feel any particular obligation to accept your father's invitation. I never do anything I don't want to do." He stared at her coolly, his head cocked to one side. "I would never have thought you were an inverted snob, Katy Donovan."

The needling taunt stiffened her spine. She held her head high and turned to face him. "You must surely know that your father would not even have considered coming to this house for dinner. And if my father had been foolish enough to extend an invitation, I have no doubt he would have been put in his place, very quickly and very firmly." Katy soft voice was trembling with icy indignation. How dare he call her a snob!

The hazel eyes narrowed ominously. "One thing you'd better learn, Katy, and learn quickly. I am *not* my father." The low fury in his voice sent a shiver through her. "We saw eye to eye on practically nothing. So whatever preconceived notions you've formed about me, you can just throw out the window. I won't be tarred with the same brush, Katy. I'm my own man."

Confused by the harshness of his words and his determination to make her believe them, Katy mumbled a quick, "I'm sorry," and turned back to the stove. As she opened the oven door and slid in the tray of biscuits she felt his eyes boring a hole in her back. Finally, without a word, he turned and walked back into the living room.

A few minutes later her father bustled into the kitchen to prepare the drinks he had promised. Katy turned on him. Her eyes were brimming with tears.

"How could you do this, Dad? You knew I didn't want that man here. How could you?"

The anguish in her voice brought his movements to a halt. He put down the two glasses he had taken from the cupboard and turned to her. Big, paw-like hands cupped around her face to tilt it up for his inspection. Smiling down into her troubled eyes, he saw the fear and anxiety there and shook his head sadly.

"Oh, Katy, Katy." He sighed heavily. "Darlin', Trace won't hurt you. He's a good man. Can't you see that? Why, over the past week he has earned the respect and admiration of every man on the place." Tom's weathered brow creased with worry as he searched her face. Lowering his voice, he spoke to her soothingly, tenderly. "Believe me, sweetheart, if I didn't know I could trust him, I wouldn't let him near you."

Katy swallowed hard and lowered her eyes. Her chin quivering, she stared at a button on the front of his shirt. "All right, Dad. I won't say any more. It's too late now to do anything about it anyway."

The meal, and the rest of the evening, passed very smoothly, despite Katy's jittery nerves. Trace and her father consumed their food with the hearty appreciation of men who have spent the day out of doors doing physical labor. Katy barely touched hers. The talk centered around the farm—which mares were due to foal, which pastures were in need of attention, the cost of grain. It was strictly man talk and she was happy to sit back and let it all wash over her.

After the meal Katy served the men their coffee in the living room, then returned to the kitchen to do the washing up, grateful for the excuse to escape. She washed each dish carefully and slowly to draw out the chore as long as possible. As her hands went about the familiar task she stared past her reflection in the window at the dark shadows of the woods behind the house.

A storm was building up in the distance. Above the bare branches the sky glowed intermittently with eerie flashes of white as lightning streaked downward from a livid line of black clouds. Katy eyed it hopefully. If it moved this way, perhaps Trace would leave.

She sighed as she placed the last dish in the drain rack and pulled the stopper from the sink. What was the reason for his sudden friendly attitude? She thought about his taut anger when she had apologized for her father's presumptuousness in inviting him here. Was that it? Was he trying to demonstrate that he was not a carbon-copy of his father, that he had no intention of following his lead? If so, was he doing it out of sheer obstinacy, a determination to go against his father's wishes? Or did he really want to develop a better working relationship with his employees?

Henry Barnett's haughty lord of the manor attitude had always irritated Katy. Her father liked it no better than she, but he managed to shrug it off. He knew his worth, and he loved this farm and his work too much to be bothered by his employer's social prejudices. Thomas Donovan had a way with animals, particularly horses. He had worked with them all his life, both in Ireland and the states, and his knowledge and experience were unsurpassed. Henry Barnett had not liked him, had thought him too proud by far for a mere working man, but he had been no one's fool. He had known exactly what kind of manager he had in Tom Donovan.

Katy supposed she should be grateful that Trace treated her father with the respect and deference his age and experience deserved. Drying her hands, she hung the towel on the rack in the pantry. The low rumble of male voices drew her gaze toward the living room, and her lips compressed into a bitter line. At least with Henry they hadn't had to worry about him dropping in any time it suited him.

There was hardly a pause in the conversation when Katy entered the room and slipped quietly into a chair. She doubted that either man had even noticed her presence, which, for some perverse reason, annoyed her intensely.

While they continued their discussion about the work schedule and the various changes Trace wanted to make around the farm, Katy took a half-finished needlepoint pillow cover from her sewing basket and concentrated fiercely on the in and out movements of the needle she was stabbing through the canvas. She was making an absolute mess of it. Tomorrow she would have to pick out every single stitch. Tonight, however, she needed something to divert her attention, anything that would keep her gaze from straying to the large, lean man across the room.

He gestured with his hand suddenly and Katy glanced up, her eyes drawn by the movement. She studied him thoughtfully through the long sweep of her lashes. He sat deep in the chair, his long legs stretched out lazily in front of him, one arm hooked casually over the back. His sleeves were rolled up, revealing tanned, muscular forearms, covered with a generous sprinkling of short, light hair, bleached almost white by constant exposure to the sun. Irresistibly, her gaze traveled over his long, powerful body, noting the way his jeans were molded over his narrow hipbones, the curling chest hair visible at the V-shaped opening of his shirt, the breadth of his shoulders. It seemed to her there was a careless sensuality in his every move. When her gaze lifted to his firm, masculine lips an icy shiver feathered up her spine, and she tore her eyes away.

Katy frowned down at the hopelessly knotted canvas in her lap. What was there about Trace? All evening long her gaze had been drawn to him, like steel to a magnet. It was unnerving. Why was she so intensely aware of him? Most men she simply ignored, their presence never penetrating the icy shield she had formed around herself. But somehow Trace had. And she didn't like it. Since that moment in the cemetery, almost a week ago, when she had looked up and met those glittering hazel eyes, her defenses had begun to crack.

It was a little after ten when the rumble of thunder began to make itself heard. The sound drew Trace's attention and he rose, reluctantly.

"I guess I'd better be going. If I don't leave now, I'll be caught in the deluge." At the door he turned back and gave Katy a slow smile. "Thank you again, Katy, for a delicious meal. I enjoyed it." His gaze shifted to her father. "Tom, I'll see you at the stables in the morning."

Katy and her father barely had time to say a quick good night and he was gone. The suddenness of his departure and his casual, almost distant attitude toward her all evening left her slightly bemused, a feeling that was rapidly replaced by relief.

Two hours later Katy lay staring at the ceiling above her bed, listening to the rain drumming on the roof. She couldn't sleep, and she knew why. Every time she started to drift off, she was haunted by a pair of taunting hazel-green eyes, laughing at her. As much as she hated to admit it, Katy knew Trace was responsible for this indefinable, restless longing. For three years her normal sexual urges had been suppressed, anesthetized by shock. In that time she had felt nothing for any man—no pull of the senses, no heady awareness, not even dislike. She had been completely numb. But now, slowly and surely, Trace was pulling her out of that undemanding, unfeeling state, simply by the force of his presence. His raw masculinity was too potent to be ignored. It was awakening in her responses she did not want to feel, making her acutely aware of her own femininity. It didn't help to tell herself she didn't want a relationship with any man. Her healthy, young body simply would not listen.

She raised herself up on one elbow and punched her feather pillow into a soft cloud, but it didn't help ease the tension. Stifling a moan, she rolled onto her side and stared into the darkness. The small mantel clock in the living room had chimed two o'clock before her eyelids finally fluttered shut.

Chapter Three

Moving the vacuum cleaner back and forth in long, sweeping strokes, Katy slowly made her way across the braided oval rug. A red paisley bandanna was tied around her glistening black hair to protect it from the dust. A red halter top and cut-off jeans made up the rest of her housecleaning attire.

When she reached the end of the rug, she bent down and flicked off the switch, and the vacuum cleaner whined to a stop. Sighing in relief at the cessation of the noise, she walked to the wall socket and pulled the plug. When the machine had been returned to its place in the hall storage closet, Katy padded barefoot into the kitchen.

Taking a glass from the cabinet, she filled it with cool water from the tap and drank it down thirstily. As she placed the empty glass on the counter her gaze automatically wandered out of the window above the sink to the rolling, tree-covered acreage beyond the backyard. In just three weeks the view had changed completely. Every branch was now draped with the lush, intensely green foliage of early spring. Wild flowers of every color and description edged the forest and spilled over into the open meadow. Berry vines twined their way over the fences and through the undergrowth.

Katy sighed and turned away from the beauty of the warm spring day. Tomorrow she would go roaming, but today she had chores to finish.

The dryer buzzed as she stepped out onto the small, screened-in porch which doubled as utility and laundry room. At almost the same moment, the washing machine ended its spin cycle and whirred to a stop. Pulling the warm clothes from the dryer, Katy dumped them into an empty wicker basket, then transferred the damp laundry from the washer to the dryer. When it was again humming, she hefted the basket to the small utility table and began methodically to fold the clean clothes.

A pickup rumbled to a stop in the drive, and a second later a truck door was slammed. The sounds sent Katy's glance through the open doorway to the kitchen wall clock. It was only a few minutes past four. A look of pleased surprise brightened her face. For once her father was home early. Actually he wasn't required to work on Saturdays and Sundays, but try telling him that. Hearing his heavy footsteps cross the tiled kitchen floor, she pushed a loose strand of hair away from her face and glanced over her shoulder.

"Hi, Dad. You're home early, aren't you?"

Tom stopped in the doorway. "Yes. I...ah...forgot to mention this morning that we've been invited up to the big house for dinner tonight. I thought I'd better warn you so you'd have time to get ready." He eyed his daughter apprehensively, waiting for the reaction he knew would come. He wasn't disappointed.

Katy turned slowly, her blue eyes huge. "You've *got* to be kidding!" The words were dragged from her throat in a hoarse whisper.

"No, I assure you I'm not. Trace invited us a couple of days ago." A faint flush darkened Tom's cheeks. "I guess I just forgot to mention it."

Her heart began to beat frantically. The startling pronouncement had caught her completely off guard. During the past two weeks, since the night he had shared their dinner, Trace had not come near her. She had seen him from a distance several times, usually in the company of her father, and he had waved and called a greeting, but that was all. With each passing day it had become more and more obvious he was not going to seek her out, and she had begun to relax, her life resuming its normal, placid routine as her worries concerning Trace receded. She had even chided herself for having been a complete and utter fool. Now this.

"Well, I'm sorry. I can't go. You'll just have to make my excuses for me," she blurted out in a panic-stricken rush.

"No, Katy. I will not."

The words hit her like a slap in the face, and her head jerked back in shock.

"You're going to get yourself dressed up and you're going with me up to the big house. You will eat dinner and make pleasant conversation and behave like the well-mannered young lady your mother taught you to be," Tom continued relentlessly. His voice was sure and firm, and there was a look on his face she had never seen before.

The washing machine was behind her and Katy stepped back, clutching at it for support. She shook her head. "But I can't, Dad. You know I can't!"

"You can and you will," he stated emphatically. "Now listen to me, Katy. There will be no excuses and there will be no more running away. I've been too lenient with you. I can see that now. Ever since that incident three years ago I've shielded and humored you and allowed you to hide from the world. I kept thinking that you would eventually get over it, that the horror of it would fade and you would resume a normal life." Tom's wide shoulders drooped, and suddenly he looked very tired, very old. "I was wrong. You haven't recovered because you haven't allowed yourself to forget. You've kept it locked inside you, and it's ruining your life." He gestured furiously with his hand. "Well, no more! Katy, you simply cannot allow one tragic incident to color your whole outlook on life. I won't allow it!"

Stunned speechless, Katy stared at him, all the color slowly draining from her face. The harsh tone of his voice had shocked her even more than his words. All her life her father had treated her with a gentleness that bordered on reverence. She could count on the fingers of one hand the times he had raised his voice to her in anger, thereby making it a most effective weapon. And there was no doubt that he was angry now.

A turmoil of conflicting emotions twisted her insides into a hard knot. She didn't want to go to Trace's home for dinner. Some deep-seated, primitive instinct warned her that to do so would be asking for trouble. Yet she depended on her father's continued support. It was absolutely essential to her peace of mind. The love and caring she'd received from her parents had been the glue which had held her shattered life together. Without it she would fly apart. There was really no choice. Swallowing her fear, Katy closed her eyes and nodded.

"Very well, Dad. I'll go," she said softly, her voice trembling.

Four hours later, pale and quivering with nerves, Katy sat beside her father as he brought their pickup to a stop in the U-shaped drive in front of the Barnetts' colonial mansion. She was strung taut, fighting down the nausea that churned in her stomach. Katy stared at the stately pillars marching across the front veranda with wide, fearful eyes. In the fifteen years during which she had lived at Green Meadows, she had never once been inside the big house. She doubted that her father had seen more of it than the study before Trace had taken over. Now, here they were, the two of them, about to have dinner with the new owner and possibly his young stepmother.

Her breath caught in her throat. Oh, God! She had forgotten all about Saundra. The woman had always treated Katy and her mother as though they were beneath her contempt. Katy could just imagine what she thought of this sudden turn of events.

"Do you think Saundra will be here?" she asked as her father opened his door and climbed from the truck.

He held the door open and looked at her across the width of the seat. "I've no idea, Katy girl. But even if she is, I want you to remember that you are a Donovan, and that is something to be proud of."

Katy smiled. Tom Donovan bowed and scraped to no man...or woman. Like all Irishmen, he was filled with a fierce, uncrushable pride, a trait Henry Barnett had found almost intolerable.

Katy was not without the Donovan pride herself. When her father assisted her from the cab of the pickup her eyes sparkled with determination. She was going to remain cool and calm, and get through this evening with her dignity intact if it killed her. After adjusting the full sleeves and scooped neck of her blue silk blouse and smoothing the imaginary wrinkles from the long blue and aqua patterned skirt, she slipped her hand through her father's arm and tilted her chin. "Shall we go?"

He beamed down at her, his eyes glowing with pride. "That's my Katy," he whispered softly.

Katy held her head high as they walked up the pebbled path. For nothing in the world would she let these people see that, inside, she was a quaking mass of nerves.

The sound of raised voices reached them when they stepped onto the veranda. Saundra's shrill tones carried clearly through the open window.

"I tell you, Trace, it simply is *not* done. Your father would not approve of this at all."

"When are you going to get it through your head that whether or not my father would have approved means less than nothing to me? This farm and this house belong to me now, and things will be done my way."

Katy cast her father a nervous glance, and he reached out a hand and rang the bell. The voices ceased. Within a few seconds, Mattie, the Barnetts' housekeeper, appeared at the door.

"Good evening, Mattie." Tom greeted the woman with a friendly smile. "I believe we're expected."

"Yes, of course." Mattie cast a worried glance over her shoulder as they stepped into the entrance hall. She took Katy's lacy white shawl and draped it over her arm. "If you'll just wait right here, I'll tell Mr. Trace you've arrived."

"That won't be necessary, Mattie."

Startled by the terse command, Katy's head swung around, her eyes opening wide at the sight of Trace, framed in the arched doorway to their left. Except at his father's funeral, she had never before seen him dressed so formally. The dark blue suit fit his long, lean frame to perfection. Against the crisp white of his shirt his tanned skin looked like polished bronze. Jane was right, Katy thought distractedly. The only word to describe him was devastating.

For just a second grim, harsh anger was visible in the lines of his face, but it faded quickly when his eyes lit on Katy.

She had taken extra pains with her appearance. Her makeup had been applied with care, and she had swept her hair into a shining knot on the top of her head. Soft tendrils were allowed to escape in front of her ears and across the nape of her neck for a softening effect.

The frank admiration in Trace's expression as his eyes ran over the more sophisticated hairdo brought a blush to her cheeks. It deepened as his inspection continued. His intent gaze traveled slowly from the top of her head to the strappy white sandals on her feet. There was a dark, smoldering look in his deep-set eyes as they returned to her face that in no way matched the coolness of his voice.

"I'm glad you could make it," he said politely, and gestured to the room behind him. "Won't you come in?"

Katy's pulse was fluttering nervously as she stepped toward the door. When Trace's large hand settled against the small of her back, her heart began to pound as though it were trying to get out of her body. She quickened her step to try to elude his touch, but the hand remained firmly in place.

The room they entered was large and well-proportioned, furnished with a harmonious collection of different period pieces. The overall effect was elegant, but definitely inviting. Katy was immediately conscious of the atmosphere of wealth and good taste all around her, but before her eyes could take in any specific details, Trace was directing her attention to the blonde woman ensconced on the sofa.

"Of course you know my stepmother, Saundra."

Katy shot him a quick glance. Had his voice held just a hint of sardonic amusement? She couldn't tell from his impassive face.

"Hello, Mrs. Barnett," she said politely, refocusing her attention on the woman.

Saundra Barnett flicked her a cool, disinterested glance and nodded curtly. "Miss Donovan." Her mouth curled slightly as her pale blue eyes slid over Katy's simple skirt and blouse. She looked pointedly down at her own elegant red chiffon dress and sent Katy a scornful smile.

Beside her, Katy felt Trace stiffen.

"Stop it, Saundra." The command was issued in a snarl, the low, steely voice holding a definite warning, and his stepmother widened her eyes in feigned innocence.

"Why, darling, I didn't say a word."

As Katy feared, the small, malicious act set the tone for the entire evening. Saundra was never overtly rude. She didn't dare risk another reprimand from Trace. She contented herself with snide little innuendos and cutting double-edged remarks. Her words were not blatantly insulting. They were designed to belittle, to embarrass, to make Katy and her father feel out of place and uncomfortable. If she had been gracious and polite, she might have accomplished her purpose. Katy's shyness and extreme nervousness might have worked against her to make her appear awkward and fumbling. But Saundra had misjudged her opponent, and in doing so, had made a bad tactical error. There was nothing guaranteed to stiffen Katy's spine more than ridicule. Her father's fierce pride, combined with her mother's quiet dignity, was a formidable weapon against Saundra's petty viciousness. Katy met every thrust with a cool composure that seemed to infuriate the older woman.

During the meal Saundra switched her attention from Katy to Trace, talking to him in a warm, sensuous tone, and touching him whenever possible, sliding her pale blue eyes over him like a hungry cat that has just spotted its next meal.

At first Katy was surprised. Then she recalled the rumors that had circulated when Trace left the farm four years ago. One of them was that Trace had been far too friendly with his young stepmother, that he had, in fact, been in love with her. It was said that when the situation had come to his father's attention they had quarreled, and Henry had ordered him to leave. Katy had not believed it at the time, but now she wondered. Saundra's attitude was definitely possessive.

After dinner, coffee was served in the living room and Katy began to glance at her watch, wondering how long it would be before they could leave without seeming impolite. They had just settled down with their coffee when Mattie appeared in the doorway.

"I'm sorry to interrupt you, Mr. Trace," she said hesitantly. "But Nate Pearson is here. He wants to talk with Mr. Donovan. He says it's urgent."

Before she had finished speaking, Tom was on his feet and heading toward the door. "That will be about Starbright," he explained quickly to Trace. "She's ready to foal at any moment. She's been behaving strangely, and I told Nate to stay with her and call me if anything developed."

"I see," Trace replied, following Tom into the hall.

Nate Pearson was waiting just inside the door. The three men huddled together in serious conversation for a moment, the low murmur of their voices drifting into the room, their words indistinguishable. Then suddenly Tom jerked open the front door and strode out, with Nate on his heels. Trace closed it behind them and returned to the living room.

"I'm sorry, Katy, but there's an emergency down at the stables, and your father felt he should be there. Since it's likely he'll be busy for several hours, possibly even all night, I told him I'd see you home."

Katy stood up, alarmed. "Thank you, but please don't trouble yourself on my account. I'm quite capable of getting home by myself."

"Nevertheless, I'll drive you."

"Oh, no! Really, that's not necessary," she protested quickly. The last thing Katy wanted was to be cooped up in a car with Trace. "I can walk. It's not that far."

"I wouldn't hear of it."

"Oh, for God's sake, Trace!" Saundra spat out irritably. "Let the girl walk! It won't hurt her. After all, she's only..."

"That's enough, Saundra!" Trace snapped. He glared at her, his hazel eyes narrowed into glittering slits of green ice. "Miss Donovan is my guest, and I'm going to see her home. I'm not going to tell you again that from now on things are going to be done my way. If you don't like that, then I suggest you pack your bags and leave."

Saundra blanched. "Trace! You don't mean that!"

"I mean it." The flat statement left no room for doubt. Turning his back on the shocked woman, he looked at Katy. "I'll get your wrap."

Five seconds after he had left the room, Saundra turned on her like a spitting cat. Her face was contorted into a livid mask of rage. "Stay away from him, do you hear me! He's mine! I should have married Trace in the first place, not his father. And now I'm going to. And I'm not going to let a stupid little farm girl stand in my way. So if you know what's good for you, you'll remember your place." Her pale eyes raked over Katy contemptuously. "You're just the daughter of a hired hand, and don't you forget it."

Katy looked back at her in sick disgust. Would Trace really marry his father's widow? Saundra was only five or six years older than he, and she was still very attractive. But she was hard and grasping, not a nice person at all. But then, Katy thought, what do I know? Maybe that didn't matter to men. Maybe they didn't see beyond the blond hair and the carefully made-up face. In any case, it was none of her business.

She tilted her chin proudly. "You're behaving very foolishly, Mrs. Barnett. I have no intention of becoming involved with Trace or any other man."

"And you expect me to believe that?"

"I really don't care what you believe."

"Why you little—" The sound of Trace's footsteps crossing the hall abruptly halted the angry tirade, and Saundra clamped her mouth shut, shooting Katy one last, furious glare.

"Here we are." Trace draped the lacy shawl over Katy's shoulders and placed a hand beneath her elbow. "Shall we go?" He ignored his stepmother completely, but Katy could feel the woman's eyes boring into her back as she allowed him to lead her from the room.

Outside on the veranda Trace paused. "If you'll wait here, I'll get my car and bring it around."

"No, please. I would really much rather walk."

"Very well. If that's what you want." Trace smiled pleasantly and extended his arm. "Shall we go?"

It was then Katy realized that he intended to walk with her. "Oh, but I meant..."

"I know what you meant, Katy," he said softly. "But I also meant it when I said I would see you home. Now, what's it going to be? Do we drive or do we walk?"

Katy looked at him uncertainly in the dim light filtering through the windows, her teeth worrying the soft inner tissue of her bottom lip. She saw the rock-hard determination in his expression and knew she was not going to be able to dissuade him.

She sighed deeply, her shoulders sagging in defeat. "We walk."

Ignoring his arm, she descended the veranda steps and started around the corner of the house to follow the path that led to the stables. Trace fell in step beside her. Katy walked quickly, her chaotic thoughts tumbling over themselves in a jumble of confusion. Her mind groped in frantic desperation for an avenue of escape, but she could not concentrate. Awareness of the tall, vigorous man at her side flooded her senses and her brain simply refused to function.

As they neared the stables, they could hear the mare's nervous whicker. A rectangle of light spilled from one of the stalls at the far end of the row. Katy heard her father's voice, crooning encouragement to the frightened animal, his tone low and soothing, the words unintelligible.

Green Acres Farm rarely called in the local veterinarian. They didn't need him. Not when they had Tom Donovan. But perhaps Trace didn't know that.

Katy looked up at him. "If you feel you should be there, Mr. Barnett, please don't worry about me. I assure you I can find my way home alone with no problem."

He grasped her upper arm and began to lead her past the row of stalls. "Give it up, Katy. It won't work. I'll check the progress at the stables later, but right now I intend to walk you home. So no more arguing."

Behind the stables the road wound through a small stand of trees, and when they entered it, they were immediately enclosed in almost total darkness. Katy's heart began to thud painfully. You fool! You utter fool! Why did you insist upon walking? she berated herself silently. It would have taken no more than five minutes to get home by car. Instead, here she was, walking along a dark, country road with a man who terrified her.

A thick layer of pine needles carpeted the dirt road, muffling the sound of their footsteps. As quiet as it was, their approach startled a small, nocturnal creature, and it scurried deeper into the woods, amid a frantic rustle of brush. From nearby came the low, mournful hoot of an owl. The small sounds added to the feeling of complete isolation, and Katy felt gooseflesh rise along her arms. She shivered and drew the shawl closer to her body.

"Are you cold?"

The sharp question gave her a start. "What? Oh . . . no . . . that is . . ." The days were now pleasantly warm, but the early spring nights still held a biting chill. It had nothing to do with her reaction, but it provided a convenient excuse. "It's just a little cooler than I thought it would be."

The hand that gripped her elbow slid up her arm, and she shivered again. "You *are* cold. Here, wear my coat."

"No, I couldn't . . ." she began, but before she could stop him, Trace had shrugged out of his suit coat and draped it across her shoulders.

"There, that should help."

"But now you'll be cold," Katy protested. She didn't want to wear his coat. It was still warm from the heat of his body, and smelled faintly of tobacco and after-shave. She felt suffocated in the engulfing, wide-shouldered garment. It was almost like being held in his arms.

"Don't worry about me. I've been living in the high country for the last four years. I'm used to the cold."

"The high country? Where is that?" she asked cautiously. The question was not prompted by curiosity, but by a desperate hope that conversation would dispel the intimacy which seemed to surround them.

"Colorado. I bummed around for a time after I left the farm, then I ran into an old friend. One of my college buddies. To make a long story short, we ended up going into the ranching business together. Using a part of my inheritance from my grandmother, along with what Hank had been able to scrape together over the years, we bought a small spread, fifty head of cattle, and a good seed bull." He laughed softly. "It's been an uphill struggle all the way, but now our herd is considerably larger and we're finally beginning to show a profit."

Katy held her breath for a minute, then asked the question that was tormenting her. "Are you going to go back?"

The road opened suddenly into the meadow. In the weak, silvery light of a crescent moon, Katy saw Trace's mouth curve with ironic amusement. "No. At least, not for a while. And then probably just on flying visits."

He looked up at the dark, velvet sky, his eyes skimming over the bright clusters of stars. "When I got the call from our family attorney about Dad's death I came here intending to stay only long enough to attend the funeral and pick up the remainder of my personal belongings." He looked down at Katy and shrugged his broad shoulders, smiling. "I think I was more surprised than anyone to learn that Dad had left the farm to me. I suppose he finally suffered an attack of conscience."

"Well, after all, you *are* his son."

"Yes, I am that." He sighed wearily. "But I think the real reason he did it was because I'm my mother's son. You see, it was her money that saved the farm." Katy's start of surprise drew a bark of bitter laughter from Trace. "As I understand it, my grandfather was a very poor business man with very extravagant tastes. By the time my father inherited the place, it was mortgaged to the hilt. So... he married my mother. Her family had just struck it rich in the oil business, and with their help he was able to get the farm back on its feet and recoup the family fortune, even increase it. Unfortunately, he was never able to forgive my mother for being one of that contemptible breed known as the nouveau riche, a group of upstarts with no pedigree to speak of. It seemed to embarrass him.'' He paused, then continued bitterly, ''I remember waking up one night to hear them quarreling. He took great delight in telling her he'd never loved her, that she was socially inferior, and he would never have married her if it hadn't been for her money.'' His voice hardened and deepened. ''After that she was never the same.''

Katy was horrified. Temporarily her fear of Trace was forgotten, submerged under a huge, engulfing wave of compassion and pity, something she had never expected to feel for this man. It was difficult for her even to imagine growing up in such a cold, bitter environment. The love that had existed between her mother and father was warm and deep and constant. Katy had grown up secure in the knowledge that she was the wanted and cherished result of that love.

In the pale light of the moon Trace's expression was cold and formidable. How awful it must have been for him. He had adored his mother, that much she remembered. Was that why he had rebelled so against his father? Was his wildness, his open defiance, Trace's way of fighting back, of striking out at the man who had hurt her? It was possible. Still, it had nothing to do with her.

''You really shouldn't be telling me all this, Mr. Barnett. It's none of my business.'' She preferred to keep their relationship an impersonal one, the way it had always been. If he persisted in telling her the intimate details of his childhood and his parents' marriage she couldn't do that.

"I want you to know, Katy. I want you to understand," Trace said softly.

They had reached the house, and shrugging off his hand, Katy turned and walked quickly up the brick path to the porch. "I do understand. Believe me, I won't again make the mistake of assuming you share your father's opinions and values." Rummaging through her purse for the house key as she climbed the steps, Katy was extremely conscious of Trace walking beside her, his eyes on her down-bent head.

At the door, without warning, his hands descended on her upper arms and he turned her around. Instinctively, Katy hunched her shoulders forward and tried to pull free of his hold, but found herself trapped between the door and Trace's hard body. She raised frightened eyes to search his face. A silent plea shimmered in their blue depths. She had left a light burning in the living room, and from the soft glow spilling onto the porch, she could just make out his expression. It held a strange mixture of tenderness and determination, with just a touch of impatience.

"Oh, Katy. How long are you going to ignore it?" he asked softly, his voice edged with exasperation.

The feel of his warm hands on her shoulders was so unnerving that she could barely concentrate on his words. She shook her head as if to clear it and stared at him, transfixed. "Ignore what?"

"This thing there is between us."

Alarm bells began to clang in her head. "I—I don't know what you're talking about."

He gave her a little shake. "Stop it, Katy. You're as aware of me as I am of you. Don't deny it." Lifting one hand, he ran his knuckles gently down her cheek. "It started four years ago. I wanted you then, very much, but you were so young and so painfully shy, I knew I had to wait. Then I quarreled with my father. At the time I was grateful nothing had developed between us, because I couldn't stay after that." His voice dropped to a low, husky pitch, while his eyes burned possessively over her frightened face. "When I looked up and saw you at my father's funeral, all those feelings I had four years ago came rushing back, only stronger this time. I'd made up my mind to stay, even before I knew I had inherited the farm. I wasn't going to let you slip through my fingers again."

Wide-eyed, Katy stared at him. She shook her head wordlessly, feeling the familiar, cold fear unfurl itself deep inside her. It was happening all over again. This man wanted her. He admitted it openly. And he seemed to think all he had to do was reach out and take her, that she would accept that, even be pleased. That he could even think such a thing filled her with a deep sense of shame and humiliation. What was there about her that made men think she was theirs for the taking like some pretty toy? It was so unfair! She wanted to cry and rage at the same time.

"You don't know what you're saying!" she cried desperately. "There's nothing between us! There never has been and there never will be! So why don't you just leave me alone?"

"Oh, no, Katy," he said quietly, determinedly. "I'm not going to let you hide behind that pathetic little shell you've built around yourself. I've tried to be patient with you, to let you get used to having me around, and it's gotten me absolutely nowhere. Well, no more." He pulled her close, and Katy's hands came up to push him away, but it was useless. His arms slid around her back and tightened, molding her slender body to his hard

one, her soft breasts crushed against the muscular wall
of his chest.

Katy's first instinct was to fight. She wanted desperately to lash out and claw and kick, to inflict as much
injury as possible, but she had learned, to her sorrow,
that that was not the way to handle an explosive situation. Instead, she held herself rigid. Like a tethered animal watching the approach of a hungry predator, she
stood perfectly still, her eyes huge in her white face, as
Trace's head began its slow, purposeful descent.

"No, please don't," she whispered helplessly, and
heard him give a soft laugh an instant before his lips
settled over hers.

It was a tantalizing kiss, soft and gentle, and infinitely sensual. He explored her lips with a controlled
passion that made no demands, yet established, beyond a doubt, his absolute possession. Katy was
stunned by the complete lack of brutality in his lovemaking. It was something she had expected, had braced
herself for, and its absence left her confused and diso-
riented. She felt weak. Boneless.

Trace's mouth moved unhurriedly over her lips, persuasively teasing and nibbling at their trembling softness until they parted without her being aware of it.
When the tip of his tongue touched hers, a tingling shaft
of excitement streaked through her, and she shuddered
violently from head to foot. Feeling her reaction, Trace
ended the kiss. He drew his mouth slowly from hers and
smiled down at her bewildered face.

"You see. That wasn't so bad, was it?" he mocked
gently.

Numb with shock, and something else she couldn't
even attempt to define, Katy could only stare at him.

She was weak and shaken, and knew, vaguely, that her condition was not due entirely to fear.

Trace cupped her face in his hands and ran his thumb over her parted lips. A searing blaze leaped in his eyes as he watched them tremble beneath his touch. Regretfully, he let his hands slide down to curve around her shoulders and dragged his gaze away from the sweet temptation of her mouth. Katy's heart turned over at the virile, passionate look in his eyes as they roamed over her face. "I may as well tell you right now, Katy me darlin'. I mean to have you. And nothing you can do or say is going to alter that."

He lowered his head once more and bestowed a swift, hard kiss, then took the key from her nerveless hand and opened the door. "Now, go to bed, Katy. I'll see you tomorrow." A hand in the small of her back gently pushed her inside, then the door was closed behind her.

It was only as she stood, stock still, in the middle of the living room, listening to the sound of his receding footsteps, that she realized his coat was still draped over her shoulders.

Chapter Four

Warm spring sunshine caressed Katy's face as she paused on the church steps. Usually she came away from the Sunday morning services with a feeling of tranquillity and peace. But not today. The scene with Trace the night before had left her so upset she couldn't concentrate on anything else. She had gone through the religious rites by rote, her emotions in turmoil, her mind a million miles away.

Pulling the lacy scarf from her head, Katy slipped it into her purse, then stepped to one side and watched the crowd of worshipers file by. She was in no hurry, because she had absolutely nowhere to go. With Trace's "I'll see you tomorrow" still ringing in her ears she didn't dare go home. Katy descended the shallow steps and started slowly toward her car. She had to find something to keep her occupied, something that would keep her away from the house all day. But what?

She was still asking herself the same question as she eased the car out of the parking lot and turned in the direction opposite to the farm. It was hot and stuffy in the car and Katy rolled down her window and opened the vents. Immediately the heavenly scent of roses swirled around her. She breathed deeply and let her eyes wander over the vast rose fields lining the highway on either side. They were just coming into first bloom, acre upon acre of almost every variety and color of rose grown. It was a source of great pride to most Tyler residents that their east Texas town was known as the rose capital of the world. More than half the field-grown rose bushes in the United States came from the immediate vicinity. From April to October the rose fields, which virtually surrounded the town, were a riot of color and scent. To Katy there was no more beautiful sight.

A sign pointing to Tyler lake drew her attention and, with a shrug, Katy decided it was as good a place as any in which to while away a Sunday afternoon.

Spying a fast food restaurant just ahead, she flipped on the turn indicator and swung into the drive-through lane. A few minutes later she pulled back onto the highway, a sack containing a juicy cheeseburger and a large, icy Coke on the seat beside her. The appetizing aroma filling the car made her nose twitch appreciatively.

At the lake Katy drove around the shore until she found a secluded picnic table among the towering pine trees. She parked her car in the space provided and carried her lunch to the table. Insects scattered before her, clicking noisily as she walked through the ankle-high grass. Overhead, a family of bluejays flitted through the pines, scolding angrily.

A gentle wind ruffled the surface of the lake, sending tiny wavelets lapping against the shore. Sunlight sparkled on the rippled water like thousands of glittering diamonds. Far from shore a lone sailboat leaned before the wind, its sail billowed and full, a taut red triangle against the blue of the lake and sky. Katy propped her elbows on the picnic table and nibbled on her cheeseburger, watching the scene abstractedly.

It was pure cowardice, running away from Trace like this, but she didn't care. She wasn't ready to face the confrontation that had to come. First she had to talk to her father. He would make Trace understand that she wasn't interested, that he was wasting his time. He *had* to.

There had been no opportunity to speak to her father that morning however. He had come staggering in at dawn, exhausted by his night-long vigil at the stables. After a mumbled greeting he had fallen into bed and, within minutes, had sunk into a deep sleep. His heavy, rumbling snore had followed her as she tiptoed out of the house.

Katy's musings were interrupted by the arrival of a mother duck. A slow smile curved her mouth as she watched the haughty, feathered female waddle imperiously toward the lake, emitting a constant stream of querulous quacks and trailing behind her a wavering line of downy yellow ducklings. As she led her entourage by the table, she eyed Katy as though daring her to move and proceeded toward her destination at the same majestic pace. Reaching the lake, she waded a few feet into the shallows, then lowered her body with a plopping splash and glided gracefully away. One after the other, the bits of yellow fluff followed suit, paddling effortlessly in their mother's wake.

Katy drank the last of her Coke and tossed the cup in the trash barrel, then picked up the remainder of her cheeseburger and wandered down to the shore. She laughed as she watched the mother duck dive in search of food, leaving only her feathered rump sticking out of the water, straight up in the air. Clicking her tongue, Katy tore off small pieces of bun and tossed them into the water. Immediately the ducks snapped up the crumbs of bread eagerly and when they were gone, swam toward the shore and audaciously demanded more. Katy laughed aloud and obliged. She watched them scrabbling after the scattered tidbits with a certain amount of envy, thinking wistfully how uncomplicated their lives were compared to hers.

When the bun was gone, Katy wandered along the shore. The ducks followed hopefully for a while, then turned back in disgust when it became apparent there would be no more handouts. The breeze off the lake rustled the pine needles overhead as Katy strolled aimlessly along. She couldn't understand why Trace upset her so, but he did. After all, he couldn't force her into a relationship she didn't want. Several men had made a dead set at her before, and she had simply ignored them. So why couldn't she ignore Trace? The question was unanswerable, but one thing she knew for certain. Trace affected her like no other man ever had, and that alone frightened her. She didn't like the sensations he aroused—the fluttering in the pit of her stomach; the slow, heavy thud of her heart; the weak, watery feeling that threatened to buckle her knees. Troubled, Katy trudged on, wrestling with the problem for almost an hour before finally turning back.

It was only a little after three when she climbed into the car and headed toward Tyler, much too early to go home. The only other place she could think of to go was Jane and Frank's.

It wasn't until she had already rung the Cawleys' doorbell that the first pangs of doubt began to nag at her. Jane was as sharp as a tack. Katy wasn't in the habit of dropping by on the weekends, and Jane was bound to wonder why she had today. The bell pealed inside the house several times without any answer, and feeling something akin to relief, Katy turned to go. Before she had taken two steps the door was jerked open.

"Katy! Well, this is a surprise. What are you doing here?"

Katy turned and smiled. "Oh, I was just at loose ends and I thought I'd see if you were busy."

"No. Of course not." Jane stepped back and opened the door wide. "Come in, come in. Everyone is out back around the pool. Come on out and join us."

Katy hung back. "Maybe I'd better not. I don't want to interrupt your Sunday with your family."

"Nonsense!" Jane reached out and grabbed her by the arm. "There's no reason in the world why you can't join us. As I recall, you left one of your swimsuits in the pool house the last time you were here. Besides, we all think of you as a member of the family anyway."

Frank and the kids were in the pool playing a game of catch with a beach ball when Katy and Jane stepped out onto the patio. They paused just long enough to chorus a quick "Hi, Katy," before returning to the game, playing fast and furious, as though their very lives depended on the outcome. The Cawleys' fifteen-year-old twins, John and Jason, were on one side, teamed against Frank and the seventeen-year-old Martha on the other.

"Good grief! It makes me tired just to watch them. How do you keep up with this crew?" Katy asked as she sank down onto a padded lounger.

"It isn't easy, believe me." Jane sighed and plopped down on another lounger. Arms stretched out behind her, she leaned back on her hands, then turned her head and gave Katy an inquiring look, her brown eyes narrowing shrewdly. "So, tell me. What happened at the farm to send you scurrying into town?" she asked with typical directness.

"Nothing." Katy kept her eyes on the game of catch and avoided looking at her friend. "It's just that Dad was up all night with an ailing horse, and he's exhausted. I thought I'd say away from the house and give him a chance to catch up on his sleep."

"Mmmm, and that's all there is to it, huh?"

"Yes, of course. What else could there be?"

"What else, indeed." Jane sniffed. "Only the most eligible, best-looking man in the county, that's all. And don't sit there and give me that big-eyed look. I know perfectly well that Trace Barnett is involved in this somehow."

"Of course he's involved. It was his ailing horse."

"Katy Donovan! Don't try to con me. I know good and..."

"Hey, Katy!" Jason called from the edge of the pool. "Why don't you get into your swimsuit and you and Mom join us? We'll have a three-man relay. Girls against the boys. What do you say?"

Katy grabbed the chance to escape Jane's inquisition. Jumping up, she headed for the poolhouse. "Sure. Just give me five minutes," she called as she skirted the pool. "We gals are going to beat the pants off you, you'll see."

* * *

A feeling of intense relief washed over Katy when she arrived home and turned into the empty drive. Though it was after nine, she had half expected to find Trace's pickup parked next to the house, but there wasn't a vehicle of any kind in sight. She relaxed and drove around to the back where she parked the car next to her father's pickup.

She smiled as she climbed from the car and started toward the house on slightly unsteady legs. She was feeling pleasantly exhausted by the afternoon and evening spent with the irrepressible Cawley clan. They had played water games until hunger had forced them to call a halt. Then, among a storm of unmerciful teasing and lighthearted squabbling, they had grilled hot dogs over the barbeque pit and stuffed themselves like ravenous wolves.

Katy had stayed as long as she had dared without raising Jane's suspicions any further. But by nine, after all the mess had been cleared away and the children had wandered off, Jane once again began to ask probing questions, and Katy had beat a hasty retreat.

A long rectangle of yellow light spilling from the kitchen lit her way as Katy climbed the back steps and opened the door to the screened-in utility porch. The soft tap-tap of her heels on the board floor announced her arrival even before she called out, "Hi, Dad. I'm back."

"Katy me darlin'! It's about time you were home," her father answered from the living room. "Where the devil have you been all day?"

"Most of the time I've been at the Cawleys'. We swam and pla . . ." The words froze on Katy's lips, and she came to a stunned halt just inside the living room as her eyes lit on the long, lean man sprawled in one of the fireside chairs. His narrowed stare seemed to slice right through her as she stood rooted to the spot.

"Trace! Wh-what are you doing here?"

"He came to see you, my girl. Trace was under the impression you were expecting him."

There was a gruffness in her father's voice that Katy hadn't noticed before, and when she turned to him and saw his reddened, bleary eyes and disheveled appearance her heart sank. He had been drinking again. Heavily.

"I—I—must have forgotten. I—"

"Don't worry about it, Tom." Trace cut into her stammered explanation and sent her a knowing look that made her scalp prickle. "I probably didn't make my intentions clear last night." He paused and a slow grin curved his mouth. "That's a mistake I won't make in the future, I assure you."

The softly spoken words hit Katy with stunning impact, and she took a step backward, reeling under the implied threat. Her breathing was shallow, her chest tight. Cold, icy fear was racing through her veins. Her eyes darted to her father, but he seemed sublimely unperturbed, his gaze trained on the glass in his hand.

Trace stood up, and Katy jumped. Her involuntary reaction brought his brows together.

"Is anything wrong, Katy? You seem..." he paused, his eyes narrowing on her white face, "nervous."

It was a politely worded question but Katy didn't miss the thread of steel in his voice. It made her even more nervous. She didn't want him probing for the cause. The fewer people who knew, the better.

Forcing a smile to her lips, she shook her head. "No. Of course not. I'm just tired, that's all."

"I see," he said thoughtfully. "In that case, I'll be going." He picked up his hat and gave her father a grim smile. "Tom, I'll see you in the morning."

Katy sagged with relief. She followed him happily as he headed for the door, barely able to believe she was getting rid of him so easily. Her deliverance was short-lived however. At the door he grasped her elbow and sent Tom an inquiring look. "You don't mind if Katy walks me to the gate, do you, Tom? I'd like to speak with her for a moment."

"Sure, sure." Tom waved his hand dismissively. "You two go on. Me, I'm going to bed." So saying, he rose to his feet and staggered toward the hall door. Wide-eyed, Katy watched his retreating back with something akin to panic.

"Oh, but . . ."

Her protest was cut off as Trace transferred his hand from her elbow to the small of her back, its forward pressure propelling her through the open door. Without engaging in an undignified struggle, she had no choice but to go with him.

Katy walked stiffly beside him. The pressure of that guiding hand on her back was burning through her clothing like a branding iron. She was shivering with reaction to this frighteningly masculine man, a combination of fear, anger and resentment, and had no doubt that he could feel the tremors that quaked through her.

At the gate he stopped and turned her to face him. Partly out of fear and partly out of sheer stubbornness, Katy kept her eyes fixed firmly on the third button of his shirt. His first words, however, brought her head up sharply, her eyes widening in dismay.

"How long has Tom been drinking like this, Katy?"

In the pale glow of light from the house she couldn't see his expression clearly. She looked at him with huge, stricken eyes, searching his face for some sign of compassion or understanding. Oh, dear God! Don't let him dismiss Dad, she prayed fervently. Not now. Not after everything else. Please, God, please!

Her gaze wavered beneath his penetrating stare, and Katy lowered her head. Her soft lips trembled as she whispered huskily, agonizingly, "Ever since Mother died. You see . . . he loved her so, he can't bear to go on without her. It's killing him, little by little, day by day." The last was choked out on a rising sob, and she averted her head, blinking rapidly to hold back the tears that threatened. Katy's chin quivered as she fought to suppress the emotions churning inside her. Her throat ached with the effort.

Trace drew in a deep breath and expelled it very slowly, in a long, resigned sigh. "That's what I thought," he said, his tone grim. "I've noticed he doesn't seem the same as I remembered him, even sober."

"No, he's not. When Mother died, something in him died too. Some vital spark." Katy stood with her arms crossed over her midriff, rubbing her elbows in agitation. "He's . . ."

Tom's deep, rich baritone, raised in song, halted Katy's words. They both turned to stare at the house, unable to speak as a hauntingly sad song floated out on the still night air.

The piercing sorrow in her father's voice snapped the precarious control Katy had over her emotions, and huge, scalding tears welled up to blur her vision. Biting her lips, she widened her eyes and tried to hold them back, but it was no use. One by one, they trickled over.

She turned to Trace then, clutching desperately at his arm, her tear-drenched eyes unconsciously beseeching. "Trace, please. He never drinks during working hours. I swear it! You've got to believe me!"

At first her desperate pleading seemed to shock him. Then a look of pure anguish flickered across his face. "Oh, Katy, Katy," Trace breathed sadly, cupping her face between his hands. Rough, calloused thumbs brushed back and forth across her cheeks, wiping away the steady flow of tears. "Do you really think I would dismiss your father? Do you have so little faith in me? Right now Tom is like a wounded animal, and he's easing his pain in the only way he knows how. I can't condemn him for that."

Katy stood rigid before him, blinking her eyes to stem the tears, staring at him in growing wonder. She could scarcely believe what she was hearing.

A dejected look entered the hazel eyes and Trace shook his head sorrowfully. "Katy, don't you know that Tom has always been more of a father to me than my natural father? It was Tom who bailed me out of trouble countless times during that period when I was behaving like a reckless fool. It was Tom who gave me good, sound advice. It was Tom who understood how I felt." He paused and darted a look toward the house, then sent her that lopsided smile, and Katy's heart gave a queer little lurch against her ribs. "Anyway, I'm not stupid. Tom knows and handles animals better than any man alive, drunk or sober. So don't worry, Katy. I'm not going to dismiss your father just because he's hitting the bottle. We simply have to give him time and hope he eventually snaps out of it."

The rush of gratitude she felt almost overwhelmed her. The vivid blue eyes were swimming with emotion as she looked at him, her chin wobbling. "Thank you, Trace," she whispered unsteadily.

His face became pensive and he stared at the house again. "I know losing her was a terrible blow, but still, it must be wonderful to share that kind of love." The wistful longing in his voice was unmistakable, and something deep inside her stirred. His gaze swung back to Katy and he smiled. His fingers slid into the hair at her temples, the calloused skin snagging the silky strands. "And it must be wonderful to grow up surrounded by that kind of love."

"Yes. It is."

"That's want I want for my children," he said with a soft fierceness that tugged at her heart strings. "That's what I'm determined to give them. And myself."

For a moment Katy was able to ignore the caressing movements of his hands. Pity for this man overwhelmed her as she compared his cold, loveless childhood with her own. When she was much younger, she had been envious of Trace, admiring the big house, the high life-style, and all the material things he possessed in such abundance, when all along she had been the lucky one. There had never been a day in her life when she had been made to feel unwanted, never a moment when she hadn't been surrounded by love.

Against her will, she could feel herself softening toward him. As Katy stared into the rugged but somehow vulnerable face, she wanted desperately for Trace to know that kind of deep, abiding love, and her eyes clearly reflected her feelings. "I hope you can, Trace," she said with soft sincerity. "I truly hope you can."

Trace smiled. "Oh, don't worry, sweetheart. I fully intend to. And that brings us back to the original reason for my visit."

He brought his face closer to hers, and Katy's eyes widened with renewed fear. She gripped his wrists and tried to pull back but he tunneled his fingers deeper into her hair and held her immobile. Katy's throat went dry as she met the determined gleam in his eyes.

"You knew I was coming here today to see you, didn't you, Katy?" The question was asked in a pleasant tone that, nevertheless, held a warning challenge, but Trace didn't give her a chance to reply. "I very considerately waited until late afternoon so I wouldn't disturb your father," he continued silkily. "And what do I find when I get here? Katy me darlin' has flown the coop. Well, running away won't do you any good, my love. You won't escape me that easily." His voice went low with warning. "Try it again, and I'll come looking for you."

His fingers tightened against her scalp, forcing her head up. Stunned, shaking with fright, Katy could only stare with huge, stricken eyes as his mouth moved closer, closer. When she felt his warm breath mingle with hers, she uttered a strangled "No!"

It was too late. He brushed a soft kiss against her parted lips, then another, and another—delicate butterfly caresses that sent her blood racing through her veins.

Trace raised his head and smiled down at her. "Good night, Katy." Bending swiftly, he dropped a kiss on the end of her nose. In the next instant he was striding away down the road.

The deafening roar of her heartbeat pounded in Katy's ears as she stared into the darkness that had swallowed him up. How did one fight a man like Trace? His gentle persistence was like the changing seasons, the steady ebb and flow of the tides—a gradual, inexorable force that would not be denied. The thought sent a shiver rippling through her. Hugging herself tightly, Katy stared up at the brilliant pinpoints of light in the sky and drew in several deep breaths. Well, she wouldn't give in to him. She wouldn't!

"Are you sure we can't give you a lift, Katy? It would be no trouble, really."

"Jane's right, Katy," Frank added his support to his wife's offer as the three of them walked down the hall toward the office. "Green Meadows isn't that far. Besides, I'd hardly call a drive into the country on a glorious day like this a hardship."

"Thanks. I appreciate your offer. But Dad said he'd be here at six to pick me up." Katy smiled back over her shoulder at her two friends as they stepped, single file, through the door into the office.

"Well, I just wish you had told us your car would be in the garage for a few days. There's no need for your father to run back and forth like this." Jane stopped in the middle of the room to rummage through her purse and finally extracted a large ring of jangling keys. She opened the door, motioning for the others to go through ahead of her. "If it's not repaired by Monday, just tell him we'll bring you home," she ordered imperiously.

"Yes, mother hen." Laughing, Katy stepped through the outer door, then came to an abrupt halt that sent Frank and Jane skidding into her.

"What the..." They had cried out in unison, but the startled exclamation died on their lips at the sight of the tall, sandy-haired man leaning against the wall, just outside the door. Three pairs of rounded eyes stared at him, and Trace smiled back, a hint of devilish amusement in his expression.

"Trace! What are you doing here?" Katy choked out the words through a tightly constricted throat. But even as the question was asked she had a sinking feeling what his answer would be, and her eyes began to dart around in search of her father.

Trace pushed himself away from the wall, closed the distance between them, and slipped his arm around Katy's waist. Before she realized his intent, he lowered his head and gave her a quick kiss on the mouth that unnerved her. While she was trying to gather her scattered wits, he turned and extended his hand to Frank.

"Hello. I'm Trace Barnett," he said pleasantly.

"Frank Cawley," the other man answered with wary caution, accepting the proffered hand. "And this is my wife, Jane."

Katy's heart lurched at the dazed expression on Jane's face when Trace turned that devastating smile on her.

"You must be Katy's boss. Tom was telling me how much she enjoys working for you. I understand the two of you have become good friends."

"Yes. Yes we have," Jane replied distractedly. "Katy's a dear."

Smiling, Trace looked down at Katy and pulled her closer. Belatedly she became aware of the familiarity of the embrace and tried to pull free, but his fingers bit warningly into the soft flesh of her midriff. "Yes, I quite agree," he concurred in a husky, intimate tone, as his possessive gaze wandered over her. "Very dear."

For a moment Katy could only gape at him. Trace was deliberately trying to give the impression they were romantically involved! She darted an uneasy look at Jane and Frank, and her heart sank all the way to her knees. From their surprised, but very definitely pleased expressions, it was obvious that was exactly what they thought.

"Trace, you can't . . ." she began worriedly, but the muscular arm pressing against her back turned her toward the steps and urged her forward.

He smiled at the startled couple as he guided her past them. "Sorry to run, but I promised Tom I'd bring Katy straight home. Perhaps the four of us can get together soon," he tossed over her shoulder. "I'm anxious to get to know Katy's friends." And with that, he led a shaken Katy swiftly down the walk.

"I'm parked about a block away," he informed her as they reached the city sidewalk and turned right. "When I arrived, the drive in front of the school was filled with waiting mothers, and I didn't feel like joining the queue." He gave her his most beguiling smile. "You don't mind walking, do you?"

But she did mind. She minded very much. It wasn't enough that he had kissed her in front of her friends and given them a totally false impression of the relationship. Now he was leading her down a public street with his arm curved possessively around her waist in full view of the whole town. Several passersby were staring quite openly. Trace Barnett was a well-known figure in this town, and since he had inherited Green Meadows, speculation about him had been running rampant. With a sinking feeling in the pit of her stomach, Katy accepted that news of this little episode would spread like a brush fire.

Just when she thought things couldn't get any worse, she looked up and caught sight of the Whittingdale sisters bearing down on them from the opposite direction. Katy closed her eyes and groaned. The Whittingdale ladies were the nerve center of the Tyler gossip network. Two wealthy spinsters, they lived their lives vicariously through others. Who was doing what with whom was of vital interest to them, and Katy knew they had always found Trace's escapades particularly titillating.

"Trace, will you let me go," she whispered furiously, while desperately trying to dislodge his hand from her waist. "Flora and Irene are coming this way."

"So? Let them come," he answered, with a distressing lack of concern.

"Let me go! What are you trying to do? Ruin my reputation? You know as well as I that if they see us like this, within five minutes they'll have me branded as one of your women."

"Not *one* of my women. My *only* woman."

The calm pronouncement brought her to a jerking halt. Wide, distressed blue eyes searched his face in growing panic. "Wh-what do you mean? What are you trying to do, Trace?" Her voice rose to a shrill pitch when she noticed the smug expression on his face.

The encircling arm was removed from her waist, and he turned her fully toward him, his big hands cupping the curves of her shoulders. Katy was uncomfortably aware of the rapid approach of the Whittingdale sisters, but knew it was useless to fight against the steely hold. She stood staring at him uncertainly.

"It's really very simple, Katy," he drawled with a complacent smile. His hands tightened and he drew her closer. "I'm staking my claim. I'm giving all the other single males fair warning that Mary Kathleen Donovan is spoken for."

The stunning words, the quite tone, the deadly serious look in his eyes, all combined to send an icy chill trickling down her spine. Automatically, without her even being aware of it, her head began to move from side to side in frantic, insistent denial. And all the time, Trace was drawing her closer. Mute with fear, Katy could only watch helplessly as his head bent slowly toward her. With his lips poised directly over hers, he paused and glanced over her shoulder.

"Good afternoon, ladies," he said pleasantly, when the Whittingdales drew abreast of them. And then, ignoring their scandalized gasps, he lowered his mouth to Katy's.

It was a long, lingering kiss, not brutal, but demanding nevertheless, the insistent pressure of his lips prying hers apart and forcing her to accept his warm, thrusting tongue. Katy writhed beneath the searing kiss and tried vainly to twist away, but Trace slipped his arms around her and pulled her tightly against him. His previous kisses had been brief, fleeting affairs, ending before she'd had time to panic, but now she was suffocating under his devouring male dominance, hysteria boiling up inside her, choking her.

The nightmare was happening all over again. The horrid, vicious pictures flickered through her mind, and she couldn't shut them out. She was being used, humiliated, stripped of her will as though it were of no importance, forced to accept a man's hot, demanding mouth and the insolent touch of his hands, like some worthless, mindless nothing. And she knew only too well that if she resisted, those same hands could turn violent, could hurt her. A dark, black terror gripped her, and Katy began to shiver uncontrollably, her knees buckling.

Helpless tears ran down her face from beneath her closed lids. They trickled against Trace's lips, and when he tasted their salty wetness he broke off the kiss to look down at her. Shock froze his features at the sight of her ghastly pallor.

"Katy! My god! What's wrong?"

She sagged between his hands, her head drooping forward until her chin touched her chest. A dizzying blackness swirled around the edge of her consciousness and her stomach churned. "I...I...think I'm going to be sick," she whispered weakly.

"No, you're not."

Bending, he scooped her up in his arms and covered the short distance to the car with long, ground-eating strides. Somehow he managed to open the door and thrust her inside. Then his hand was on the back of her neck, pushing her head down between her knees.

"Take deep breaths, Katy, and let them out nice and slowly. That's my girl." He crooned the soothing words as she obeyed. He was squatted down on his haunches beside the open door, bending protectively over her, his hands tender as they stroked the back of her neck and shoulders.

Katy remained bent over for a long time, drawing in deep, reviving gulps of air. Finally her heartbeat slowed, and the dizzying sickness began to fade. She lifted her head and gave him a wan smile. "I—I think I'll be all right now," she said in a weak, quivering voice.

"Are you sure?" Trace very gently cupped her jaw with one hand and scanned her white face. Worry and puzzlement flickered in his eyes.

"Yes. Yes, I'm sure."

Over his shoulder Katy noticed the clutch of people gathered on the sidewalk, gaping at the spectacle she'd provided, and turned her head away sharply, her humiliation deepening. Good Lord! By tonight the story would be all over town.

If the embarrassing situation bothered Trace he certainly didn't let it show. He pulled a handkerchief from his pocket and very tenderly wiped the perspiration from her face, pushing back the disheveled strands of glistening black hair. When finished, he fastened the seat belt around her, stood up and closed the door firmly, then walked around to the other side and slid in behind the wheel. He didn't even glance at the crowd of people on the sidewalk. Pausing briefly, he cast her a quick, assessing look, then flicked the ignition key and pulled away from the curb.

A merciful numbness settled over Katy and she sat huddled against the door, staring out the side window with dry, sightless eyes. The rose fields whizzed by in a long streak of blurred rainbow colors.

"All right, Katy," Trace said quietly, but determined. "I think it's time you and I had a serious talk. What happened back there?"

"Nothing. At least, nothing that concerns you," she said with a zombielike flatness. "Just leave me alone, Trace. That's all I ask. Just get out of my life and leave me alone."

"No, Katy. I won't do that. I *can't* do that. Haven't you realized that yet?"

Katy didn't answer him, and after a few minutes he sighed. "Okay. If you're not ready to talk yet, I won't press. But when we get back to the farm we're going to have this out. It's gone on far too long. Something is wrong, and I intend to find out what."

Katy's only answer was a cool, level look. So they were going to have a talk, were they? she thought resentfully. Just like that. Whether she agreed or not. Well, think again, Mr. Trace Barnett.

He didn't look at her, and finally she returned her gaze to the passing scenery. She felt raw and vulnerable, exposed. Trace's very presence scraped against her nerves. Why couldn't he just leave her alone? She'd had her life under control before Trace returned, but somehow he had managed to penetrate her protective shell of indifference. More so today than usual, because his sudden appearance had come as a shock. On Monday he'd flown to Colorado to settle his affairs there, and she had not expected him back so soon.

The car had barely come to a stop in the drive when Katy reached for the door handle. She scrambled out and dashed for the house, but Trace was too fast for her. He moved across the yard like a shot and took the porch steps in one leap. Before she could get the screen door completely open he was beside her, grabbing her arm and shoving the door shut again.

"Oh, no, you don't, Katy. You're not going to run out on me now," he said determinedly.

"Let me go!" she demanded. "You have no rights over me! I'm not part of the farm property!" Katy was fighting for control. She knew if she didn't get away from him soon, she was going to explode. She was hovering on the raw edge of panic, and it would take very little to push her over. Her frayed nerves simply couldn't stand any more strain.

"I never said you were. But for God's sake, Katy! Why won't you tell me what's wrong?"

"Because it's none of your damned business!" she shouted wildly. Twisting her arm free, she snatched at the screen door again, but Trace slammed his hand against it with a splintering force that made the wooden frame tremble.

He grabbed her shoulders and gave her a little shake. "Dammit, Katy, you—"

"What the devil is going on here?" Tom Donovan's massive bulk loomed up on the other side of the screen door. His brows came down in a thunderous scowl as he noticed his daughter's distraught face, and his narrowing gaze swung to the man holding her. "Take your hands off her, Trace," he commanded with quiet menace. "Now."

Defiant anger flared in the hazel eyes as they locked on the older man. A muscle jerked beside the grim line of his mouth, and for a moment Trace looked as though he were about to argue. Then, his jaw tight, he slowly, reluctantly, let his hands fall to his sides and took a step backward.

Pushing open the screen door, Tom stepped out onto the porch and silently gathered Katy into his arms. He held her close, his huge frame absorbing the violent tremors that quaked through her, his rough, paw-like hand tenderly stroking the silky head lying against his chest. He fixed the younger man with a hard, demanding stare. "What did you do to her?"

"I kissed her."

Some of the anger seemed to go out of Tom. "I see," he murmured. Tired gray eyes gazed down at the trembling girl cradled in his arms, and he shook his head sadly. "Well, that explains it."

"What's wrong with her, Tom? And don't tell me she's shy. There's more to this than just shyness. A woman doesn't get sick just because a man kisses her."

Before her father could answer, Katy twisted around. Her blue eyes were icy as she glared at Trace. "I told you it's none of your business! Now please leave me alone."

"I love you, Katy. And I want to marry you," Trace stated flatly. "That makes it my business."

She sucked in a hissing breath and her eyes grew dark, the pupils expanding until there was only a thin ring of blue around the outer edges. "You can't be serious," she breathed out shakily. "I'm not going to marry you! I'm not going to marry anyone!"

Trace held her terror-stricken gaze for a moment, then looked at her father. "I meant what I said, Tom. I love her. I have a right to know."

"Trace, my boy," Tom began doubtfully. "You've only been back a few weeks. How can you be sure of your feelings so quickly?"

The hazel gaze didn't waver. "How long did it take you to realize that you loved Kathleen?"

Tom's brows rose in mild surprise, then a faraway look entered his eyes, and his craggy features softened. Shaking his head, he gave the younger man a rueful smile. After a tense pause, he heaved a sigh. "All right, Trace. I'll tell you."

Chapter Five

"**D**ad, no! You can't! I won't let you!" Katy's face lost every vestige of color as she stared up at her father.

"Katy girl, listen to me," Tom urged softly.

"No! No, I won't! You can't..."

"Stop it, Katy!"

He grasped her by the shoulders and shook her, then brought his face down to within inches of hers. "Now listen to me, Katy girl. And listen good. Trace is right. Can't you see that? He loves you and wants to marry you. If you refuse, he deserves to know why. If you accept him, he *should* know what happened. Either way, *he has the right to know!*"

Tom's expression grew infinitely sad as he looked down at her frightened face, and his voice dropped to a low, husky pitch. "Oh, Katy, Katy. Don't you understand? This isn't just for Trace. It's for you too. Not once since it happened have you shed a tear, or even spoken of it directly. You keep it all locked up tight inside you and try to pretend it never happened. Well, it *did* happen, Katy, and you're entitled to your tears and anger. Let's bring it all out into the open and let it go. You'll never get over it until you do."

The air on the porch was thick with tension. Katy could hardly breathe. She didn't want to talk about it. She didn't even want to think about it. But deep down, she knew her father was right. For a long time she simply stared at him, and then, finally, closed her eyes and nodded.

Tom's face relaxed, and he pulled her close. "That's my Katy," he whispered huskily against the top of her head.

By silent agreement, the three of them filed into the house. Katy went directly to the sofa and curled up in the corner. Propping an elbow on the armrest, she pressed her balled fist against her mouth and turned her face away from the two men. Her slender body was quivering with tension.

Trace remained standing and watched Tom pace restlessly in front of the fireplace. When at last he came to an abrupt halt and swung around, his face was stiff and pale.

"About three years ago," he began in a voice that shook with controlled fury, "Katy was attacked by two men."

The bald statement made Trace's body jerk as though he'd been touched with an electric prod. His jaw clenched, and his fists curled into white knuckled fists at his sides. He stared at the older man, his throat working convulsively, and it was several seconds before he could ask the question that hovered in their air. "Did they . . ."

"No!" Tom answered quickly, shutting off the dreadful word. "No, not that. Thank God." Katy's soft crying made him wince, but he gritted his teeth and went on. "They had dragged her into the woods, but your father and I were returning from town and we heard her screams. We got there in time to prevent . . ." He closed his eyes and waved away the rest of the statement. "But she'd fought them and they had hit her. By the time we arrived she was unconscious." Tom's face contorted with remembered pain and anguish, and he turned away sharply, unable to continue.

"Who were they?" Trace demanded through his teeth.

Tom's face twisted with bitterness as he looked back over his shoulder. "They were guests here at the farm."

"What were their names?"

"I don't know."

"What the hell do you mean, you don't know?! Weren't they prosecuted?"

"No."

"*No?* Didn't they receive *any* punishment?" Trace demanded incredulously. "Didn't you at least give them the beating they deserved?"

Tom braced both arms against the fireplace mantel and hung his head, dejection in every line of his body. "No," he whispered hoarsely.

"Do you mean you let them get away scot free? You did *nothing?*" The questions came out slowly, menacingly, the low, savage tone chilling.

But Tom had had enough. He swung around and confronted the younger man with blazing eyes. "What do you want from me, lad? Don't you think I wanted to tear them limb from limb for what they'd done to my Katy? Of course I did! But I couldn't. At least, not then. Katy needed medical attention." Tom ran an agitated hand through his white hair. "By the time I got back from town, your father had spirited the two men away," he said grimly. "He said if we tried to prosecute his friends, he'd testify on their behalf. He'd swear in a court of law that Katy had enticed them into the woods. It would have been our word against his."

"And you continued to work for a man like that?" Trace ground out in a seething rage. "My God, man! What happened to that fierce Irish pride?"

"I swallowed it for once in my life!" Tom roared back. "And believe me, it was a bitter pill. Look at me, lad. *Look* at me! I'm sixty-three years old. Who's going to hire an old man like me? I had a wife who needed constant medical attention. What choice did I have but to stay?"

Trace looked like a wild man. His eyes were two glittering slits of green fire. His jaw was clenched in anger, and a muscle jumped spasmodically in his cheek. He looked ready to explode.

Swearing violently, he swung around and brought his fist down hard on the back of a chair in a fit of frustrated rage. He stood with his back to the other two, his big frame shaking as he fought for control.

Katy was crying openly now. Wordlessly Tom sat down beside her and gathered her into his arms once again. Her deep, wrenching sobs tore at him, and he laid his cheek against the top of her head, his face ravaged with pain, as the silent tears squeezed from beneath his tightly closed lids.

The three remained that way for a long time, no one daring to move, until finally, finally, the weeping gave way to a series of jarring hiccups, and Katy sat up and wiped her wet cheeks with the back of her hand.

The movement seemed to release Trace from his frozen stance, and he turned slowly. He took a step forward, then stopped when she flinched away from him.

"Katy...I—I don't know what to say. Words can't express how sorry I am...or how ashamed I am of my father's part in what happened. I know that doesn't help but..." He gestured weakly with his hand, then let it fall back to his side.

Katy's chin trembled as she looked down at her hands. Her fingers worked nervously at the skirt of her blue cotton sundress, creasing the material into tiny pleats. She pressed her lips together, unable to speak.

"But, Katy, none of this changes anything," Trace rushed on urgently. "I love you, and I want to marry you. I—"

"No! Don't say that! For God's sake, don't say that! Just leave me alone!" she cried as she turned and buried her face against her father's chest.

"Katy..." Trace took another step toward her but Tom held up his hand and shook his head.

"No, Trace. Not now, lad. Not now," he cautioned softly. "Let her be. She's had enough for one day."

Helpless frustration tightened Trace's muscles, and for a moment he looked as though he were going to ignore the command. He stared at Katy's huddled figure for a long time, then sighed and nodded reluctantly. "All right. I won't say any more. But I'll be back."

The screen door banged against its frame as the heavy thud of boots hammered across the wooden porch. Then there was only silence.

Tom unfolded the newspaper, turned a page, then refolded it with a snap. The dry, rustling sound drew Katy's attention, and she looked up from the magazine she was reading. A tender expression settled over her features as she watched her father, scowling at the newspaper through the reading glasses perched on the end of his nose. He was such a *good* man, and so extraordinarily patient with her.

Not once since Trace had stormed out yesterday had he even mentioned the discussion or the traumatic events of three years ago. He had said his piece and brought it all out in the open. Now, how she handled it was up to her. She knew without asking that she would always have his love and support, and, if she wanted it, his advice, but he would push no more. Yesterday, when he had insisted upon telling Trace the whole sordid story, had been one of the few times he had ever pressed her into something against her will.

Katy's gaze returned to the magazine in her lap, and she idly turned another page. Her eyes were slightly out of focus as she stared at the phony, professional smile of the girl in the toothpaste ad. As usual he had been right. Listening to him tell that awful story had been difficult, painfully so, but the long overdue tears had been a catharsis. Three years of built up tension, fear, and anger had been purged from her system, and when her hiccuping sobs had finally ceased, she had felt drained, both physically and emotionally. At her father's insistence she had gone directly to bed and had fallen immediately into the deep oblivion of exhausted sleep. When she awoke this morning she had felt more at peace than she had in years. The business with Trace wasn't over yet, she was aware of that. But perhaps now that he knew the reason for her attitude he would accept her rejection of him.

So immersed was she in her thoughts that she didn't hear the soft fall of footsteps across the porch. When the knock sounded she jumped, her eyes flying to the door.

Her father lowered his newspaper and gave her a quick, concerned glance, then tossed it aside and rose from his chair to answer the summons.

"Good evening, Trace."

"Tom."

A hinge squeaked noisily in the tense silence as the screen door was opened, then closed. Katy felt Trace's presence in the room as surely as if he had touched her. The changing sound of footsteps told her that the two men had left the hardwood floor and were crossing the braided rug, but she kept her eyes on the blurred image in the magazine.

"I know you're here to see Katy, so why don't I just make myself scarce for a bit," Tom offered politely.

Katy's head jerked up, but before she could open her mouth to protest, Trace was speaking.

"No, don't go, Tom. I think it would be best if you both hear what I have to say."

"Very well, lad. If that's what you want." Tom extended his hand toward the other fireside chair. "Have a seat, then."

Katy's heart was beating against her ribs like a newly caged bird as she watched Trace lower his long frame into the chair facing hers. Leaning forward, he placed his elbows on his knees and trained his eyes on the faded, work-stained Stetson that his hands were restlessly turning. Then, without warning, he looked up, straight into Katy's eyes.

"Will you marry me, Katy?" he asked with a curious, dull flatness.

She stared at him for a moment, knocked off balance by the suddenness of his question, then, swallowing hard, turned her head aside. "I—I'm sorry, Trace. I...can't," she stammered painfully.

There was a moment of thick silence, then he expelled his breath in a heavy sigh. "That's what I thought you'd say."

Katy looked back at him, drawn by the grimness of his tone. "I can't!" she said more urgently. "Surely you can see that?"

"No, Katy. It's not that you can't, but that you won't. Unless you're forced to."

"Don't be silly." She laughed nervously. "You can't force someone to marry you."

"Can't I?" His eyes bored into her with hard determination and, strangely, what appeared to be regret.

"No. No, of course not," she asserted with more conviction than she felt. She had the strangest sensation that control of the situation was rapidly slipping from her hands.

He looked at her for a long time, the hazel eyes narrowed and intent, then asked blandly, "Tell me, Katy, where do you think your father got the money to pay your mother's medical bills?"

Whatever she had expected him to say, that was not it, and she blinked in surprise. "Why, I suppose he borrowed it from the bank. Why do you ask?"

"Because the money didn't come from the bank. It came from the operating capital of this farm. Week by week, over a period of several years, your father borrowed what in total amounts to well over twenty-five thousand dollars." He paused to let that sink in, then added softly, chillingly, "They were unauthorized loans, Katy."

Her breath hissed through her tight throat, and for a moment she could only stare at him. Then her incredulous gaze swung to her father.

"Is this true, Dad?"

"I'm afraid it is," he admitted regretfully.

"But—but why? *Why?*"

"If there had been any other way, I would've taken it. But the banks wouldn't loan me the money. They all said I was too old, and the amount was too great. I asked Henry Barnett for a loan, but he turned me down flat. So I took what I needed. It wasn't difficult. Henry never bothered to give the books more than a cursory glance. As long as the farm was showing a healthy profit, he was happy." Tom paused, then his voice hardened. "I'm sorry I had to do it that way, but I would've taken money from St. Peter himself to ease my Kathleen's last days."

A feeling of utter despair engulfed Katy as the seriousness of her father's actions began to penetrate. She rubbed shaking fingers across her forehead and closed her eyes. "Oh, Dad. What have you done?" she murmured helplessly.

"If I had been here, I would have given your father the money, Katy. I hope you believe that. I think you should know, also, that he's been paying the money back in regular monthly installments," Trace said quietly, and Katy's eyes flew open.

"Does that mean you're not going to prosecute him?" she asked, her face alive with hopeful expectancy.

Pain flickered in the hazel eyes. "No, I'm not going to prosecute."

The moment the words were said, Katy slumped back in the chair, nearly faint with relief, but the reprieve was short lived. His next words hit her like a spray of buck-shot.

"But if you won't marry me, I'm going to have to dismiss your father."

"No! You can't mean that! You'll get your money back. Dad will keep up the payments and—and now that I know, I can help," she cried desperately. "That way it will be paid back twi—"

"It isn't the money, Katy," Trace interrupted in a flat, hard voice that stopped her cold.

Her confusion was evident, and seeing it, he continued in a softer, more caressing tone. "I love you, Katy. If I can't have you as my wife, I don't think I could bear to see you every day, to know that you were here at the cottage, just a few hundred yards away, yet completely out of my reach."

"The lad's right." Her father spoke up before Katy could voice the protest on the tip of her tongue. "I know how he feels. If you aren't going to marry him, then we must move on."

"But...Dad! You love this place!"

"Aye, that I do. And I'd hoped to live out my days here. But if we must go, we must." She started to speak but he held up his hand and cut her off. "No, Katy. I sympathize with Trace wholeheartedly. Had your mother refused to marry me I couldn't have borne to see her every day. It would be an act of cruelty to stay, and I have too much respect and admiration for Trace to be a party to that."

Stunned, Katy stared at her father, barely able to breathe. A frightening sensation of utter helplessness began to seep into her, penetrating to the very marrow of her bones, and she felt her stomach muscles twist into a hard knot. There was no way out but one, and her mind shied violently away from the thought. If her father lost this job, he would never find another, at least, not one that would pay well enough for him to handle the enormous mountain of debt that loomed over them. And certainly her own meager salary would be of little help. She loved her father dearly and would do anything to help him . . . but to marry Trace, to live intimately with him. . . . A steel door clanged shut in her mind, blocking out the frightful images, and Katy closed her eyes, her body shuddering in remembered terror.

"Katy, listen to me."

Trace's voice came from close at hand, and when she opened her eyes, she found him crouched in front of her chair, his hands braced on either armrest. Instinctively, she shrank back into the cushions. His nearness was oppressive. Katy could feel the heat from his body, smell the clean, male scent of him. His earthy masculinity was a powerful force that wrapped itself around her, making her acutely aware of her own fragile femininity as no other man ever had.

Her reaction brought a quick thinning of his mouth, but Trace pressed on doggedly. His eyes locked with hers, and Katy felt her mouth go dry. She tried to look away, but there was an earnest plea in the green depths that held her mesmerized.

"Katy, I promise you, I give you my solemn word, if you accept my proposal, the marriage will not be consummated until you are ready."

Surprise flickered in her eyes. "You—you mean it would be a marriage in name only?" she asked, her expression guarded.

Wry amusement tugged at the corners of his mouth as his head moved from side to side. "No, Katy. This will be no marriage of convenience," he stated unequivocably. "I love you, and I want very much to make love to you, and I'm confident I shall one day, but not until it's what you want also. I promise I'll not force you or seduce you. You have my word on that. But I reserve the right to do everything in my power to make you want me too. However, you will be in complete control. When our marriage becomes a real one it will be at your request."

Katy noted his use of the word *when* instead of *if*, and silently marveled at his self-confidence. How could he be so positive? And why would he want to take such a risk? She glanced instinctively toward her father, seeking his advice, but his face remained unreadable. Her gaze swung back to the man crouched at her feet. A worried frown creased her delicate brow. "Trace... what if that never happens?"

"That's my problem, Katy. Not yours. All you have to do is trust me. And you can," he added softly, persuasively. "Believe that."

He picked up her clenched hands and gently pried them apart. Long, brown fingers stroked back and forth over the silken skin in a loving caress. "One day, my love, we'll look back on this and laugh. I refuse to believe the love I feel for you could possibly be one-sided. It's too strong, too deep. The problem is that your emotions have been encased in a block of ice for so long they're numb. But the ice cracks a little more every time I touch you. We both know that. With time and patience, it will melt completely, and I think you'll find that you love me too." He stared at her intently, willing her to believe him. "I'm betting my whole future on it, Katy."

Confusion clouded her blue eyes. She felt torn in two directions. Fear still held her in a tight grip, but Trace's words pulled at her heart like a powerful magnet, stirring long-buried dreams. As a child she had woven wonderful fantasies of someday having a marriage like that of her parents, of sharing that kind of deep, boundless love, of having a home of her own and a small brood of beautiful, happy children. That dream had died three years ago. She had buried it so deep that she had not believed it could ever be resurrected. But it had happened. The old yearnings stirred inside her.

Honesty forced Katy to admit that she did feel some sort of basic attraction for Trace. Her body had recognized it long before her conscious mind had accepted the fact. What if he was right, if all he'd said was really possible? Could she love him, wholeheartedly, in every sense of the word?

"Katy, I don't expect an answer now." Trace's voice broke into her thoughts. "But I want your promise that you'll think about it. Will you do that?"

"I—I—" She stopped and chewed worriedly at her lip, her eyes wide and wary. Finally, she took a deep breath and whispered, "Yes. I'll think about it."

"Good. That's all I ask." He patted her hand and stood up. Katy remained in the chair and watched, dazed, as her father saw him to the door. He pushed the screen door part way open, then paused, and turned back to face her. "Just remember, Katy. It's a chance for happiness for both of us. Don't throw it away." Then he was gone.

"Well, my girl, what do you think?" Tom asked as he returned to the sofa.

Agitated, Katy stood up and began to pace the floor in front of the hearth, her heels clicking impatiently against the hardwood floor. She retraced her steps several times, then stopped and flung out her hand, a harried expression on her face. "Oh, I don't know! I *just don't know!*"

"Well, I'll say this. You'll not be gettin' a better proposal than that, me darlin'."

The thickening of his brogue lifted the corners of Katy's mouth. It told her more clearly than words ever could how deeply concerned he was for her.

"I know that, Dad." She folded her arms over her midriff and resumed her pacing. "That is, if he keeps his promises. That was a very pretty speech, I'll admit, but, supposing I did accept, what's to prevent him from claiming his rights after we're married?"

"His word, that's what."

"And you think I can put my trust in that?"

"I know you can. He's a good man, Katy. Believe that."

Shaking fingers raked the silky mass of blue-black hair away from her face, then returned to massage her throbbing temples. "Oh, Dad," she sighed wearily. "How can you be so certain? I keep remembering how wild he used to be. The crazy, impossible things he used to do."

"Aw, Katy, Katy," her father admonished with soft severity. "In those days he was hurtin' badly. The lad was lashin' out at the world in the only way he knew how. Can't you understand that?"

Katy stared at him, transfixed. Less than a week ago Trace had said something very similar about her father. Perhaps the two men were even more alike than she had thought. Was Trace really like her father? Was he one of those strong, rugged men whose masculinity is merely enhanced by his deep capacity for tenderness?

Katy had heard it said that every little girl wanted to marry a man just like her daddy when she grew up. In her own case she knew that was true. She could imagine no finer man in the whole world than Tom Donovan. If Trace was really like him...Katy deliberately thrust the thought aside. It was silly, wishful thinking. She had to be practical and level-headed about this.

"Oh, Dad, I just don't know what to do." She sighed in weary confusion.

"Katy, listen to me. Even in his wildest, most hell-raising period, Trace was absolutely trustworthy. When he gave his word, he stood by it, even if it meant taking a thrashing from old Henry."

One corner of her mouth lifted in a rueful smile. "It sounds as though you think I ought to accept Trace's proposal."

"I'll tell you truly, my girl, if I had the privilege of hand picking a husband for you, I'd choose Trace. He's a good man, Katy. None better. And he loves you deeply. He'll make a fine husband and father, and he'll take good care of you."

"But I don't need a husband to take care of me," she argued.

Tom looked at her sadly, and patted the cushion beside him. "Come here, lass," he ordered, and Katy obeyed. He picked up her hand and squeezed it gently, his tired old eyes warm on her trusting face. "Look at me, darlin'. I'm an old man. I won't be around much longer. I want to know that you have someone, that you won't be alone when I—"

Katy pressed her fingers against his mouth, shutting off the dreadful words. "No! Dad, don't say that!" she cried, but Tom merely shook his head and removed her hand.

"Don't look so stricken, darlin'. Truth to tell, without your mother, I don't much care. You're the only thing that's kept me going this past year." Raising a large, calloused hand, he tucked a lock of hair behind her ear, then trailed his knuckles along the elegant line of her jaw.

"Lookin' at you is like seein' my darlin' Kathleen as she was twenty years ago," he murmured softly. "And you're like her in other ways too. Some women could have shrugged off that attack and gone on with their lives. Some it would even have hardened. But not you, Katy. You're soft and gentle and very vulnerable. You need the love and protection of a good man. I want that for you, Katy, more than anything in this world," he whispered fiercely. "Love, the kind your mother and I had, is life's greatest reward. If you've got that, nothin' else matters."

"But, Dad, I don't love Trace," she protested.

"How do you know that, darlin'? For years you've kept your emotions locked up tight inside you. You haven't let yourself feel anything for any man. Let go, Katy," he urged. "You'll be surprised how good it feels." He gave her hand another squeeze and smiled coaxingly. "And I'll admit, I'd rest easier knowing Trace would be takin' care of you after I've gone."

Tears pushed against her lower lids, then slowly trickled over, leaving wet tracks on the satin-smooth cheeks. As she stared at the lined, weathered face, Katy was forced to accept what her mind had refused to see for the past few years. Her father *was* looking extremely old and tired.

"Oh, Dad." Her voice wavered as she forced out the words. "I suppose, if it means that much to you, and you're sure he can be trusted, I'll marry him. I haven't much choice anyway. If I don't you'll have to give up your job."

Tom reached up and framed her face with his large, work-roughened hands. His brows were drawn together in a concerned frown as he stared into her tear-drenched eyes. "Don't be doin' it for me, Katy darlin'. Do it for yourself. I've known him, man and boy, and I'm tellin' you, you'll not find a better man, or a better husband, than Trace Barnett."

Chapter Six

"You're going to *what!*" Jane squeaked.

"I said I'm going to marry Trace," Katy repeated huskily, keeping her head down, her eyes firmly fixed on the small cup she was washing. She could feel Jane's shocked stare boring into her, but couldn't make herself meet her friend's eyes.

"I *know* what you said. What I want to know is *why?* Less than a week ago you were still avoiding him like the plague, and now you calmly tell me you're going to marry him. Good grief! I'd heard that Trace was a fast worker, but this is ridiculous!" Jane dried another cup with swift, agitated movements and shoved it into the cabinet above the counter. "Oh, I know he put on a good show when he picked you up last Friday, but it was obvious that you were still running scared."

Katy glanced up and smiled wanly. "Trace is rather hard to resist when he wants something badly."

"That I can well imagine!" Jane retorted. "Don't get me wrong. Frank and I were delighted that he was interested in you. It's high time you came out of your shell. But we thought he'd have sense enough to court you slowly and carefully, the way you deserve to be courted. We were even betting that it would be the end of summer before he broke through that wall of reserve. And then probably several months more before things started getting serious between you two. Now this! I tell you, Katy, it looks to me as though you've been bulldozed into something against your will, and I don't like it! Not one bit!"

Katy's hand was trembling as she placed the last dish in the drain rack, and Jane pounced on the betraying reaction like a cat on a mouse.

"Ah-ha! Look at that!" she cried triumphantly, as Katy plunged her hand back into the sudsy water. "Your nerves are as tight as a fiddle string. Don't tell me that's a normal reaction for a radiantly happy bride-to-be, because I'm not buying it."

Jane hung her dish towel on the rack at the end of the counter, then turned to face Katy with her hands planted firmly on her hips. "Now, I want to know what's going on. You're my friend, Katy, and I don't want to see you hurt. And I can tell you, I'm picking up some very peculiar vibrations."

Sighing, Katy dried her hands on a paper towel and turned to meet her friend's demanding stare. She should have known she couldn't fool Jane. Why had she even bothered to try? Jane was very sensitive. She had an instinct about people, especially those to whom she was close. There was nothing else to do but tell her the truth, and that meant starting at the beginning, three years ago. It seemed incredible that the secret she had kept locked inside her for so long was about to be told again, for the second time in the space of just a few days. But, somehow, strangely, it didn't seem to matter anymore.

"All right, Jane. I'll tell you." Katy walked across the room, sank down onto the couch, and motioned for the other woman to join her. "It's rather a long story, so you'd better have a seat."

"Sounds ominous," Jane said, as she curled herself into the opposite corner of the couch. The bristling aggression slowly drained from her as her gaze probed Katy's pale face. Leaning back against the armrest, Jane watched worriedly as Katy struggled to get the words out.

At last she began, slowly and hesitantly, her voice barely more than a whisper, her throat aching. Katy kept her head lowered, her eyes trained on her hands as she began to recite the horrifying story. Several times she had to pause to gather her composure, but she told it all. Forcing the words out in a flat, dull monotone, she described the attack, her father's timely arrival, Henry Barnett's threat, even her own withdrawal into emotional numbness. Then, with the worst behind, her voice grew stronger as she told of Trace's relentless pursuit, her father's desperate action, and, finally, of the incredible proposal.

The air was heavy with emotion when the strained narrative ended, her words vibrating in the deathly silence. The tension was suffocating. Katy's chest was so tight it hurt to breathe. Finally, gathering her courage, she looked up and found that Jane was staring at her with anguished brown eyes, her cheeks wet with unchecked tears.

"Oh, Katy," she choked out, and in the next instant moved across the empty cushion to clasp the younger girl in her arms. "Katy, dearest, why didn't you tell me before? I knew something was wrong, but I never dreamed . . . Oh, God! Katy!"

"I—I just couldn't."

"Mmmm, it took someone as determined as Trace to pry it out of you. And thank God he did!" she declared fervently. "I take back all the things I said about him. My opinion of that man has just gone up like a rocket."

Katy pulled back and looked at her friend. Her eyes were wide with surprise. "Just a few minutes ago you were ranting about this sudden engagement. Now you sound as though you approve."

"Now that I know the whole story, I do. Wholeheartedly!" She smiled and reached up to brush a stray curl away from Katy's face. "Katy, love, if you haven't gotten over the trauma of it in three years, you're not ever going to. Not by yourself, anyway. You need someone gentle and patient to teach you about love, the way it should be. Someone who cares for you deeply. From what you've just told me, I'd say that Trace is that man."

"Thanks for the vote of confidence."

The deep, masculine voice came as a complete surprise to the two women, and both jumped in alarm. Katy whirled around, her eyes widening.

"Trace! What are you doing here?"

"We were going to shop for an engagement ring today. Remember?"

"I thought we were going to do that this evening. After I finish work."

"The stores will be closed by then, love. Or had you forgotten?"

She hadn't. In fact, she had been counting on it. Buying an engagement ring made it seem so official, so final. She had been hoping to delay the purchase for a day or two, to give herself a chance to get used to the idea. From the sardonic amusement in Trace's expression, she was fairly sure he had known exactly what she was up to.

A warm blush started at the base of her throat and surged upward. "Trace, I don't think I'd..."

He stepped forward and took hold of her hand, drawing her to her feet in one smooth motion. When she was standing he dropped his arm across her shoulders and smiled down at her. "I doubt very much if your boss would begrudge you an hour or so to shop for your engagement ring." His persuasive gaze switched to the petite woman on the couch. "Would you, Mrs. Cawley?"

"Of course not. And, please, do call me Jane," she replied instantly. "You couldn't have chosen a better time, as a matter of fact. We just put all the little angels down for their afternoon nap. It will be another hour or so before the organized chaos starts again."

"Good. That should give us plenty of time. Thanks, Jane." Trace turned Katy toward the door and urged her forward.

During the ride to the jewelers, Katy sat rigid and silent. Every cell in her body was quivering with tension. This was the first time she had been alone with Trace since accepting his proposal, and the enormity of her decision had suddenly begun to overwhelm her. The rest of her life. She had committed herself to this man *for the rest of her life!*

She slanted him a wary glance from beneath her lashes. Today he was dressed in an impeccable light gray suit, teamed with a dazzling white shirt and a gray and wine striped tie. Evidently he thought the occasion warranted a certain degree of formality. Ruefully, Katy glanced down at her own simple black and white, geometric-patterned sundress with its short, white jacket. She felt positively dowdy by comparison.

As if he were a magnet, her eyes were drawn to him again and again. He looked exceptionally handsome, Katy had to admit. But not even the sophisticated elegance of his attire could conceal the leashed power in that long, lean body or the sheer virility that radiated from him. Just being near Trace made her uneasy. He was so... so rawly male.

A shiver rippled through her like an icy wave. What if her father were wrong? What if Trace couldn't be trusted? The dreaded fear began to unfurl itself deep inside her, and Katy felt suddenly cold and clammy. Closing her eyes, she took several deep breaths and forced down the panic that threatened to consume her. No! No, she wouldn't think like that. Her father was a good judge of character, wasn't he. And so far, Trace's behavior had been exemplary.

The night before, when she had told him she would marry him, his eyes had flared hotly with some dark, intense emotion, but it had been only a fleeting reaction that had faded before she'd had a chance to become frightened. Surprisingly, he had only smiled that slow, heart-stopping smile and said softly, "Thank you, Katy. I promise you won't regret it." Other than giving her one, brief kiss on the cheek, he had made no attempt to touch her.

Determined to live up to her end of the bargain, Katy clamped down on her rising panic. Her resolve wavered slightly when, a short while later, Trace slipped the stunning marquise-cut diamond solitaire on her finger. The unaccustomed weight of the ring and the blatantly possessive look in Trace's eyes brought back some of her doubts. Katy's heart began to beat with a slow thud. Things were moving too fast. For a hysterical moment she actually considered running for the nearest exit.

As though sensing her thoughts, Trace placed his hand under her chin and tipped her face up. She knew her fears were visible in her eyes, but instead of becoming angry or impatient, he sent her a smile of such tender compassion that her heart gave a queer little jerk.

"It's too late for second thoughts, darling. If our jeweler friend hasn't already spread the word, I'm sure the newspaper staff has. You see, I called this morning to have a formal announcement placed in the paper. Besides that, there are several other very good reasons for rushing," he informed her, smiling indulgently into her wary eyes. "Not the least of which, I'll admit, is the fact that I am very anxious to make you my wife. But there's something else, too, something you said the other day that made me realize it would be best if I made my intentions clear."

"Something *I* said?"

"Yes. Katy, I'm well aware of my reputation in this town, especially where women are concerned. I don't want anyone to have any doubts about my feelings for you, or what your position is in my life. For that reason I want this engagement made public as soon as possible."

No matter how hard she tried, Katy could not sup—press the warm glow Trace's words had brought. It stayed with her all the way back to the nursery school. It also perplexed her. Why should it please her so much that he obviously cared for her and wanted the whole world to know? It was a difficult question, one that made Katy feel uneasy and somewhat guilty.

Now that she had committed herself and had begun to accept the situation, she realized that their arrangement was actually very one-sided. Trace was being extremely patient and understanding and receiving little in return. In all honesty, she had entered into the bargain with her eyes wide open and really had no cause for complaint. She had given her word and accepted him on his terms, and she might as well make the best of it. It would be pointless not to.

With that decision firmly in mind, she made no protest when Trace accepted Trace's invitation to dinner that night.

They arrived at the Cawleys' front door promptly at eight, to the sound of heavy, discordant rock music issuing from the house at a volume that threatened to shatter the walls. Darting Trace an uncertain glance, Katy reached out to ring the doorbell. The melodious chimes didn't make a dent in the orchestrated bombardment.

Amusement crinkled Trace's eyes. "I think a firmer approach is called for." He practically shouted the words in her ear while reached around her to pound on the door with the side of his balled fist.

A moment later it was opened, and Frank grimaced apologetically as he motioned them in. Miming for them to follow, he marched into the room where Jason and John lay sprawled on the floor in front of the stereo and turned the volume down.

"Hey! What did you do that for!" they squawked in unison, turning identical, outraged faces toward their father.

"I don't think our guests would care to go deaf before dinner," Frank replied with a complete lack of concern. "If you two think you can manage a vertical position for five minutes I'd like you to meet Katy's fiancé. Trace, these two juvenile delinquents are our sons, Jason and John. Boys, meet Trace Barnett."

"Trace Barnett!" they squeaked together. "You mean the guy who owns Green Meadows Farm?"

"'Fraid so," Trace admitted laconically.

They stared at him for a moment, goggle-eyed, then Jason gave Katy a broad wink and nudged his brother in the ribs. "Boy, I'll say one thing for you, Katy"—he snickered—"when you do something, you do it up brown."

Katy was spared the necessity of answering that because Jane walked into the room, followed closely by Martha.

The Cawleys' eldest was dressed in purple jeans and a pink T-shirt. The lurid message scrawled across her breasts made Katy do a quick double take, then hurriedly turn away, her cheeks a bright pink. She was profoundly glad when the girl sailed right on past them.

"Sorry. Can't stop to chat now," she called over her shoulder, taking the stairs two at a time. "My date will be here any minute."

Jane's mouth twitched. "Revolting, isn't it."

"Absolutely," Katy agreed, rolling her eyes.

Jane laughed, then switched her attention to the man at Katy's side. "Don't panic, Trace. I guarantee it won't be like this all evening."

"That's right." Frank added his assurances. "Tweedledum and Tweedledee here are going to the movies, and Martha is going out with her latest heart-throb."

"*Heartthrob!* Yuck! That word went out with the biplane," John groaned. He clutched his stomach and staggered toward the door. "I think I'm gonna be sick!"

"Yeah, me too," Jason agreed as he trailed after him. "And the only cure for it is a giant box of popcorn and a root beer."

"That's quite a family you've got," Trace said, laughing, when the door closed behind the two boisterous teenagers. "Is it like this around here all the time?"

"No, not always. Sometimes it's worse." Jane waved her hand toward the sofa. "Why don't we sit down and have a nice, relaxing drink before dinner. I don't know about the rest of you, but believe me, I need one."

Frank had no sooner handed out the drinks and taken a seat than Martha came bounding back down the stairs. "Hi, Katy. Sorry I couldn't stop earlier, but I'm going out with this fabulous new fella, and he gets absolutely furious if I keep him waiting." She quickly eyed Katy's rose silk dress and sighed expressively. "Gee, you look terrific."

"Thanks. You look pretty good yourself." Katy was relieved to see that the jeans and T-shirt had been exchanged for a bright yellow and green sundress with a matching jacket. The petite brown-haired girl was the image of her mother, all pixie charm and bouncing enthusiasm. On her, the brilliantly patterned dress looked perfect.

After introductions were made, Martha, with a directness that rivaled her mother's, studied Katy and

Trace intently, her head cocked to one side. For a moment her eyes darted back and forth between them, then she shook her head, as though slightly dazzled by her discovery. "Boy, are you two ever going to make good-looking babies together," she stated with a bluntness that brought instant silence to the room.

Becoming suddenly aware of the four stunned faces staring at her, Martha swept them with a disgusted look. "Well, they will!" she insisted defensively. "It's all in the genes, you know. We learned that in Biology I, for heaven's sake!"

Before anyone could find his tongue, the doorbell rang. Martha let out a squeak and ran to answer it in a flurry of skirts and long, shining hair, her startling observation immediately dismissed from her mind. "That'll be Phillip. See you guys later."

There was a brief, taut silence after the door slammed, then three voices burst out laughing. Katy closed her eyes and turned beet-red.

Her flush deepened when Trace leaned close and whispered, "You see, darling. There's one more reason for us to marry."

"I'm sorry, Katy," Jane sputtered helplessly. "But you know how Martha is. She just says whatever comes into her head."

"Yes. Like someone else I could mention," Frank drawled pointedly.

"Well, subtlety never was my long suit. At least with us Cawley women you always know where we stand." Jane stood up and motioned for Katy to follow. "Come on. We'll give these two a chance to get acquainted while we finish dinner."

The meal went smoothly. Jane had prepared everything in advance so that it could be served with a minimum of fuss—a simple, well-planned menu of green salad, a dish of veal and rice, and broccoli in cheese sauce. For dessert there was a light chocolate-mint pie.

The table conversation was pleasant, sometimes bantering. Trace fit easily into the relaxed atmosphere of the Cawley home, joking and laughing with her friends as though he had known them for years. By the time they retired to the living room for after-dinner coffee, even Katy had relaxed somewhat.

"Tell me, Trace. When is the wedding?" Jane asked interestedly, as she handed him his cup.

The unexpected question brought Katy's head up, and she found that Trace was studying her thoughtfully. She looked away quickly and took a sip of coffee to cover her nervousness. She hadn't yet adjusted to being engaged. The thought of actually fixing a date paralyzed her with fear.

"We haven't discussed it, but I'm hoping it will be next month," Trace said quietly, his intent gaze fixed on Katy's downbent head.

The long curtain of black hair swung outward in a rippling arc when Katy's head snapped around. "Next month! But that's too soon!" The china cup clattered against its saucer, and Katy bent over to place it on the coffee table. Clasping her hands together tightly to stop their trembling, she turned to Trace with wide, troubles eyes. "We can't get married that quickly, Trace. I— I—"—her mind groped for an excuse, any excuse to delay—"Th-there's so much to do before a wedding. I can't possibly be ready in time."

Smiling, Trace ran a finger lightly over the curve of her cheek. "All right, darling. Six weeks. But not one day longer. In three weeks we'll have an engagement party, and three weeks after that we'll be married."

"An engagement party!" All thought of the wedding vanished with the introduction of this new threat. "Oh, do we *have* to? I don't know the first thing about giving a party like that. And...and I don't know any of your friends or relatives. I'd make a hopeless mess of the whole thing."

"Don't worry about it, sweetheart. Saundra can handle the party. That's the one thing she's good at," he said with a caustic bite. "Just give her a list of the people you want to invite, and I'll see that she takes care of the rest."

"Speaking of Saundra," Jane drawled in an elaborately casual tone. "How did she take the news of your engagement?"

Mild surprise flickered over Trace's rugged features. "Actually I don't suppose she's heard about it. She went to Dallas to visit friends while I was gone, and she hasn't returned yet."

Probably because, like herself, she hadn't expected him back this soon, Katy thought in a sudden burst of angry cynicism. The mention of Saundra deepened her growing sense of dread. Like a fool, she hadn't given the woman a thought, but there wasn't a doubt in her mind that Saundra would be livid when she heard the news. Suddenly Katy's stomach muscles tightened into a hard knot. She didn't think she could deal with Saundra's vicious anger on top of everything else.

"Will Saundra continue to live at Green Meadows after you and Katy are married?"

"Jane! That's none of your business," Frank ground out warningly. "You have no right to ask questions like that."

Jane tossed her head defiantly and shot her husband a quelling look. "I know that. But Katy has a right to know. After all, it affects her future. But knowing her as well as I do, I'm fairly sure she would never ask. So I'm doing it for her."

"Nevertheless, you shouldn't..."

"That's all right, Frank. I don't mind answering Jane's question." Trace looked at her and shrugged, his features screwed up in a rather self-conscious grimace. "Actually, I've never given the matter a thought. Saundra has lived at the farm for so long that it just never occurred to me to ask her to leave. But I wouldn't worry about it too much. She'd always enjoyed being mistress of Green Meadows. Once Katy and I are married and she has to relinquish that position, I doubt she'll stick around very long."

Katy was appalled. Weren't things bad enough without this additional complication? She had no desire to be pitted against Saundra in an open confrontation. Did he really expect her just to walk in and wrest control of the household from that spiteful, vicious woman? Or perhaps he didn't. Perhaps this was all lip service. Her eyes narrowed in sudden suspicion as she studied him through the veil of her lashes. Maybe he didn't believe she could win in a battle of wills with his stepmother. Maybe he didn't want her to win. She couldn't believe he was unaware of Saundra's interest in him. He might now want to marry his father's widow, but he certainly didn't seem averse to having her around.

The progression of her thoughts made Katy's stomach churn, but she was powerless to stop it. That could explain why he was so unconcerned about the physical side of their marriage. No doubt, Saundra would be quite happy to satisfy his male appetites. It was even possible that she was already sharing his bed, if rumor were to be believed.

The rest of the evening passed in a blur. Lost in her own thoughts, Katy sat back and let the conversation flow around her. She was puzzled by the violent emotions that tore at her. Even if her suspicions were correct, why should she care? She didn't love or want Trace. She should feel relieved that he might turn to another woman for physical satisfaction. Shouldn't she?

During the ride home she remained quiet, trying to come to grips with the confused jumble of emotions that plagued her. She had the strangest sensation of being swept along on a tide of events over which she had little or no control. It was very disturbing.

It was only when Trace brought the car to a halt in the drive beside her home that Katy's mind came back to the present. When he switched off the engine and turned to face her, the sudden quiet seemed oppressive and threatening, and she blurted out the first thing that came into her head.

"I'm sorry if Jane's questions embarrassed you."

"I wasn't embarrassed," he said with gentle amusement. "They're very nice people, and they care for you very much. I'm glad of that." His voice deepened to a husky caress. "I want only your happiness, Katy. I happen to love you very much."

She turned to look at him then, her blue eyes wide and searching, probing his face intently. "Do you, Trace?" she asked doubtfully. "Do you really?"

He seemed surprised by her skepticism. His brows rose sharply, and he looked back at her in blank astonishment. "Do you doubt it?"

"Oh, I don't doubt that you *think* you love me." She shrugged one shoulder. "But I can't help but wonder if you're not just reaching out for a fantasy."

Instead of becoming angry, as she had half expected, Trace merely looked at her broodingly for a moment, then smiled. "You're a very perceptive lady," he said softly. "I'm only human, Katy. I have all the same weaknesses and needs as other mortals. I won't try to deny that you epitomize all that I've ever longed for. Not only are you beautiful, and the most exquisitely feminine woman I've ever known, but you've also had the advantage of a loving upbringing by parents who were totally committed to one another and to you. That makes you all the more special, Katy. I want what only you can give me. I need it." His voice hardened to a soft violence that made her skin prickle. "I'm going to have it."

His words did not erase her doubts, but deepened them. Katy stared at him apprehensively. Her fear was reflected in her eyes, and seeing it, Trace frowned.

He paused, as though considering his next words carefully, then asked, "Have you ever wondered just what love is, Katy? Have you ever tried to define it, to put it into words?"

She shook her head mutely, staring at him with wary eyes.

"I've always thought love was finding that one someone who could fill a need in you that no one else could." His mouth curved in a self-derisive grimace. "Everyone has those needs, those desperate longings, that incomplete feeling. When you find that one person it's like finding your other half, and she fills the emptiness, completes you like the missing piece of a jigsaw puzzle. To me, that's love."

He framed her face between his hands and looked into her eyes, his gaze probing the very depths of her being. "And believe me, Katy, my very soul cries out for you. You're what has been missing from my life, all my life, and I need you very much.'' The deep, dark velvet voice stroked over her, soothing and caressing, wrapping her in its warmth. ''But love isn't altogether selfish. It also means caring more for the happiness and well-being of the loved one than you care for your own. And that's how I feel about you, sweetheart. I could never be happy unless you were.''

Katy stared at him, her throat tight with emotion. She felt helplessly drawn by the desperate yearning in his voice, the deep need, the exquisite tenderness. In that moment she knew she was totally, irrevocably committed to this man. Katy knew with a deep certainty that she felt something for him, and that she needed him just as surely as he needed her. She didn't want it. She wasn't ready for it. But it was there all the same. It was that irresistible, magnetic pull she had feared from the beginning. She also knew that if she entered into a marriage with Trace, no matter how platonic, she could never endure the kind of sordid arrangement she had envisioned earlier.

Watching the play of emotions cross her expressive face, Trace smiled gently. He bent and brushed a feathery kiss over her lips. It was possessive and loving, and heart-stoppingly tender. Light as it was, Katy felt it all the way to her toes.

When he raised his head his eyes caressed her face in a way that made her bones melt. ''I love you, Katy,'' he whispered. ''Don't ever doubt it.''

Chapter Seven

"If you don't hold still, Dad, I'll never get this thing tied," Katy admonished, while her father shifted restlessly from one foot to the other. She thought he looked very handsome and distinguished in his formal evening attire, with his shock of white hair neatly brushed and his deeply tanned skin glowing against the crisp white shirt. But Tom was obviously uncomfortable.

"Humph! I still don't see why I have to get rigged up in this monkey suit," he grumbled, his face like a thunder cloud.

"You have to wear it because this is a formal engagement party. And you may as well get used to wearing it because in the future you'll probably be attending quite a few affairs like this."

Tom's scowl deepened. "The devil you say! I'll be doing no such thing!" he denied vehemently.

"Oh, yes, you will." Katy's voice was calm and placid, as though she were soothing a fractious child.

She straightened the loops on the black bow tie and patted it into place, then looked up at her father and smiled. "You were the one who was so anxious for me to marry Trace. Didn't you realize that as his father-in-law you will be expected to attend any social functions we may have in the future?" Eyes twinkling, she reached up and patted his cheek. "Anyway, I know you'll want to come, if for no other reason than to give me moral support—which I shall probably need in large quantity."

Tom's expression altered quickly, concern darkening the gray eyes that searched her face. His hands came up to grasp her shoulders as his brows drew together in an anxious frown. "Katy darlin', you're not marrying Trace for my sake, are you? Because if that's all it is, I won't have it. You're not a sacrificial lamb, my girl. You're my daughter and I want your happiness above all things. I won't deny that I think this marriage is the best thing that could happen to you. But if it isn't going to make you happy, I'll admit to being an interfering old fool and go see Trace right now and call the whole thing off."

The smile faded from Katy's face and her eyes grew distant as she chewed worriedly on her bottom lip. It was a temptation. Her father could go to him and put a stop to the arrangement immediately. Then she could return to the safe, calm life she had led before his return. Couldn't she?

But even as she asked herself the question Katy knew deep down inside that it simply wasn't that easy. She was bound to Trace now in some strange, indefinable way that had nothing to do with concern for her father or even a longing for security. Her mind shied away from examining her feelings too closely, but she knew that her future lay with Trace. It was as though on that day at the graveside, almost two months ago, when she had looked up and met his eyes, the thread of her life had become inextricably woven with his.

"Answer me, Katy. Why did you agree to this marriage?"

Her father's concerned voice brought her out of her thoughts. She shook her head and gave him a wan smile. "I—I honestly don't know. At first I told myself I was doing it for you, so that your future would be secure, and because it would make you happy. But now, I'm not sure. I'm just . . . not sure."

Tom lifted one hand and cupped her cheek. A gentle smile replaced the tense anxiety in his face. "Don't worry about it, darlin'. Just follow your instincts. You won't go wrong."

He kissed her on the forehead, then turned her around and gave her a little push. "Now then, go get your things, girl, and let's be going. Trace wanted us there half an hour ago. He's going to think you got cold feet at the last minute."

In her room Katy deliberately took her time, unnecessarily recombing her hair and checking her appearance for perhaps the tenth time. She had no intention of arriving at the big house any earlier than she absolutely had to. The less she had to endure of Saundra's company the better.

The woman was impossible! On the surface, at least in front of Trace, she had been the soul of politeness and congeniality, seeming to accept the engagement with good grace, if not enthusiasm. But whenever Trace was not around Saundra's tongue dripped pure poison. She needled Katy constantly with malicious little remarks about her lack of sophistication and her modest family background, hinting that she was only kidding herself if she actually believed the marriage would take place. Saundra seemed confident that Trace would call the whole thing off before the wedding day arrived. Since that was only three weeks away, it seemed unlikely, but still, the malicious little innuendos were getting under Katy's skin.

Katy had not mentioned the matter to Trace. She had wanted to, several times, but whenever she worked up the courage to discuss the situation she was suddenly besieged with tormenting doubts and questions. What if they really were having an affair, as Saundra had implied on several occasions? What if he had no intention of cutting his stepmother out of his life after they were married? As far as she knew, during the three weeks since they had become engaged, he had done nothing toward persuading Saundra to move out of the house. And the woman certainly acted as though she were a permanent fixture.

It was a situation that could not be allowed to continue. Sometime between now and the wedding Katy knew she was going to have to talk to Trace and settle the matter, once and for all. She could not...she *would* not share either a husband or a house with Saundra Barnett!

When they pulled up in front of the big house Trace was waiting for them, nervously pacing the front veranda like a caged lion. Before Katy could locate the handle and open the door, he was beside the truck.

"What took you so long, darling?" he asked anxiously, as he helped her out. "I was beginning to get concerned."

Katy opened her mouth to answer but the words stuck in her throat when she saw the uncertainty in

Trace's eyes. He looked terribly worried. Frightened almost. For the first time she realized that he was very vulnerable where she was concerned, and the knowledge made her heart contract with a strangely pleasurable pain. Did he really love her? Until now she hadn't put much stock in his avowal, but his attitude seemed to confirm it. It was a heady thought, and for a moment she could only stare at him, her pulse throbbing wildly in her throat.

The lines of strain slowly eased from Trace's face as he drank in the sight of her. A small flame leaped in the hazel depths when his eyes met hers and clung.

"Well, my boy, I'm sorry we're so late," Tom said, breaking into the strange spell that locked them together. "But you know how it is when women get to primping. I hope none of the guests have arrived yet."

"No, not yet. But they should start arriving any time now." Holding both of Katy's hands, Trace stepped back and let his warm gaze roam over her from head to toe, then back again. "And I must say, your daughter is well worth waiting for."

A warm blush flooded Katy's cheeks when she met that intent, possessive stare. Blatant, male appreciation written in every line of his ruggedly handsome face, Trace repeated his inspection, slower this time.

Her chiffon dress was a pale powder blue at the top, where the simple draped bodice, supported by two thin straps, lovingly clung to her breasts and waist. From there the flared, floating skirt gradually deepened in color, reaching a dark midnight blue where it swirled like a delicate cloud around her ankles. It was an utterly simple, devastatingly feminine dress that gave her skin a pearly cast and brought out the color of her eyes.

It was part of the new wardrobe Trace had insisted upon buying for her. It seemed to Katy that she had bought more clothes in the past three weeks than she had in her entire adult life. With Jane's help, she had scoured all of the Tyler dress shops and a good many in Dallas as well. She had been hesitant about accepting his offer, but now, seeing the look in his eyes, Katy was glad she had. In any case, she knew that, as mistress of Green Meadows, she would need presentable clothes, and her father certainly couldn't afford to pay for such an elegant trousseau.

Smiling, Trace placed his hand lightly on the back of her waist and urged her toward the house. "Come inside. If we hurry, I'll just have time to give you your engagement present before our guests start arriving."

"Another present? Trace, you shouldn't have done that. You've given me so much already."

Her protests fell on deaf ears. Inside the house, Trace ushered her into his study and closed the door behind them. While she stood uncertainly in the middle of the floor he went to his desk, unlocked it and removed a square, flat box from the top drawer.

"I hope you like it," he said softly, as he placed it in her trembling hands. "When I saw it, I thought of you."

Katy lifted the lid and gasped. "Oh, Trace. It's beautiful."

In the velvet-lined box lay a necklace of brilliant sapphires and diamonds. In the finely wrought setting they resembled a chain of exquisite flowers, each vivid blue stone surrounded by a circle of diamonds and nestled in a bed of platinum leaves. The clusters were connected by an entwined strand that resembled a delicate, trailing vine.

"Here, let me put it on for you," he offered, as she continued to gape at the sparkling necklace.

Katy obediently turned around, and as the cool stones settled against her skin, she tilted her head forward and pulled the long fall of hair over her shoulder, exposing the nape of her neck. The feel of his warm fingers brushing against her flesh made Katy shiver.

Trace guided her to the wall mirror and stood behind her, his hands on her shoulders. His eyes met hers in the mirror. "Do you like it, Katy?"

"Oh, Trace. How could anyone not like it? It's the most beautiful thing I've ever seen."

"Does it deserve a kiss?"

She stared at his reflection, her heart pounding against her chest. During the past three weeks he had made no attempt to kiss her, other than brushing his lips across her forehead when he told her good night. He had touched her often, his hand cupping her elbow, or lightly pressing against the small of her back when they walked together, or sometimes just holding hers, but never in any way that frightened her or made her unduly nervous. But now he wanted to kiss her. Though she didn't find the idea totally repugnant, Katy wasn't sure she wanted their current, easy relationship to change.

Seeing the indecision in her eyes, Trace took it for refusal. "Forget it, Katy," he said with soft regret. "I didn't mean to press you."

Strangely, his quick retraction made up her mind for her, and, turning around, she placed her hand on his arm. "No, Trace, I—I didn't . . . I mean . . . if you want to kiss me, you may," she offered hesitantly.

"Are you sure?"

She wasn't. She wasn't sure at all. But it was too late to back out now. Swallowing her fear, she nodded.

Very gently, very cautiously, Trace slipped an arm around her waist and drew her close. His other hand came up under her chin and cupped her jaw, tilting her head up. An incredibly tender light glittered in the deep-set hazel eyes as they roamed over her face, touching on each delicate feature like a caress.

Trembling within that gentle, possessive embrace, Katy was acutely aware of the warmth of his body against hers, that clean, masculine scent she had come to associate with Trace alone, and the heavy throb of his heart beneath her hand. Her own heart was racing so fast she thought for a moment she was going to faint. But then, as his head began a slow, purposeful descent, Trace whispered, "I love you, Katy," and her eyes fluttered shut.

The kiss was soft, and infinitely gentle. His lips caressed hers with a tender passion that was rigidly controlled, tasting and exploring their trembling softness almost reverently. Katy was shaking, but she knew it was not altogether from fear. An almost unbearable excitement tingled through her like an electric current.

Trace made no effort to deepen the kiss and, after a moment, drew slowly away and smiled down into her face.

"Did you find that too unbearable?" he asked huskily.

"No." The surprise in her voice was plain, even to her own ears, and Trace's smile widened.

"Good. That's an encouraging sign."

Frowning, Katy opened her mouth to speak, but at that moment there was a sharp rap on the door, then it was thrust open and Saundra stepped inside.

Her expression grew hard when she spied the embracing couple. It grew even harder when her eyes lit on the necklace encircling Katy's throat. "For heaven's sake, Trace! This is hardly the time for kiss and cuddle," she snapped, and Katy felt her face crimson. "The first carload of guests has just driven up. I hope you don't expect me to entertain them alone."

The next half hour was spent greeting the steady stream of guests. Katy stood at Trace's side, a stiff, polite smile pasted on her face as she was introduced to one stranger after another. It wasn't long until the house was overflowing.

It seemed that all of Trace's relatives, no matter how distant, had come to take a look at the woman he had chosen. Katy squirmed under their intent scrutiny. Her stomach was fluttering with nerves. In addition to his family, he had also invited all his friends and business acquaintances. The only people Katy knew were Jane and Frank, and the other farm workers and their families.

Saundra had been livid over the inclusion of the workers, but Katy had very quietly and firmly insisted that they be invited, and in the end she had won. She and her father had no relatives in the United States. Except for the Cawleys, the other workers and their families were her only friends, and she was determined that they should attend the party. All Saundra's protests had fallen on deaf ears, and her appeal to Trace had met with equal failure. He had backed Katy to the hilt.

During the entire evening Trace remained close to Katy's side, his arm curved possessively around her waist, or draped over her shoulders as they circulated among the guests. Katy met so many new people that she was positive she would never keep the names straight and after a while even stopped trying. She was acutely aware of the many covert glances they received and could not help but wonder if they looked like a happily engaged couple. Trace certainly appeared happy, but Katy was very much afraid her own apprehension was plain for everyone to see.

The formal announcement of their engagement was made around ten o'clock. Katy suffered deep embarrassment at being the cynosure of every pair of eyes in the room, but at least when it was over she felt that the worst was behind her, and her nervous tension began to ease somewhat.

After the toasts were made and the good wishes were received, Trace maneuvered them through the crowd to join the Cawleys and Katy's father, standing a little to one side by the open French doors that led onto the patio.

"Katy, dearest, you look absolutely gorgeous tonight," Jane said, smiling up at her when they joined the group. "And I must say, you've handled this whole affair quite well. Before you know it, parties like this will be old hat to you."

"Not if I have anything to say about it," Trace interjected. "We'll entertain occasionally, a few close relatives and friends, but nothing on the scale of the parties that my father and Saundra gave. I prefer a more quiet life, and I think Katy does also." He waved his hand in an encompassing gesture. "This party tonight is a once-in-a-lifetime occasion."

Katy sent him a grateful smile. "I'm so glad to hear you say that. I don't think I could endure this sort of thing too often."

"Don't worry, sweetheart, you won't have to. I've no intention of getting caught up in a mad social whirl. That was part of my quarrel with my father, one of the reasons why I left the farm four years ago. Our priorities didn't mesh at all. His idea of what was important and mine were diametrically opposed."

Katy looked up at him, surprised. This was the first time he had mentioned the quarrel with his father. Though she didn't want to believe it, she couldn't help but wonder if his other reason for leaving had to do with Saundra.

"I echo my daughter's thanks, Trace," Tom said in a relieved tone. "She informed me tonight I'd have to attend whatever parties you two hosted, and I'll confess I wasn't looking forward to becoming a social butterfly at this late stage in life."

Trace laughed aloud at the look of outright distaste on the older man's face. "We'll make it as easy on you as we can, Tom."

Katy felt as though a load had been lifted from her shoulders. Smiling, she turned her head to speak to Jane and froze, the words dying on her lips as she caught sight of Saundra making her way toward them, her arms linked familiarly with the two men on either side of her. Shock widened Katy's eyes and drained every hint of color from her face. Her features working convulsively, she began to shake her head from side to side, a stark, mindless terror gripping her.

The violent tremors shaking her body were transmitted to Trace through his encircling arm, and he looked down at her quickly, alarm leaping into his eyes at her tormented expression.

"My God! What is it, Katy? What's wrong?" he demanded in a frantic voice.

But Katy was incapable of speech. Looking at her panic-stricken face, Trace realized she hadn't even heard him. Fear had her by the throat; she was oblivious to everything else. When she tried to back away Trace wouldn't let her, his arms tightening protectively around her as his eyes made an urgent, sweeping search of the room, seeking the cause of her distress.

It was then he noticed Tom's aggressive stance. His huge frame was taut and poised menacingly. His hands were bunched into tight fists at his sides. A low, vicious growl rumbled from the older man's chest. He was like a wild animal tensing for attack.

Trace tracked Tom's murderous gaze to the approaching trio, then swung back sharply, his eyes narrowing in dawning comprehension. His face grew hard, his body stiffening as he unconsciously drew Katy nearer.

"They're the ones, aren't they?" he asked in a dangerously soft voice.

Both Jane and Frank looked at him in wary confusion, sensing the deadly threat in his tone and wondering at the cause. Wisely, both remained silent.

"Yes." Tom spat the word out. His rage was almost a tangible thing.

"Trace, darling. Look who's here," Saundra called, her eyes sparkling with malicious glee.

Paralyzed with fear, Katy stared at the two men, bile rising in her throat as she met their nasty, knowing smiles. Never, *never* would she forget those faces. At the moment they wore the haughty, bored look common among the idle rich in Saundra's social circle, but Katy could still see the vicious anger that had twisted those aristocratic features three years ago, the terrible, ugly violence that had flared out of control. Tearing her eyes away, she tried to force back the ghastly, terrifying memories, but it was no use. She could feel their eyes on her, and her skin crawled.

There was no remorse in them, no apology, no guilt. They didn't even bother to hide their amusement, their vindictive, slightly lustful eyes sliding insultingly over her.

"This is Vince Wilby and Edgar Hollis. Two very dear, *very* close friends of Katy's," Saundra continued in an insinuating voice. Her smile grew wider when her attention switched to the ashen-faced girl in Trace's arms, her brows arching in feigned surprise. "Why, whatever is the matter, Katy? Don't tell me you're shy? Surely not! Not after the...ah...intimate relationship you shared with Vince and Edgar a few years ago?"

The poisonous innuendo tore an anguished cry from Katy's throat. Turning blindly, she buried her face against Trace's chest.

His hand came up to cradle the back of her head and press her closer as he strained to absorb the convulsive shudders that racked her slender frame. Burning anger radiated from him in white-hot waves.

"Did you invite these men here?" His eyes stabbed through Saundra with the deadly precision of cold steel.

Saundra could not ignore the barely leashed fury in his tone, or the protective way he held the frightened girl in his arms. Her carefully made-up face grew hard, her eyes glittering with hatred. All pretense of friendliness was dropped.

"Yes!" she flared defiantly. "Did you really think I'd just stand by calmly and watch you make a fool of yourself by marrying this...this *nobody?* She's nothing but a cheap tramp. Just ask Vince and Edgar. They can tell you..."

"Shut up, Saundra," Trace snarled.

"No! I won't shut up! Did you know that your precious fiancée is nothing but a tawdry little tease? That only a few years ago she deliberately lured poor Vince and Edgar here into the woods and—"

"That's enough!" Trace's hard-boned face was white with anger, his nostrils pinched, his mouth a hard line. A muscle twitching in his cheek warned of his tenuous control over the rage building within him. "I have never hit a woman in my life," he grated through clenched teeth. "But I swear to you, Saundra, you say one more word against Katy and I'll slap you silly."

Saundra blanched and stepped back. It was no bluff, and she knew it.

The two men at her side stirred restlessly, their eyes shifting with uncertainty between Saundra and Trace. The leering grins had disappeared.

Very slowly, with dangerous deliberation, Trace turned to Jane and handed Katy into her care. "Take her to the study and give her some brandy, will you? I'll be there just as soon as I've cleared out the vermin."

He turned his cold, implacable gaze on Saundra. "You've got exactly thirty minutes to pack your bags and get out. If you're not gone by then, I'll throw you out bodily, with a great deal of pleasure."

"You can't do this to me!" she protested angrily. "This is my home!"

"Correction. This is *my* home. And you're no longer welcome here."

Saundra sputtered and fumed for a moment, but Trace's hard, unblinking stare finally silenced her. With one last, furious glare in Katy's direction, she spun on her heel and stalked out.

Vince and Edgar turned to follow, but Trace stopped them. His voice was ominously soft, an unmistakable, steely threat running through the velvet tones.

"Oh, no. I think not. We have some unfinished business, I believe." He bared his teeth in a travesty of a smile as he met their startled glances. There was no doubt of his intent.

"Now see here," the man called Vince began to bluster. His eyes darted nervously to his companion for support. "If you think we're going to stand still for this . . ."

"I don't think. I know." Trace's voice cut across his protest like a well-honed axe. The finality in his tone was chilling.

Stepping to one side, he gestured toward the patio doors. "Shall we step outside. Unless, of course, you'd like me to wipe up the floor with you right here in front of the other guests."

The two men turned a sickly gray, perspiration beading their faces. Edgar Hollis swallowed hard and ran one finger around the inside of his collar. "Come now, Mr. Barnett, can't we talk this over? There's no need for violence."

"Oh, there's a need, all right," Trace assured him, softly, dangerously. "I feel a fierce need."

Shrugging out of his jacket, he handed it to Frank, his eyes never leaving the two cowering men. With slow, deliberate movements, he began to roll up his shirt sleeves. "Now, you two can either walk out that door in the next five seconds, or I'll haul you both out by the scruff of the neck. The choice is yours."

"Do you need any help?" Frank asked as the two men moved reluctantly toward the door. Having heard the story from his wife, Frank had worked out the reason for Trace and Tom's anger, and his own slow-rising temper had flared hotly.

"Thanks, but no. This privilege belongs solely to Tom and me." Trace smiled and looked at his future father-in-law, his eyes glowing with anticipation. "I think we can handle this. Don't you, Tom?"

Tom brightened instantly. He rubbed his hands together, a slow, eager smile splitting his face. "You know it, lad. You know it."

Katy could barely recall being led through the crowd of interested spectators, or drinking the glass of brandy Frank had pressed into her hand. Reaction had set in. She lay curled in a tight ball on the leather sofa in Trace's study, her fist jammed against her mouth. Her eyes were strangely blank and her skin looked like alabaster. She made no sound. No move.

Jane sat beside her on the couch and stroked the silky black hair away from Katy's temple. Her eyes were clouded with worry. Now and then her gaze sought her husband, as he paced restlessly up and down the room, but neither said a word.

Finally, after what seemed like an eternity, the door was thrust open and Trace entered. His eyes went immediately to the huddled figure on the couch. In three long strides he crossed the room and knelt beside her. There was a slight tremor in the hand that gently cupped her face.

"Are you all right, darling?" he asked with soft urgency. His gaze roamed restlessly over her face, worry and concern tightening his rugged features.

His words seemed to break through the trance that held her. Katy turned her head slowly and gave him an anguished look. Her chin quivering, she closed her eyes against the threatening tears and nodded.

In the next instant Trace stood up and gathered her into his arms, then sank back onto the couch and settled her on his lap, hugging her close. Neither noticed when Jane and Frank slipped discreetly out the door and closed it behind them.

Trace rocked Katy back and forth, his hands roaming soothingly over her body as he pressed soft kisses over her face. Katy, feeling truly safe at last, burrowed deeper into the security of his warm embrace.

"Oh, Katy," Trace breathed raggedly against her temple. "I'm so sorry, sweetheart. If I had only known what she was up to, I would have put a stop to it. But I can promise you, nothing like that will *ever* happen again. Saundra is gone from our lives for good, and after tonight her two friends won't dare show their faces around here again."

Something in his tone sent a shaft of fear through her, and Katy grew still. Slowly, she pulled back and searched his face with wide, apprehensive eyes. For the first time, she noticed his hair was disarrayed, and there was a tiny cut at the corner of his mouth. When he lifted his hand to stroke the side of her face she saw that his knuckles were scraped and bleeding, and her stomach clenched sickeningly.

"What did you do to them, Trace?" she whispered.

He grinned. "Your father and I gave them just a small portion of the punishment they deserved," he said with hard satisfaction.

"My father? You let my *father* fight them? Trace! How *could* you? He's an old man. He could have been seriously hurt!"

Trace laughed heartily. "Katy, love, Tom may be sixty-three, but he's as strong as a bull." His eyes twinkled at her. "I'm just glad he was on my side."

Katy stared at him, appalled. There was an aura of suppressed excitement about him, a triumphant joy at having beaten two men senseless, and she found it terrifying. Were all men the same? Did they all find violence exciting? The thought sent a cold trickle down her spine.

"You enjoyed it, didn't you?" she burst out agitatedly, unable to hide the bitter accusation in her voice. "You enjoyed it, and that makes you no better than those two men."

"Katy!" Trace looked as though she had slapped him. He stared at her with disbelieving eyes. "Katy, you're not frightened of me, are you?" he asked finally, and groaned when she nodded. He closed his eyes for a second, a look of intense pain flickering across his face. "Oh, Katy," he whispered sadly. "Don't you know I'd never hurt you? *Never!* You have to believe that, darling. You have to."

Katy's heart thumped with a slow, heavy beat. She looked at him uncertainly. Did she dare trust him? She had always been frightened by his raw masculinity, his overwhelming virility, but this new threat was even worse. What if he became angry or frustrated when their marriage remained platonic, as she fully intended it would? Would he turn violent? Did she dare risk that? The wedding was only three weeks away. If she was going to back out, she had to do it soon. Yet, how could she?

As though reading her mind, Trace pulled her close. "Don't walk away from me, Katy," he whispered urgently, burying his face in the cloud of hair at her neck. "Give me a chance to make you happy. To make us both happy. Trust me, darling. Please."

Katy remained rigid in his arms for a few seconds. Then, slowly, she relaxed against him, and rested her head on his shoulder.

Chapter Eight

Katy looked beyond the airplane's wing to the faint, rosy glow on the horizon, where the ocean met the sky. They had been chasing the sun for hours, but it had steadily outdistanced them, and the fiery ball had sunk majestically into the blue Pacific only moments before. Pulling her eyes away from the gathering dusk of early evening, Katy sighed.

As though drawn by a magnet, her gaze lowered to the rings on her left hand. She touched a finger to them gently, almost fearfully. Well, she had done it. That morning, on her father's arm, wearing her mother's creamy white wedding dress and her grandmother's veil, she had walked down the church aisle and joined her life, irrevocably, to Trace's. She was committed now. There could be no turning back.

Of the ceremony she remembered very little. The sea of faces watching her had not registered, nor had the profusion of flowers in the church, nor the stirring chords of the wedding march that had thundered from the organ. The only thing she had been aware of was the tall, incredibly handsome man waiting for her at the end of the aisle, watching her approach with an intensity that made her already shaking knees go weak as water. If it hadn't been for her father's support, she would have crumpled to the floor in a little heap of satin and lace and quivering flesh. From the moment she stepped into the church, Trace's eyes had seemed to pierce right through the misty cloud of tulle that billowed around her head and shoulders, his expression so warm and tender, so blatantly, proudly possessive that her heart had leaped up into her throat and stuck there.

Katy supposed she must have spoken her wedding vows, though she couldn't recall doing so. When Trace had taken her icy, trembling hand in his, her mind had gone blank. It wasn't until he lifted the veil over her head and kissed her softly on the lips that she had come out of her daze.

The reception afterwards had been an ordeal, and she had been profoundly grateful when Trace had suggested that they leave.

Katy sighed and returned her gaze to the window. Now, here they were on their way to Hawaii to begin a honeymoon that wasn't to be a honeymoon at all. She hoped.

There was a soft ping, then the stewardess's voice was informing them that they were beginning their descent into the Honolulu airport and asking everyone to please buckle their seatbelts. Immediately Katy stiffened.

She had never flown before. Earlier, during the short flight from Tyler to Dallas, she had been pale and shaken. But when the jumbo jet had roared down the

Dallas runway and strained into the sky, she had been petrified.

Katy felt the plane slip downward and closed her eyes tightly, then jumped as Trace's warm hand covered hers.

"Relax, darling," he whispered. Smiling, he gently pried her white-knuckled fingers from the armrest. Still holding her hand, he slipped his other arm around her and pulled her close. "Just shut your eyes and lean on me. We'll be down before you know it."

Katy complied gratefully, feeling ridiculously secure with his arm wrapped around her, her face pressed against the fine material of his dark, three-piece suit.

After receiving the traditional Hawaiian greeting, Trace guided them through the hustle and bustle of the airport with a minimum of fuss. Within minutes, Katy was sitting in a taxi, fingering the lei of white ginger blossoms that encircled her neck.

The hotel Trace had chosen for them was one of the most plush on Waikiki Beach. When they entered the lobby, Katy was pleased to see that it was moderately full. Somehow she felt safer with other people around. Which was why, when Trace left the choice up to her, she had elected to come to Hawaii for their honeymoon. It was beautiful and exciting, but more importantly, it was packed with people. She didn't want to be alone in some isolated, romantic spot with Trace.

Katy stood nervously by and watched as he signed the register, a satisfied smile curving his mouth as he wrote "Mr. and Mrs. Trace Barnett" in a clear, bold hand. By the time they entered their ninth floor suite her stomach felt as though it contained a thousand butterflies.

The suite was elegant and beautiful, but Katy was too keyed up to notice. She was acutely aware that this night would prove whether her father's trust in Trace was justified, and with every second that ticked by, her doubts grew, stretching her nerves to breaking point.

What if he had been wrong? What if...?

When Trace and the bellboy disappeared into the adjoining room, Katy stumbled to the balcony doors and tugged them open. Her breath was coming in short gasps as she crossed to the waist-high railing and clutched it desperately. A soft breeze gently lifted the heavy tumble of hair off her shoulders. The moon painted the midnight-blue ocean with streaks of silver, illuminating the frothy, lace-edged waves as they slid onto the sand far below.

Katy stared blindly at the romantic scene. God! She'd been a fool to enter into this crazy arrangement! What did she really know about Trace, other than that he wanted her and seemed willing to go to any lengths to get her? Even her father didn't really know him. After all, Trace had been gone for four years, and people could change a lot in that time. No! No, she wouldn't think that way. She couldn't! She'd go mad if she did.

Taking long, deep breaths, Katy forced herself to remember how tender Trace had been with her, how considerate, how concerned. Yet on the heels of that thought she recalled how violent he could be when angered, his fury a cold, frightening menace. So far he had only shown her his gentle side, but she knew there was another. She had glimpsed it the night of their engagement party.

"So this is where you disappeared to. You had me worried there for a minute."

Katy flinched at the sound of Trace's voice, just behind her, then flinched again when his hands closed warmly around the curves of her shoulders. She held her breath and fought to control her trembling body. Her knuckles were white as she gripped the railing. The slow movement of his hand, though meant to be soothing, did little to help.

"There's nothing to be frightened of, Katy," he murmured softly as he felt her reaction. "You must believe that."

Unable to speak, Katy swallowed hard and nodded. She felt brittle, ready to shatter.

There was a moment of tense silence, then Trace continued in a deliberately lighter tone. "You hardly touched your meal on the plane. Would you like to go downstairs for dinner?"

"No, thank you. I'm really not hungry."

"Well, in that case, why don't you go in and get ready for bed. I know it's fairly early here, but our bodies are still on Texas time. I suggest that we get a good night's rest, so we'll be in shape to start our tour of the islands in the morning."

Katy turned slowly to search his face, and met only tenderness and understanding in the hazel eyes. Her heartbeat began to slow to normal. "I—I think I will," she stammered weakly. "I'm very tired. It's been a long day."

Smiling, Trace put his arm around her shoulders and led her inside, releasing her as they reached the bedroom. Katy gave him a wan smile and stepped through the door, only to come to a skidding halt just inside, color draining from her face at the sight of the huge, king-sized bed that dominated the room.

There was a loud roaring in her ears as the blood began to pound through her veins. Dizzy with fear and rage, she whirled around to find Trace's large frame filling the doorway. He was very still, watching her intently.

"You lied to me!" she screamed, backing away. "You've been lying from the very beginning."

"I didn't lie. You've known all along that I meant for us to share a bedroom."

"A bedroom, yes! But not the same bed!"

"Yes, Katy, the same bed. Both here and at home."

Panic clawed at her. She took another step backward, her head moving slowly from side to side, her face distraught. Her heart was beating so hard she was almost suffocating. "No! No, I won't do it! I won't let you do this to me! You promised you wouldn't..."

"Stop it!" Trace covered the distance between them and grasped her by the shoulders, shaking her gently. "Stop it, right now. You're becoming hysterical. I have no intention of breaking my word to you. I'm not going to make love to you, Katy, until you ask me to. But I *am* going to hold my wife in my arms when I go to bed at night." He pulled her close and wrapped her in an unyielding embrace, holding her terrified eyes with an intent, unwavering look. "Oh, darling. Don't you see? If our marriage is ever to have a chance we've got to get you accustomed to being close to me, to touching and being touched. It's normal and natural." He stopped and gave her a teasing smile, lifting one hand to trail his knuckles down the line of her jaw. "And once you get used to it, I think you'll find it quite enjoyable."

Katy swallowed hard. Her heart was still banging away at her ribcage. "Th-that's all? You won't..."

"No. I'd never take advantage of you," he assured her quickly. He stared at her, willing her to believe him. The sincerity in his expression was unmistakable. "I don't just want your body, my darling. I'm greedy. I want your love, and I want you to give it to me freely."

He released her and turned her toward the adjoining bath. "Now, get ready for bed, woman. We have a busy day ahead tomorrow."

Katy stumbled into the bathroom on rubbery legs. She showered, slipped into her nightgown, brushed her teeth and hair and creamed her face, all in a frozen daze. The thought of spending the night in Trace's arms made her feel faint. How could she possibly do it? Yet, what choice did she have? She had accepted his terms six weeks ago, and so far he had lived up to his side of the bargain scrupulously. She could hardly do less.

Katy slid the white silk and ecru lace negligee over her matching gown and tied the bow just under her breasts. Then, her throat dry, she reached for the doorknob.

Only a dim pool of light from the bedside lamp lit the room, but it was enough for her to see that Trace was already in bed. His muscular chest was bare, and in the soft light, the curling mat of hair that covered it gleamed like burnished gold. Against the white sheets his skin was a deep bronze, his shoulders unbelievably broad. Katy's heart took off like a jackhammer. She stood rooted to the spot.

A slow smile curved Trace's mouth as he turned back the covers and held out his hand invitingly. "Come to bed, my darling," he whispered.

As though pulled by an invisible string, Katy walked slowly toward him, unable to look away from that intent, hazel stare. Trembling violently and flushing a deep crimson at the appreciative gleam in his eyes, she took off the thin negligee and dropped it across the end of the bed, then slid in beside him. At once Trace's arms closed around her.

Her body stiffened as she felt herself drawn against his hard length, but when she tried to strain away his arms tightened.

"No, don't tense up like that, sweetheart. Just relax and put your head on my shoulder." The encircling arm held her close, his hand cupping her hipbone and rubbing it rhythmically, while the other gently, but firmly, curved around the side of her head and pushed it down until she felt the warmth of his skin beneath her cheek.

Katy could scarcely breathe. The incredible intimacy had every nerve in her body wound to violin-string tautness. The warmth of his flesh seared her from forehead to toes. The musky, masculine scent of him was all around her, invading her body with every shallow breath she drew, making her giddy. She felt warm and protected, and cold and afraid, all at the same time.

The lamp clicked off and the room was flooded with darkness. Trace's breath stirred the hair at her temple as he placed a soft kiss on her forehead. "Good night, darling. Sleep well," he murmured.

She almost giggled hysterically. Sleep well? *Sleep well?* How on *earth* could she sleep when she felt as though she were about to explode into a million little pieces?

Long after the caressing hand at her hip had ceased its motion, Katy lay rigid at Trace's side, staring into the darkness, listening to the slow, strong thud of his heart beneath her ear, feeling the steady rise and fall of his massive chest. How could he sleep? She certainly couldn't. But then, Trace was probably used to sleeping with a woman in his arms. The thought was painful, and Katy's mind immediately shied away from it.

For what seemed like hours, she lay perfectly still, not daring to even blink. But finally, little by little, her taut muscles began to go slack, and her lashes fluttered downward, brushing against the bronzed shoulder that cradled her head. The small, tight fist which lay across the masculine chest slowly uncurled. Smiling, Trace covered the delicate hand with his own larger one, and pressed it tightly to him.

When she opened her eyes, the room was filled with sunshine, and Trace, propped up on one elbow, was smiling down at her.

"Good morning, wife," he greeted cheerfully, then laughed aloud as a tide of deep color rose from her neck all the way to her hairline.

Flustered by his nearness, and acutely aware of her vulnerable position, Katy's eyes darted around in a frantic effort to avoid the muscular chest, just inches from her nose. It was an impossible task. Finally she gave up and focused intently on the hollow at the base of his throat.

"Good—good morning."

Her stammered reply brought another chuckle from Trace. Then he reached out a hand and brushed the tousled strands of hair away from her face. "Do you know you're even more beautiful when you're asleep? You look so soft and cuddly with your face scrubbed and clean, and all that glorious hair spread out on the pillow." The words seemed to be drawn out of him slowly, a low husky passion roughening his voice.

Katy lay mesmerized, unable to look away from that hard, sensuous mouth as it drew inexorably nearer. Warm breath feathered against her skin as he added softly, "I don't know how I managed to wait this long for my good morning kiss."

Then his mouth found its target. The kiss was exquisite, his lips moving over hers with great tenderness, coaxing, imploring, enticing. The tip of his tongue traced back and forth between her slightly parted lips, only just penetrating into the sweet moistness within, yet the tiny invasion was excruciatingly sensual and explosive. Its shock waves rocked Katy to her toes. Her soft mouth quivered beneath his as fear and intense pleasure battled for control.

Meeting no resistance, Trace leaned closer. His bare chest brushed the tips of her breasts through their thin covering as one hand closed possessively around the inverted curve of her waist. For an instant Katy's trembling fingers hovered just a scant inch from his chest. Then, drawn by a power beyond her control, they settled against the hard, muscled flesh and threaded hesitantly through the crisp hair that covered it.

Trace's instant response was a shuddering moan. The hand at her waist stirred as the pressure of his mouth increased.

Katy felt like a tightly wound spring, her body taut and quivering with conflicting emotions. She was terrified; she was thrilled. She wanted the kiss to end; she wanted it to go on forever. She wanted to wrench herself out of his arms and scream at him to leave her alone; she wanted to burrow closer, to melt into him, to become a part of him, to never let him go. It was hell; it was heaven.

Through the haze of fright and pleasure, Katy became aware of Trace's hand, moving slowly, caressingly up the side of her ribcage, then halting just under her arm, the heel of his palm against the side of her breast. Pressing ever so slightly inward, his hand began to move in tiny circles, massaging the soft flesh with a sensuous rhythm.

A choked gasp was wrenched from Katy's throat as she felt her breast swell against his palm. She stiffened, and instantly Trace withdrew.

The hand was removed as he raised his head and smiled down at her. "You see. That's all it takes, my love. I'll never push you farther than you want to go."

He lowered his head and brushed a feathery kiss across her mouth, then astonished her by throwing back the covers and springing out of bed. As he walked away toward the bathroom Katy's dazed eyes roamed over the rangy frame, noting distractedly that the thin pajama bottom hanging low from his hips did little to conceal his blatant masculinity.

When the door closed behind him, Katy stared at it in perplexity. How could he just turn his emotions off at will like that? She certainly couldn't. Every inch of her body still tingled from his touch. Of course, she was grateful that he had ended the embrace before things got out of hand, she told herself quickly. It was very reassuring to know that Trace truly did intend to keep his word.

Her eyes widened as she realized that was exactly what Trace had intended. His demand that she share his bed and this morning's warm, provocative lovemaking were his method of proving to her, right at the onset, that he could, and would, keep his word.

In the bathroom the shower started, and over the rushing noise she could hear Trace singing slightly off-key. Katy slid back down under the cover, smiling to herself as the tension began to slowly seep out of her. For the first time since she had accepted Trace's proposal, she actually began to feel optimistic about their future together.

After breakfast, which, to Katy's delight, was eaten on the balcony, Trace left the choice of activities up to her. Katy elected to spend their first morning on the beach. She had never even seen an ocean before and was as excited as a child when they stepped onto the white sand of Waikiki Beach. She even forgot to be self-conscious about appearing before Trace in a bathing suit, until, slipping out of the thigh-length beach robe, she looked up to find his eyes running over her hungrily, as though he would like to devour her on the spot.

She was wearing a form-hugging maillot in a shimmering, vivid blue that exactly matched her eyes. When she had tried it on at the store it had seemed perfectly modest, but now, as she watched Trace's eyes widen and flicker with some strong emotion, Katy was very conscious of the way the clinging material molded her high breasts and boldly defined the curving line of waist and hip.

In her heightened state of awareness Katy could actually feel the touch of that hazel-green gaze as it traveled the length of her body, from the thick ebony plait that lay over one shoulder, all the way down to the pink toes curling into the sand. When he raised his eyes to hers, Katy's heart jerked to a halt, then took off with a crazy, erratic beat. The look on his face was one of such desperate longing, such intense, burning desire that she felt her mouth go suddenly dry.

"My God, you're beautiful," he groaned huskily. "Even more beautiful than I imagined."

Katy stood frozen, oblivious to the other people on the crowded beach, her gaze caught and held by the liquid green fire in his. Her lips parted, and the tip of her tongue slid over them in unconscious provocation.

Trace drew a sharp breath, took a jerky step forward, then brought himself up abruptly. Shaking his head, he heaved a sigh. His mouth twisted in a rueful smile. "Come on," he murmured hoarsely, reaching for her hand. "Let's go for a swim before I do something I'm sure I'll regret later."

In the next instant he was racing toward the surf, dragging Katy along behind him. They hit the water at a dead run, and she squealed with shock at the coolness of it against her heated skin, but within seconds Katy felt as though she were surrounded by soft, warm silk.

Trace released her hand and they both dived into an oncoming wave. She made no attempt to keep up with him as his powerful body cleaved through the water ahead of her. Turning parallel to the beach, she swam at a leisurely pace, feeling marvelously free and relaxed. She kept at it as long as she could, but finally tired muscles forced her to stop for a rest. As she trod water Katy's eyes idly searched for Trace. When she failed to locate him she merely shrugged and flipped over onto her back.

A short while later, floating along with her eyes closed, completely lost to the world around her, Katy was brought suddenly and rudely awake when something closed around her ankle and tugged her downward. There was barely time for a short, terrified scream before the blue-green water closed over her head.

As she kicked out in blind panic her leg was released and a hard, sinewy body slid up hers. A pair of strong arms wrapped themselves around her waist, and with a powerful kick, Trace sent them both shooting upward toward the spangled sunlight.

Sputtering and gasping, they broke the surface. It took Katy several seconds to realize what had happened, but when she did her eyes shot sparks.

"Why you—you beast! You scared me half to death!" she ranted. She hit the water with the flat of her hand and sent a stinging spray into his grinning face. Trace quickly retaliated in kind, and the battle was on. With an indignant cry, Katy lunged forward and upward, coming down on his shoulders with all her weight, dunking him soundly.

For the next hour they played like two boisterous children. With mock anger, they tormented and teased one another unmercifully. It was an exhilarating new experience for Katy. Never before had she shared that kind of lighthearted fun with anyone, most especially not with a man.

Only once during their play did even a hint of sexuality break through, and that was so brief, so nonthreatening that Katy had no time to object.

Popping up suddenly in front of her, Trace had pulled her against him and planted a swift, hard kiss on her mouth. Drawing back only slightly, he traced the tip of his tongue around the outline of her parted lips.

"Mmmm, delicious," he murmured thoughtfully. "A trifle salty, but delicious all the same." He held her close for just an instant, running his hands over the wet silkiness of her body with shocking expertise. Then, with a grin, he released her and streaked away.

Bemused, Katy stared after him. She tried to work up a bit of anger, but it simply would not come. Trace in this teasing, carefree mood was impossible to resist. Slowly, a small, wicked smile curved her mouth. With a decidedly determined gleam in her eye, Katy took a deep breath and set out after him.

Finally, exhausted, they stumbled from the water and collapsed onto the woven mats Trace had placed side by side on the sand earlier.

Katy's chest was heaving from her exertions as she patted herself dry. "I can't remember ever having so much fun," she said breathlessly. Her eyes sparkling, she tossed Trace a happy smile.

He stopped his own drying to give her a long, intent look. His expression was suddenly very serious. "That was only a taste of what it's going to be like for us, sweetheart," he said in a soft, sure voice. "I'm not saying our life together with be all fun and games, but it's going to be good, babe. I promise you that. Because, whether you know it or not, we belong together, Katy."

Katy felt a fluttering, uneasy sensation begin in the pit of her stomach. Trace's quick change of mood brought her down off the euphoric cloud with a bang. To cover her confusion, she picked up the bottle of suntan lotion and began to rub the creamy liquid methodically onto her arms and legs, letting the silence lengthen. She had no idea how to reply to his statement, so she simply said nothing.

She had finished anointing the front of her body and was about to recap the bottle when Trace took it from her.

"Roll over and I'll do your back," he instructed.

"Oh, no, I'll—"

"Don't be silly, Katy. You have very delicate skin, and I don't want to see it burned. And you needn't be afraid to let me touch you. I'm your husband. Remember?"

Reluctantly, Katy did as she was told. She felt the cool squiggle of lotion trail down her spine, then Trace's hands were moving, slowly, hypnotically over her skin. The maillot was practically backless, cut well below her waist. Trace made sure every inch of exposed flesh was covered. Katy's breathing was shallow, almost painful, as she felt the caressing touch of those calloused hands work the lotion over her shoulders and spine.

Suddenly Trace sat back on his heels and gave her a slap on the bottom. "Okay, now it's your turn."

When Katy looked up, startled, he stretched out on his stomach and handed her the bottle. "Be sure to put a lot across the top of my shoulders, will you," he instructed blithely. Ignoring her shocked expression, he rested his head on his crossed arms and closed his eyes.

Suspicion sparkled in her narrowed gaze as it ran over his bronzed form. Surely skin that deeply tanned didn't need any protection? Tight-lipped, Katy squeezed a generous mound of the white lotion into her palm and slapped it between his shoulder blades.

She had meant to keep her movements brisk and impersonal but as her hands made contact with his flesh, she faltered. The feel of hard muscle and bone beneath warm skin was strangely pleasurable, and Katy's hands, as though with a life of their own, began to move in a slow, massaging rhythm across the broad-shouldered back, her slender fingers kneading and flexing as they smoothed on the slippery lotion.

She became mesmerized by the task. She was only dimly aware of the other supine bodies stretched out on the sand, the steady rush and retreat of the rolling waves against the shore, the dry rattle of tattered palms. Entranced, she watched the hypnotic movements of her pale fingers against the tanned skin. A few loose tendrils of hair around her face lifted in the soft breeze. The sun was warm against her bare back. She breathed in slowly, deeply, her senses swimming. All around her were the smells of sand and sea, of warm masculine flesh and coconut-scented tanning lotion.

How long she continued the sensuous massage Katy had no idea, but suddenly she realized that Trace had fallen asleep. Oddly piqued, she jerked her hands away. She recapped the bottle and stowed it in her beach bag, then stretched out beside him on her back. Her heart was thumping.

Through slitted eyes Katy watched the puffy clouds floating overhead. Honesty forced her to admit that she had enjoyed touching Trace. She hadn't expected to, but she had. What was it about Trace that made him so different from other men? Why did one man's touch evoke revulsion and fear, while another's offered pleasure and security? Was it merely a matter of technique—violent demand versus gentle enticement? Katy mulled the thought over for a moment, but finally came to the conclusion that there was more to it than that. There was something about Trace she found irresistible, something that beckoned to her, despite her attempts to ignore it.

Turning her head, she studied his strong masculine face. Her searching gaze traced over the network of tiny lines that rayed out from the corners of his eyes, the stubby lashes that looked almost white against his bronze skin, the hard, sensual mouth that had softened appealingly in sleep. It was a surprising, disturbing thing to face, but there was no escaping it; she was strongly attracted to her husband, mentally, emotionally, and physically.

* * *

That night when she slid into bed beside Trace, Katy felt only the vaguest flutter of fear in the pit of her stomach. Surprised, she told herself she was simply too exhausted to be afraid.

They had spent the entire afternoon sightseeing, beginning with a walking tour of Chinatown and the Cultural Plaza. Amazed and delighted by the wide variety of wares, Katy had gone from shop to shop, looking at rare pottery, turquoise, jade, silks, and herbs. In one of the food shops she had stared in wide-eyed amazement when shown one of the greatest of Chinese delicacies— an egg which was a century old and which looked and smelled every single year of it.

After Chinatown came a quick visit to the Falls of Clyde, the world's only surviving one-hundred-year-old, full-rigged, four-masted sailing ship. From there they toured the State Capitol building and the Iolani Palace, where the last two Hawaiian monarchs had lived.

That evening they had enjoyed dinner and a spectacular Polynesian show in the hotel dining room.

Now, feeling pleasantly tired and sleepy, Katy couldn't summon up the strength to resist when Trace gathered her into his arms and pulled her close.

With her head resting on his arm he placed the other hand under her chin and tilted her face up. "Tired?" he questioned, chuckling softly as he met her drowsy look.

"Mmmmmm."

"Happy?"

Surprise widened her eyes. She frowned as she considered the question for a moment, then a slow smile curved her mouth. "Yes," she admitted, with a discernible trace of astonishment in her voice.

Trace dropped a soft kiss on her mouth, then pulled back and smiled. Tenderly, his fingers stroked the silky black strands at her temple. "Good. I want you to be happy."

All the love he felt was clearly visible in his eyes, in his strong-boned, handsome face, and Katy reacted to it instinctively. Feeling warm and cherished cuddled against Trace's hard strength, her body weak with a delicious languor, she had no defense against the powerful attraction that drew her to him. Without thinking, she lifted her hand and stroked his cheek, smiling sleepily.

Trace drew in a sharp breath, then his head swooped. He kissed her long and hungrily, with a tender passion that made her heart swell in her chest until it nearly suffocated her. By gradual degrees the kiss grew stronger, deeper, more demanding. He parted her lips with ease and slid his tongue into the sweet moistness of her mouth, rubbing it against hers in a rough, sensuous caress.

Katy felt feverish, her body trembling from the strange erotic sensations pulsing through her. The soft, exquisitely sensual kiss seemed to penetrate to her very soul. A small nagging voice in the back of her brain told her to push him away, but she didn't have the strength or the will.

Trace abandoned her mouth to bury his face in the curve of her neck, nibbling at the sensitive skin. Katy's senses were alive with pleasure as she docilely gave herself up to the passionate embrace.

The large hand at her waist began to move slowly upward, but this time, instead of resting against the side of her breast, it cupped the warm soft mound possessively.

When Katy stiffened, the hand stilled instantly, but did not release its prize. For long moments the only sound in the room was the harsh rasp of their disturbed breathing. At last, when she made no further protest, Trace began to caress her, tentatively at first, then growing gradually bolder. Katy closed her eyes and held her breath as her nipple puckered into a hard bud of desire. A soft moan escaped her tight throat.

Encouraged by her passive acceptance, Trace reclaimed her lips with a scorching demand, his tongue probing relentlessly into the intimate recesses of her mouth, while his hand slid downward. Katy's stomach muscles clenched as his flattened hand spread out over her quivering abdomen, edging steadily downward, moving in slow circles.

When the caress threatened to become unbearably intimate, Katy wrenched free of the drugging kiss and grabbed his wrist. "No, Trace. Don't," she cried in panic.

Rolling over onto his back, Trace pulled her close and gently stroked her arm and the side of her face. His breathing was ragged and the heavy thunder of his heart roared in her ear. "Don't worry, sweetheart. Everything is fine," he assured her in a soft, crooning voice.

Katy shivered against him as Trace repeated the soothing caress over and over, with infinite care and patience. When at last her breathing returned to normal and she relaxed against him, he placed a warm kiss on her forehead. "Good night, darling."

Long after sleep had claimed Trace, Katy lay staring into the darkness. Two days ago, if anyone had told her that she would allow Trace the liberties he had taken tonight she would have told him he was crazy. Yet, she had not only allowed them—she had enjoyed them.

And that scared her more than anything. That her own body could betray her came as a definite shock. She had been so *sure* of her invincibility.

Sighing, Katy snuggled her head more firmly against Trace's shoulder and determinedly closed her eyes. She was simply too exhausted to worry about it now.

Chapter Nine

To Katy's amazement, the honeymoon she had dreaded turned into the most thoroughly enjoyable two weeks she had ever known. Each day in the Pacific paradise brought a wonderful new experience, and somehow, Trace's stimulating, yet undemanding companionship seemed to increase her pleasure.

When they weren't sailing or snorkeling or just lazing on the beach, they went shopping or sightseeing. One morning they took the tour boat out to the Arizona Memorial in Pearl Harbor, and from there visited the Punchbowl, the huge crater known as the Cemetery of the Pacific. Both came away from the sobering sights deeply affected. To shake off the somber mood, Trace took Katy to a charming, open-air restaurant on the beach, where they ate lunch amid the throbbing pagan beat of Polynesian music. Afterward they spent a leisurely afternoon wandering through the Bishop Museum.

Though at first put off by the rather forbidding appearance of the Victorian stone building's armory-like exterior, Katy was soon delighted as she viewed the amazing collection of treasures housed inside, especially the huge whale hanging from the ceiling in Hawaiian Hall.

There were artifacts of tortoiseshell, whalebone, and beautifully carved wood in striking contrast to the ornate thrones of the Hawaiian monarchy. But most impressive of all to Katy were the priceless red and yellow feather cloaks and capes worn by Hawaiian chiefs.

"Oh, Trace. Aren't they gorgeous," she breathed ecstatically, when they stopped in front of the first display. "Just look at those colors. They haven't faded a bit, even after all these years."

"Very impressive," Trace agreed. "But then, they ought to be. Those things were handmade from feathers of exotic birds which are now extinct. And since each bird produced only one feather that was considered brilliant enough for a chief's garment, it took years just to complete one robe."

"How do you know that?"

"Oh, I read it somewhere," he said with an air of offhanded superiority. Then his eyes twinkled. "I think it was in one of those brochures the hotel provides."

"Oh, you!" Katy gave him a sharp poke in the ribs. "And there I was, all set to be impressed with your vast store of knowledge."

Laughing, Trace flung his arm around her shoulders and led her toward the next display.

The casual embrace was something he did often. No matter where they were or what they were doing, he always managed to touch her in some way. If his arm wasn't draped across her shoulders or hooked around

her waist, his hand was tunneled under the heavy fall of
ebony hair and curved around her nape, his fingers absently massaging the tight muscles.

At first the constant contact made Katy nervous, but
after a few days she became resigned to it. By the end of
the first week, the feel of his arm around her seemed the
most natural thing in the world.

They spent several days driving around the island,
exploring remote beaches, visiting extinct volcanoes,
orchid nurseries, and pineapple and sugar plantations.
On one of their trips they stopped to picnic at Makaha,
better known as Surfer's Paradise, and watched in awe
as muscled young men on surfboards rode the forty-
foot waves in to shore.

Every evening they ate at a different restaurant in order to sample the wide variety of ethnic cuisine the islands offered. After dinner they either enjoyed
Honolulu's fantastic nightlife or went for long walks on
the beach. Rarely did they return to their suite before
midnight. But no matter how late the hour, each night
when they relaxed in the king-sized bed, Trace gathered Katy into his arms and made gentle, persuasive
love to her.

Knowing that she had only to give the slightest sign
of resistance and Trace would stop, Katy did not panic
when his caresses gradually became more and more intimate. By the end of their stay, though she still had no
intention of allowing him to consummate the marriage, Katy could no longer deny that she enjoyed
Trace's lovemaking.

On the morning of their departure, while Trace had
gone down to the lobby to settle their bill, Katy gathered up their last minute articles and added them to the
cases she had packed the night before. She took one last

look around the suite for anything she may have missed, then closed the cases and snapped the locks shut.

Restless, with nothing more to keep her occupied, she slid open the glass door and stepped out onto the balcony. Her eyes were sad as she leaned against the railing and gazed down at the beach. At this early hour there were only a few heads bobbing in the blue water.

Katy sighed. How she hated to leave. Their stay had been ideal—a period out of time when the problems facing them seemed far removed. As she thought back over the last two weeks, a small, self-derisive smile tugged at her mouth. Well, it had been ideal from her point of view at any rate. She doubted that Trace would describe their rather unorthodox honeymoon in quite the same way.

But in any case, it was over now and reality was about to intrude. Katy had the uneasy feeling that it was going to be much more difficult to keep her husband at arm's length once they returned to the farm.

The soft swish of the sliding door alerted her to Trace's presence, and Katy cast a quick glance over her shoulder. A wan smile of greeting flickered over her face before her gaze returned to the horizon.

"Feeling sad about leaving?" Trace asked perceptively. Stepping up behind her, he slid his arms around her waist and pulled her back against him, resting his chin on the top of her head.

The blue of sky and ocean merged into a wavy blur as her eyes suddenly welled with tears. "I guess so," she replied in a wavering voice. Katy swallowed hard on the lump that rose in her throat. Good Lord! Why was she behaving so emotionally? Anyone would think she was a starry-eyed bride who couldn't bear for her honeymoon to end!

A low rumble of laughter vibrated against her back. "Well, as much as I'd love to stay just here and enjoy the lotus-eating life with you, I'm afraid I have a horse farm to run." Trace bent his head and pressed a feathery kiss against her temple. "But don't worry, sweetheart, we'll come back someday. In fact, I'll make you a promise right now that we'll return on our twenty-fifth anniversary for a second honeymoon."

Katy turned within the circle of his arms and gave him a troubled look. "Oh, Trace. Do you honestly believe—"

A sharp rap on the door cut her off and drew an impatient look from Trace.

"That'll be the bellhop."

Katy stared after him as he stepped back into the sitting room, her expression thoughtful. What were the chances of a platonic marriage surviving twenty-five years? Practically nil, she admitted to herself sadly. Especially when the husband was a passionate and virile man like Trace.

Refusing to dwell on the tight knot of pain that twisted in her stomach, Katy glanced at the ocean one last time, then resolutely stepped inside.

Her father was waiting for them at the Tyler airport when they arrived that evening. The despondent mood that had clung to her all day disappeared like a wisp of smoke at the first sight of his craggy face. When he grinned and opened his arms wide, Katy flung herself into them.

"Oh, Dad, I'm so glad to see you!" she cried as he lifted her off the floor.

"And it's glad I am to be seein' you, Katy darlin'," Tom replied huskily. For a moment he hugged her tightly against his chest, as though he could not bear to let her go, the big hand spread across her back patting her with rough tenderness. When he finally put her on her feet, he held her at arm's length. Tom's face beamed as he noted the healthy, sun-kissed skin and the happy sparkle in her blue eyes. "Well now. I'm thinkin' marriage agrees with you, Katy girl. You're more beautiful than ever."

His gaze went beyond her to the man who stood waiting. The look on Tom's face spoke of admiration, respect, and fondness, but most of all, of a deep, profound gratitude. Releasing Katy, he stepped forward and held out his hand. "Welcome home, Trace," he said warmly.

"Thanks, Tom. It's good to be back."

All the way to the baggage claim section the two men talked business. Katy walked along between them, smiling contentedly. Her spirits seemed to rise a little with each step. Suddenly it felt very good to be home.

When Trace left them to claim the luggage, Tom turned to his daughter with a questioning look. "Well, now. Tell me, Katy girl, was I right to trust that young man?"

A faint twinge of pink swept over Katy's face. Her father had never once doubted Trace's integrity. "Yes, Dad. You were right. Trace is a man of his word, just as you claimed all along. I'm sorry I ever doubted you or him."

"Don't worry about that, sweetheart. You had a perfect right to be apprehensive. The important thing is you're learning to trust him. That's absolutely essential if you're going to have a good marriage." Tom smiled gently and patted her arm. "Give him a chance,

Katy girl. He loves you very much. He'll make you happy, if you'll let him.''

Katy's answering smile was wan. What did that mean? Did he want her to accept Trace as a husband, in the fullest sense of the word? Even knowing what he did?

He was watching her intently, as though waiting for her reply, but Katy didn't know what to say. Her feelings for Trace had altered during the past two weeks. But not *that* much.

Glancing over her father's shoulder, she was relieved to see that Trace had recovered their luggage and was striding toward them. He had a bag in each hand and two more under his arms. His powerful body showed no sign of being burdened by the load, but Tom quickly relieved him of two of the cases.

''I'm parked right outside,'' he said, nodding his head toward the exit doors. ''We'll just load these into the trunk and be on our way. I'll have you home in two shakes.''

''Good,'' Trace replied, smiling warmly at Katy. ''I'm anxious to get home and carry my bride over the threshold.''

Surprise widened Katy's eyes for just an instant. For a brief time she had forgotten that she would now be living in the big house. In the weeks prior to the wedding the problem of where they would live had seemed very minor, compared to all the other things that had been worrying her. Now it seemed to loom very large. The thought of living in the huge, pillared mansion filled her with apprehension. Katy wasn't at all sure she was capable of taking Saundra's place as mistress of Green Meadows. Or that she even wanted to.

Tom was already walking toward the door and Trace moved to follow him. Two steps away he stopped and turned back to Katy, a questioning look on his face. "Coming, sweetheart?"

After the briefest of hesitations, Katy nodded and picked up the two tote bags full of souvenirs which sat at her feet. With one in each hand and a stiff smile on her face, she took the few steps that brought her level with her husband. Side by side, they walked across the crowded lobby and stepped out into the warm Texas night.

All of Katy's fears soon proved groundless. Within a month she had settled into the big house and her role as its mistress as though she had been born to it.

She had expected the house to be a constant reminder of Henry and Saundra, but Trace, with the sensitivity she was coming to expect from him, eliminated that problem almost immediately. The morning after their arrival he took her on a tour of the house. Very tactfully he pointed out the furnishings which had been in his family for years, especially those items that had belonged to his mother. The rest, he explained tersely, had been selected by Saundra.

After viewing only a few rooms Katy could easily spot which was which. Evelyn Barnett had chosen elegant period pieces with clean, classic lines, while Saundra's taste ran more to the ornate.

Halfway through the tour Trace surprised her by saying, "I want you to redo the house to suit yourself, Katy. You can have a free hand to change anything you want, in any way you want. My only demand is that you get rid of every item that belonged to Saundra. I want that woman's presence obliterated from our home just as soon as possible."

"Oh, Trace, I couldn't do that!" Katy protested quickly. "The house is lovely, just as it is!"

"That may be, but I think a house should reflect the taste of its mistress." He lifted her chin with one finger and smiled to her anxious face. "I keep remembering how warm and inviting your father's cottage is. There's a wonderful, homey feeling there that this place lacks. I like that, Katy. I like it very much. And I think you do too."

A wry smile twisted one corner of her mouth. "Well, yes. Actually, I do. But I somehow can't imagine this house with homemade braided rugs and chintz-covered furniture."

"Maybe not. But I'm sure that whatever you choose will be perfect. Keep anything of Mother's that appeals to you, but get rid of Saundra's. Then just let yourself go."

Katy continued to resist the idea for a time, but in the end, Trace was adamant. Once started, she tackled the project with enthusiasm, spending countless hours looking at furniture catalogues, paint samples, and upholstery and drapery swatches. In some rooms she made sweeping changes, in others only small ones, which, nevertheless, managed to subtly alter the tone of the decor. Within a few weeks the house had begun to take on a new personality.

Much to everyone's surprise, Katy returned to her job at the daycare center. It was what she wanted to do, and Trace didn't mind. Mattie certainly didn't need her help caring for the house.

Gradually her life settled into a pleasant routine. The days were spent helping Jane with the throng of irrepressible but delightful children. The evenings were spent quietly with Trace. Several times a week Trace persuaded her father to join them for dinner, and Katy was deeply touched by the thoughtful gesture. The fact that her husband and her father liked and respected one another filled her with a deep sense of contentment.

Katy knew that to others they appeared to be the typical newlywed couple. Trace certainly made no effort to hide the fact that he adored his wife, and Katy would have been less than human had she not responded to the constant attention he showered on her. When he looked at her in that special way, or simply touched her gently in passing, she felt warm all over. All of her doubts about Trace vanished under his consistent, loving care.

As the weeks passed Katy began to realize that she was happier than she had ever been in her life. If there were times when she felt a twinge of regret at the look of hungry yearning she often glimpsed in Trace's eyes, or when her own body stirred with restless longings, she quickly suppressed the feelings. She didn't want anything to disturb the even tenor of their relationship.

For a long time it looked as though nothing would. Then one night, about two months after their return from Hawaii, she arrived home to find Trace packing.

Katy froze in the bedroom doorway and stared at the open case spread out on the bed. A cold feeling of dread clutched at her. Her frantic gaze went to Trace, where he stood bent over an open dresser drawer.

"Where are you going?" she asked bluntly, her voice breathless with anxiety.

Surprise and pleasure lit Trace's handsome features when he swung around. "Hi, darling. I didn't hear you come in." Carelessly tossing a stack of clean underclothes into the open case as he passed the bed, he crossed the room and took her into his arms, kissing her long and lingeringly on the mouth.

Normally Katy melted under the soft persuasion of his kiss, but tonight she stood rigid within his arms, her lips cold and unresponsive. All that registered on her mind was that half-filled case. The moment he released her, her eyes went back to it. "Where are you going?" she repeated urgently.

"I'm leaving early tomorrow morning for California. I received a call from Ed Tillman this afternoon. You remember him—the California rancher who was here a few weeks ago looking over some thoroughbred stock? Well, it seems he's finally made up his mind. He's buying the black stallion and six mares, and he wanted me to deliver them to his ranch just as soon as I can."

"I see," she said quietly. "And how long do you think you'll be gone?"

"Oh, about ten days, I'd say. I'm going to take it slowly, and stop often to exercise the horses. Their legs tend to swell on long hauls like this, and I want them to be in top shape when we arrive, so I'll probably take four or five days to make the trip. Then I'll have to stay a few days to make sure they settle in okay. I should be back by a week from Friday. But don't worry if it takes a bit longer."

"Do you have to go? Why can't you send someone else?"

"Normally I would. But Ed is very influential among California's horse set, and this is the first time he had bought any of our stock. I want to be sure everything goes well."

Ten days. She wouldn't see him for ten days. Katy felt her stomach plunge as though she had suddenly swallowed a ten pound rock. Distressed by her reaction, she pulled out of his arms and walked briskly over to the open case.

"My goodness, just look at this mess." Her voice came out high and unsteady, sounding nothing at all like her. "I don't understand why you men are so helpless when it comes to something like packing. None of this will be fit to wear by the time you get to California." Shaking her head, she pulled the jumble of clothing from the case and began to refold it. "Why don't you just get out whatever else you want to take, and I'll pack it for you."

"I was hoping you'd say that," Trace said, chuckling.

Katy kept her head down as she carefully repacked each item, blinking rapidly to fight back the threatening tears. She was furious with herself. Why should she mind that Trace would be gone for almost two weeks? Or that he hadn't asked her to go? Only a few months ago she would have been relieved. So she had gotten used to spending her evenings with him. So what? It wasn't the end of the world. There was no reason for her to be lonely just because Trace wouldn't be here for a few days. She could spend every evening with her father. The way she used to. She probably wouldn't even notice that he was gone.

As Katy put in the last item and straightened up she felt Trace's hands slide around her waist from behind, as his lips nuzzled aside her hair and nibbled at her neck.

Katy relaxed against him, and for just a moment, reflected irrelevantly on how easily she had grown accustomed to his touch.

"You know, honey, I've been thinking. It's about time we gave a party, and this would be a good time for you to plan it—while I'm gone and out of your hair."

"A party? Why do we have to give a party?"

Trace turned her slowly and locked his hands in the small of her back. There was a devilish gleam in his eyes and his mouth was twitching. Katy leaned back against his arms and eyed him suspiciously.

"Well, it's the custom around these parts for newlyweds to give some sign to their family and friends that they're ready to leave the bedroom and rejoin the rest of the world," he stated with a perfectly straight face, then laughed aloud as Katy blushed furiously. "Surely you've noticed that we haven't had any visitors or received any invitations since we returned? They're all waiting for us to indicate that we wouldn't be averse to a little socializing. A party would accomplish that."

Her face still warm, Katy stared at the top button on his shirt. "What kind of party?" she asked with a decided lack of enthusiasm. She hated the very thought of giving a party. The last one they'd had ended in disaster.

"Oh, just something casual. Maybe a barbecue around the pool. And don't worry, we won't invite too many people. After dinner tonight I'll make up a list of the ones I feel we should ask, and you can add anyone else you want. Mattie can help you with the food and decorations. She's an old hand at this sort of thing. Plan it for two weeks from Saturday. I'm sure to be back by then." He tilted his head to one side and gave her a slow, coaxing smile. "Okay?"

Resentment smoldered in Katy's blue eyes as she stared back at him, but there was no resisting Trace when he turned on the charm. Finally she released a long, resigned sigh and nodded. "Okay."

Katy turned her head and glanced at the illuminated dial of the bedside clock. One fifteen. With a disgusted sigh she threw back the covers and slipped out of bed. The silken folds of her nightgown fluttered soundlessly around her ankles as she walked barefoot across the carpet to the window. Drawing back the lacy curtains, Katy stared morosely out into the darkness.

Moonlight filtered through the huge oak tree by the drive, casting a dappled pattern of light and shadows across the manicured lawn. From behind the house, hidden in the dense forest, came the incessant, high-pitched hum of a thousand nameless insects. A movement caught her eyes, and as Katy watched, a small furry animal scampered across the grass and disappeared into the shrubbery.

The quiet was nerve-wracking. Katy shifted restlessly and stared up at the black velvet sky.

This was the fourth night in a row that she hadn't been able to sleep. And she knew why. The simple truth of the matter was that she missed Trace. Dreadfully.

She had grown accustomed to falling asleep in his arms, with the sound of his strong heartbeat beneath her ear and the warm comfort of his hard body pressed against hers. Without him that enormous bed was just a cold empty space.

And it wasn't only at night that she felt this grinding loneliness. She missed him every minute of the day, even during those times, like at work, when she normally didn't see him. Since the moment he had disappeared down the drive, pulling that long stock trailer full of horses behind his truck, she had walked around feeling as though her heart were encased in lead. And she hadn't been in the least successful in hiding her feelings. Jane had noticed her unhappiness only that morning. In her usual, forthright manner, she had gotten right to the heart of the problem.

"Sweetie, if you don't like the pattern on these dishes, just say so and I'll buy some new ones. There's no need to scrub it off."

It took several seconds for Jane's voice to penetrate, but finally Katy turned her head and gave her friend a blank look, her blue eyes slightly out of focus. "What?"

"You've been washing that same plate for the last five minutes," Jane explained with exasperated amusement.

"Oh! I'm sorry. My mind must have been wandering." Hastily, Katy swished the dish through the rinse water and placed it in the rack.

"Your mind isn't wandering, doll, it's taken a hike. You've been off in some world of your own for the past three days. What's the matter? Did you have a fight with that dreamy man you married?"

Katy pulled the plug in the sink and watched the water whirlpool down the drain. "No, of course not. Anyway, that would be a bit difficult, since he left Tuesday morning to deliver some Thoroughbreds to a rancher in California."

"Ah-ha! Now the light dawns!" Jane crowed in triumph. "I knew it had something to do with Trace. For two months you've been absolutely glowing with happiness. Now, all of a sudden, the light has gone out of you and you're walking around like a zombie." She cocked her head to one side and narrowed her eyes shrewdly. "You're missing that man like hell, aren't you?"

"No—yes—I mean..." Katy's stammered denial trailed away to nothing in the face of Jane's smug grin. Sighing heavily, she walked to the couch and sank down in one corner, her shoulders drooping. Her eyes remained fixed on her plucking fingers as they toyed absently with a loose thread in the upholstered arm. She sent up a prayer that one of the kids would wake up and give her an excuse to escape. There wasn't a hope in hell that Jane would just let the matter drop.

Katy risked a quick glance at her friend, then wished she hadn't. Jane was still standing there with her hands on her hips, watching her with that I-dare-you-to-deny-it smirk on her face.

"Oh, all right. You win. So maybe I do miss him a little," Katy admitted grudgingly. "We've been married over two months now and...and"—she paused and shrugged—"we've become friends and I'm used to having him around. That's all."

"Horse feathers!" Jane snorted succinctly. "When a friend goes on a trip you say 'so long, Charlie' and go on about your business. Only when you're in love do you count the days until a man returns."

A high-pitched wail from the nursery drew Jane toward the door. With her hand on the knob, she stopped and looked back at Katy's stunned face. "Think about it, Katy," she said softly.

Well, she'd thought about it all right. With a sigh, Katy let the lacy panel fall back into place and turned toward the lonely bed. Since Jane had made that astounding observation she had thought of nothing else.

And slowly, relentlessly, the truth had forced its way to the surface. She was in love with Trace.

Katy stretched out full length on the bed and stared through the darkness at the ceiling. How had it happened? When had she lost her fear of Trace? In two months' time she had gone from lying in his arms like a slab of granite, to the point where she could not sleep without him by her side.

Looking back on the past two months, Katy realized there had been no one occasion that had marked the change in their relationship; it had been a gradual process. With infinite care and patience, Trace had shown her repeatedly that she could trust him. As that trust had grown, her fear had receded. Those horror-filled moments in the woods would probably always haunt her to some extent, but she knew now that she could no longer equate Trace's touch with the vile, unspeakable things those two men had tried to do to her. There was not even the vaguest similarity between their violent lust and her husband's tender, passionate love.

Once her fear had been conquered, it had been impossible to hold in check the powerful attraction that had always existed between them. Each night, when Trace held her in his arms, it became more and more difficult for her to pull away before their lovemaking reached its ultimate conclusion. Her body ached for the fulfillment only Trace could give.

A delicious shiver raced through Katy's body as she recalled the heart-stopping sensations Trace could so easily arouse in her. With a look or touch he could turn her bones to water. When he held her and kissed her as though he would draw her into his very soul, nothing else in the world mattered.

Yet, for a while, Katy had stubbornly refused to admit that the attraction between them was anything more than physical. It was easier that way. Physical attraction could be denied fulfillment; love could not.

But she could no longer ignore her feelings. It had taken only these few days apart for her to realize that without him she was miserable. What was it Trace had said? When you find that one right person it's like finding your other half? Katy smiled. He was certainly right about that.

Rolling onto her side, Katy buried her face in Trace's pillow, then groaned. Mattie had changed the sheets that morning and the clean linens smelled only of soap and the freshness of outdoors. Now even Trace's scent was missing.

Her longing for him had reached an intensity that was painful. As she lay there staring into the darkness, feeling sick with need, Katy made the most momentous, most difficult decision of her life. It could no longer be avoided or postponed. When Trace returned she would let him know that she loved him, and that she was ready for their marriage to be a real one. *How* she would do it, she hadn't the slightest idea. She couldn't quite see herself just walking up to him and blurting it out.

With a sigh, Katy hugged his pillow against her chest. Somehow she'd find a way. They couldn't go on like this.

Chapter Ten

Late in the afternoon on the day Trace was due to return, Katy stood at the kitchen sink, deftly peeling potatoes. Every few seconds her restless gaze darted out the window toward the stables. He would have to go there first to unhitch the horse trailer, she knew. The thought of seeing Trace again made Katy almost faint with excitement.

Her eagerness had made her haunt the kitchen all day, since the windows in that room afforded the best view of the stables and back road. After about her tenth visit, Mattie had finally become so exasperated over finding her underfoot constantly that she had tied an apron around Katy's waist and put her to work. Katy didn't mind. She was grateful for an excuse to stay.

As she reached for another potato, Katy's eyes were drawn irresistibly to the window once again. The familiar blue truck was just rolling to a stop beside the stables. Her heart gave a little leap and the potato peeler clattered into the sink. Katy stood frozen for a moment, then her feet were carrying her toward the back door. En route the apron was snatched off and tossed over the back of a chair. Oblivious to Mattie's knowing grin, she pushed open the screen door and loped down the back steps two at a time.

Katy's heart was pounding with anticipation as she started across the yard. With each step she was walking faster and faster, until by the time she was halfway there she was running.

Trace was just rounding the front of the truck as Katy approached the stables. Catching sight of him, she was suddenly overcome by a fit of intense shyness and skidded to a halt several feet away.

Trace spotted her at the same moment and stopped too, his eyes flaring like dry kindling. "Katy." Her name came out on a breathless sigh. Katy wasn't even sure she'd heard it.

They stood absolutely still, staring at one another. An expectant silence hung in the air between them.

For the past week Katy had planned exactly what she was going to say, exactly how she was going to behave when Trace returned. Now, every carefully rehearsed word flitted right out of her mind. Her brain simply refused to function.

The hazel-green eyes made a quick, avid search of her face and figure. Surprise flickered in their depths as he noted her heaving chest and flushed cheeks. Then, slowly, a devastating smile curved his mouth, and he broke the tense silence with a husky, "Hello, Katy."

Katy stared back at him with wide, hungry eyes. His sandy hair was windblown into an attractive disarray. The chambray work shirt, stretched taut across his hard, muscled chest and broad shoulders, seemed to emphasize his primitive masculine appeal. His loose-jointed stance was deceptively casual, but his eyes were alert as he watched Katy's silent struggle.

Her insides were fluttering like snowflakes in a storm. The desire to touch him was so strong it was almost irresistible, but her feet seemed to be rooted to the spot. She couldn't force a sound through her aching throat.

From the corner of her eye she saw her father emerge from the stables. Taking in the situation at a glance, he stopped short and placed his hands on his hips. "For heaven's sake, Katy girl!" his gruff voice chided. "What are you waiting for? Give the man a proper welcome."

Katy's uncertain gaze went from Trace to her father, then back. The look in the hazel eyes echoed Tom's words, and when Trace opened his arms wide she obeyed the command. With a joyful cry, she sped across the intervening space and flung herself against his chest.

She was lifted clear off the ground as their lips met in a long, burning kiss. His arms crushed her so tightly that Katy could barely breathe, but she didn't care. Winding her arms around his neck, she thrust her hands into his hair and pulled him closer.

Katy's uninhibited response seemed to release a floodgate in Trace. He kissed her with all the pent-up need of a man long denied, the fierce, driving hunger of the past months surging to the surface. Katy responded instinctively, glorying in the possessive, passionate demand.

Finally, the initial torrent spent, the kiss gentled into a long, exquisitely tender exploration that left them both weak and trembling. When at last their clinging lips parted, Trace allowed her body to slide downward until her feet touched the ground. His arms remained around her, holding her close, as he buried his face in the silky fall of her hair.

"Oh, sweetheart, I've missed you like hell," he muttered raggedly against her neck, breathing in the very essence of her. "But, dear heaven! It was worth every lonely hour just to have you greet me like this."

Katy smiled as she snuggled deeper into his arms. His shirt was unbuttoned halfway to his waist. Without conscious thought, she wound her arms tightly around his lean middle and pressed her face against his chest. A delicious shudder rippled through her as she buried her nose in the cloud of curling hair and inhaled deeply of his masculine scent. Trace's arms tightened, and Katy closed her eyes, utterly content. This was where she belonged.

The truck engine roaring into sudden life jolted them back to their surroundings. Surprised, they turned to find Tom beaming down at them from the pickup's cab.

"Don't mind me," he drawled. "I'm just going to take the trailer down to the barn and clean it out." With a casual wave, he put the truck in gear and drove away, the empty horse trailer bouncing and rattling along behind.

The knowing twinkle in her father's eyes had brought a flush to Katy's face but Trace didn't seem in the least disconcerted. Smiling that crooked little half smile that made her stomach flutter, he drew her close and fitted her tightly against his side. With his arm curved around her shoulders and hers around his waist, they turned and walked toward the house.

Later that night, as she sat before her dressing table, mercilessly dragging a brush through her hair while she waited for Trace to emerge from the bathroom, Katy was as taut as a drawn bow.

It was one thing to decide, with the safety of hundreds of miles between them, that the time had come to make their marriage a real one. Following through on the decision was something else again. She loved Trace. She had no doubts about that. And her body pulsed with a deep, burning need that only his complete possession could satisfy. Yet fear, insidious, mind-choking fear, was slowly twining its curling tendrils through her.

It wasn't a fear of Trace; she knew that he would never hurt her. It was fear of the unknown. Giving yourself completely over to another person, experiencing the ultimate intimacy, was something Katy had never even contemplated until a week ago.

The sudden opening of the bathroom door brought an end to her self-torment. Katy's heart kicked painfully against her ribs as she watched Trace's mirrored image become inexorably larger.

He was clad in only a towel, which draped low from his hips. The sculptured beauty of his chest and shoulders made Katy's pulse race. In the soft light from the bedside lamp his naked skin glowed like polished bronze, its smooth surface broken only by the V-shaped pattern of burnished gold chest hairs.

Purposefully, relentlessly, his intent gaze never once leaving her, he moved across the lush carpet. When he came to a halt, only a few inches separated them.

A shiver rippled through Katy as their eyes met in the mirror and his hands settled warmly on her bare shoulders. She inhaled the intoxicating mixture of pine soap and clean male scent that emanated from him. Through the thin silk of her gown she could feel the heat of his body all across her back.

There was no mistaking the message in his eyes. Trace had not misread the silent invitation in her uninhibited greeting, in the hungry looks she had given him all through dinner.

"Let's go to bed, Katy," he whispered with husky sensuality. "I want to hold you."

For a painful few seconds Katy's lungs refused to function. Then, mesmerized by the burning look in those deep-set eyes, drawn by a need even stronger than the curling fear in the pit of her stomach, she allowed him to lift her from the stool and lead her, trembling and silent, to the bed.

The light covering was thrown back, and as Katy slid obediently into the enormous bed, the lamp was clicked off. There was a soft plop as the towel hit the carpet, then the mattress tilted under Trace's weight. Powerful, sinewy arms reached out and gathered her close, molding her intimately against the hard, masculine body, his naked flesh burning its imprint into her through the silk gown.

"Oh, Katy, Katy. I feel as though I've waited all my life for this," Trace breathed against her lips just before his mouth claimed them.

The kiss was both passionate and tender, demanding and entreating, and Katy's lips blossomed under it like a bud unfurling beneath the sun. A soft moan escaped her as he explored the silken sweetness of her mouth with excruciating sensuality. She felt his tongue tracing her lips, delicately probing the sensitive membranes on the inside of her cheek. Trace had kissed her passionately many times but always before there had been that element of restraint, of rigid control. No more. He made no effort to curb his desire, and under the questing kiss, Katy felt her own control slipping, the last remnant of doubt and fear fading into oblivion.

"Oh, God, how I love you," he murmured thickly as his mouth trailed across her cheek. Katy was beyond reply, her body shivering deliciously as his tongue traced the convoluted swirls of her ear. His broad hand ceased its rhythmic caress of her hip to glide slowly upward. It paused briefly at the indented curve of her waist, then again to cup the warm fullness of her breast, before moving, with sure determination, to her shoulder. One at a time, the thin straps of her gown were moved aside, and the slippery material was lowered to her waist.

He drew back to look at her. Moonlight filtered through the lacy curtains at the window. In its dim, silvery glow his eyes burned feverishly.

"Beautiful. You're so beautiful."

His hand curved possessively around one breast, his fingers stroking softly over the curving slope.

Then Katy gasped and her mind went spinning out of control as his lips captured the rosy tip and tugged gently. Her flesh responded instantly, forming a hard bud of desire, achingly tight and tender.

Palm flat, fingers extended, his hand moved onto her quivering stomach, and instinctively Katy's body arched upward, liquid heat surging through her veins. Her hands moved restlessly over the corded muscles in his neck and shoulders. "Trace. Oh, Trace," she moaned softly, lost to everything but the driving need that pulsed through her.

"I know, sweetheart. I know."

Abandoning her breasts, his mouth forged a moist trail upward, pausing on the way to delicately trace her collarbone and nibble at the underside of her jaw. Katy was caught in the exquisite rapture of the slow, tantalizing caress, and she waited breathlessly for his mouth to reclaim hers.

It was a few seconds before she realized that his hands had stilled, the softly spoken love words had ceased. Through the haze of passion clouding her vision Katy saw that Trace had pulled away and, propped on one elbow, was looking down at her expectantly. Heavy lidded eyes blinked once, twice, but he continued to watch her in that intent way, as though waiting for an answer to some unspoken question. Or had it been unspoken?

"Wha—what..."

"Tell me what you want, Katy," Trace urged in a low whisper. "I have to know, for both our sakes."

Confusion clouded her expression for a moment, then, slowly, the meaning of his words sank in, and her eyes widened. Trace wanted her to *ask* for his lovemaking!

Shock rippled through her. She couldn't! She simply couldn't!

But, looking into his face, Katy knew, with sickening certainty, that if she wanted a real marriage, she must. From the very beginning Trace had put the burden of decision on her, and he wasn't going to relieve her of it now. There would be no claims of coercion or seduction or misunderstanding later. If she wanted her husband, she would have to tell him so.

Gathering her courage, Katy swallowed hard and tried to force the words through her constricted throat, but they simply would not come. The inhibitions of a lifetime were just too strong. Feeling her happiness slipping away, Katy gazed back at him in mute desperation, tears welling up in her eyes.

Abruptly, Trace rolled away from her. Moving to the edge of the bed, he sat hunched over, elbows on knees, his head cradled in his hands.

Something about the rigidity of his back, the utter, absolute defeat in every line of his body, sent a chill through Katy. A panicky fear, worse than any she had ever know, began to build inside her, and she reached out to touch him.

"Trace, I..."

Violently, he jerked away.

"For God's sake, Katy, don't touch me! My control does have its limits!"

Flinching from the stinging lash of his angry voice, Katy drew back and huddled motionless against the pillows.

Trace reached out and flicked on the bedside lamp. Lifting a hand, he raked it through his hair, rumpling it even more than Katy's fingers had.

"I'm sorry, Katy. I didn't mean to snap. None of this is your fault," he said in a flat, dejected tone. Grim-lipped, he clasped his hands together between his knees and shot her a brooding look over his shoulder. "You tried to warn me that this might happen, but, arrogant fool that I am, I was positive I could make it work. I love you so much that I thought all I had to do was show you and give you time, and eventually you'd come to me. Tonight, when you seemed so happy to see me, I assumed... Oh, hell! What difference does it make now."

Snatching up his robe from the end of the bed, he slid it over his shoulders and stood up. Katy felt cold and sick inside as she watched him walk away toward the dressing room. At the door he stopped and turned back to her with an odd, defeated smile on his lips. "I think, under the circumstances, I'd better sleep in the dressing room. No matter what the future holds for us, I don't want to break my word to you, and I'm afraid my control has been stretched to its outer limits. Good night, Katy."

The door clicked shut behind him, and Katy lay frozen. Why had she lain there like a statue? Why hadn't she found the courage from somewhere to tell him what he wanted to hear? Instead, by her silence she confirmed his mistaken assumption that she didn't love him or want him.

Turning her face into the pillow, Katy let the thick down muffle her sobs. She wept long and bitterly, her shoulders shaking as the terrible, wrenching cries tore from her throat, until finally the emotional storm was spent and she was drained.

Hours later she still lay, dry-eyed, staring at the ceiling, her emotions in utter turmoil. Like a swinging pendulum, her anger switched from herself to Trace, then back again. Couldn't he see, by her greeting, by the way she responded to his slightest touch, that she was his, totally? Why did he insist that she put her feelings and desires into words? That was asking too much. Couldn't he *see* that?

She sighed deeply. No. No, it wasn't asking too much. Trace had told her from the beginning how it was going to be. She just hadn't realized he meant it quite so literally. Or, more to the point, she had never truly expected the situation to arise.

She was a fool. A blind, stupid fool. For almost two weeks she had yearned desperately for him, had practically counted the hours until she could lie in his arms and know his love. Now, here they were on his first night home, in separate beds.

The dressing room door drew her longing gaze repeatedly. She had only to knock on that door and utter a few simple words and all the barriers would be gone. Yet she couldn't.

Chapter Eleven

Standing on the patio, among the group of gaily dressed, laughing people, Katy was filled with a strange sense of unreality. That she could smile and talk, or even function at all, after the miserable week she had just endured, seemed something of a miracle.

Taking a sip of her drink, she let her eyes wander. Like a homing device, her gaze automatically sought out and zeroed in on Trace. He was with a group of people on the other side of the pool, his back to her. How symbolic, Katy mused bitterly.

The pain that followed that thought almost made her cry out. Determinedly, she jerked her gaze away. This was neither the time nor the place to indulge in a fit of self-pity. Tonight marked her debut as mistress of Green Meadows, and pride, if nothing else, demanded that she give a good accounting of herself. Mentally squaring her shoulders, Katy exchanged her watery drink for a fresh one, pasted a stiff smile on her face, and started toward the nearest cluster of people.

Somehow she managed to carry out her duties as a hostess. Moving from one group to the next, she made introductions, saw that everyone had a drink, and exchanged inane small talk, not one word of which she could recall five minutes later. And through it all she was vitally aware of Trace and the fact that he seemed deliberately to be keeping a careful distance between them.

And that, much to her dismay, was exactly what he had been doing for the past week. Katy had expected, or at least hoped, that Trace would return to their bed, once passions had cooled and they had both recovered from that debacle of a reunion. It had not happened. Trace still slept in the dressing room, while night after night she tossed and turned alone in that huge bed, sick with unhappiness and the steadily building fear that she was losing him.

On the surface nothing had changed. As always, Trace treated her with great care and consideration and was unfailingly pleasant. Yet there was a subtle difference in their relationship. There were no more warm, teasing looks, no more gentle bantering conversations, and worst of all, no more attempts at lovemaking. Trace hadn't so much as touched her, even accidentally, since the night he returned from California. They were polite strangers, occupying the same house.

Katy knew the situation could not continue for long. The strain was intolerable. Aware also that the solution to the problem lay in her own hands, she was consumed with guilt and self-disgust.

Dozens of times during the past week she had steeled herself to face him and tell him exactly how she felt. But each time her courage had failed her at the last moment. It was maddening! She wanted to tell him. Knew it was what he wanted to hear. But she just couldn't!

Katy absently twirled the ice cubes in her drink and pretended to listen as Trudy Bledsoe described her teenage son's latest football injury in great detail. Trudy was the wife of one of Trace's old college buddies. Even listening with only half an ear, Katy had already learned that Trudy's whole life revolved around her husband, John, and their three children. In a sudden fit of self-torment, Katy idly wondered if she would be around long enough to become friends with the talkative, but otherwise pleasant, woman.

From across the pool, Trace's deep laughter rang out, drawing Katy's gaze like a magnet. Her mouth tightened when she saw the way a willowy blonde was clinging to his arm as though she couldn't stand without his support. Katy turned away sharply, and when Trudy paused to draw a breath she quickly excused herself, saying that she wanted to speak with Mattie about serving dinner.

Once inside the house, Katy ignored the kitchen and went directly upstairs to the master bedroom. In the adjoining bath she rummaged through the medicine cabinet for the aspirin, and finding them, downed a couple with a glass of water. After two hours of watching that woman drape herself all over Trace, the dull ache in her temples had become a full-fledged tension headache.

The moment she arrived Monica Traverse had thrown her arms around Trace and kissed him full on the lips. Much to Katy's chagrin, he hadn't objected in the least. When the long, passionate embrace was over, Trace had laughingly disentangled the woman's arms and told her to behave herself. Then, without the slightest hint of embarrassment, he had turned to Katy and introduced her as his cousin, a relationship which the lovely Monica had quickly discounted as having no importance.

"Fourth cousins, darling," she had drawled seductively. "That hardly constitutes next of kin. Anyway, our relationship has always been more in the 'kissing cousin' category, wouldn't you say?" Giving him a heavy-lidded look that spoke volumes, she smiled slowly and purred, "Don't tell me you've forgotten all those long summer afternoons we spent in the hayloft?"

The sly innuendo sparked an instant reaction in Katy. Anger, hot and strong, surged through her, and for the first time in her life, she felt an urge to commit physical violence. The dislike she had felt for Saundra was nothing compared to the hostility this woman aroused. Hayloft indeed!

But if she found Monica's remark offensive, Trace certainly didn't. Throwing his head back, he let out a bark of delighted laughter.

"You little devil. You haven't changed a bit, have you? Stirring up trouble is obviously still your favorite pastime." Trace grinned at the blonde in a way that made Katy's heart lurch painfully. "Well, this time it won't work, sweetheart. My wife isn't in the least jealous. Now, mind your manners and say hello to Katy."

"Hello, Katy," Monica parroted, smiling archly as her green eyes swept over Katy in a quick, head to toe inspection. "I really should hate you, you know, for stealing this gorgeous man the minute my back was turned. If I hadn't been touring Europe this summer, you would never have gotten away with it."

Ignoring Katy's startled expression, Monica slipped her hand through Trace's arm and gave him a reproachful look. "And I really shouldn't even speak to you, you naughty man. How *could* you marry someone else, when you know I've been lusting after you for years? I'm heartbroken!"

"Maybe I just got tired of waiting to catch you between husbands," Trace teased.

"Oh, you! Just for that I'm not going to let you out of my sight all evening."

And she hadn't either, Katy reflected grimly.

She tried to tell herself she had nothing to fear. After all, Trace loved her. He had proven that in a thousand different ways. But still a niggling doubt persisted in the back of her mind. She kept remembering that when she had pointed out to Trace the possibility that the marriage might never be consummated, he had told her that was his problem. He hadn't, however, explained how he would deal with it. The mere thought that he might have the marriage annulled, or take a mistress, made Katy sick at heart.

Giving herself time to regroup her forces, she sank onto the bench in front of the dressing table and began to brush her hair with slow, soothing strokes. Then she swept it back high over her temples and secured it with two amethyst-studded combs. After she had touched up her lipgloss, Katy stood and surveyed her reflection. She adjusted the full sleeves of her gauzy, burgundy blouse and tucked it more securely into the waistband of the long, matching skirt. Then, with no further excuse to delay, she made her way back downstairs to the party.

When Katy stepped outside, she discovered that during her absence a space had been cleared at one end of the patio for dancing, and Trace and his "kissing cousin" were now wrapped in each other's arms, swaying to the slow, seductive music that poured from the outdoor stereo speaker.

The tightness in Katy's chest increased. Pivoting on her heel, she stalked back into the kitchen and informed Mattie, rather curtly, that it was time to serve dinner.

"Who's the blond bombshell?" Jane asked her a short time later, when Katy joined the Cawleys at one of the tables scattered around the back lawn.

Katy didn't need to ask who she was talking about. Her eyes went immediately to the table where Trace and Monica were seated, and her set expression became even stiffer. The woman was practically sitting in his lap!

"That's Monica Traverse, Trace's cousin," she replied, striving for indifference, then completely spoiling the effect by adding, "she's been in Europe for the last six months and now she'd making up for lost time."

"She certainly is," Jane agreed heartily, not even bothering to comment on Katy's incensed tone. "And if I were you, my girl, I'd put a stop to it. Pronto!"

"What am I supposed to do, threaten to scratch her eyes out if she doesn't back off? I'm sure Trace's snooty relatives would *love* that. I get the distinct impression they're all just waiting for me to make some horrible social blunder."

"Well, you'd better do something, sweetie, because that woman has got the hots for your husband. And if he decides to take what she's so obviously offering, you won't have anyone but yourself to blame."

Frank's scandalized "Jane!" had no effect at all.

"I mean it!" his wife continued pugnaciously. "It's time Katy realized that she's married to a passionate, virile man, and if she continues to keep him at arm's length she's going to lose him."

Katy didn't need Jane to tell her something she already knew. The same worrisome thought had been running through the back of her mind all week, like some blurred, flickering film. Tonight's little episode merely brought it into sharper focus.

Eyes fixed on her plate, she listlessly poked at the savory barbecue with her fork, and murmured, "I know."

The wavering note in Katy's voice brought Jane's head around with a snap. After a search of her face she quickly changed the subject.

The meal seemed interminable. Seated not more than ten feet away from Trace, Katy couldn't miss the provocative gleam in Monica's eyes whenever she looked at him or the way she seemed to be plastered against his side. Every time the woman's husky laughter rang out, Katy's jaw clenched tighter. By the end of the meal her teeth were aching.

Later, when Trace and his cousin returned to the improvised dance floor, and the woman literally melted against him, Katy watched through narrowed eyes and indulged in a delightful fantasy in which she shoved Monica, fully clothed, into the deep end of the pool.

Katy was slow to anger. She could count on the fingers of one hand the number of times she had truly lost her temper. But that was not to say she didn't have one. When pushed long enough, and far enough, she could explode into a magnificent fury that was all the more shocking for its rarity. An evening of watching Trace accept the cloying attentions of another woman, while virtually ignoring his wife, had her doing a slow burn. By the time the party began to break up, she was nearing flash point.

Predictably, Monica was the last to leave. Katy had just closed the front door after saying good night to her father and the Cawleys when Trace strolled into the entrance hall with the woman clinging to his arm.

"I'm going to walk Monica to her car, darling," he announced in a casual tone that set Katy's hackles up. "I won't be but a minute—why don't you go on up to bed. Mattie and the others just about have everything cleaned up, and I know you're tired."

His solicitude grated on Katy's nerves like a fingernail scraping on a chalk board, but her blistering glare was wasted. His attention had already returned to the woman at his side.

"It was a lovely party, Katy," Monica cooed. "I can't remember when I've had such a good time."

It was all Katy could do to restrain herself. Gritting her teeth, she barely managed a tight, "Thank you," before pivoting on her heel and stalking up the stairs. If Trace thought her behavior rude, that was just too bad! At that moment polite platitudes were beyond her.

Katy marched into the master bedroom and, in a very childish, but totally satisfying fit of temper, slammed the door with a force that rattled the pictures on the wall. Seething, she began to pace the room. Every time she passed the bedside table her eyes went to the clock. How long did it take to say good night, for heaven's sake! Imagination stoked the fire of her jealous anger, and with every tick of the clock the pressure built higher. Twenty minutes later, when Trace strolled into the room, she was ready to let fly.

He stopped just a few feet inside the door and stretched, flexing his broad shoulders and giving vent to a huge yawn. "Boy, am I bushed," he commented lazily. Releasing a long sigh, he gave Katy a friendly smile and headed for the dressing room, absently unbuttoning his shirt on the way. "All things considered, it was a nice party, don't you think?'' he tossed over his shoulder.

He didn't seem to notice that Katy had jerked to a halt at his entrance, or that she now stood in the middle of the room, still fully clothed, glaring daggers at him.

''Oh, just terrific!''

Trace had taken two more steps before he caught the snapping sarcasm in her voice. Faltering to a stop just as he reached the dressing room door, he turned slowly and shot her a quizzical look. The beginnings of a puzzled frown creased his forehead.

Too incensed to say another word, Katy swung away and stalked to the dressing table, where she angrily snatched the combs from her hair, flung them into a drawer and slammed it shut. She then went to work on the amethyst earrings.

Trace's frown deepened.

''Did you enjoy the party?'' he asked, more cautiously this time.

Her lips tightened as she met his gaze in the mirror. ''Enjoy it? I just spent six hours talking to a group of people I didn't know, while my husband completely ignored me. And you want to know if I *enjoyed* it?''

''I'm sorry if you feel that I ignored you, Katy, but as the host I had an obligation to entertain our guests. We both did.'' Pulling his unbuttoned shirt from his trousers, he let it hang free while he stood, hands on hips, watching her intently, his expression wary.

''Entertain the guests? Is that what you were doing?'' She spun on one heel and stormed across the room, coming to a halt just inches from him, her eyes shooting blue flames as she glowered up into his surprised face. ''As far as I could see the only person you bothered to entertain was 'cousin Monica,'" she sneered, while angrily working open the buttons on her long sleeves. Without waiting for a reply, she turned and stalked back across the room.

Trace's brows jerked upward, and his expression froze. Then, slowly, noting her stiff, angry movements, his features began to relax. Amused satisfaction glittered in his eyes as he said, coaxingly, "Now, come on, Katy. Be fair. I circulated among the guests all evening. I'm quite certain I talked to everyone, at least twice."

"Yes! And the whole time you had that woman plastered to your side!" she snapped, ripping the blouse off over her head. She flung it into a chair beside the bed and retraced her steps. "And speaking of time, just why did it take twenty minutes to say good night when you walked your dear cousin to her car?" she demanded, poking his bare chest with one slender finger.

"Monica wanted to talk to me about something. I guess time just got away from us."

"Talk to you! *Talk* to you! She had all evening to talk to you!" Katy railed. "Although I will admit, talking wasn't what she seemed to have on her mind. That woman was all over you, and I didn't see you objecting. Not once!" The finger jabbed again. "Well, let me tell you something, Trace Barnett. I will not be treated that way. While you were playing footsie with Monica I spent a ghastly evening deflecting pitying looks from your friends and trying to ignore the knowing smirks your uppity relatives cast my way. It was humiliating! And I don't intend to put up with it. That woman is not to set foot in this house again! Is that clear?"

Whirling around, she marched back to the bed, kicked off her shoes and wiggled out of the burgundy skirt and matching half slip, nearly sizzling with fury. With a careless toss, both garments joined the blouse in the chair. Head held high, she stalked to the dresser and removed a clean nightgown.

"Come on, Katy," Trace said, chuckling. "Monica doesn't mean anything to me. For heaven's sake! We grew up together."

Katy threw her nightgown on the bed, incensed by the so-called explanation. She faced him with her fists planted on her hips, eyes blazing, oblivious to the fact that she was clad in only a scanty, lace and silk, burgundy teddy, which revealed a great deal more than it concealed. She was much too furious to give a thought to her state of undress.

"Oh, I've heard all about the way you grew up together," she snarled. Pelvis thrust forward, hips swaying provocatively, she sauntered up to Trace in an exaggerated imitation of Monica's seductive slink.

Trace's eyes roamed avidly over her scantily covered body, a flame leaping in their depths as they studied the milky gleam of her breasts, where they strained against their sheer, lacy confinement.

Giving him a sultry, feline look, Katy mimicked huskily, "Don't you remember all those long summer afternoons in the hayloft, darling?"

Her face hardened. Abandoning her seductive pose, Katy threw her head back and glared at him, her lip curling in disgust. "Grew up fast, didn't you."

Trace's mouth quivered suspiciously. With studied nonchalance, he stripped off the shirt and tossed it at the hamper behind him. Then, crossing his arms over his chest, he leaned a bare shoulder against the door frame. "Keep that up and you're going to wear a rut in the carpet,'' he said, addressing the words to her re-treating form as she stomped back toward the bed.

If Katy heard the remark she chose to ignore it. She was much too caught up in her satisfying tirade to be sidetracked. It felt wonderful, absolutely marvelous, to spew out all the anger that had been boiling up inside her for hours, and she wasn't about to deny herself the pleasure.

''Now you just listen to me,'' she continued pugna-ciously, as she fumbled with the ribbon ties that held the bodice of the teddy together. ''If you think I'm going to put up with you carrying on with that woman, or *any* woman, you can just think again. I won't stand for it! You forced your way into my life, refused to take no for an answer, and practically bludgeoned me into mar-riage. Well, you got what you wanted, Trace, and now you're stuck with me. There will be no other women in your life *or* your bed. I'm...''

A choked sound behind her brought her whirling around, the unfastened teddy falling open to below her waist. Her jaw dropped at the sight of Trace, strug-gling manfully to contain his laughter.

''Don't you *dare* laugh at me, Trace Barnett!'' she shrilled at him, stamping her foot in outrage.

Caught red-handed, unable to hold it in any longer, Trace threw back his head and let the sputtering chuck-les blossom into rich, full-bodied laughter, a warm, ex-ultant sound of pure joy.

''Trace, you stop that right now or I'll—I'll—''

Her irate threat succeeded in choking off his laugh-ter, but did nothing to dim his euphoric joy. Bristling with indignation, but too stunned to move, Katy watched with open-mouthed astonishment as Trace strolled toward her with a ridiculously happy grin splitting his face.

"Oh, Katy, Katy. You're such an adorable little goose."

Frowning, she plucked at the hands that settled on her waist. "I'm *not* adorable and I'm *not* a goose," she retorted testily. "Now, let me go! And stop grinning like an idiot!"

The hands at her waist tightened and Katy's feet suddenly left the floor. Frantically, she clutched at Trace's shoulders as he whirled her around in circles. When he finally stopped her head was spinning.

Still holding her aloft, he grinned triumphantly. "Ahhh, but you are *very* adorable, my darling. Especially when you're in a flaming rage and haven't the faintest idea why."

"Haven't the fa..."

That was too much! Fists doubled, Katy rained blows on his head and shoulders. "Put me down! Put me down this instant!" she shrieked.

"Of course, my love." Grinning, Trace tossed her onto the bed. In a blink he followed her down and pinned her to the mattress with his body, his mouth closing over hers in burning possession.

Katy writhed beneath him. She was determined to fight the instant pleasure his touch evoked. Squirming and pitching, she tried to evade his insistent mouth, but Trace did not let up until, at last, she quieted.

Then, slowly, cautiously, he lifted his head and stared down at her. A gentle smile curved his mouth but his eyes were quite serious.

"Now, as much as I'm intrigued by the sleeping tigress I somehow accidently let loose, I want you to calm down and tell me, in plain, straightforward language, what it is you really want. I think we both know, but I want you to say it anyway.''

Katy glared back at him, her expression a mixture of pride and defiant anger. When she remained stubbornly quiet Trace gave her a little nudge.

"Come on, Katy. Say it."

"All right, dammit! I love you! And I want you!" she snapped in a completely unlover-like tone. "Is that what you wanted to hear?''

Trace sucked in a deep breath and closed his eyes. He remained perfectly still for a moment, as though in the grip of some agonizing pain. Then, slowly, he relaxed, and on a heart-felt sigh, breathed, "At last."

With exquisite tenderness, he lowered his head and kissed her again, his lips tasting, coaxing, caressing. Katy felt all the fight go out of her, and with a moaning sigh of surrender, she wrapped her arms around him and held him close, returning the delicately passionate kiss with an eagerness that instantly brought a growling response from Trace.

They touched and tasted, exploring each other with sensuous delight, reveling in the new freedom. In mere minutes Trace had shed his remaining clothes and the ridiculous wisp of silk and lace was smoothed from Katy's body.

His lips and tongue played over her, kissing and tugging at her breasts, stroking the silky, quivering skin of her belly. Katy returned the caress, shyly at first, then with growing sureness, her heart swelling as she felt his shuddering response.

The driving urgency of their need for one another could not be restrained for long. When neither could bear the exquisite torture any longer, Trace rose over her. Hesitating, he looked down into her flushed face.

"Are you very sure, Katy?" he asked, with a vulnerability that tugged at her heartstrings.

A tremulous smile curved her mouth as she took his face between her palms and pulled his head down. Against his lips she whispered, "Love me, Trace."

He took her gently, guiding her through that first, fleeting moment of discomfort with tender care, then, passion blossoming freely, they moved into a realm Katy had never even dreamed of. Together they climbed higher and higher, until the almost unbearable pleasure reached its peak and exploded in a shower-burst of ecstasy. In the shuddering aftermath, they clung to one another and drifted slowly down to earth, spent and utterly replete.

"Did I hurt you, darling?" Trace asked some time later.

Katy nuzzled her nose against the side of his neck, a soft smile tugging at the corners of her mouth as she caught the thread of concern in his voice. "Only a little. But it was worth it." Her arm tightened on his waist. "Oh, darling, I had no idea it would be like that. I feel so foolish, putting both of us through all that torment for so long."

Trace tipped her chin up and smiled lovingly at her contrite expression. "Don't worry about it, sweetheart. It was something you had to work through. I've always wanted you. I don't deny that. But I wanted you free of fear, and loving me as much as I love you." Cupping the side of her face, he stroked her bottom lip with his thumb, while his eyes ran over her wonderingly. "I swear to you, Katy, it's never been like that with anyone else. Never."

"And it never will be," she retorted spiritedly. "Because I warn you right now, you've landed yourself a very jealous wife, like it or not."

Trace laughed delightedly and hugged her close. "Oh, I like it, I like it. But I must admit I'm still in shock. I had no idea my sweet, gentle Katy had such a fiery temper."

"I do when provoked," she informed him with a stern, narrow-eyed look. "And if 'cousin' Monica gets within ten feet of you again she'll find herself on the receiving end of it."

"Calm down, spitfire. Monica is a nuisance but you have no reason to be jealous of her. She simply likes to stir up trouble, then sit back and watch the fur fly." He gave her a devilish look. "Though I will admit, had I known the effect she would have on you I would have invited her over long ago. She accomplished in a few hours what I haven't been able to do in months. But for the record, no matter what she implied, Monica and I have never been lovers." He planted a quick kiss on her mouth and grinned. "Satisfied?"

"I'll be satisfied as long as you love me," Katy whispered.

Rolling her over onto her back, Trace framed her face between his hands and stared intently into her eyes, his own burning. Katy's heart turned over at the love she saw there. "That will be forever," he promised huskily.

* * * * *